TINTAMARRE!

BRIAN LLOYD FRENCH

 Published by:

RAI Books -

165 Lee Avenue

Toronto, ON M4E2P2

416.803.5301

This book is a work of fiction except for descriptions of historical events. Names, characters, organizations and personalities of historical figures are fictional and any resemblance to persons living or dead is entirely coincidental.

International Edition 2015

ISBN-13: 978-0-9937688-2-8

What readers are saying about Tintamarre!

From Ronnie Gilles Leblanc - Acadian Historian Emeritus: *"Good to learn that the book is well received by Acadian descendants, and I can understand why. You have captured their attention by presenting another picture of the Deportation and how it affected people individually. I look forward to reading the book again."*

From NEW YORK TIMES Best-selling Author: Carsten Stroud (Niceville): *"Outstanding historical fiction with a rock-hard substrate of lived lives! Read this and be overwhelmed with STORY! Man can write, and needs to be READ."*

From Descendant of Beausoleil Broussard - Kelley B.: *"Through the magic of your words, you are shining a much needed light on the history that should never EVER be forgotten - made light of - or just abandoned in a time as some sort of forgettable history. Outstanding job - You have done them proud - You have done us proud - and I just so very much commend you, sir."*

G. Robinson: *"This is a must read book if you are an Acadian descendent. I recommend it to anyone, but if you want to understand what our ancestors really went through, take the time buy this great book and read it then pass it on to your families."*

Norm Cormier: *I`m almost finished reading it. It`s one of the best books I`ve ever read. I see that I`m getting near the end of the book and I find myself wishing it had double the number of pages.*

Frank Cormier: *I am enjoying every page and learning at the same time about what my family went through. I will be passing this history on to my grandchildren so what they went through will never be forgotten.*

DEDICATIONS

This book is dedicated to Kathy, as always, who forgives me for spending family time in front of a laptop and ...

to my Mom, Charlotte Matilda Kaluza French, who passed away at the age of 98 while I was writing this book, as well as my late brother Tony who was a pretty good writer himself ...

and to my beloved, late Sister Wanda Girouard and her husband Alfred as well as Acquila and Mae Girouard.

ABOUT TINTAMARRE!

The Terror and Triumph of an Acadian Family

In 1750 the road to Quebec leads through a small Acadian settlement called Tintamarre. The English order a final solution.

From the author of "Mojito!" comes the epic story of an Acadian family caught in the middle of the war for Canada...
Mathilde and Acquila Girouard are raising their family in a pastoral paradise. Then the English come.

Mati and 'Quila are at the mercy of the English Empire, pushed around by pestilent priests and pursued by violent rangers that keep count of their victims with scalps.

When Mati and the children are captured by the English to be sent far away from home, all appears to be lost. Then Acquila and the Acadian resistance hatch a plot to rescue them from under the nose of the entire English army.

Ile
Royale
Ile St. Jean
Louisbourg
Baie Verte
Chipoudie
Beaubassin
Remsheg
Cobequit
Grand Pre
Piziquit
Port Royal
Chebucto

ACKNOWLEDGMENTS

Ronnie Gilles Leblanc – Historian Emeritus – Parks Canada: Ronnie Gilles is a walking compendium of all knowledge on the Acadians and how they lived. He was an enormous help with my research and I will thank him eternally. Francois Leblanc from University of Moncton.

Dr. Ruth Whitehead - formerly staff ethnologist and assistant curator in history at the Nova Scotia Museum. Dr. Whitehead was very generous in sharing time by educating me on how aboriginals lived in Acadia.

Late Dr. Bernie Vigod and Late Professor Ken Windsor at UNB. Dr. Phil Buckner at UNB. Colin Leonard, Teacher at TRHS.

Juliette Bulmer – Historian – Parks Canada: Fort Beauséjour.

David Mawhinney at Mount Allison University for more background and guidance.

Ron Trueman – Beauséjour Historian and Pointe de Bute Resident. Ron's Grandfather wrote one of the most authoritative books on the Tantramar area and Ron has continued this legacy and is a walking authority on the land and where things happened.

Don Colpitts – Beauséjour Historian and Pointe de Bute Resident and Colin MacKinnon – Marshes Ecologist and Historian.

Allan Balser – Pointe de Bute Resident - My sister's partner who owns an ancient farmhouse overlooking le Loutre's "new" aboiteau on the Riviere Au Lac and gave me shelter when treasure hunting.

Readers: Frank Cormier, Patricia Geoffroy, Claire Peterson, Bertica Robinson, Sari Ruda, Sue Chamberlin Emery, John Estano DeRoche, Norm Cormier, Gary & Gayle Robinson, Susie Richard and many others.

New York Times Best-selling Author, Carsten Stroud, for cheerleading...

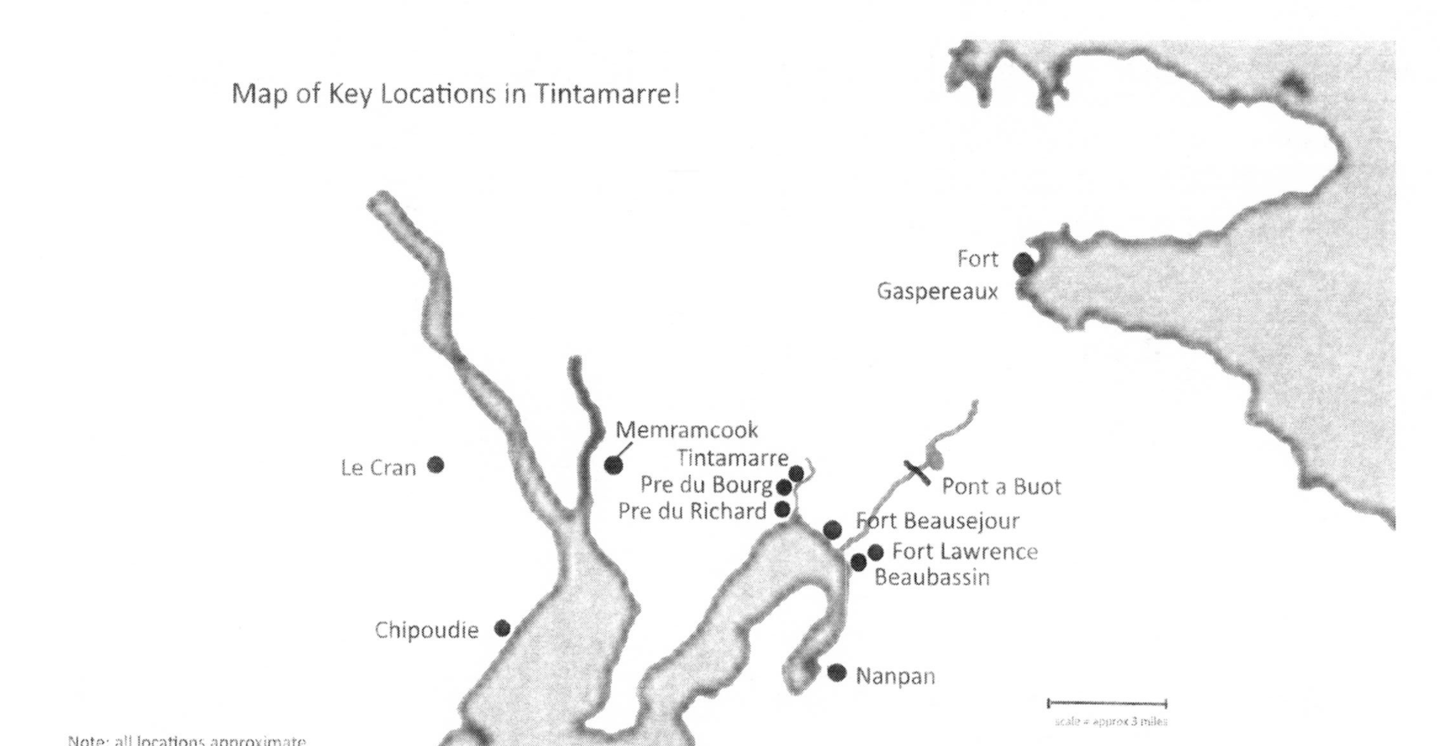
Map of Key Locations in Tintamarre!
Fort
Gaspereaux
Memramcook
Tintamarre
Pre du Bourg
Pre du Richard
Le Cran
Pont a Buot
Fort Beausejour
Fort Lawrence
Beaubassin
Chipoudie
Nanpan
scale = approx 3 miles
Note: all locations approximate

PROLOGUE

Six women, some with flames smouldering on their clothing, tried to escape into the wooded area, but in their long dresses they were slow and a couple tripped. Six muskets took aim and fired and three of the women fell; shot in the back.

Danks saw no value to a terror campaign if there was no one to tell the story. "Hold yer bloody fire! Let them go."

Danks yelled at his subaltern, "King!"

A young clean-cut ranger came running toward him, "Capt'n."

"Look inside the buildings and see if there are any bairns. Bring them out if there are. We shan't kill them, and we won't let them burn. Put them in the animal barn. The women will return and find them, I expect."

"Yes, Capt'n." King hurried off. Danks filled and lit his pipe and withdrew a skin filled with whiskey and enjoyed a long drink of the fiery liquid. He lit his pipe and watched his rangers finish their day's work.

One of his men gathered the scalps and brought them to the Captain. He added them to the existing twenty that were festering and stinking in the bag hanging about his waist.

1 – UN

Mathilde Girouard brushed the top of her oversized loaves of bread with butter and liberally sprinkled it with coarse salt, the way her grand-mére had taught her. Her husband, Acquila, had travelled many miles to the area called Remsheg to dig the salt where the seasoning rose from the very ground. She stood back and admired her "boules" and put all four of them on a cooking rack in the fireplace that 'Quila had made for this singular purpose.

Mati loved the way her husband always came up with inventions that made her life easier or better able to do things for her family. Her kitchen was the envy of almost every other woman in Beaubassin and sometimes it was difficult for her to not brag about how happy she was about how her life had turned out.

She hummed a little ditty that she had heard one of the local musicians play on his wooden whistle after mass the previous week.

She also loved the simple beauty of making her bread; how 'Quila put in his time with the other men to plant and harvest the oats and wheat seeds on the low lands, mill the grain into flour and pack it into barrels. There was something extremely fulfilling, almost sensual, about being the one to finish the work of many people and being able to give something back. She felt a little guilty about how she would get the credit for the final result when she believed that she had the easiest job of anyone involved in the lengthy and strenuous process of bread making.

Mathilde was born in Nanpan, a small settlement only a few miles from where she now lived. She had never ventured further than the return trip to visit her mére, Domithilde, et pére, Charles. She and Acquila had lived with them when they were first married as her parents had lived with their parents. Her brother Jacques had married, stayed at home and was still raising his family there.

Acquila had started building this house when they had been first married. It had taken an entire summer to lay the foundation and cut, saw, and season all the wood. When he had finished all this, the other men in Beaubassin had worked together to assemble and finish it. By then, they had three children.

Her father's family, the Leblancs, had been in Acadie for over a century and were among the first settlers in the area of Tintamarre.

Looking out the window, she could see that the men were burning the marshes to eliminate the dead hay and allow better for new growth. The appetite of flames for the dry grass brought to her mind one of the most vivid memories of her childhood. It was the telling of a story to her by her grand-mére, Louise Poirier:

"When I was small, younger than you, we were living closer to the river, us. One day mon pére, he came running into the yard in a great hurry. He was very upset, him. He grabbed ma mére by the arm and told us all to run into the forest and keep running until we could run no more and then hide.

"I looked back, when I was running, me, and I saw the church, it was burning and I could hear loud sounds that were muskets, I think.

"We ran into the woods, a mile, maybe more, and we hid until dark. In the moonlight, we returned home and looked at the settlement from the edge of the forest. It was all on fire, every building. And the only people walking they wore red coats, like the devil.

"There were many bodies on the ground and I saw one of the red coat devils walk over to one of the bodies. And that devil, him, that devil, he cut the hair from the head of that body.

"We slept all night in the forest, and we waited until all the red coat devils had left and then we returned. And ma mére, she turn over the dead body that the red coat devil had desecrated. And it was mon pére."

Ever since being told that story, even though she had never met even one English, Mati had nightmares of monsters that wore red coats and brought death and fire to her people.

Their house was at one corner of the village of Beaubassin that was just above the gentle slope of the ridge that led down into the marshlands. These drained marshes stretched for miles to the north between the ridge on which their settlement was built and another; on the other side of the Mésagouèche River.

The house was a good size with private sleeping areas in the attic for her and Acquila and another for the two boys. Their daughter Béatrice, who was only five, slept on a small cot at the foot of her parents' bed.

The wind always roared off the bay and up the hill so the door and windows were on the side facing away from the valley. Her kitchen was on the right side of the front door when entering so that the prevailing winds would not enter their home and disturb the fire.

The huge fireplace had a large slate hearth that her husband had found and hauled back from a beach beneath the cliffs many miles away and hardwood was neatly stacked on it. Along with the built-in bread frame, the fireplace had inside hooks where 'Quila hung and smoked pieces of venison, large salmon, ducks and other meats that were plentiful in the area.

There was a cold room dug in the basement and 'Quila would carry down blocks of ice in the spring to allow some foodstuffs to keep longer. Her staples: potatoes, turnips and apples, were kept in barrels in the cold room. Mati grew cabbage in her garden, sliced it up and combined it with salt in earthen ware containers in which it fermented into choucroute. It was a welcome addition to the diet in the winter with dried meats and potatoes. She also had a barrel of salted herring and another barrel of pigs' feet and pork shoulders pickling in vinegar she had made from apples.

Mathilde was sure that no one else in New France ate better than her family did and she delighted when her boys would ask for more food and she had enough for them until they stopped asking.

She noticed that her boys' beds had not been made and she thought she would soon need to make Emile's pants a little longer. When she thought of her oldest boy, who was an exact replica of his father, she remembered the first time that she and 'Quila had set eyes on each other.

Acquila, had come to Nanpan as an adult. Mati thought back to when she was a young girl living with her parents, brothers and grand-mére...

*****

It was Saint Benedict's Day and as always on such days there was a fast followed by a feast. The village residents all convened in the village church for the party and each family shared in provisioning the event as well as enjoying it.

The men each had their own specialties in libations and there was always a more than adequate supply of wines made from dandelions, gooseberries and chokecherries. One settler, Bertrand Haché, who was the only local Acadian from eastern France, had figured out how to distil various local grains into rough liquor that was also used by older people in the area to alleviate their joint pain.

In the summer months, the fête moved outside and the local musicians brought along their whistles, jews harps, homemade fiddles and rough-hewn banjos and the entire village celebrated late into the night. Many revellers without instruments added the stomping of their feet and oral sounds to the rhythms.

At one of these events, when Mati had just turned 16, she noticed Acquila Girouard. He was rowdy and got into a wrestling match with one of the other young men. He managed to get the other fellow on the ground and hold him there but let him up so the match could continue.

Both men took off their shirts and Mati couldn't help but notice sweat drop from Acquila's swarthy brow onto his muscular chest. She had strangely felt weak and felt a shudder go down her spine.

When the two men finished wrestling they brushed themselves off and 'Quila lifted the other man's arm in victory even though it was obvious that 'Quila was the winner of the match.

He smiled at her but she turned her eyes away. Her grand-mére often expressed her hope that Mati would devote her life to God as a nun, since she had no other granddaughters. And Mati, although she was a devout Roman Catholic, really didn't want to. But, as a devoted daughter and granddaughter, she couldn't bring herself to express her hesitancy and say never.

Then 'Quila came to call on her.

She was spinning wool in the living area of their house when her father answered a knock at the door. She heard the mumbles of conversation and took a peek out of the window. Then her father raised his voice and slammed the door and she quickly got back to her spinning wheel.

'It was him…'

Her heart beat a little faster but she forced herself to calm down. Her father came in with a stormy expression on his face and she didn't dare to look up. He stomped to his chair, sat and crossed his arms across his chest. Glowering.

'Surely, Papa can't be mad at me?'

Her father stood, marched over to her, started to say something… and then stomped back to his chair, sat and lit his pipe, and glowered some more.

A short while later Mathilde's mother returned home and she and Mati's father had a loud argument in the kitchen, while Mati carefully and quietly kept spinning. After a few minutes her father had stormed out.

Her mother started making poutine rapée dumplings, which was something she often did when she was upset. It always served to cool her down when times were difficult or she was worried. She added some water to flour in a wooden bowl, some salt and worked it with her hands. She grated several potatoes and added them to the mixture.

She took handfuls of the pastry and wrapped a bit of salted and fatty pork in each one and dropped them in an earthenware bowl of heavily salted water. She would leave it there to season and gain flavour. When she was done she walked over to Mati, adjusting her apron and her bonnet. She sat down on a stool while Mati continued spinning.

"Mathilde. This is a difficult discussion but one that every mother has to have with every daughter." She had a handkerchief in her hand and daubed her eyes, which were slightly teary.

"No father likes to see his daughter grow up and be lost to another man. So every father acts the way yours did this afternoon, when that time comes. He doesn't want you to see Monsieur Girouard. He says that Acquila is too old for you and that he does not know his family."

"But, Maman…"

"Ecouter, ma petite."

"Oui."

"I told your father that he has to allow his little girl to grow up. He got very angry when I said this. I asked him if he would be willing to meet this young man and perhaps get to know him."

"Oh, merci, merci, ma mére."

"But he said no."

Mati's heart fell.

Her mother daubed at her eyes again. "But I have been with your father since I was of the age you are now. And I asked him where he would be today if my pére had not allowed him to meet me."

"That's when he got angry and left."

Mathilde felt her eyes start to tear from frustration and disappointment.

"But don't cry, Mati. Your father will be angry for a while. That's the way he is. But he is wise and he will know that I am right. And I have no doubt that he will agree to meet Monsieur

Girouard and perhaps get to know him well enough to offer his approval."

Mati turned toward her mother on her stool and reached out to her. Her mother embraced Mati and whispered in her ear, "Mati, Chér, you will always be our little girl even when you have little boys and girls of your own."

The first opportunity for Mathilde to meet Acquila was at church the following Sunday. She washed and starched her church clothes and bonnet and demurely applied a little raspberry juice to her cheeks just as they were about to leave. She noticed that her mother had put two gigantic pies on a shelf high up in the fireplace. Mati thought that this was very curious.

Her mother and father were very devout, as were all the residents of Nanpan. Attending church was the way that they proved their devotion to God and their commitment to their community. Mathilde's youngest brothers Joseph and Pascal had their baths in the morning in the kitchen and their hair was greased and carefully combed. Her oldest brother, Jacques, was twelve and had bathed the evening before. Her grandmother donned her Sunday clothes that she had worn for over forty years that had been constantly patched and maintained so, as always, they looked like new.

When the bells started ringing her grand-mére led the family procession to the church, followed by Mati's parents, then the children by descending age. Little Pascal, as he always was, had been distracted by the rabbits being interrupted by all the human activity. Her father had needed to give him his look of impending punishment to get the six year old to stay in line.

In only a couple of minutes the family reached the church located in the centre of the only road that was populated on both sides by houses. The church was farthest from the brow of the hill that dropped down into the Riviere Hébert to the south.

As always the wind was blowing strongly off the river and all the women tightly tied their bonnets and were holding their skirts against their legs. It was remarkably warm for a spring day and the grasses were starting to turn green. The road, which had been paved with logs decades before, was almost completely dry.

Several men were outside of the church smoking and talking.

Mati noticed Acquila among the men and he noticed her and nodded. She hadn't dared to nod back but she smiled and noticed out of the corner of her eye that he had smiled back to her.

Her mother signalled to Mati and the two boys to move ahead into the line of parishioners being greeted by Father Bourgeois. Her father left the line and walked away; toward Acquila. Mati was careful to not pay any attention as this might have troubled her papa and that might have made him even more stubborn.

She, her mére and the two boys said their greetings to the priest and entered the small chapel. It had been constructed after New Englander Colonel Benjamin Church had burned the original church, and settlement, at the beginning of the century. The roughly hewn pews made of elm wood had survived the burning, were now as hard as iron, and worn smooth by over a century of worshippers' bottoms.

The interior had barely enough room to accommodate the settlement's population of just over eighty. There was a simple but ancient granite stoup of holy water just inside the entrance and the Leblanc family, minus Papa, but including little Pascal, each touched the water and made the sign of the cross. Mati had never forgotten how dear the little boy had looked, trying so hard to mimic the adults. They went to their row, genuflected to the ark and took their seats.

One of the few salvations from Church's terrible attack, that had cost one acolyte his life, was that the crucifix and other items used for the Eucharist were rescued before they could be stolen by the English. The skull of the murdered acolyte, Roger Arseneaux, was kept in the altar in the reliquary. Survivors of the raid reported that his spirit had warned families who had been fishing a few miles away to not go home. Many of the residents of Nanpan still prayed every morning and evening to Saint Roger of Nanpan and his skull was placed on the altar on the mass closest to every anniversary of the raid.

A rumbling came from the back of the church and Mathilde turned around to see her father and Acquila enter together. After they had completed the sign of the cross, her father joined them while Acquila sat in the back row. Mathilde noticed that her father whispered something in his mother's ear. Domithilde glanced sideways to Mati with just a tiny hint of a smile.

Mati was almost exploding with curiosity. What had her father whispered to her mother? Was it about Acquila? Why had her mother baked such large pies?

Mati understood almost no Latin, so at Mass had always participated in the liturgy by rote. At this mass she was always a step behind in kneeling and reading the responses. She couldn't pay attention and she had gotten a pinch from her grand-mére for her mistakes. The mass couldn't end soon enough for her.

When Father Bourgeois called for the dismissal, she could hardly wait to leave. He asked all the men to stay behind to make an announcement. The women and children stood, genuflected and left.

* * * * *

Acquila Girouard stayed behind with the other men although he was anxious to be formally introduced to the girl he now knew was named Mathilde.

The priest, holding a piece of parchment that looked very formal, called to all the men: "Please come to the front of pews." Acquila moved to the front and was curious as to what Pére Bourgeois might have to say that was so important.

"Mes Amis, les seigneurs de la village de Nanpan, I was given this letter to read to you by a courier who came from the English government in Annapolis Royal. I will read it in French, although it is, of course, written in the language of our occupiers.

"This letter is addressed to all residents of Nova Scotia, by the acting Governor of the colony, same being Colonel Richard Philips, Esq. on behalf of His Majesty King George, King of England, all of its colonies including the Province of Nova Scotia.

"Be it known by all present that as of the date and time of the reading of this notice that all residents, tenants and property rights holders in this colony of Nova Scotia are hereby required

to swear their unconditional fidelity and loyalty to the King of England and that they will on demand by a legitimate authority bear arms on behalf of the King of England against any aggressor, be they Aboriginal or French or of any other race or creed.

"Thus, I command all residents of Nova Scotia to make the following oath:

"I promise and swear on my Christian faith, that I will be faithful to obey His Majesty George II whom I recognize as the sovereign of Acadia or Nova Scotia. So help me God.

"Signed,

Col. Richard Phillips, Governor (Acting)

"There is nothing for me to add. If any of you wish to come and sign this oath before me, then do so."

There was a rumble among the men, but no one came forward.

2 – DEUX

Mati and her mother and grand-mére and brothers started home. Her mother said, "Jacques, I want you to run home and take a bag down to the beach and find us one or two of those big red bugs there, and collect as many of those closed shells as you can carry and fill the bag with as many of the crevettes as you can catch and bring them back."

"Oui, Maman," Jacques said, and started off at top speed to fulfill his chore. Mathilde said, "Maman, what is happening? Why are you making such a large meal? What did papa say to you?"

Her mother gave her a stern look and held her finger to her lips. "Attender, ma petite." So Mati managed to control her curiosity, but only just, but when they had gotten out of earshot of the church she asked again.

"Your father told me that he had a discussion with Monsieur Girouard." She pronounced his name in the Acadian dialect; as "Geerwaw".

"About what? What did he say? What did Acquila say?"

"Calm down, I will tell you. He said that he invited Monsieur Girouard to work with him in the aboiteaux maintenance this week so they might get to know each other."

"That's all?"

"Well… he also invited Monsieur Girouard to join us for dinner this afternoon."

Mati's spirits rose and a huge grin lit up her face. "Oh, Maman! What will I do? What will I wear? How will I act? What will I say?"

"Mathilde," her mother said in a firm voice but with a suppressed smile, "I expect you will act like yourself and that you will be polite and that you will wear what you always wear for Sunday dinner and that you will mind your tongue and not allow yourself to act like a silly, lovesick fool."

Once the three women and the little boys arrived home, Pascal and Joseph were ordered to change into their normal clothes and go outside to play with the other children. Mati's grand-mére, Louise, and her mother immediately changed but Mati was told to stay in her Sunday clothes.

Her mother started a roaring fire in the fireplace and put her cauldron, half-filled with water, on a corner of the grillwork. She also put quantities of greens in a pot of water to boil when the other items were finished. Mati watched as the two older women started fussing around the kitchen. Her grand-mére went down in the cold room and returned with the dumplings Domithilde had made the day before.

Jacques arrived dragging a burlap bag. He released it on the floor and his mother said, "Merci, mon petit chou."

Her grand-mére said, "Mathilde, come and see how I prepare the ragoût."

Mathilde's grandmother used all her strength to lift the bag and drop it on the table. Mathilde helped her empty it which revealed two lobsters the size of small dogs, a pile of clams and oysters, a bunch of crabs and a healthy pile of thumb-sized shrimp.

"First, Mathilde, we make our soup." Her grand-mére had a huge hand axe, grabbed one of the huge lobsters, chopped off the claws and tail with a huge whack each and dropped the remaining body in the steaming cauldron and proceeded to do the same with the second lobster. Then she chopped off all the large crab claws, chopped the bodies in half and dropped them in the pot as well.

Her grand-mére pulled down a couple of smoked sausages hanging from the ceiling and a smoked pork hock while her mother went out to the yard and emerged with a chicken that Jacques had killed and plucked clean of feathers the day before. Louise made short work of the chicken, cutting it into a dozen pieces and salting and flouring it thoroughly. She placed a skillet on the cooking grill, tossed in a piece of lard, and then started frying the chicken. She covered it with a handful of dried peppers that came from the French-owned Caribbean islands. A couple of sausages and the pork hock were chopped up and were also thrown in the mixture.

Then Mati's grand-mére chopped up onions and added them to the meat then added the shellfish to the boiling pot. She kept her eye on the clams and oysters and removed them and set them aside the minute they popped open and dropped in the immense lobster tails and claws and shrimp.

"Le grande finale, Mathilde!" With that her grand-mére dumped the entire contents of the skillet into the cauldron. She replaced the skillet on the cooking grill and dumped in a quantity of lard, waited for it to melt and then added a cup of flour. "To thicken the ragoût, Mati." She stirred it for several minutes until it browned, then lifted the huge skillet once again and poured the mixture into the stew. "C'est ca." She used a utensil to give the stew a good stir.

At that very moment there was noise outside,

"Vite… Mathilde, go upstairs." Mathilde hurried.

The door swung open and Acquila preceded her father, Charles, into the house.

"Monsieur Girouard, these are our sons, Jacques, Pascal and Joseph." The boys bowed very formally and Acquila bowed just as formally back to them. "And this is my mother, Louise Leblanc, and my wife, Domithilde".

"Thank you for inviting me for dinner, Madame Leblanc and Madame Leblanc. Among my keepsakes from my mother that were saved for me were these, I hope you will find some use for them." He handed a package in a lace doily to Louise who smiled and handed them to Domithilde who opened the package, removed four small silver spoons and gasped.

"Oh, mon Dieu, Monsieur Girouard. These are very precious and you must value them very much. Thank you, very, very much."

"It is my pleasure and I am sure that ma mére would prefer that they find a home in a family instead of hidden in a rough man's luggage."

While Mati was waiting upstairs, sitting on the edge of her grandmother's bed, she could hear the sound of spirited conversation, mostly in feminine voices interrupted by throaty male monosyllabic responses. She was filled with curiosity. She suspected her father and the young man would be talking about the work that remained to be done on the dykes and sluiceways, the aboiteaux, as well as the regular maintenance program.

Finally, after what seemed like an hour, she heard, "Mathilde, come downstairs, we have a guest for dinner."

Mathilde resisted hurrying, the worst thing would be to tumble downstairs, and she calmly gathered herself and walked down the narrow and steep staircase into the main living area.

When she arrived, everyone was standing in front of the door. "Mathilde", her father said, "this is Monsieur Acquila Girouard, he is working with me now and I invited him to join us for dinner. Monsieur Girouard, this is our daughter, Mathilde Leblanc."

Mati didn't really know what to do, but she walked toward Acquila and, based on her limited experience, curtsied, bending slighting at her knees.

He spoke first.

"Mathilde, I am very pleased to meet you," he bowed.

She nodded demurely.

"Domithilde, please show our guest to his place at our dinner table."

Acquila held up another package. "Madame, first…may I?" Domithilde nodded.

He gave a package to Mathilde who didn't open it, but beamed in anticipation.

Her mother said, "Mathilde, perhaps you can open M. Girouard's gift after dinner. We need to eat before the food gets cold."

Mati came to her senses and noticed that her mother had set up a small table for the two little boys to leave the dinner table for Jacques and the adults. Her grand-mére directed the boys to their seats and served them first.

As always, her Papa was at the head of the table and Maman sat at the other end. Acquila sat with Jacques on one side while Mathilde and her grand-mére would share the other. Each place was set with a plate and bowl.

Mati had sense enough to be a focal point of the dinner service and she got busy. She filled a bowl with fiddlehead fern greens and another with crow's feet greens and put them on the table and beside them smaller bowls of home-churned butter and homemade vinegar.

Meanwhile, Charles started the conversation, “So, Monsieur Girouard, how was it that you came to our village?”

“Monsieur, I came because I had no reason to stay in France. My family is from a little village along the Riviere Loire, named Gennes. We were not holders of lands, my parents died; I did not wish to join the church or the militaire. I have cousins in Grand Pre whose family has been here for over one hundred years, so I came here for adventure.”

Mati glanced at him and thought his eyes looked huge and she was intrigued by the way he seemed to smile as he talked.

“Have you found adventure?”

“Oh, very, very much, Monsieur Leblanc. Here I am making my own way and I pursue my own destiny.”

“That is good. Men who come to this place have to be very strong and determined. It is no place for weaklings or those with soft hearts and hands.”

Mati’s mother and grandmother brought a huge bowl of the stew to the table and another of the poutine rapée and a third of mashed turnip. There was a large ewer of cider and another of milk that had been chilled in the cold room in the basement.

Mati wondered if her mére had planned to have this banquet happen, or if it was accidental. Knowing her mother, she thought, probably the first. She would know that handsome young men are few in the settlement and would try her best to find one for her little girl.

Her father said, “Mathilde, why don’t you join us? Asseyez vous.”

Mati took her place as did her mother and grand-mére. The enormous quantity of different foods was passed around and, after plates were filled, Charles said grace.

The table they were dining at was long and narrow to best fit within the house and Mati found herself only a few feet across the table from her possible beau and she was thrilled and had a problem concentrating on her food. She didn't even notice if her father had yet said grace! Mati's father poured Acquila a mug of cider, then filled his own and said, "M. Girouard, what do you think of what Pére Bourgeois revealed to us today?"

Acquila replied cautiously, as he had worried if his host would wish him to discuss such serious matters as politics and religion. "Monsieur Leblanc, I always listen carefully to whatever our priest tells us, but it seems that he did not offer us guidance, non? May I ask your opinion?"

Charles took a deep draught of his cider and refilled his mug after offering a refill to Acquila who declined. "We can not trust the Maudits, ever, I think. And I am a farmer not a soldier, so I intend to take up arms against no one. Certainly not against my fellow farmers and not against soldiers who are better shots with muskets than I am."

Knowing now Charles' point of view, Acquila was comfortable to reply. "I agree, Monsieur Leblanc. Our enemies are bad weather, high tides and the little black flies."

Charles broke into a loud and animated laugh as did his wife, while Mathilde, still a little shy, only smiled, and covered her mouth with her napkin. Acquila was a second late and leaned back in laughing and accidentally kicked Mati in the shin with his wooden sabots. She took in a deep breath to try and repel the immediate pain, but looked across at him.

"Oh, Mademoiselle, I am very sorry. Did I hurt you?"

She shook her head and smiled.

"I would never hurt you, Mathilde."

Domithilde then looked at her husband and they both smiled. Then little Pascal spilled his stew all over the table and the moment was lost and the two women rushed to clean up the mess. Charles stood.

"Will you have a pipe outside, M. Girouard? I have some raspberry brandy I made that you might enjoy."

"Oui. I would enjoy that very much." Acquila stood and Charles went to the fireplace to take a small jug from the mantel and to light a length of fuse.

"Madame Leblanc et Madame Leblanc et Mathilde, I hope you will accept my appreciation for feeding so well a starving soul that is used to catching and killing something and cooking it badly. It was all very delicious and I will not have to eat for another day."

The two older women nodded and smiled until Charles returned. "Acquila, Venez avec moi. You have your pipe?" Acquila nodded.

They went outside to a circle of driftwood chairs around a small table in front of the house, sheltered from the wind. Both men removed their pipes and Charles produced a pouch of tobacco, which was a cheap and well-appreciated benefit from trade with the English colony in Virginia. He filled and lit his pipe while Acquila filled his and then accepted the fuse. Charles realized he had forgotten cups for the brandy so went back inside and quickly returned and sat.

"Your family, your parents, you said they have passed, how did they die?"

"There was a flood and mon pére tried to save a sheep that was being swept away and ma mére tried to save him and they were both lost. I was eleven years of age and became a servant to the local priest, who was a very good man. My sisters were all dispersed to relatives and I have not since seen them."

"That is very sad."

Acquila shrugged. "It's the only life I ever knew. I was sad, then, but I was very young and moved along with my life. It did give me a fear of water, which I overcame by coming to Acadie in an old leaking boat in November."

Charles laughed. "Bien sûr!

What are you intentions here, Monsieur Girouard?"

"To settle here in Beaubassin, live well, work hard and raise a family to look after me when I am old."

"Those are good intentions. What about our daughter, Mathilde, who is very dear to us?"

"She is very wholesome and intelligent and seems to be well trained in looking after a home, Monsieur Leblanc."

"She is also close to the age when she might consider having her own family."

"Would it be improper, M. Leblanc, to ask you for permission to see Mathilde with the most respectful intent?"

"You will be working with me in the aboiteaux. Perhaps after a week or two I will provide you an answer to your request."

While the men were outside smoking, Domithilde said with excitement, "Mati, quick, open your gift from M. Girouard!"

She did. It was a single pearl in gold fitting and necklace that she treasured every day thereafter.

* * * * *

Ten days later, Acquila and Charles were covered in muck at the end of a long day spent building a new aboiteau in a new dyke on the other side of the Riviere Nanpan.

It was a huge undertaking, but over the previous century the frigid and unstoppable tides of the Baie Beaubassin had worked its way around the existing series of dykes and was starting to pool sea water on the northwest area of the marshes. These pools could eventually reclaim the ocean from fertile farmland that had been formed over decades by agonizing work of several previous generations.

Work could only be done at low tide, which meant they could only work on days with low tide and then only for less than five months in the late spring to early fall. Weather willing. So the men worked feverishly and without a break from dawn to dusk in the period between planting and harvest to maintain the intricate system of dykes that protected their farmland and livelihoods.

Charles sat on the wooden aboiteau that was waiting to be installed once the digging was finished and watched Acquila complete the last few shovels. The tides would do their work overnight, and in the morning they would need to re-do much of the work they had done today. The tides were eternal.

"Enough, Girouard. We need to leave before the tides return."

"One more." Acquila pushed his dyke spade once more into the earth and removed one more shovel load, then used the tool's square blade to push him out of the hole high enough so that Charles could give him a hand out. The hole they had dug was already filling with water.

The men walked briskly to the other side of the marsh, back toward the village, and firmly stored their spades in the soil of the dyke adjoining the Nanpan River ready for tomorrow's labour.

While the settlement was less than a few hundred paces away, the river and its muddy shores created a considerable barrier. So now they had to deal with the slippery hazard of making their way down and up mucky banks that had in the past ended the lives of other men just as strong and careful as they.

But barging was much less work than going far enough up the muddy stream to be able to ford it. Acquila made his way down the rope they had tied to the barge and Charles passed him the pole they would use to navigate the few dozen yards to the other shore. They were exhausted but careful to not slip and after ten minutes were tying up the raft on the other side and pulling themselves up the slippery bank.

After they were walking back Charles said, "Good job, mon fils. You are a good worker."

"Not yet as strong as you, Charles."

"But you haven't been eating my wife's cooking that gave me this strength. You know, Mathilde is as good a cook as my wife?"

"Non."

"Perhaps you should clean up and come to visit tonight to

meet with Domithilde and our family."

Acquila had been hoping for this invitation and he was thrilled.

3 – TROIS

Benoni Danks and his corps of two dozen irregulars had come by schooner from Machias in the Province of Massachusetts, not far from the border of the northern colonies. The trip was unpleasant even with a stop on Grand Menane Island and the spring gales resulted in the scuppers being filled with vomit. When they arrived all of the men were out of sorts and arguing with each other.

He had been summoned by Colonel John Gorham, to bring his company of rangers to Nova Scotia to provide some level of protection for the English outposts and respond to attacks by the local Indians who seemed to be led by a renegade priest of some sort.

Their tents were next to a small brook. It was sun up and two of the men were using jerry-rigged fishing poles made of alder branches to capture small speckled trout. They had a sizable pile of the ten inch long fish next to them which a third soldier was cleaning while smoking a white clay pipe.

His scrappers were mostly unwelcome in their civilized New England towns and if they had not volunteered to come on this mission; most would have found a home behind bars. Danks and his raiders were rangers; not quite British regular army and not quite civilian militia. His group, and a few others, had been formed to try and defeat the savages loyal to the French at their own game. They had uniforms of a sort, dull browns and blues with a blue, and usually filthy, Tam O'Shanter and canvas leggings. Several of the men who had joined the crew in Boston had done so just for the pair of boots and a bowl of porridge.

His second in command was Hezekiah King, and Danks called for him. "King!"

The young, red-faced Yorkshireman appeared. "Capt'n."

"Have the men complete their breakfast and be packed for travel. Have the scouts bring me their report."

"Yes, Capt'n."

King had already prepared the men to move on. In his several months with Danks previously in New England and now Nova Scotia, he had learned to anticipate his Captain's decisions and his mood swings and his sometimes irrational orders.

In a minute the two scouts, twin brothers, Charles and Virgil Labreque appeared. They were local men, half red skinned, who were descendants of the wars with the English from a few decades earlier. They had been abandoned, left in the woods to die by their Miqmaq mother, but had been rescued by a French settler woman and given to a local priest.

As the twins had grown up the priest had treated them horribly and as soon as they were able they ran away from the settlement. They had grown to adulthood living off the land while getting to know every hill and stream.

They despised both the Indians that had abandoned them and the French priests who had been their torturers. They took special pleasure in the ugliest side of their new current English employer's mission and treated brutally every French person with whom they dealt.

For Danks the brothers had been irreplaceable since they had joined his rangers. In just two weeks they had taught his men how to live off the land and had just returned from scouting out a Miqmaq camp they knew was nearby.

"Boyos, come forward."

"Captain."

"Pray tell me, lads, where's the Mikymakys?"

Charles, who was outfitted as if a Miqmaq in rough wool

sweaters and deerskin breeches, spoke in his patois, “It’re tree leagues and have abouts dirty peoples, mostly mens. One pries’. All rest injuns, not widemen.”

“How well are they armed?”

“Dee injuns have bowsarras, a few musket, dem. Dat all.”

“Go get yer things, boyos. Ye’ll be guiding us to them as soon as we get our orders and make our way back.

Danks stood and called. "King! Have the men fall in."

"Done, Capt'n"

"Order 'em up."

“Rangers, two abreast!”

“F’ard, By the left, March!’

* * * * *

Mathilde poured herself a mug of tea and remembered how her mother had bustled around her before her wedding to Acquila. At times it seemed like yesterday, other times it seemed as if it had happened to someone else.

It had been mid-day and her mére had been like a mother hen: polishing her little girl's shoes, making last minute adjustments to her dress and preparing her cosmetics. She remembered how her grand-mére, Louise, had crocheted a wedding bag that would accept gifts from the guests and was finishing the white cake that they would serve to guests at the end of the fête…

Mathilde had wished she could do something, anything, to relieve her tension. All the men and boys had been told to remove themselves and she was sitting in her underwear.

"Mama... Do you think that Acquila is a good man?"

"What do you think, ma chou?"

"I... think so."

Domithilde laughed. "Well, Chér, that is all that matters. What you think. But I think I agree with what you think."

Mati forgot her worries for a second and smiled, covering

her mouth.

"Smile, ma Chér! It is the happiest day of your life!"

Mathilde smiled more broadly.

"What should I know, Mama?"

"You will know, Mati, when the time comes."

Outside there came the sound of bells; the priest and his deacons were walking through the small village ringing hand bells to signify it was time for the wedding service to which all community members were of course invited. Domithilde knew from past weddings they had about a half hour before the parishioners would be seated and ready for the arrival of the family.

"Well, Mati. It is time."

Her grand-mére stood and fluffed Mathilde's petticoats, that she had worked on since Mati had been born, in the air to freshen and expand the many frills and folds and increase its volume. "Ici, Mati."

Mati stood and gave her grand-mére a warm embrace and received the petticoats and stepped into them and pulled them up to her waist. Domithilde expertly did some adjustments with her needle and thread and made sure that they fit well and would stay in place. She held up the wedding shift for Mathilde's approval and helped her pull it over her head, adjusted Mati's hair and held it in place at the back of her head with a comb. Then she placed a shawl around her shoulders and veil over her head.

Domithilde said, "Tres, tres, jolie, Mathilde. Your soon to be husband will be very pleased to see you and I am very proud to be your mére."

"Merci, ma mére. You have filled me with love all of my life and I promise you that I will share it with my children as you did with me and all my generations will remember you in their prayers."

Domithilde passed Mati a bouquet of wildflowers and said, "You are a loving and beautiful woman, Mati. Mais, allons-y. It is time for my little girl to become a woman and start her new life."

The rest of the day and the ceremony were a blur in her memory. She remembered the fête in the church hall and the music played by Acquila's friends and the men of the village dropping coins in her grand-mére's crocheted bag to dance with her and the hilarity of the women of the village each dropping a small chick into a pen at the entrance of the hall to provide her and her family fresh eggs every morning, forever.

And then she and her husband spent their first night together; and they had never spent another apart since.

* * * * *

Danks' Rangers made their way overland toward the new English headquarters in Chebouctu on paths cut through thick pine forests, avoiding distractions in the interest of a more critical event; a meeting with their commanding officer and new Governor.

Eventually they came to a small English outpost along a large inlet and were supplied with a canoe that allowed Danks to accelerate his travel to the new headquarters. They stayed overnight and were up at daybreak to finish their travel. Danks ordered his company to make camp until they returned.

"King, bring Hollis. We'll go."

Hezekiah and the other sub-altern, Charlie Hollis, took the oars and they canoed and portaged until eventually, in the dark, they reached their destination. They manoeuvred the canoe to shore and held it steady while Danks stepped on dry land. It was pitch dark except for the one fire toward which they had paddled.

The three began walking up the rocky slope, past the gallows and stocks, until they came to the village palisades. They approached the guard on duty, the junior officers saluted, the guard saluted to Danks. Josiah presented the guard with their commander's orders and they were escorted to a junior officer on duty.

He welcomed them officiously, "Lloyd, Captain. That is Benjamin Lloyd, Ensign Benjamin Lloyd. I expect you men would like to be given quarters and something to eat. The first is easy; we have visitor quarters in the barracks, the second more difficult; Cook is off for the night and likely asleep or inebriated."

Danks said, "Just a bed will do for now, Ensign Lloyd."

The Ensign guided them to the barracks. "I expect you might find Colonel Gorham in the local, Captain. He is often the last person to depart. It's just outside the southern entrance." He took them inside the barracks, it was filled with snoring, belching and farting soldiers; like military barracks in every camp.

Lloyd led them to one end of the structure where there were a dozen or so empty cots. "Here you are, Captain. Parade is called at break of day."

The three men dropped their kit at the foot of their assigned beds. Danks said, "I'm going to try and find the Colonel as well as some rum. A naval place like this one should have an ample supply."

"Can we come along, Captain?"

"If ye wish, but don't repeat what ye might hear and don't say anything ye'll regret later."

The captain led the trio out the door. He told them to be quiet. Danks led his small company south, along a couple of back streets, to the exit from the palisade and explained their mission to the guards and were allowed to pass. They came up to a door with a two headed black bird roughly painted on the door. Danks opened the door and let the two juniors precede him inside.

There were a half dozen men in the small public house, five at one table; John Gorham, sitting by himself at another.

"Colonel."

"Captain Danks. Please join me."

"Ye mind, Sor, if me lads sit with us."

"Not at all, providing they mind their manners and pay their own way."

The barkeep arrived.

"A small cask of rum."

"A shilling in advance, sir."

“What’s the world coming to?” Danks reached in a pocket and tossed one to the server.

“Three glasses, unless the colonel wishes some.”

“Make it four.”

Gorham offered Danks a small cigar, which he accepted and lit from a candle on the table. Danks looked at Gorham; he appeared washed and civilized.

“What’s going on with the politicians, Colonel Gorham?”

“I think that the new Governor has all sorts of trouble lined up for the Crapauds and their Indians. They've been slaughtering some of our settlements.”

Hollis dared speak, “What about their oath?”

“The French are born liars, lad. Boy, you can tell when they lie when they move their lips.

"How was your trip? I expect ye’ll want to visit the Paymaster in the morn. How many?”

“Two score.”

“Good start.”

“Ye’ll meet with the new governor, Cornwallis the Younger, tomorrow. Figger first light. Be on yer best behaviour. He’s not used to living outside of luxury yet, and he tends to look down his nose at anyone that ain’t wigged and perfumed. The Paymaster is in the church.”

Gorham drank back his rum and stood. “In the morning, Captain. Lads.” He opened the door and walked out.

Danks thought for a brief time about following Gorham to his bed. But he had not fallen asleep sober in years, and he thought this wouldn’t be the best time to start. He finished most of the cask, allowing his subs a mug each, then led them back to their quarters.

* * * * *

Danks awoke with the dull thickness behind his eyes and under his tongue to which he had grown accustomed. He found that when he didn't drink a substantial amount during a night he would have splitting headaches in the morning. He preferred the thickness to the pain.

He had slept in his clothes. He sat up on his bed, turned up the bedside oil lantern, and lit a cheroot with his fuse case. He stood, walked to the barracks entrance, opened the door and looked outside. There was a chill in the air from a wind blowing off the ocean down the harbour.

The smoke and the cool air woke his aides who greeted the day by coughing; the barracks were coal heated that gave off fumes even worse than the older man's cigars. The lads were wearing long night-dresses that they quickly removed, rolled up and stowed in their kits.

"Come on, Lads. Get yer arses movin'. I have some business to do and then we'll see the guv'ner."

He had asked Gorham where the Paymaster office was and he had been told that his office was in the church. He led his charges the few dozen yards to the small steepled building and knocked on the side door.

It was opened by a small, foppish, red-headed man with tiny spectacles who was still wearing his bedclothes.

"And who might you be?"

"I be Captain Benoni Danks of the provincial Rangers and I'm here to collect me bounty."

He threw his scalp bag on the wooden steps.

"Oh. I'm Willigar, the Paymaster and the Quartermaster. Very unpleasant. Let's do the count outside. Please don't ask me to touch them."

Danks picked up the bag and started tossing the scalps in a pile in the street while Willigar counted.

"Very, very unpleasant, but very impressive. That is forty two times fifty guineas. That is a considerable amount, Captain Danks. Might I suggest that we sign a promissory note to you for most of it, and you can collect the currency when you are going to a place to spend it."

"I'll take ten in pound sterling and fifty in local now and the note. But I want the note registered."

"Well, I'm also the official registrar, so that will be done."

"Do up the paper work and I will return after me meeting with the guv'ner."

Danks turned and led his men by the church and along the parade ground that was already showing signs of life. They passed the courts heading south and then turned east a block to the Governor's simple single story residence.

The doorway had guards with wigs and full military dress at its front. Danks turned toward one of the guards and gave him his orders. The guard read the missive and opened the door for Danks and the others followed. There was a small anteroom with an aide seated at a finely crafted desk. The room itself had been whitewashed and there were a number of very expensive pieces of furniture. One wall had an enormous mirror with a gilded frame, another a full scale portrait of a finely dressed nobleman, undoubtedly one of the new governor's ancestors.

An aide in proper attire looked up and offered an expression of disgust.

Danks passed him his orders; the aide looked at them and said, "We had expected you later in the day, Captain Danks."

He cast his eyes toward a group of three fine chairs against one wall and started to say something then stopped.

"Please wait, Captain Danks, I will see if the Governor is disposed to see you."

In a moment the aide returned and sat at his desk in silence. Danks and his two juniors waited, standing for close to an hour. Then the front door opened and John Gorham entered.

"Danks. Good morning. I trust you slept well."

"Well enough, Colonel."

"Hinshelwood, please see if the Governor will see us now."

"Yes, Colonel."

Hinshelwood returned in a half minute, "Colonel, Governor Cornwallis will see you now."

Gorham and then Danks followed the aide into the Governor's private chamber. It too was ornately furnished but had walls that were simply whitewashed.

Cornwallis was seated and didn't rise.

"Please sit, Colonel Gorham."

He held a handkerchief to his nose, obviously bothered by the odour emitted from his visitors. He was uniformed, wigged and powdered and, although seated, appeared to be tall.

He stood and spoke as he looked out a side window. "Colonel, we have to correct the Acadian situation. I have tried my utmost to have them accept allegiance to King George, that they could keep their homesteads and become loyal Britons.

"That place where they have settled, this Beauséjour or Tintamarre or whatever they call it, it is a very important place in our plans to control the northern part of this new world. We need to cross that damned little stretch of swamp to deliver our soldiers and our material to Canada in the winter.

"But with the interference of that damnable priest the Acadians have refused our overtures, have refused to swear their allegiance and are interfering with our master plan. Not to mention that just last week they scalped and beheaded six of our men cutting boards for the new settlement in Dartmouth."

"And now, they, or at least their Mickymackys, have taken arms against our people. By right of law, this Nova Scotia is a colony of England and is under the rule of good King George the Second. Is this correct?"

"Substantially, your Excellency."

"And, as King George's appointee to see that this colony is properly managed as a dependency of England, then I have every right to take action as I would if the Acadians were rebels in England, itself. Yes?"

"That would be so, your Excellency."

He turned back toward the men. "Then action, it is, that I will take." He smiled and showed his dirty teeth, while reflecting a sinister, almost wolf-like, attitude.

"I have tried my best, well beyond the standard level of effort, to have these farmers stay in our colony. We would prefer to not have to bring boatloads of Germans here to populate this place, but these Frenchmen are . . . incorrigible.

"They will never be welcome settlers in our Nova Scotia,

Colonel, although we have offered them every kindness. I have here," he held up a document, "a denial by one thousand Frenchman to ever agree to submit their loyalty to our throne. These peasants… these farmers… write that they will leave this land rather than swear to an oath of loyalty to us.

"We find this to be an act of treason. We will not treat with these savages; nor will we follow the normal courtesies of civilized warfare. We will expand our bounty to all Indians, men, women and children and we will visibly expand our presence on this peninsula. I want fortresses in Annapolis Royal and here in Halifax to be strengthened and I have ordered fortresses to be built in Chignectou, including what the French call Grand Pré, in Piziquid and in Beaubassin. I will see a road built to better allow this.

"I have ordered Captain Cobb to pursue the arrest of the leader of French uprising, the priest, Le Loutre who is behind this insurrection. I have also given him full royal authority to take as hostage any and all wives and children of rebel French subjects in Nova Scotia to enforce the loyalty of these French peasants.

"Your orders, men, are to prepare these sites for our occupation with soldiers and civilians by eliminating the non-loyal subjects resident there. These orders are to be executed forthwith. And eliminate that damned priest if you have the opportunity, in such case you will be well rewarded, as well as arrest those Frenchmen that supported these terrible events.

"You shall muster with your commander, Lieutenant Colonel Charles Lawrence, in the parade grounds at noon hour to begin your mission.

"That is all. Good day to you." Cornwallis turned, sat at his desk and started looking at papers.

Gorham and Danks and the subalterns left the Governor to prepare for their mission. Gorham said, "Bit of a prig, is he not?"

Danks replied, "Looks like my granny in that wig and with that doily."

"The well bred, generally aren't; bred, that is. Or at least not often enough."

Danks snorted. "Nothing like an inherited title to encourage oneself to talk like a lion and look like a unicorn."

Gorham snorted back.

The two senior officers went to the Paymaster and Danks signed his X to finalize his paperwork and get his promissory note. With just a few weeks work he had a tidy fortune.

Within an hour the quartet reassembled at the parade ground and went to the adjoining mess for a meal prior to their travel.

They each had a plate of beans and a smoked herring. Each packed a couple of additional fish in their kits to accompany them on their voyage and they left to meet their ultimate commanding officer.

When they got outdoors they faced a parade ground almost filled by a battalion of several hundred troops all dressed in red coats and wearing the tricorns and mitre caps of the Fortieth Foot. At their front was a stocky officer who eyed the newcomers before he turned command over to a junior officer and walked toward them.

"Gorham, I presume."

"Lieutenant Colonel." Gorham and the others saluted.

"You know of your orders." Lawrence spoke this as a command not a question. "What problems do you see foresee for us?

"Colonel Gorham, I think their Indians will, of course, be in our way. They are called, Mikymakys, and are quite fierce. And there is the priest."

"What do you know of this priest, Colonel Gorham?"

While Gorham appeared to have a higher rank, it was with the Rangers and it had no value to the regular forces. Lawrence actually showed Gorham considerable respect by using it at all.

"His name is Le Loutre. He makes his base in the centre of the province, mostly in Cobequid, but he is very mobile and causes mischief across much of the province. He is very unorthodox and controls almost all the redskins, who follow his commands expeditiously."

"Well then, we shall need to make an end of him. You have heard of the slaughtering last week, I presume?"

"Yes, Colonel.?

"Well, your immediate command is to appropriately penalize the Indians that did this. Where are your men based?”

Gorham said, “Not far from Piziquid, Danks?”

Lawrence turned his attention to the Captain of the Rangers with obvious distaste.

“My men are currently camped near Mines, Milord.”

“I am a Lieutenant Colonel in King George’s army, Danks, you will address me as such.”

“Yes, Sor. Yes, Lieutenant Colonel.”

“Soon I will be taking this regiment with me to Chignectou to finally deal with the French. Two hundred more men are already en route aboard four sloops loaded with everything we will need to build a fortress to end this French and Indian problem.

“Colonel Gorham, are you ready to proceed?”

“Yes, Lieutenant Colonel.

“Very well. That is what you will do. You are so ordered.”

4 – QUATRE

The Girouard house in Beaubassin was outfitted with a cistern above the animal lean-to that was kept full by the frequent rains in the Chignectou isthmus. Even in the winter there were often mild winds that would blow down the bay and keep it from freezing. It was next to the chimney, which also kept its contents in liquid form.

Mati used lye soap to wash the afternoon meal dishes in a wooden tub and rinsed them in a slow dribble from a tap on a wooden pipe leading from the cistern.

Quila had built stables against the same side of the house as the fireplace that was large enough for their sow and boar and Jacques the Ox. With the warmth provided by the family fireplace the animals had easily made it through a season of snow and sleet blowing horizontally along the marshes. Along with the animals they kept, the family had six sheep in the communal herd as well as three and a half cattle, the half being a milking cow named Eleanor they shared with the Landrys, another young couple in the village. They had started to slowly but surely increase the size of their herd of cattle last year by keeping one calf per year.

Forage crops from the marshes were plentiful for Jacques the ox and the pigs lived on slop from the kitchen. The sheep foraged and provided the wool for their socks, which made their wooden sabots more comfortable when they wore them instead of their moccasins.

The Girouards had moved to Beaubassin two years after getting married and having their two boys in Nanpan, while living with her parents. The village had pulled together to frame, roof and side their house in Beaubassin. Béatrice had been conceived and born here. Whenever either one of them could, they would make improvements to their home and property.

'Quila had seemed distracted when he had left the fields for his dinner. He had barely spoken except to say that there were rumours of troubles of some kind. Usually he was always jovial and telling funny stories. Today he had barely spoken except to offer his thanks to God for the meal. He hadn't even played with the children who were now out and playing with others.

She took the dishes inside and carefully placed them on her kitchen shelves.

She stopped and thought. 'What is troubling him?'

She walked around the house and to the brow of the hill leading down into the marsh and the fields. The two boys Emile, eleven, and Maurice, nine, were down in the fields with some other boys; while little Béatrice was sitting in the shade of a tree just to the left of the main door to the house with a doll, play acting a drama of some sort that only a six year old girl could imagine.

The fields in which the Beaubassin men worked were reclaimed from marshland by the residents over many decades. They first had needed to dyke against the tides and then build drainage ditches with a mechanical flap that allowed water to flow back out into the bay, but not back in. They called this invention an aboiteau.

The inbound tide left behind extremely fertile silt and the area was incredibly productive farmland. The men grew wheat and oats that were milled into flour as well as ordinary hay that was used for animal feed. The clay in the soil was also very useful for making pottery.

Most of the families had developed an area of artisanship that allowed them to produce things to trade. Bertrand Haché's son had moved to the village from Nanpan and he continued on with his father's hooch recipe, while a few other families made wines, some produced wool or linen clothing and others made tools. Mathilde and Acquila made pottery; bowls and mugs and the children helped out by working the pottery wheel or painting simple designs on them.

All of the families cooperated on the dyke and aboiteau construction and maintenance, herding and growing and caring for the fruit trees. Each family grew vegetables in their own gardens. In a season enough fruit and vegetables were usually grown to last almost through the entire year if properly stored or preserved. Mathilde could pick out 'Quila and waved to him, although she knew that he wasn't looking at her. The men were all busy, working strenuously on maintenance work on an aboiteau.

Acquila was working alongside Simon Bourque and Camille Robicheaux. Acquila looked slim and wiry next to the two older men who both had boxy shapes of bulk and muscle mass.

It was warm and they were sweating profusely and frequently drinking from their water skins that were being kept cool in the bay, tied to posts in the dykes.

The men had been resisting discussion about what they had been told earlier in the morning. Acquila broke the silence. "Mes amis. What do you think the meeting is about?"

Simon said, "He is a priest. He is always calling for meetings, him. They almost always mean more work for us."

Simon, who was the least devout of the three, added, "We do a lot of work to save our poor souls."

'Quila said, "Our souls are all we have to look forward to, mon ami. I suspect when we get to heaven we will still have an eternity of hard work before us."

Simon said, "But I don't think we will be getting the joys of our wives' blueberry pies and their boudoirs for all eternity."

The men laughed. Camille said, "I will go to the meeting tonight. If the Holy Father from Rome tells me to jump naked into the bay, then I will jump in the bay naked. If the Priest in Beaubassin who comes from Limoges tells me to jump in the bay

I will keep my clothes on."

The men laughed again.

* * * * *

As Mati was stirring the hearty turnip, potato and salt pork soup she had made the door opened and Acquila entered. He looked a little angry, which was very unlike him.

"'Quila, sit down, I've made a soup for you."

He said nothing and sat at the table. He took out his pipe, filled the bowl and lit it. It was unusual for him to do this immediately on arriving home.

The children had already eaten and were playing loudly outside in the dwindling natural light.

"'Quila, what is wrong?"

"Mati. It's about the English, I think."

This suggestion of the English doing something made Mati's blood feel cold. She thought of watching the burning marshlands in the morning and the story her grand-mére had told her. "What about les maudits?"

"I don't know what. We men have to meet with the priest this evening."

"Why?"

"I don't know. Another priest is to join him, we will find out then."

She called the children inside and to the table and brought her husband a generous bowl of her soup and poured him a mug of tea with herbs. "Thank you, ma Chér".

"Père, je vous remercie pour cette nourriture que vous fournissez à notre famille."

A rule that Acquila had brought with him to Acadie, that was not shared by Mathilde's family, was that family discussion was to be held after dinner, not during. So Mati served herself and they finished their evening meal in silence, other than the horseplay and banter from the children.

When they were finished ‘Quila rose and collected the parts of their candlestick lanthorn. It had a pottery base with a leather windbreaker that covered the front part so he could walk with it. Mati’s grand-mére had made the candles. He lit it with a taper from the fireplace. The church bell began tolling.

He walked to Mati and kissed her cheek, “I will be back soon, ma Chér.”

* * * * *

Danks carefully belly-crawled to the top of the low ridge and found a small clump of fallen pine boughs behind which he could ensure his movements would be hidden against the edge of the horizon. He raised his spyglass and pointed it through the clump to closely examine the small settlement about fifty yards away.

He saw eight structures. One with a cross on its peak was almost certainly a chapel, one roughly hewn one was likely a barn for livestock, another was a sawmill and the remainder would be residences. The building construction was the same as Danks had seen in other settlements; they were made of logs with the chinks filled with, “bauge”, the clay and straw that was plentiful in the tidewater rivers nearby. This made the structures fairly durable and able to resist musket fire. He thought he would need to burn them out when the time came.

There were two cows grazing on the sparse grass that were now looking around and lowing, possibly sensing the raider’s presence.

There was a large fire pit in the middle of the small settlement and from its grill came the scent and smoke of cooking meat; probably wild animals from the surrounding woods. Danks’ mouth watered at the smell; he and his men had recently mostly lived on jerky, smoked fish and dried apples so as not to generate smoke that would reveal their position.

It was mid day and there was little movement in the settlement. Candles and lamps could be seen through the oil-skin covered windows in the houses and glassed windows of the mass house. A trio of Indians were sitting on logs near the grill, smoking pipes and dipping porringers into a cask likely filled with an alcoholic beverage. A small Miqmaq lodge about thirty yards from the houses, closer to the inlet from the Bay of Fundy, was on the edge of the treed area. A handful of Indians were outside their lodge sitting and talking with much larger and smokier pipes. He scanned the wooded area and saw more Indians hiding; possibly having noticed the English and readying an ambush.

He signalled King, Hollis and John Gorham to join him.

“Sor, the savages are as sharp eyed and eared as foxes. We need to be very quiet. I recommend we put six marksman in range to fire on those in the bushes and another six to fire on the ones in the clearing. After their salvo have them rush and finish the job with axes. We will stay back and hold our men in reserve to finish them off if needed.”

“Aye, Capt’n, that makes sense.”

"Hez, your crew will fire on the bushes, Hollis, yours on the others. Make it so on my signal."

The sun was almost at its peak in the sky and Danks checked both of his pistols as well as his musket. They were all loaded. He was sure that all his men had done the same. He removed his war hatchet from a sheath on his side and shoved it into his belt next to one of his pistols.

His signal, an almost silent whistle, would start the attack.

He looked briefly at the sun. His men would be anxious, like hounds waiting for the beginning of the hunt. He took out a narrow reed and held it to his mouth. He whistled into and through it.

Instantly a dozen muskets fired causing birds surrounding the settlement to take flight. Almost a half dozen Indians fell to the ground, dead or soon to be. A couple started running into the woods and another toward the buildings but none made it to safety. The cattle were shot in their tracks as they were about to bolt from the noise.

After the shooting there was a second of dead silence then the rangers started rushing their adversaries. Quickly they realized it was a trap; musket fire was coming at them from another grove of bushes. Gorham yelled, "Take cover in the sawmill!"

The men all changed direction to seek cover with several running toward and into two of the other structures. One wild Indian came running at Danks from behind, the captain turned when he heard his war cry. The attacker's hair was greasy and filthy and he carried a large war axe. Danks swung his musket and shoved the butt into the savage's face, then swung the barrel across the side of his head. He pulled out his knife and grabbed the stinking hair and started to cut it when he was shocked to see that under the hairy face was a filthy priest's collar. He was a French churchman and there was a rosary around his waist. Danks finished the job and removed the greasy hair. Danks offered priests and aborigines no mercy. Frenchmen might be allowed their lives if they confirmed their allegiance to the King of England; but not a lying, thieving, priest who had gone native.

Danks and Gorham, were almost at the sawmill when Gorham fell, "I'm shot!"

Danks went back to help Gorham and they stumbled with a half dozen other rangers in the mill. Around them was the sound of doors and window shutters being slammed and secured by the remainder of the company.

There was a pause while all reloaded. "Colonel? Ye shot?"

"In my arse. Bleeding bad." Gorham's face was ugly in pain and he reached down and tore open his breeches. "But I'll live."

Danks gave Gorham his satchel to bite on, pulled out his fighting knife and dug into the wound until he had removed the ball. Fortunately, it hadn't penetrating very deeply and was probably a ricochet. He pulled out his grimy handkerchief and tied it around the wound.

After the initial battle, things quieted down enough that Danks sent out one of the Labreques. It took several minutes for him to attract a shot and return. It seemed that the Indians were willing to wait them out.

"Colonel, how ye stand?"

"I'll survive. But we need support. Send some men to

Chebouctu and get Clapham and Bartelo here to spring us. Get them to bring a field gun."

* * * * *

On the way to the meeting at the church Acquila met up with Simon and Camille.

Camille said, “Why are we required to meet at night? I sleep at night.”

Simon said, “Mon ami, they only give us daylight to work in, not to enjoy ourselves or even to go to meetings at the church.”

Acquila said, “Simon, you always find the words that seem to make our futures look dim. You should cheer up!”

“Quila, I think the sinners have all the fun.”

Acquila replied, “I wouldn’t know. I haven’t met any sinners.”

Simon said, “No one is so blind as he that will not see.”

The men reached the small church. Along with the bell, there was a flag flying to indicate that the parishioners were to attend a meeting. The church was brightly lit and already almost full. It seemed that all the men in the village, anyone who worked in the fields which included fifteen year old boys and older, were in attendance. There were about three dozen men already seated. Father Le Guerne gave the three new arrivals a bit of an angry look for being a little late, but he greeted them warmly and welcomed them in.

In front of the altar, with an Indian on one side and a markedly handsome Acadian man on the other, was a short but very solid cassocked priest. Acquila thought that he had a very large head and wondered if it was really big or if his body was actually small.

Men were being offered mugs of wine mixed with herbs and spices and Acquila accepted one. As in every group of men, there were talkers and there were listeners. Usually Simon was the big talker, but this time he was too worried to tell jokes or complain about the weather.

After a few moments Father Le Guerne directed the men to sit. He then moved to the front of the room.

"Men of Beaubassin. Our guest, Abbé Le Loutre, is visiting from Cobequid. He is accompanied by Monsieur Joseph Brossard, dit Beausoleil. Abbé Le Loutre has an announcement to make."

Le Loutre spoke loudly, "Messieurs. We Acadians face a very great risk from a very evil enemy.

"This enemy is Godless and at this very moment is taking the land of your fellow Frenchman and Roman Catholics. They are killing French women and scalping French infants here in Acadie, now. And it will only get worse. You and your family are in serious danger."

The speaker paused.

The men were all transfixed by his power and passion.

"They are coming here. The wars overseas between France and its enemies including Angle Terre will be fought here as well as Europe.

"Les Anglais have built fortifications in Port Royal and in Chebouctu. They are coming to build one here. They will kill all of you, they will kill your wives, they will put your livestock on their dinner plates and they will scalp your children."

The Abbé paused for effect.

One of the older men started to speak, "Father, we want no part of the war, many of us signed an oath to les Anglais that we would not take up arms against them, if they did not force us to take arms against other Frenchmen."

Another spoke up, "But many of us also signed a document that l'Abbé Le Loutre gave us that said we would never live under the yoke of the English and that we would leave if we were told to rather than live under les maudits."

Le Loutre interrupted the man and said, "We cannot stay here, on this side of the river. In days, weeks or a few months, perhaps tomorrow, les maudits Anglais will be here. They will use this place as a fortress to exercise control over this part of l'Acadie. You cannot stop them and if you try, you and your wives and your children will be killed."

Le Loutre moved closer to the men. His head looked even larger. “We will relocate this community. Before next Sunday you will move your family and livestock and whatever you can carry to temporary shelters on the high land on the other side of the marshes. On the other side of the Riviere Mésagouèche where the British do not stake as strong a claim. We will provide you sustenance, food and shelter for three years when you relocate their. We expect to receive some assistance from our soldiers in Louisbourg to assist us.”

There was a rumble among the men and not surprisingly Simon spoke up, “What will happen to our houses.”

“You will burn them, or I will. We will not allow them to stand and be used by the damned English for their comfort. They will be set to flame. And if you choose to stay in the land of the damned English than you will be anathema; an enemy of God and an enemy of France and you will die at the hands of our aboriginals and be buried in unholy ground.”

“What if we try and stop you?” Simon said.

“Then you will go to hell.” Le Loutre said. “Tomorrow you will start to move whatever you can to the new settlement and you will start work on your new house across the river.”

The Priest left the church without another word, striding loudly on the church’s plank floor.

5 – CINQ

Acquila and the other men left behind in the church sat stunned for several minutes. They were all devout, some more than others, but all would do what their priests told them to. Their devotion was what had sustained them and allowed them to accept hardships.

Camille, Simon and Acquila left the church together. The two older men had a much longer commitment to Beaubassin; they both still lived in the houses that they had grown up in as children. But this might be a disadvantage, thought 'Quila. They had never had to start with nothing as he and Mathilde had. It would be more troubling for Simon's wife, and he had no doubt that Mati would be very upset. Acquila said, "Amis, what will we tell our wives?'

"We could try the truth," Simon answered, then snorted, "That has never worked before."

Acquila said, "Well, I will tell the truth."

Simon replied, "Girouard, you will go straight to husband heaven."

The two other men said their goodbyes and Acquila was left to march the final fifty yards in solitude. They had built their house with blood, sweat and tears along with the generosity of their neighbours, only a decade before. He supposed they could keep all their livestock without any problem, and if the men all worked together and worked efficiently, they could rebuild the new settlement faster. Especially if the French soldiers were present to help out.

He entered his house, there were a couple of candles burning; the children were not present so he thought they must be in their beds.

Mati was sitting in her favourite chair to the left of the door. She was repairing some children's clothing in front of a large candle. When the door opened she was a little startled and dropped her work on the floor. She rose to meet with her husband.

"Acquila, what was the meeting for?"

"Les Maudits are moving up the coast toward here."

"Oh my God! What will we do?"

"The Church has told us that we will relocate north of the river. He says the English will not touch us there because they have no claim to the land."

"And what will these English do."

"The Abbé said that they are treating we French cruelly, that they are savage and brutal and showing no mercy."

Mathilde scowled. "The Abbé… Puh…"

Mati hated it when priests acted like nobility. The idea of leaving behind what they had worked so hard to build angered her, but the Church had said so. And she was devout and would eventually do what the priests told her to, even if she grumbled about it.

She opened the door and started to walk outside. Acquila started to follow but she turned toward him and said, "Alone, please." There was a full moon and she looked down the slope to the marshes.

'Quila and the other men of Beaubassin over generations had turned the marshes into a paradise of sorts. They had built canals to drain the water and dykes to keep it out. Over decades its alkaline had been depleted and it had become an incredibly fertile place to raise crops and grow animals fat and healthy.

For Mathilde, the drama to come to her family was far too real. She had no doubt that the English, Les Maudits, would cause great turmoil and pain when they came. It accompanied them like a bad smell. She had been told in horrific detail how those in red coats brought suffering. The wars in other countries and on oceans in another world were coming to this tiny village thousands of miles away from both London and Paris.

She went back inside the house; Acquila was smoking his pipe and reading his Bible. She glanced at him at the same moment that he glanced back. She went upstairs and he joined her in a few minutes. She felt drained and needy and pulled him close. And then even closer.

* * * * *

Acquila and Mathilde got out of bed at the break of day. She brewed some herbal tea made from local roots and herbs that they both liked. They took mugs and walked outside. She looked across the marsh to the ridge on the other side that extended out into the bay that a Frenchman known for his generous hospitality had lived upon that was called "Beauséjour".

It was a warm and sultry day at its beginning and as always on such days she was accompanied by a swarm of mosquitoes that flourished in the damp environs. She slapped at a few; for some reason they never seemed to bother Acquila. She thought with a smile, 'he was made to live here.'

He pointed across and she could see that there seemed to be a flurry of activity at the highest point of the land, there was a great deal of smoke arising and it looked like foliage was being burned.

They turned around in response to noise from further down their own village's main street and they saw Father Le Guerne walking in their direction, surrounded by a dozen or so villagers. They were moving as if they had a purpose.

"Monsieur Girouard!"

"Bonjour, Pére Le Guerne!"

"Bonjour. I have brought together our men to help design the means of relocating our settlement to Point Beauséjour. What do you think? Is there a route through the swamplands and rivers that will be most efficient? Do we need to travel all the way to the bridge?"

"Père, I don't know what the other men are saying. What do they say?"

"Well a few say, the hell to the Anglais let's stay and fight, a few others think we should take the long high land route. Simon and Camille, ici, say that the soldiers should do all the heavy work. What do you think?"

"Well, I think that this time of year even with the early melt and warmer weather, the grasslands are still very wet. Pulling heavy wagons and moving heavy livestock is sure to be very difficult and the river impassable. We could use boats for as much of our property as possible, but I think that the tides are wrong now and the mud would be very difficult."

The priest nodded.

"The herd animals, I think that if they are properly led and are outfitted with swamp boots, they might be able to avoid the wettest spots, but they will still need to get over the river or around it, maybe we can build a closer bridge at a narrow point. Otherwise we can walk them an extra league and cross it at Buot's bridge. To make it easier, we can either quickly build a bridge closer to the village by filling a section with logs. But this will not survive the high tide, I think. Roger's bridge is the least risky but longest to accomplish."

"I think that is good counsel, M. Girouard." There were general sounds of agreement. But Acquila continued.

"But I would not disagree with making the soldiers, peut-être les générales, do the carrying, because they have made the reason for the move."

The entire group erupted in laughter. Le Guerne had only smiled at 'Quila's humour, but he nodded agreement. He said to the group: "Everyone present your household items in front of your houses. If you have a cart, use it. I will be examining the possibility of using boats, but if this is not possible then we will travel with the livestock.

"Acquila, can I ask you to recruit the livestock drivers to

take the herd animals to the other side of the river. Even the children can help out with this. Everyone can bring along their own pigs and milk cows. Chickens can be bagged and carried."

"Yes, Father."

"Allons y. Let's go!"

Acquila thought the best people to move the herd animals would be the women, older men and children. They would need to move the herds a full league until the Mésagouèche River wasted away to just a small stream. This was where Buot had built his bridge and Roger Casey, an Irishman who had married an Acadian girl, had built his trading post and tavern.

It would be dirty work to move the hundreds of cattle and pigs, but not difficult.

"Mathilde," he said, "Can you have all the women pack up their family items and goods for transport? I will get the older men and children to work on herding. Get any owners of the dogs that can herd to also come along. I think if we work hard today, we can get the job done by nightfall."

Acquila called to Camille and Simon and they all met in the centre of the settlement. He told them to bring their oxen and axes to the copse of trees near where the Mésagouèche narrowed at Buot's Bridge.

* * * * *

In Beaubassin, it was not much work to get the older men and children out of bed. Members of the herding party, once they were awake, had quickly dressed and been told of their jobs. Once outside it took each of them only a minute or two to find a whippy alder branch to encourage the livestock to move along.

The old men and their grandchildren happily walked down the slope to the herds; not many had attended the meeting with the Priest the night before so they didn't know why. But it was a distraction from their normal routine that they appreciated. They were soon joined by younger men bringing along dogs. The dogs accompanied their owners and were yipping and snarling in their play while preparing to follow the missives of their masters until they begin to nip at the heels of the cattle to move them along.

After leaving the settlement Acquila met his friends and their oxen at a copse of spruce trees only a few dozen yards from where the Mésagouèche narrowed at Pont à Buot. There had long been a small log bridge across the river at this point that allowed small groups of people and single file animals to cross. But it was inadequate to allow carts and large numbers of livestock to do so.

The three men set to work to enlarge it. They drove the oxen hard and soon they had a sufficient number of logs, after they had been limbed, to fill in and expand the bridge cross the small stream and provide a reasonably smooth passage for carts and animals to the safely, for now, French side of Acadie.

There was a small trading post, of a type, on the other side and the original owner, Roger Casey, had sold liquor, tobacco and blacksmithing services to travellers. All the adult men in Beaubassin had visited at one time or another to tell secrets to each other or escape their family responsibilities.

Now it was managed by Jean Jacques Cyr and his wife Marie-Josephe, and their two daughters, Marie and Françoise. The young women attracted and fascinated younger, single men in the settlement, but none had money for libations so they offered their manual labour in trade for enjoying the cider while trying to seduce the daughters.

Acquila and his friends waited at the bottom of the hill in the grazing pasture for things to happen. Advancing were several hundred cattle and off to one side a similar number of sheep and to the other over a hundred pigs. The latter had a problem being herded, but 'Quila didn't have a better idea to get the stubborn pigs to the other side of the river than to push them or hope they followed; so he led their masters in whipping and making noises. They could always butcher them and salt or pickle the meat if they misbehaved. A few of the smarter children were leading pigs over the bridge by holding carrots in front of their noses.

Mathilde and a couple of the other younger women pushed a cart down the hill filled with water-skins for the workers. Knowing that it would be dirty work, they also had brought along as many cloth rags as they could spare.

Acquila went over to his wife and thanked her. "Mati, can you make the other women pack up their households. Many will be afraid and some will not be able to move or act. And you will have to make them. None can be left behind. Can you, ma Chér?"

"I will try, 'Quila. I will try."

"Merci, Mati." They embraced and she began hurrying back on the long walk across the grasslands and up the hill with the another younger woman.

She thought of how she would get the other women to do what needed to be done. Many had already suffered through terrible heartbreak and would be on the edge of giving up. Others would not believe that anything would happen and would be difficult. Some of the women would refuse to be directed by a younger woman. She could only do her best.

6 – SIX

Father Le Guerne was trying to organize water transport for all the assets that didn't have legs or wheels. They had three large flat-bottomed boats that were designed to carry crops in the canals, not barrels of flour and heavy wooden furniture on the bay with the most violent tides in the world. So he was a little apprehensive about whether they could do it.

Looking down at the marsh, the river and the bay that they would need to traverse, it didn't seem as easy to do as they thought. There was a bend that slowed the Mésagouèche down, but it was also the most slippery and muddy at that point. The effort and time to load and unload might be more difficult than the long two league overland route to cross the bridge. Using barges around the mouth of the river was one possibility, but with low tide it would be impossible and at high tide, dangerous.

He decided that it was impossible to do and that they might even lose lives in the exercise. He walked back to the other side of the village to see how the move of the livestock was coming along.

He saw a steady stream of brightly dressed people pushing large carts and carrying large objects and whipping and moving their animals along while they were followed by others pushing carts with huge wheels. He was surprised with the ability of his flock to respond to an event that would probably devastate most people. They were giving up their homes that they had built with their own hands because of their faith in the Church; in God!

He was humbled by the authority that the Lord had vested in him.

He wondered if it was futile to even try move the contents of over sixty households to the other side of the river. It was a massive job as almost everything that the residents had built or gathered in their time here assumed that it would never need to be moved. Yet all things were precious and bought with a dear share of their small amount of wealth or created with a massive investment of their limited time. It would be shameful to leave their household items behind, especially if they were destined to be used by les maudits.

And even if they did get their belongings moved across the river, they still did not have a roof to cover their heads.

'They are blessed people, these Acadiens. They are brave and intelligent and ... unsinkable,' he thought. 'Like the flat bottom boats that they used. And they are so devout, how could le Dieu do anything but honor them with his love and gifts?'

He looked above, crossed himself, clasped his hands and thanked God for putting him in this place and asked Him for guidance to help him follow His will.

* * * * *

The relocation was a massive undertaking. Each person likely had ten times their body weight to be moved. They decided that the most probable way of getting the greatest amount of material moved was also the slowest; to carry or cart it to the point where the Mésagouèche River was narrowest, at Pont à Buot. Once they had their items across the river they could go back for more; it was safe from the English on the north side. It wasn't necessary to move it all to the top of the hill; at least not now.

Acquila Girouard was a miracle. Father Le Guerne watched him pushing carts several times his weight along swampy ground when others had given up. He kept the pushers and carriers laughing while they too moved more things more quickly than they likely ever thought they could. 'He has formed the dozens of carriers and pushers and herders into a choir,' Le Guerne thought, 'with each singer performing perfectly.'

Dark had arrived and the job was not yet finished. While he didn't know for sure, Father Le Guerne suspected that Abbé Le Loutre would decide early in the morning to burn the settlement, or even worse, that the English would arrive and not only burn, but kill.

Acquila continued urging the oxen drivers to move carts a foot, two feet closer to the destination; convincing husbands that they could carry or roll one more barrel across the bridge; convincing wives that they could carry one more chair or one more basket of food.

But finally, even Acquila was done in. The moon was three quarters full and he looked to see what they had accomplished in their fifteen hours. And it was nor enough. More than half of the goods that had been brought down the hill still were on the side claimed by the English. And what had been delivered to the other edge of the river needed to be moved along to make room for more.

But there was no more that could be done, this night. Acquila hoped that Mathilde was safe and back in their home with his children for what might be their last night in the house they had built. He went to join her.

Acquila went to bed and immediately fell asleep. He was awakened by the sound of the small birds announcing their presence and snuggled close to Mati. With all the recent events they hadn't the energy to spend intimate time together and he wanted to renew their bonds and release his tension with their union.

She stirred and responded to his attention.

For a few minutes they travelled away and flew above the threats to their existence. They were stronger as one.

* * * * *

When they left their bed they stared reality in the face. While helping everyone else move all their personal things, they hadn't touched anything of their own. Even their own children had helped drive the animals and hadn't packed or prepared anything for being moved.

"Mati, we need to decide what we must bring with us and what we can leave behind. When you can, try to set aside the items that we need to survive and sustain our souls."

'Quila dressed and walked outside, the settlement was just starting to rise and there were signs of other households stirring. The sky was clouding up which, if it resulted in rain, would make a difficult day impossible. He felt he needed to cross the river and see where they could build temporary shelters. He needed to know what it would be like; if the settlement would be able to feed its children tonight and tomorrow.

He knew that the Abbé would arrive this day or the next and Acquila had no doubt that the priest would set fire to the houses whether or not the settlement was emptied out or not.

"Mati, I have to cross the river and see what awaits us when we move. Can you ask Father Le Guerne to continue working to move goods across the river? And can you see if you can push the herders to finish moving the livestock? Once across, have the people continue to move them toward the hill on the other side. They need to create space for the rest of us."

"Yes, 'Quila. Be careful."

She moved toward him and they embraced.

"Chér, I am always careful."

"'Quila, be careful."

"Bien sûr, Chér. This time I will."

They shared a long kiss and he left.

He walked briskly down the slope and toward the point where the river narrowed enough to allow him to leap over it. He kept a pole there to use as a shortcut to cross without the long walk to the bridge. He estimated the distance he would need to travel across and gripped the pole, accordingly positioned it midway across the river and pushed it ahead, moving his hands higher on the pole as he gained momentum in crossing. He easily cleared the river and landed safely on the other side. He left the pole on the bank for his return trip.

He started trotting to the area for the temporary settlement and arrived in less than a half hour, the last few minutes were up a fairly steep hill and he was winded. There were a number of large bell shaped tents on the flat part of the high ground and he walked toward them. The wind was blowing strongly from off shore and he was chilled as he was sweating heavily.

He looked over the bay and there were dark clouds that were gathering.

He looked around and saw that a number of trees had been taken down and limbed and that it seemed that whomever was in the tents were starting to build large shelters. He opened the flap of one of the tents, “Bonjour!”

One of the men, just awakening and wrapped in heavy furs, stirred. “Oui.”

“Monsieur, I am one of the residents. What are you doing here?”

“We were sent from Ile Royale to come and build a settlement on this hill and a small fortress at the bridge. That is what we are doing here.”

“Can we talk about this?”

“Oui, un moment, s’il vous plais.”

Quila closed the flap and waited.

The man emerged wearing breeches and boots and a white cotton undershirt. His hair was very long. “I am Grenadier Louis-Thomas Jacau de Fiedmont from Ile Royale, Monsieur.”

“I am Acquila Girouard from Beaubassin, Acadie, Monsieur. You were born here?”

“I was born in Louisbourg, Monsieur. And my wife and my children were born there. So we are here to help you, Monsieur Girouard.”

“How many of you are here?”

“We have eight men.”

“And how, monsieur, will eight men assist over one hundred people to build places to live and relocate all of their households and livestock in one day?"

"We are very hard workers, Monsieur Girouard."

"Then I suggest you all rise from your beds and begin working very hard, Grenadier de Fiedmont. I need your men to help us move all of our families and all of their goods and livestock to this side of the Mésagouèche River immediately, once we have done this, then we can all begin building shelters. But, Monsieur de Fiedmont, if we do not relocate our settlement before it rains, then we will not need any shelters."

"I understand."

"Then, let's go."

"Oui." de Fiedmont went among the tents, rousing the soldiers and ordering them to get dressed. In just a few minutes, without too much grumbling, the men were dressed and ready.

"Men, this is Monsieur Girouard who is the leader of the settlement across the river. He has ordered us to assist them in relocating the livestock and the family belongings from the old settlement before we begin the construction of the new one. So we will follow him and do his bidding. Since it looks like it might rain, we should start now."

Acquila got things started by beginning to walk quickly away from the soldiers and looked back to make sure they were following.

They were. He was relieved; a number of strong young men would offer a great benefit to getting the relocation completed.

It was already getting warm and the air was very humid. He led them to his vaulting pole and they each took turns making the leap without any falls and walked up the hill. Acquila noticed that the people were working hard; every corner of the small settlement seemed to be busy with activity. He looked around for Mathilde but couldn't find her.

Grenadier de Fiedmont wasted no time in directing his men to move carts and wagons as quickly as possible. This morning, with the additional urgency, the men of Beaubassin had gotten as many oxen tied to as many carts as possible and there was already a line up waiting to make the transfer over the river at a point barely within sight.

Acquila looked at the skies, at the frantic activity in the village and the movement of the line to the river. If God granted them only this single day, then they just might make it. He looked for Father Le Guerne and hurried toward the church. The priest was just leaving it. Acquila waved to him and Father Le Guerne hurried toward him.

"What is it, Acquila?"

"Father, we must ask the Holy Father to assist us this day. It is very important that the rain holds off for us to get our work done."

The priest placed his hand on Acquila's shoulder. "I have already prayed to our Father to sustain us today, Acquila. The weather, and all of us, are in his hands. He will dispose of us as He will."

* * * * *

In Beaubassin, the addition of the eight strong soldiers had a strong influence on the motivation of the workers; the new workers were business-like and helped lift and push where needed and looked for opportunities to streamline the movement of materiel.

By mid-morning the livestock, hundreds of sheep, cows and pigs had been moved across the river and were being driven toward the higher ground.

There was a line of carts back a half league from the bridge that carried household items waiting their turn to cross. The path being used: along the ridge that the settlement was on for most of the trip, then a diagonal through the chest high grasslands, could easily be identified from a distance. It was becoming a road.

Acquila thought there was a chance that they might actually be able to do it even with the risk of rain and the tides that were already pushing their way up the river. Especially since, for whatever reason, there seemed to be many fewer than thirty or so households being moved. He thought perhaps that the contents of as few as a dozen had actually been moved to the crossing point based on the number of beds he had counted.

He wondered what had happened to the rest. Had they decided not to move, to force the Abbé to not fulfill his pledge to burn them out? Had they decided to go somewhere else?

He returned to the settlement to try and find Mati. When he had left, she had been busy working with some of the older women. He saw his two boys helping out by putting items on sledges that they would be able to pull across to the other side.

"Emile! Where is your mother?"

"Papa! She is across the river, I think."

"Hurry, get as much as you can over the river, I think it will start to rain soon."

Acquila decided that with the line of material being steadily moved, that he could see about getting some shelters built before nightfall. He hurried back to their house and collected his axe.

The first drops of rain fell when he walked down the hill and started trotting toward his vaulting pole.

The tide was on its way in and it was about three quarters of its way up the muddy bank that was about five paces across. He swung the axe and tossed it to the other side. He was a little troubled by the rain on his pole; it would be slippery.

Far down the river he could see the line, but not whether it was moving or not. He needed to get to the site where temporary shelters would be built and chop down more logs to get them built. For now, it was important to get a roof over the heads of the residents, especially the children. And the foodstuffs that could be harmed by water, flour and grains would also need to be covered.

He used his normal routine with the pole and vaulted the water to the other side.

He picked up his axe and started walking across the oxbow in the river toward the higher ground where the temporary settlement would be built. They would need to accommodate at least a hundred people. He would look for two parallel lines of trees on level ground that he could limb and use as uprights. Then he could cut long, straight trees and use them as cross members. Then they could tile half rounds of birch bark to keep out the elements until more substantial shelters could be made. But at least the most precious things and people would be kept dry.

* * * * *

Mati had spent the day helping women pack up their households for transport. But when she visited Amélie Gallant she was surprised that she and her family had prepared very little for the move.

"Amélie, do you need some help to pack?"

"Mathilde, there is no point. We are leaving Beaubassin."

"Why? To where?"

"To Ile St. Jean. We want peace, Mathilde. There is no end to the turmoil here. You may not have noticed, but there have been many, many families from the area that have already left. And more are leaving now."

"I haven't noticed, but I understand."

"Even the holy church is against us and will burn our homes underneath and over the top of us."

"I don't think they would really do that."

"With that insane priest, I have no doubt that they would burn our homes even with us locked inside, Mathilde."

"Amélie, it is blasphemy to accuse a priest of this. You must be careful of who hears you."

"Would you tell?"

"No. Of course not."

"Then we will be safe on our voyage. Mathilde, thank you for being a friend."

"Do you need any help?"

"Yes, very much, but we will be able to travel to Baie Verte. We will take very few things with us."

"Well, God be with you and your family, Amélie."

"And yours, Mati."

"A la prochaine…"

"Oui."

Mati left her, saddened. She wondered how many of her other friends would not follow her to the French side of the river. The rain was starting to fall and she walked to their house to get her rain bonnet. She put it on and walked back to see how the work was going. While she could only get an impression because of the distance, it seemed that the line was getting shorter on this side and was spreading out on the other.

She looked across the marsh and she could see Acquila walking back toward the village, his axe over his shoulder. As he got closer to the edge, he swung the axe and it flew back to the near side of the river. Then she watched him take his vaulting pole and begin his normal practice. He rose over the rapidly rising water.

And he almost made it.

His feet landed on the near side, but her heart almost stopped and she screamed in anguish when she saw him fall backwards and into the slick mud of the banks of the Mésagouèche River.

Mati kicked off her sabots and ran headlong down the hill toward 'Quila not paying attention to the ground beneath her, nor her skirt and aprons, and she fell face first and slid on the growing wetness of the ground. She collected herself and continued on, ignoring brambles and thistles, moving as fast as she could in her rapidly soddening clothes.

She arrived.

'Quila was barely keeping his head above water by scrambling and kicking with his feet and trying to dig his hands into the muddy banks. He was only recognizable because Mati knew it was him; he was fully covered in dark brown muck.

"Quila, I will try and find something!"

She looked around to see what she could pass to him, but as far as she could see there was nothing but marsh grasses. Thinking in desperation, she took off her woolen skirt; it looked like it might reach him but, if it didn't, 'Quila would almost certainly die.

"Hold on, mon Chér!"

"Vite, vite!!"

Even with 'Quila's panic, she decided to spend an extra few precious seconds and tied her apron as tightly as she could to her skirt. 'It might work', she thought and she tossed her heavy skirt toward him.

Quila began to slide away, the tidewaters were increasing by the second and water was already to his chin and any second he might start to breathe in water. But just as he was about to go under, one hand grabbed firmly on Mati's dress and he started to pull, but she was only a little more than half his weight. She could feel herself losing her own grip on the shore which was getting wetter and more slick by the second. She began to lose hope, and her desperation made her pull more desperately, and she screamed at the top of her lungs, "St. Roger! Help Me! Help Me!"

At that very second, 'Quila's efforts at kicking and digging reached a layer of rocks and gravel and he was able to get a purchase and with whatever strength he had left he pushed with his foot and moved so close to the shore that he could almost touch her and she reached for him. But he started to slide back, but found the solid rock again and with both of them pulling and pushing at the same second he got his chest over the bank and made it to shore, on top of Mati's legs.

For minutes they stayed that way, bereft of the slightest amount of physical and emotional strength, shivering with cold and relief. Mati started praying, thanking God and Saint Roger for rescuing her husband.

'Quila was almost totally encased in slippery mud and Mati was almost totally naked except for her rain bonnet and underskirt. Once he began recovering some strength he rolled free of his wife and removed his shirt and gave it to her to wear.

"Chér, we have to find the children." He stood up and helped Mati cover herself and together they exhaustedly began the few hundred stride walk across the field and hundred more to the settlement.

They came to their homestead but the children were not around. Mati cleaned herself as well as she could and went to look for them. Acquila stripped his remaining clothing off, cleaned himself and followed her, catching up in a few minutes.

He was fully exhausted but there was still work to do that started with finding his own children and making sure they were safe.

7 – SEPT

Abbé Jean-Louis Le Loutre was marching, head down, pushing his way through the rain. His cassock was soaked and hung heavily from his shoulders, but he didn't notice the hindrance or discomfort. The worst inconvenience were the infernal black flies that got under his clothing and couldn't easily be discouraged because of their huge numbers. He thought they were not unlike the many hundreds of English now en route to suck the lifeblood out of his Roman Catholic French village.

He and Chief Jean Baptiste Copit were leading a group of fifty warriors to Beaubassin to destroy anything that the English might use as a resource to further control Acadie. It was unfortunate that they had to threaten and relocate their own people, but this settlement, among them all, had been less interested in building a French Catholic nation and more interested in being farmers. Few had lifted a finger to assist in defending the French homeland; none had participated in the attack of the English at Port Royal.

He had heard that at the same time many had been very stubborn in accepting their rule by the English and that the English would do them no favours when they arrived. These residents of Beaubassin were very insubordinate and difficult people.

They had marched from Cobequid to the edge of Beaubassin starting at first light of day. But it was very heavy and difficult travel and while they had expected to arrive and begin the destruction, if necessary, in the early evening, they would arrive after nightfall. They didn't wish to burn fellow Frenchmen unless absolutely necessary. The rain would make them delay the burning, he hoped still before the English arrived. He had no confidence that the small garrison and his few Indians could stop a full-scale assault led by a well-experienced force.

They had come across signs of a similar sized military force traveling in the same direction and the Abbé thought it possible that the other group would win the race if they had the same destination and were adversaries. This would complicate his mission considerably.

The priest had ultimately decided that the weight and numbers of les maudits would take the peninsula as they intended to; there was little hope that the French could keep their land here, they might only make it less easy for them.

But the people could move to the northern part of Acadie, off the peninsula, nearer to the part of this primitive land that was theirs for eternity, Quebec.

For his Miqmaq allies, however, it was different; they were fighting for their very survival as a people. For all of his dozen years in New France the Abbé had devoted every waking moment to saving the eternal souls of these savages. At least when they went to their destiny they would go as blessed and without sin.

Le Loutre had been called to service by Christ as a young man, an orphan, and his calling was to rescue souls that would otherwise be lost to Satan. He served God in a God-forsaken place where what he did mattered. His warriors were special; each had Christian names and each was saved and they all fought the English heretics with a special savagery.

Le Loutre had made this trip many times so he recognized the landmarks that told him they were close to their destination. They stayed under cover of the fir tree forests as long as they could until they came to the marshlands at the first of the four main rivers that crossed the Chignectou area.

He left his Miqmaq warriors under cover to be called on as necessary and carried on to the settlement. He did bring along his Miqmaq leader, Jean Baptist Copit, for security.

When he arrived at the village he was quite impressed with the progress that had been made. Someone was making these Acadians follow his instructions. Although he suspected he and his Miqmaq would still need to do the burning, there was a chance he might not need to burn any people.

He walked toward the church, which had been created well before he had come to New France, and marvelled at how passion for the Almighty had provided energy to the supplicants to build such a tribute. He looked above, closed his eyes and said a brief prayer of thanks and asked for strength for what he had to do next. He entered the church.

Father Le Guerne was prostrate on the floor, his arms extended from his shoulders to form the shape of a cross. He rose when he heard the door open and walked to meet his visitor. They exchanged pleasantries.

"Father Le Guerne, a most impressive start to your mission to remove the settlement as a resource for les maudits. You should be congratulated."

"I think we both know who should be praised, Abbé Le Loutre, and He needs not the honour as He is honour. His hands were not mine as much as a young man in the village."

"And who would that be, Father."

"He is a young man from France, not born here, who has a family who were. His name is Acquila Girouard. A fine young man very devout, and, as you will see, very hard working. He has been organizing the move, pushing the families very hard to get the work done. Everyone likes and respects him."

Le Loutre said, "He sounds like he would make an excellent priest. It's unfortunate that he was not approached when he was a child. He might be an excellent associate of our campaign. Is he one we can trust?"

"To protect our people, our church and our country?"

Le Loutre nodded.

"Yes. He is very dedicated."

"Let us go and meet this hero of Beaubassin."

* * * * *

Once progress had been made on building the temporary settlement across the river, the French army engineers had gotten back to work in meeting their main objective; to construct a small redoubt that could house and protect a garrison of as many as hundred men. They were building this just north of the Pont à Buot that les Acadiens were now traversing.

They'd cleared an area behind the redoubt to serve as a parade ground and a tent encampment and there were already a few dozen tents in place. They were building a triangular structure, really just trenches, fortified with a low, double reinforced palisade to stop musket fire.

Nearby others, who had just arrived from Louisburg, were building a men's barracks and a smaller building for officers. The tavern and trading post, which had existed for decades, was doing a booming business supplying the engineers and workmen with grog, beer, bread, sausage and cheese.

Acquila had washed up and was exhausted from his fall in the river, but he got together a dozen men from the village to continue to work on the temporary shelters on higher ground. The rain had stopped and residents were continuing to move their goods closer to safety.

The men all brought their axes and in an hour had cleared an area twenty paces long and about four paces wide bounded by elm trees that been stripped of their lower branches and were in a relatively parallel line.

The men then found thin and straight birches that they chopped down and fastened to the line of elms, one side being a foot or two higher. They then laid birches across the top and tiled the roof with half cylindrical cuttings of birch and other barks.

They cut down other trees to serve as walls on the back and either side to create a long house, and then started on another. While it wouldn't do for a winter, it would work fine for to keep the elements off of precious items that could not easily be replaced. Family members were already starting to arrive to the temporary settlement area, with the earliest arrivals getting the choicest spots. They would all continue to live in their homesteads until they absolutely had to leave, but were thankful that when the worst happened, they would at least be dry.

Meanwhile, more French soldiers were arriving over the course of the day and there were now several dozen soldiers, all stripped to the waist, working with axes and huge saws and putting the logs in place for the redoubt. One large company of men that arrived from Quebec went to work with oxen in building a more permanent structure on the slope rising from the Baie Francaise, named Beauséjour, further west from the tavern and bridge.

Grenadier de Fiedmont was glad that the work here was almost finished. He noticed that the redoubt structure wouldn't be impressive, forty feet square with four rows of foot wide spruce trees interlocked to at least be able to defend against musket fire and smaller ball artillery. It could also serve to protect artillery if this was required to repel an attack.

Acquila tracked down Mati and the children after they had crossed the river. They were helping to move their own goods under the cover of the shelters.

He asked his wife, "How are you?"

"Quila, I am very tired. I will be happy to see the bed tonight. How are you, mon Chér?"

"I'm tired, but am so happy to have my life, thanks to you, to be able to share it with you."

"'Quila, will we be safe here?"

"As safe as I can make it, ma Chér. Perhaps we can return home for one last night with our family." They collected their children and made their way home.

Neither had the energy to vault the river so they took the long route across the bridge, being careful not to disrupt or slow down the steady stream of goods, animals and people crossing the Pont à Buot. After an hour they climbed the hill approaching the settlement. Coming toward them, looking a bit like a rhinoceros, was a cassocked priest along with Father Le Guerne. Acquila wondered if they were coming for him. Why?

They met at the crest of the hill. Acquila greeted them, "Pére Le Guerne? Bonjour."

"Bonjour, Monsieur Girouard. C'est l'Abbé Le Loutre."

Acquila, of course, had seen this man a few days earlier and he went down on one knee in supplication. "Bonjour, Monseigneur."

"Arise, my son. I understand, if anything, that I should be offering honours to you. This is Madame Girouard?"

"Yes, Father, this is my wife, Mathilde." Mati curtsied; she had much less respect than her husband for churchmen, she believed they might well be behind all the turmoil that was going on in her family and settlement.

"Madame," said Le Loutre. "Might I suggest that you tend to your relocation and your family, we have important discussions to have with your husband."

This angered Mati. She had little use for the church and its bullies. Even less for this one. She turned toward Acquila and kissed his cheek without speaking or even acknowledging the priest's insulting command. Nothing good could from this. She went to find her children.

Le Loutre spoke, looking across the marshes to the activity that could barely be seen. "Monsieur Girouard, I understand that you are largely responsible for the progress made in relocating the settlement.

Acquila started to speak, "Monseigneur, I had very little . . ."

"Monsieur Girouard, neither the Heavenly Father nor I have any use for false modesty. You, with the inspiration of our Lord, have been responsible for the success of this mission, oui?"

"If it pleases the Lord, I have had a part in it."

"You have been blessed by and spiritually carried in your achievements by the Heavenly Father, oui?"

"I suppose so, Father."

"Then you are truly a man of God, my son, and you shall be rewarded for this. You must accept this reward modestly, but for the glory of God. And in the name of God, I appoint you as my assistant in the coming struggles. You will answer only to me and do nothing without my knowledge and approval."

Acquila wondered what he had gotten himself into. Why couldn't they have tried to vault the river and perhaps missed this encounter? Yes, God came first in his life, but spiritually, not temporally. On this earth, not the hereafter, his family was most important to him. He must always put his family first. How could he do both? How could he meet his responsibility to his family, yet comply with the orders of the most powerful priest in Acadie? For now, though, there was no action he could take or decision he could make.

"I understand, Father, and I will do as you request, in the name of God."

"That is good my son, God shines his glory on you. Let me tell you what God requires you to do."

* * * * *

Over the course of the day more soldiers arrived steadily from Quebec. Most were hard-nosed veterans of battles abroad and at Louisbourg: "old moustaches" and "Vrai Bougres" who were commanded by Chevalier Jean-Louis La Corne.

La Corne was sweating profusely and found his collar extremely tight in the damp climate. He had been in Acadie for a year, moving from camp to camp, interviewing Acadien refugees and training some to act as militia and support what was sure to be more intensive engagement with the English in the coming months.

He had recently also been hand-picked to organize the French response to les Anglais at Beaubassin.

His first few hours in the camp were to be spent with Abbé Le Loutre and he was impressed with the activity that the priest had already arranged with les Acadiens, Miqmaq and half-breeds in organizing the removal.

He thought he would have some time to prepare for the English attack that was sure to come.

He was checking out the construction progress on the redoubt at the bridge. It appeared to be proceeding well and it was the least of his concerns.

He already had over one hundred men under his command, many of whom spoke different dialects. He had no idea who his subaltern officers were, or even how to identify them. He called on the only subordinate officer he knew, his Ensign who had traveled with him, Tremblay, who was visiting Acadie for the first time.

"Ensign."

"Chevalier, I am at your command."

"I want you to wander around the motley gang of soldiers here and order any and all officers to muster at the redoubt construction site in sixty minutes. They need not be in full uniforms. We have no time for formalities, I think."

"Oui, Chevalier."

La Corne saw a bit of a commotion coming toward him. It was a small retinue that seemed to be gathering people as it moved along. He thought of the terrible fairy tale from his childhood of the piper, who attracted children to follow him, whom he killed and ate.

Finally he could see the group more clearly and saw that there was a sturdy priest at the line's head and he seemed to be emotionally armed for bear, blustering and laughing at the same time, dismissing some people coming up to him while embracing others.

La Corne saw that the priest had noticed him as well and the priest had started walking toward him. He could feel the Abbé's intensity from fifty feet away and wondered how their conversation might unfold. He did not look like the type of man who would either provide or receive calm counsel and exchange ideas in a friendly manner.

By the time the priest arrived his retinue had decreased to just two men, another priest and a slender, younger man with a shock of black hair hanging over one side of his forehead.

"I am Le Loutre, Abbé to the Miqmaq people in Acadie, who are you?"

"Bonjour, Monsieur. I am Chevalier Jean Louis La Corne, Order of St. Louis and commander of this French fortress."

"Welcome to Tintamarre, Chevalier La Corne. We are pleased that you and your men have arrived."

"Who are your aides, Abbé Le Loutre?"

"This is Father Le Guerne, padre to the local people here and Monsieur Acquila Girouard, commander of the local Milice l'Acadien, whom I have just appointed to his position."

Acquila was shocked, the Abbé had told him he would be an assistant, but not that he would be expected to fill a military role. He was honoured, but also apprehensive. What would Mathilde say? How could he create a militia while building a suitable home for his family and seeing that they were fed and protected?

La Corne nodded to Father Le Guerne and saluted to Acquila, who awkwardly returned a salute.

La Corne said, "let us sit," and he led the group to a cluster of log ends that had been trimmed from the redoubt construction that could be used as stools. He withdrew his smoking packet from a pocket and filled and lit his pipe.

"Abbé, I can inform you that military dispatches from Cap Sable tell us that the British have a fleet of at least twelve ships on its way to le Baie Beaubassin. We have no expectation that they would head anywhere but here."

"Captain La Corne, I have been anticipating this, as you can see, we have already relocated much of the settlement to the north side of the River Mésagouèche, and we are preparing to raze the settlement tonight to ensure that not one kindling of a roof and not one ounce of sustenance is available for the invaders' use."

"This is good, very good. And what militia resources can you offer to support our regular soldiers, Commander Girouard?"

Acquila didn't know what to say, so the Abbé said it for him. "We hope to have one hundred Acadians to support you Captain, most of whom are trained in musket and also my fifty Miqmaq warriors."

"Again, very good, Abbé Le Loutre. Might I suggest that the moment that all people and livestock are moved here that you start the razing the village. I might add that we will be immediately commandeering one half of the livestock from the settlement as well as one half of all foodstuffs for the use of the garrison. I trust this will be satisfactory."

"I expect, Captain, that your army will provide a requisition for repayment at some time in the future."

"I think the Governor's assistant, Bigot, will approve such a thing. In any case, I hear he will be visiting Fort Louisbourg in this late spring and he can be solicited for this."

"Bien, Monsieur Captain, please advise me when this happens."

"I will. You are doing an excellent job, Abbé Le Loutre." The Chevalier said, and went looking for Ensign Tremblay and any collection of officers his subaltern had managed to find.

* * * * *

Mati was trying her best to keep her temper when she left the Abbé and Acquila. No one was more devout that she, no one loved the Roman Catholic Church or God more than she did. No one was more loyal in attendance at mass or in providing food for feasts. But she distrusted priests, believing their inspiration was from greed as often as the Almighty or for the good of their flocks.

Yet here she was being treated like a nobody, like an appendage to her husband, like she didn't matter when she knew that nothing would get done in their home, in their settlement, in Acadie or in France unless women made or allowed it to happen.

And what did Le Loutre have up his sleeve? She loved her husband for all the right reasons, but she knew that any time anyone asked him to help out or do something important, that he would do it. It wasn't that he wasn't tough and direct when he needed to be, but sometimes he spent as much energy helping other families as he did on his own.

But in the settlement the beneficiaries of his generosity would always find a way of paying them back; in work, in venison or something else.

And that bastard, that priest, would take advantage of her husband and he would offer nothing in return. Nothing, except eternal salvation; which would not keep her warm at night and their children fed.

She looked around the village when she arrived back in the settlement and saw the children playing games. The boys were paired off with others the same size and pretending to be chevaliers with their sabres. The girls were making mud cakes with elaborate swirls. All the children were filthy.

This would almost certainly be their last night in their home. The place where they had shared so many delicious meals, so much laughter and so much love would be burned to the ground because of the greed of a damned priest. She shuddered she was so angry.

There was not one person from Beaubassin that cared whether they lived under a French flag or under the English one. They just wanted to raise their families in peace, grow their crops and look after their animals. They would still marry in the Roman Catholic Church regardless of any oath they gave to the English and they would still not fight fellow Frenchmen even if they were ordered to; they just wouldn't. But that was no reason to make them leave and burn their homes.

As always it was going to be about self-important men wanting more power and money.

She went over to Emile and spoke loudly over the roars of dreaming, playing boys. "Emile, you, drop your stick, you, and come home and wash for dinner. Maurice, you come too, mon petit." The boys looked at her for a half second like she was a stranger from a different country, then smiled and skipped over to her.

"Maman!"

"Come along you two, vite." Béatrice was in a different world and looked like she had been eating her muddy cakes, she was filthy from head to toe.

She led them the few dozen steps home and told the boys to strip to their undergarments and wash themselves with lye soap while under the tap of the cistern. She ended up carrying Béatrice and dropping her in the tub in the kitchen while she used all her strength to manoeuvre a huge pot of hot water from the fireplace. She tested the temperature, found it to be just right, and poured it in the tub with her little girl. She used a porringer to pour water over Béatrice's head, who, of course, screamed like a sauvage, as she always did when getting bathed. She soaped Béatrice's hair, rinsed it, and scrubbed the rest of her. There was an inch of mud in the tub when she was finished, so she got her little girl to stand up and step over the edge of the tub onto a thick cotton cloth that she used for only this weekly event. She grabbed another from a nearby shelf and scrubbed her dry. Then she pulled a nightdress over her head and gave her a tap on the bottom.

The boys came rushing in the door in their short under pants and both demanded to know, "Maman, ce qui est pour le dîner?"

"Ssssh! Get your pants on, you," and they both ran back outside and came in a few seconds later without shirts.

She said, "You little devils, you get back out there and put your shirts on."

"Oui, Maman!"

Mati followed them outside to see if there was any sign of Acquila. She walked around the house and sure enough, several hundred yards away; she could see him bravely vaulting again across the river. She thought she might have to have a word with him, but knew it would make no difference.

She went back inside and prepared the side dishes: a cold chow of vinegar, sugar, spices and green tomatoes with sliced onions and she dropped a large handful of sandfire greens into a boiling pot of water. She removed a medium sized boule de pain from the bread rack and put in on a cutting board on the table, along with a sharp knife.

The last things that they would take with them when they had to leave were her cooking implements that she needed for this dinner. Other than the cooking and cleaning pots, there were only wooden spoons with which to eat.

Using a heavy cloth doubled over several times she reached into the pie shelf in the fireplace and pulled out a large pork tortiere as the main course. She placed this on a flat stone on the table designed for the purpose.

The children took their seats and they began dinner. Mati wondered where 'Quila was.

Finally, after the children had finished their portions, without touching the greens or chow, of course, Acquila had arrived home. He grunted a greeting to his wife and children, who were cleaning up their supper plates.

"Acquila Girouard! Où avez-vous été? What does that maudit bastard priest want you to do? Enfants, go upstairs. Now!"

The children left.

"He wants me to help Compagnie d'Esgly, ma Chér."

"Puh… Compagnie d'Esgly … Puh. Now why would he want a farmer from Beaubassin to help Compagnie d'Esgly, the Royal Army of France? Yehn?

"l'Abbé wishes me to . . ."

"L'Abbé wishes you… when has l'Abbé ever wished anything. He doesn't wish. He orders. He treats you like a little puppy. What does he want? What is his order?"

"Ma Chér, I am to organize and command le Milice l'Acadien."

"You are what!?"

"Mathilde, the British will be invading and taking over Beaubassin any time now. Maybe they are in the bay now. They will have a very large force, many more than our soldiers, even with the Miqmaq Indians. The military commander needs our men."

"You mean he needs our farmers and husbands."

"Mathilde. This is our home. If the English come they will take it. And they will kill us and our children and eat our livestock."

"But it is your priest who will burn our home."

"Oui, ma Chér, I know."

Mathilde suddenly understood that in this place, surrounded by les sauvages and with mortal enemies, Les Maudits, surrounding them, that their life, their destiny, was not their own.

Then they heard musket shots.

8 – HUIT

Chevalier Jean-Louis La Corne thought he would have time **to** fully prepare for the English invasion. He was mistaken. But luckily for the French, though, the priest's Indian leaders were alert.

Even though it was early evening, the English under Lieutenant Colonel Lawrence were coming. They were almost here.

Sailing into the basin were a dozen or more large ships, probably enough to carry several hundred fighting men. The flags were English. The alarm was raised. The French had no ramparts, barely walls to defend themselves. They were surely destined to an unhappy end.

But Abbé Le Loutre and Chief Copit were ahead of Compagnie d'Esgly in preparedness; they had fifty Miqmaqs waiting for the English behind the dykes on the Mésagouèche armed with muskets and bows. They had another fifty prepared to burn the settlement to the ground and they were already beginning to awaken and mobilize the Acadians who were in their homes; they would burn the people as well as the buildings if they had to.

The ships were at least a mile offshore and waited several hours for the tide to rise. Finally, perhaps out of impatience, they began to lower some whaleboats to carry troops to shore.

Invisibly from the French position, two whaleboats had been released early in the day on the voyage from Piziquid, near some shale cliffs, and John Gorham and Benoni Danks had already worked their rangers into place on the ground to support Lawrence's main force.

The first few British boats started rowing but ran aground some distance from their destination, which was a fatal mistake. Only a few yards after they stepped off the boats they were stuck in muck almost to their knees and were slaughtered by arrows and musket balls from the shore.

Those who weren't killed put the corpses in the boat then quickly returned to their ship.

* * * * *

Acquila and Mathilde sat shocked in their homestead when they heard the musket shots. Acquila went to get his own musket and a handful of cartridges when they heard the Miqmaq war cries. He opened the door and looked outside and barely missed being bludgeoned by a Miqmaq warrior preparing to smash down the door to throw a torch inside.

Acquila dodged the club and Emile, his oldest boy, came running downstairs and grabbed their other musket from beside the door and pushed its barrel into the Miqmaq's face, directly into his eye socket. The warrior fell into the house, Quila grabbed the warrior's club and smashed in his skull. The torch flew from the warrior's hand into a basket of kitchen rags that quickly began to burn.

"Allons Y! Vite. Vite! Let's go!"

Mathilde pulled Béatrice through the door and was followed by Maurice while Acquila and Emile quickly grabbed whatever valuables they could, including a bag of musket cartridges, and the family ran toward the nearest wooded area. All around them there were screams; Miqmaq war cries and the sounds of terror of L'Acadiens trying to escape their burning homes and the arrows and torches of Le Loutre's Miqmaqs.

They made it into a copse of low maple trees without being noticed.

The Indians hadn't been told to harm the Acadiens so they didn't follow the Girouard family into the woods. Acquila said, "We will wait here until it's dark."

They watched. It was approaching dusk and the settlement, dozens of homes and barns were fully aflame and fires were reaching high into the air. The Miqmaqs were running wild, causing as much damage as they could.

All they could do was watch the devastation. Mathilde could only focus on their own home and her eyes teared up and she held her children tightly.

Acquila said, "Come."

The family made their way along the well-rutted cart path to Pont à Buot trying not to look back. They met up with more than a dozen other families and together, finally, they crossed the bridge.

They found their place in the temporary settlement and Mati put together a makeshift meal of dried sausage and her big loaves of bread that she had carried over earlier for Acquila's dinner. Everyone except Mati was famished and ate ravenously. She looked across at the fires that were consuming their homes and tried hard not to show her tears.

Meanwhile, Abbé Le Loutre, "Beausoleil" Brossard and Chief Jean Baptiste Copit and their Miqmaq followers continued to burn every building in the settlement, even the church. A special group of men were sent to rescue and transport the massive church bell; one cast thousands of miles away for just this place and just these people.

* * * * *

The British ships withdrew and waited for the tides to rise and things to settle down on shore. After several hours it seemed to be calmer and a boat under a white flag appeared and rowed to shore shortly after sunrise.

When they were close to shore they could see a small advance sentry outpost with the Fleur de Lis flag identifying it against one of the dykes.

They were able to get within shouting distance without any problem. A mid-officer shouted, "Now see here, French troops! Lieutenant Colonel Charles Lawrence wishes a parley with the commander of your forces."

A young French soldier cautiously rose above his muddy position, "Oui. Je vais demander la réponse de notre commandant." He turned and slopped as quickly as he could through wet grass and mud to the main body of the encampment. In about a half hour a command party that had travelled by horseback and under a white flag appeared, dismounted and walked to within hailing distance.

"I am Lieutenant Colonel Charles Lawrence, Commanding Officer of this British Regiment."

Captain Edward How, Lawrence's head subaltern, translated the conversation, speaking in French for his commanding officer and responding with the precise meaning of the French spoken. He had been travelling to France since he was a young boy; his mother had been born in Bretagne. This made him invaluable to English officers since his arrival a few year years before and had earned him trust of Acadians with whom he had interacted.

"Bonjour, Monsieur. I am Chevalier Jean-Louis Chapt De Louis La Corne, l'Ordre de St. Louis, and commander of this French fortress. What is the purpose of this parley?"

"My orders are to take command of the high ground on the east side of the River Mésagouèche and defend the border of Nova Scotia at all costs and to pursue whatever military missions for which I might be directed. What are yours?"

"Monsieur Lieutenant Colonel, my orders are to protect the sovereignty of the lands west of the Mésagouèche River on behalf of King Louis, to the last man if necessary."

"Then I will be landing on the east side of the river to enforce the sovereignty of King George and Great Britain."

"We will not obstruct nor inhibit your landing, Lieutenant Colonel." The Capitaine saluted, turned precisely and led his entourage back to his headquarters to prepare for whatever might happen next.

Lawrence directed his oarsmen, “Let’s go back toward the ship and continue on to the landing area with a larger force. Ensign Rose, signal the ship that we shall be taking the eastern high ground without conflict and for them to meet us and go ashore.”

While the French Army agreed to not interfere in the English landing, Beausoleil, Le Loutre and Chief Copit did not agree to any such thing.

When the first English boats landed just east of the Mésagouèche River they were immediately set upon by about two dozen of Le Loutre’s Miqmaqs and half-native Acadians. Fighting was fierce and one-sided with several British casualties until Gorham’s rangers came from behind. Then it was Copit who had to give in; his men were outnumbered and were already fatigued after the day’s adventures in burning the settlement. Many were being mowed down by musket and sabre.

The Abbé passed on the order to withdraw and all remaining French and their Miqmaq allies left the peninsula of Nova Scotia, destroying anything they could.

* * * * *

Captain Edward How stood on the slope of the ridge southeast of the mouth of the Mésagouèche River and watched the activity on both sides of the river; both were busy.

Nearby, the English whale boats and scows were emptying the stowage areas of more than a dozen English ships and carrying the materiel up past the burned carcasses of the former Acadian settlement to the site they had chosen on which to build their new fort. The stores included bell tents, sixteen-pound mortars, and hardware to begin construction of a fortification along with food staples, weapons and ammunition. Already, a half league further north on the ridge on which he stood, he could see ox teams hauling long straight logs toward him and the fortresses building site.

Across the swamp, with a spyglass, he could see past de Valliere's island and the ruins of his manor house and the settlement. He saw activity on the point directly across from him on the opposing ridge a half league away. The French were building earthworks near their access point to the basin.

With his translation ability not needed, How found himself with time on his hands.

He wandered around the construction site, saw nothing of interest and walked over to and through the old Acadian settlement ruins. Much of what he saw there surprised him. The houses had been solidly built and many, except for their roofs, were in reasonably good shape although unlikely to be easier to repair than new structures could be built from scratch. Unlike other such burned villages through which he had previously wandered; this one did not smell of burned flesh, which was a relief to him.

He was happy that there had been minimal harm to civilians so far in this encounter of enemies. Normally ordinary people would make up the lion's share of casualties.

He liked these Acadians; they reminded him very much of his mother's family members. They enjoyed simple pleasures; their families, their farming and their faith. He smiled at his poetic consonance.

He could hardly remember ever meeting a contemporary man-at-arms from the homeland of his mother and many Acadians: Bretagne and Normandie. He did know that historically they had been often in the middle of battles between English and French kings. Many of the French people from the areas had the blood of English and Welsh soldiers running through their veins.

All in all, he was relaxed and happy. He had heard that there was a tavern a league or so away, upstream. He started the walk there; perhaps he'd meet some Acadians who knew his mother's family.

* * * * *

In the new settlement of Beauséjour, new homes were being constructed for the two-dozen families who remained and the new fortress was being expanded and fortified closer to the basin, about a league from the Pont à Buot. The redoubt and other buildings at the bridge had been quickly completed and were now garrisoned with a defense force of several dozen soldiers.

For the men of the settlement, all the construction meant eighteen-hour days, heavy work from sun up to sun down. Not only were they building their own homes, but they were also being conscripted building the new fortress to offer protection.

As always, Acquila and Mathilde were among the hardest working of all the family heads in contributing to the rebuilding of the settlement.

While Acquila was working on the buildings, Mati was fully occupied in driving Jacques the Ox to pull the plough and break the earth to plant their staples; potatoes, carrots and turnips. If they were fortunate they might be able to get a crop in and grown in time to feed them over the winter. It was backbreaking and dirty work, not to mention exhausting. Béatrice was playing with her doll alongside where Mati was ploughing.

Even Emile and Maurice were helping out; they filled in gaps by milking the cow and running errands for the men working on the houses.

In a few days, the stone foundations were started for all the new houses and trees had been cut, limbed and stacked. Needing a few weeks for the timbers to dry out, Acquila had an opportunity to retrieve a valuable piece for their new home; the slate hearth that had been left behind. He set out to see about recovering it.

He walked over to Camille and Simon, "Amis, we have some free time, can you help me recover our hearthstone?"

"Bien sûr," they both responded and the three men walked toward the Girouard home site where Mati was still ploughing. She stopped when they approached. She still looked beautiful, but was sweating and her sabots were caked in mud and her skirts were muddy.

"Chér, can we take Jacques to retrieve our hearth?"

"Please. I need to feed Béatrice and the boys need their mid-day meal."

The men unhooked Jacques from the plough and led him to the nearby cart, hooked him up and then led him toward the bridge. The three friends chatted about the progress in their work, the weather and whether they would be able to cross to their old settlement without being stopped. No one had yet crossed the river, at least without doing so secretly, and they were a little apprehensive.

As they neared the bridge they noticed an English officer coming their way. He didn't appear to be armed, or to be accompanied by other soldiers.

The Englishman reached his side of the bridge, surprisingly the three friends by greeting them in French. "Bonjour, gentlemen, it is a beautiful day, is it not?"

The Maudit English had even spoken with the two older men's coastal dialect from Bretagne!

"Oui, Monsieur. Je m'appelle Acquila Girouard et mes amis est Camille Robicheaux et Simon Bourque."

The three men started crossing the bridge and met the English half way and all shook hands with him. "Je suis Edward How. How might I possibly offer you assistance."

Acquila said, "When my house was burned and my family left Beaubassin, we had to leave without the hearth of our fireplace. We were hoping to carry it back to our new home, as it will be very difficult to replace."

"Monsieur Girouard, you know that this side of the bridge is English soil and you Acadians have chosen to abandon your homes, yes?"

"We are aware of this, Monsieur How. But we have nothing to do with this conflict. We wish to live peacefully, but I would like to have my wife have the convenience of having a warm hearth for her cooking."

"So this is an order from your wife?"

Acquila smiled and nodded.

"Well then, since this is an order from a superior, then I must concede to her. I hope you will not mind if I accompany you to ensure there is no misunderstanding."

"Of course."

"Then bring your ox and cart."

Camille drove Jacques across the rough corduroy log bridge and they began the trek across the grassy field.

"Monsieur Bourque, your accent is from Bretagne, oui?

"Oui, our family is from a very small village near the ocean called Erquy, do you know of it?"

"Know of it? My friend, my mother is from St. Malo, we are practically cousins."

Camille said, "I have never been there, of course.'

How said, "I miss the place very much. But this Acadie is my home now and I hope to be able to have a family here."

The men and the ox climbed the ridge leading to the new fortress and the old settlement. Sentries stopped them and Captain How explained their reasons to visit the burned settlement and they were allowed to pass and collect the hearthstone. Acquila took the opportunity to collect a few other large items that would be useful; the cistern, the ladder that led to the attic rooms and the metal grills from the fireplace.

They took the long trek back with Captain How in their company. When they arrived at the bridge they did not notice that Jean Baptiste Copit was among the Miqmaqs at the trading post; or that he took notice of the friendly good-byes between the men.

* * * * *

Acquila wished that he had half as many workers and tools as the British to rebuild their homes. There were over twenty houses and the church to build and, including the boys, about forty men to do the work. They worked on all buildings at once.

They had found and carted enough stones for all the foundations, mixed mortar for them all, and then finished the foundations. While the mortar was setting, and Acquila and his two friends had travelled to the old settlement, other men cut, limbed and notched more long straight trees for the walls and roofs that would need to fully dry.

When the three men got back, they cruised the available trees on the high ground and marked the ones that would be used. They estimated that they could not finish all the houses using maple, oak and elm even though it was abundant. As a group, they decided that all the floors, uprights and roof beams would be made of hardwood and that the spruce and pine would be used for the corrugated walls. There was no shortage of clay and straw to fill the chinks in the walls so they would be stucco houses that would insulate against the heat and cold.

The women had pooled their tea, herbs and staples and had organized their meals for the coming week. A friend of Mathilde's, Hugette Haché, had fashioned some snares and after a few hours came back with a dozen rabbits. Another woman, Helene Fougere, had volunteered to sacrifice one of their cattle and had taken on the job of not only killing it, but also doing the butchering.

Since they had lost their cold rooms when they abandoned their homes, Helene had also taken on the job of salting and smoking the meat and making sausages to sustain the new settlement.

Other women were working hard to make the temporary shelters as comfortable as possible. They had built ditches to direct any rain water away from the lean-tos and waterproofed the seams of the bark tile roofing. They had divided the furnishings that they had rescued equally, so every family had beds and chairs as needed.

The soldiers had brought along a large ripping saw blade and Acquila was putting together the saw platform so that they could rip-saw flooring planks. He had put it on a sledge so that he could saw the trees where they fell and make them easier to transport.

"Acquila!" He turned his head to see Helene's husband, Abelard, who they all called Abel, and a couple of other elders from the village.

"Oui?"

"Can we find a quiet place to talk?"

"Bien sûr."

The men walked to sheltered place in the trees. One of the men had a bottle of apple cider that he passed around. They all lit their pipes.

Abel spoke up, "Acquila, we need to send men back across the river."

"Why?"

"We need to get some items that were left behind."

"What?"

"Did you bring your silver with you?"

"Yes, we had very little."

"Many of the families did not, and if they are to recover their savings, they had best do it before the English settle in on the land."

Acquila said, "Were such things not included in any agreement made with les maudits?"

"Would you trust either les maudits or our own soldiers?"

"No. Of course not."

"We need to get it."

Another man, Remi Hébert, said, "How would you do this, 'Quila?"

"We could do in the day or in the night. If we are found there in the day, then we can look innocent, but we will definitely be seen. If we do it at night, then we will look guilty if we are seen. Who are the people that left their silver behind?"

Remi gave him a page of parchment with six names. Each had a description of where they had buried their fortune. He noticed they were the families that had most resisted relocating.

Acquila said, "Here's what I think we do. We will get a couple of our women to do this. They will be less suspicious to the English and they look more honest when they lie than we do.

"I will ask Mathilde if she is willing."

Abelard said, "Very good, Acquila. I think that if she is successful, then each family should pay a share, say one tenth, to her for her bravery."

"That is a good thought, ami, but I think she and I would

both rather see this go to help build the new church."

* * * * *

John Gorham was to meet up with his other Ranger groups, Danks and Bartelo. He needed to give them orders about providing perimeter security for the new encampment and he found them and their sixty men lounging lazily under a collection of apple trees, now filled with ripening fruit. There were wasps buzzing around as well, but they did not seem to bother either the white Rangers or the Mohawks.

Several were biting into the apples, and some, lacking functional front teeth, were cutting slices with knives that likely had also seen duty in removing hair.

He called the two Captains out and offered them both cheroots, which they accepted. He offered them his match case and they both lit up from the smouldering fuse rope inside. Gorham lit one up himself.

"So, Gentlemen. The French seem to have retired to the west side of the river, but that does not mean that there is not mischief that will be done against us. The priest and his half breeds and Miqmaqs are not part of any arrangement we have with the French army so I suspect will continue to be a very real threat.

"So we need you to have roaming pickets, say a dozen or so men, scouting the vicinity, say within a league of the encampment. Bartelo, you'll take the first watch starting just before sundown. Best rest up until then, lads. Take light provisions for eight hours.

"Danks, you will take your turn tomorrow night. Make sure you get a report from Bartelo, here.

"Any questions?"

Both the Ranger captains shook their heads. Bartelo went to where he had been sitting, picked up his musket and signalled to a group of his men to follow him.

* * * * *

Acquila went looking for Mathilde and found her working around the temporary shelters.

"Ma Chér." He explained to her what they needed to do, she understood and immediately began thinking of ways that she might talk herself out of trouble, if she needed to.

"But Mati, ma Chér, it is not worth your life. If you believe you find yourself in danger, return here."

"I will be safe, you do not need to worry, 'Quila."

"I know that, but be careful. Can you get another woman to go with you?"

"I will be careful and I don't need any help, this is very easy."

She started to walk away, and then he stopped her. "Take this." He offered her his knife but she refused it.

"If my wit is not sharp enough when I need it, then no knife will be."

He watched her pick up a cloth bag and start walking down the hill.

She arrived back in the old settlement an hour later, passing along the river bank some distance below the English construction. The village was abandoned and several of the old homestead sites were still smouldering a little from the fires. Many of the buildings, however, were still standing although burned out.

The first one, the Doucets', had a bag of silver coins hidden under a loose slab inside the fireplace. She needed to find and use a sharp stick to prise it open and wished she had brought 'Quila's knife. She dug, found the bag, weighing probably a pound, in her bag and rose.

She took a quick look around. She was still alone.

Her next place to go was the Yvan Landry's house, two homesteads away. According to her note, they had their silver under the bottom step in their cold room. She noticed that she had soot marks on her apron. She would need be more careful.

She got to the Landry's; the roof had partially caved in but only to the level of the second floor so the main floor was almost unaffected. The door to the cold room was in the kitchen area. She entered the house, went to the trap door, opened it and reversed her direction to climb down the steep steps.

When she got to the bottom, it was quite dark and she had to feel her way around to look for the cache. The cold room had a hard clay floor and she tried to dig up the earth under the stairs with her hands and again regretted not bringing a knife. She climbed back upstairs to look for a tool of some sort and heard a noise.

She stopped her movement and held her breath.

It was the sound of two men talking, not nearby, but close. She couldn't make out what they were saying, not even what language they were speaking. She looked around for something she could use as a reason to be there.

Remi Hébert and his wife Gabrielle had left their home in a hurry and forgotten many things, she spotted a kettle hanging from the fireplace. It was one of those things that were always there and you never noticed it until your looked and they had left and never noticed it. She quickly put it in her carry bag and waited to see if the men entered. She pretended to be fussing around.

But they never came any nearer, the sound of their voices faded.

She looked around the kitchen. There was a wooden spoon on the ground near the opposite wall, she hurried over, picked it up and almost fell down the steep stairs to the cold room. She dug in the red clay behind the bottom step and stuck something hard. She cleared around it and found a wooden box. She pried it open. It was filled with silver guineas and a beautiful gold ring. She counted the coins as she put them in her bag and when she was done she climbed back upstairs.

"Who be you?" Standing in the doorway was an Indian. She knew it couldn't be a Miqmaq; they were certainly not welcome here.

"Je ne comprends pas Anglais."

He moved closer to her.

He replied back in English, “My Labreque Virgil. Who you?”

She spoke back in French. “My name is Mathilde, this was my house before it was burned.”

“You Roman Catlik? Priest Le Loutre?”

“Oui, he burned my house.”

“He is devil, him. You go.” He indicated to the door with his head.

She didn’t hurry, but left. “Thank you, Merci, Monsieur Labreque.”

She decided not to take the chance of getting any other caches. Her bag was heavy; she could manage more but it would slow her down. If she had to run, she might drop it, which would throw away her friends’ fortunes. She put the kettle back on top of her bag and left, walking as quickly as she could toward the Pont à Buot. When she arrived back at the new settlement she went first to see Gabrielle.

Mati found her working on the other side of the temporary housing. She beckoned to her friend and Gabi came to her. “Mathilde. What happened?”

“Come close, Gabi. I got your silver, where can we put it that will be safe?”

“How can I ever thank you?

“You don’t need to. You would do the same for me.”

“I will someday. I promise.”

“Come, let us find a safe place before we go to our beds.”

9 – NEUF

Danks and his crew were settled in a row of bell tents within the encampment. One of every five men had to act as sentries for a two-hour shift to make sure they stayed alert. There still could be enemies behind every bush, despite the ceding of the land a few days before.

As it was getting dark, most of the older men were puffing on pipes and drinking rough alcohol from containers of various forms. The young were playing knife games of various sorts.

They had a fire blazing with a turnip and corned beef stew being cooked for dinner. When the cook banged his porringer the crew lined up with their wooden bowls and had them filled. They were each given a thick slice of rough, slightly stale, brown bread.

The quiet of the night was moved by the chirps of crickets and the buzz of cicadas and somewhere in the encampment a sweet voice was singing a hymn: "Our God, Our Help in Ages Past". There was a hum of conversation from groups sitting in front of a hundred and fifty tents.

The soldiers in the camp were all close to exhaustion; in the past week almost all of them had spent several days and nights in a ship battling rolling waves. Many were already asleep, although just now it was getting dark.

It started with a shriek. Then silence. Then a scream of fear and cry of pain. Then, "No No No No No!" Then a long moan.

Another scream, then a cry, "Motherrrrrrrrr!"

Then, "The Lord is my shepherd . . . . . AHHHHHHHHHHH."

It went on for most of the night.

The next day the heads, without hair, were found. They had been tossed into the middle of the English camp.

* * * * *

Gorham sent a courier to bring Danks back to his tent. Almost no one in the encampment had slept the night before. Gorham did not want to wait for orders from Lieutenant Colonel Lawrence, that he suspected would be faulty or too risky.

He had expected this; the French, especially the damned priest, would not leave this land peacefully. And he pledged to himself and his dead rangers, 'none of them papist bastards and savages will ever leave here alive, damn them.' He lit a pipe although he almost never smoked in the morning.

Along with Danks and Bartelo's survivors, he had about a half hundred rangers and about a dozen or so Mohawks, out of about three hundred men in the camp. Each one of his rangers was worth ten of the red coats in this place, at this time, he thought.

He suspected that the priest and Indian had a hundred or more. And they knew the land better and had safe havens, probably fortresses of a sort. It would be a filthy business to hunt them down. But if they didn't, then they would see more occasions like the massacre last night. The savages would also likely continue to be a problem in the other English settlements being established.

Danks showed up with King.

Gorham said, "Terrible night, last night."

Danks grunted.

"Can't let them filthy savages do that to our people, Danks."

"No, Sor, we can't."

"Your job will be to clear them out now. You're to cause havoc among all the savages, be they red or French. You'll take your two dozen and my Mohawks. Savvy?"

"I savvy."

"Here's a slip to give to the Quartermaster to give ye whatever ye need in munitions and food and a few guineas for bribes if you need them. Here are your orders and passport." He handed Danks a horn tube.

"Yes, Colonel."

Danks left. Gorham puffed on his pipe.

* * * * *

Mathilde awoke, having slept well in the shelter cuddled next to Acquila on a piece of rough cloth and covered by one of their goose feathered quilts that her grandmother had made. He had dug out an indent in the soft spruce needle earth mattress at the level of their hips to make it more comfortable when sleeping on their sides.

They awoke at first light and lay in each other's arms without speaking for several minutes. There was no sign of life in their exhausted children.

"Mon Chér, I must arise and prepare the first meal."

Acquila groaned, exhaled and rolled toward her. "Me, soon."

She pecked him on his cheek and got out of their bedding.

The terror of the escape from their old home was behind them.

There was a fresh water stream about twenty yards from the shelter that ran into the Mésagouèche River. Someone, she thought probably 'Quila, had built a square canvas enclosure at a section of the stream to allow the women some privacy. She entered the room, it was vacant, and she squatted to do her toilet. Then she immersed herself in the chilly water. There was a large block of lye soap and she used it to wash. Her hair was very long and she hadn't washed it for several days, so she took advantage of her situation to suds it up and rinse it off. The water was freezing; but it made her feel alert and alive.

She towelled herself off and got dressed in her sleep clothes and returned to the shelter. Acquila was wandering around unshaven and seemed a little discomforted.

She started dressing "You look unhappy, Chér," she said.

"I'm not a good outdoor sleeper, Mati. I like comfort."

"Oh, pssshu. You're just getting old, you."

Acquila grabbed her from behind began tickling her and they both landed on their bedding, both laughing out loud until they thought about the children only a few feet away, but then one thing led to another.

* * * * *

Benoni Danks was in the encampment his rangers had set up just alongside the new fort construction area. He was holding a Virginian Cheroot, one of a few hundred he had brought with him from Massachusetts. He was sitting cross-legged in his officer's marquee tent and had just poured himself an unhealthy portion of scotch whiskey. He took the tube containing his orders, lit a small dry stick from his fire and lit his cigar first before opening the package Gorham had given him.

He coughed and used his scalping knife to open the tube and remove his orders. It was addressed specifically to him, using his formal rank. It read:

To: Captain Benoni Danks, Commander, Massachusetts Provincial Rangers

"You are ordered to cause havoc against the Acadian French and Mikmaks across Nova Scotia until you receive further orders. All are commanded to provide you any and all assistance as may be necessary."

Under authority of:

J. Gorham, Esq., Colonel"

"King!"

The young ranger ran to his tent.

"Aye Aye, Capt'n."

"We're not bloody salt arses, King. We walk to work. 'Yes, Capt'n' will do."

"Yes, Capt'n."

"King, have the lads pack their bags and muster here in one hour."

"Aye, Capt'n."

Danks knew Gorham's Mohawks were building their lodges outside the area in which the palisade was being constructed and furthest from the river and he went there. Although it was only an hour past dawn, the new fortress was already a beehive of activity with more permanent shelters and the palisades being erected.

Before he arrived at the Mohawk placement, Colonel Gorham called to him.

"Danks."

"Colonel."

"Let me be clear. Your new orders are to include the killing of every God-damned Mikkymak, half-breed and Frenchman you see along the way. Savvy?"

"Savvy, Colonel."

"Spare them no quarter. Kill every bloody last one of them you can and bring their scalps back in a bag. We'll see how that Christless bastard Copit and his power hungry priest like their own medicine."

Danks had never seen his commanding officer so animated or so angry. "Fifty guineas for each, Colonel?"

"A hundred each for the bastard redskins, Danks. Five hundred if you bring back Copit or the priest La Loot in chains."

"We'll try our best, Colonel."

"The chief of my Mohawks we call Lord Miller, he'd be the tall one missing an ear."

"On my way, Colonel."

"Do your duty, Danks. Kill. Them. All!"

"I'm your servant, Colonel." Danks saluted and left, directing himself toward the native longhouses being built on the edge of the new English encampment.

When Danks arrived at the Mohawk camp, Gorham's Mohawks were covering their lodge's roofs with large sections of bark taken from the trees that had been chopped down for the longhouse walls.

Danks walked up to the nearest group of workers, "Where be yer chief?"

They looked at the Englishman with blank faces. "Yer chief, ye God-damned heathens. Lord Miller!"

One of the men, older and shrivelled with old war paint covering much of his face, came up to Danks and waved him in a direction. Danks followed. They approached a lodge and a tall man with a single plait of long hair on an otherwise totally bald head. It was tied at his scalp with leather strands about six inches in width with the remaining two feet of greasy hair hanging to one side. He wore leather leggings, moccasins and was bare above his waist. His chest was filled with tattoos of swirls and boxes and other symbols. He was missing his left ear.

He looked suspiciously at Danks.

Danks marched aggressively toward him. "I come from Gorham. You and your warriors are to come with me."

The Mohawk looked directly at Danks. "We kill?"

"As much as you want."

"You pay?"

"I pay twenty guineas for any scalp you bring me."

"Then we go."

"I will return."

Danks walked back to his tent and found his Company of Massachusetts Rangers assembled doing what they always did when they weren't killing or drinking; smoking and talking. Some were laughing, a few others were already sneaking liquid from their water bladders.

When they noticed Danks arrival they stood, tapping their pipes on their muskets to empty the ashes.

"We're going to raise havoc, boys. We'll be on top of the bastards before they know it. Ye got yer gear? Good, let's go get the redskins."

Danks and King marched the rangers to the Indian camp. The Mohawks were ready and ran ahead of the white men who marched in cadence. With Lord Miller in the lead, the company resumed their bloody march across Acadia.

* * * * *

After their time together and getting the children dressed and out to play, Mathilde and Acquila walked toward the new fortress being built on the point on higher ground and closer to the bay.

Acquila was curious because he had heard gunfire when they were enjoying the afterglow of their intimate time. It was a warm morning and it promised to be very hot and Mathilde was unhooking the front of her top-shirt to cool off as they moved along.

"Acquila, we have more worries than getting our new house or even the war that is going on around us."

"What, ma Chér?"

"It is feeding our animals and ourselves."

He looked at her, "Quoi?"

"All of our animal feed and seeds for planting were burned with our buildings or are on the other side of the river. I don't expect that les Anglais will allow us to go digging up what they believe is their land."

"No, I don't expect they will. We will need to depend on providence, Mati."

"Providence. Puhh! Providence got us in this mess. You hear about Serge Melançon?"

"He is that old widower?"

"Oui. He was. He died yesterday when he ate a burdock root."

"People are that hungry?"

“The ones that do not know how to look after themselves are.”

As they were nearing the new fort, they heard a hubbub coming behind them on the path. It was a column of soldiers surrounded by an ox cart carrying a large chest. The men seeming to be very alert and protective. It was approaching them quickly and they hurried to get out of the way.

They noticed that Abbé Le Loutre was at the end of the parade, the first time he had not assumed prominence in such a line.

“’Quila, what can that be?”

“I don’t know. But it looks important if l‘Abbé is in the line and at the very end.”

“You need to find out, ‘Quila. Our lives may depend on it.”

“I don’t know that he would tell me.”

Mati said with a hint of cynicism, “You’re his new chief of militia, you. What does your Abbé have hidden in his gowns? Tell him you have to know what it is, to be able to protect it.”

* * * * *

While Benoni Danks and his motley group of rangers were marching east, Jean Baptiste Copit and his warriors were dogtrotting around the new English positions and toward the other Acadian villages in Chignectou.

Copit was planning to do a circle of all the other settlements in the area: Grand Pre, Mecan, Menoudy and Piziquid. He had already visited Nanpan and forced the Acadians there to disperse and had killed those who had refused.

He knew from reports from his Miqmaqs that there were still Acadians living in them, although many had obeyed the Abbé and left to go to the northern territories.

His Miqmaqs had killed and tortured and scalped two dozen English only two nights before, and burned a nearby Acadian settlement a few days before that, but they kept up a steady two league-an-hour pace. This was beyond Copit’s level of endurance, so he rode behind on a broken down gelding he had appropriated from an Acadian settlement.

While his patron, the Abbé, was a politician in Copit's eyes who would make trade-offs as necessary to protect and expand his influence, the Miqmaq chief saw the English as true devils sent by Kisúlkw to test His subjects.

While the chief had been brought up in the Roman Catholic Church, he ruled not for the French, but for his people. The Miqmaqs had been in this land since the beginning of time; the Française were just visiting. They were like the geese that spent half the year in the Shubenacadie lakes; there were very many of them, they made a lot of noise and they even wore blue, white and grey costumes.

He often came into conflict with the other chiefs who accused him of not representing them; that he was a renegade and only spoke for his own small band. But Copit believed he had a hereditary right and he accepted the responsibility that came with his inheritance.

Copit was able to get along with the French; their chief, the priest, kept his people armed with weapons and rewarded them for taking the hair of the English. He could do trade with the French.

But for the English, there was no hope. The few times he had been in their company they had been demeaning and rude and had treated him and his fellow warriors like savages that had no inherent right to live on their own land.

He minded not when his missions required him to take the blond and red hair of English.

Before the sun was fully in the sky they had left the settlement of Nanpan. The little grouping of buildings was located in a small valley of a tributary of a larger river and the haze made it difficult to see their destination. It was very quiet, it was Tqoljewiku; not even the frogs were making noise. It was difficult not to notice the disruption along the shoreline.

Chief Copit signalled to his lieutenant, Menickh, who was named after the small berries that had sustained his mother during her pregnancy with him. Menickh understood and stealthily crawled on all fours through the grasslands until reaching the top of a low rise.

For the last few steps he barely moved; making sure that his head did not disrupt the line of grass at the top of the hill. He saw what he had to see and carefully backed up and gave some hand signals to his chief. Copit moved his men forward; all intelligent enough in the ways of war to move without raising dust or making a sound.

As they got closer to the ridge, they began moving faster and accelerating. In a minute they reached the top and as a unit rose to their feet and started charging headlong down the slope, war cries in full throated screams, at an English column.

The English reacted quickly, turning toward the assault and unleashing a volley that dropped a half dozen of the Miqmaqs in their tracks. They too were accustomed to the ways of war.

In a matter of seconds, the Miqmaqs were upon them and the hand-to-hand combat was fierce; war clubs smashing against muskets and musket stocks smashing into faces. The worst violence was Miqmaq against Mohawk; their mutual hatred generations old.

Danks, being an old campaigner, tried to organize a controlled retreat; "King, take five men thirty strides to the left and reload. Double time! Lord Miller, be strong! Get yer men scrappin'. Harder. Harder. Come on men. Push back! Push back!"

And the tactic worked. King managed to get a half dozen men far enough away to have enough time to reload and their volley slashed into the sides of the Miqmaqs.

Copit, knowing that his men were tired from the previous two nights and could not sustain the assault much longer, yelled for a retreat. His men responded, stopped pushing forward, and started fighting defensibly moving back to their previous position on higher ground.

The English were happy to allow this; they too were feeling their casualties and fatigue and were happy to have it end. The Miqmaqs would take no scalps this day, though two of them were dragging an English prisoner. The English would take scalps, but the tally of their own dead was a terrible price to pay for them.

Danks sat recovering from the fierce fight they had just endured. To repulse an assault was not his mission. To hunt down and kill Miqmaqs was.

He was exhausted from his own efforts; he was in his thirties and feeling his age.

He called, “King!” His subaltern came to him. Get Lord Miller to bury our dead and our boys to scalp the redskins.

“Boyos, we have not begun. Get the rest of the men ready to hunt down and kill every one of those bastards.”

* * * * *

Acquila met the Abbé at the site of the new church, to be dedicated to Saint Louis. Adjacent to the site was the bell rescued from the now burned church at Beaubassin. Mathilde was at the temporary homestead providing the mid-day meal to their children.

Le Loutre was facing the fortress construction site where the redoubts were being dug; logs destined to serve as the palisades were being stockpiled outside of the perimeter of the area being dug out with the clay being piled on the outward side.

He seemed to sense ‘Quila’s arrival and spoke without turning toward him.

“Monsieur Girouard, the Church needs you.

"This peace will not last for long. There are things happening in the world that we do not see.” He turned around and looked directly in ‘Quila’s eyes.

"Before too many days pass these marshes will be the scene of even worse conflict than we have already seen. But for we ordinary followers of God, we might not live long enough to see this bloodshed.”

“Father?”

“We have no food, Monsieur Girouard. Not for our people and not for our livestock. If we do not cooperate now, then we will not last through the winter."

"What can we do, Father? Pray?"

"We pray every day as part of our doctrine, Monsieur. So not only pray. We will build new aboiteaux, we will prepare our lands to grow our sustenance for next year, we will build our church and settlement and we will buy our food to survive. Unfortunately, we will buy the food from les maudits that will enrich them. But they will sell us the food we need to sustain and strengthen ourselves so when the time comes we will defeat them."

"What will I do, Father?"

"You will lead our men, Monsieur Girouard. You and your fellows will prepare the ground, with God, to accept our seed next spring. You will lead them in preparing them to fight against the English invaders and you will lead them in building the aboiteaux which will sustain us as a community for eternity, until we receive our just rewards.

"The Holy Church will provide remuneration to all the workers to a level to feed their families. They will do work as I described to earn this remuneration. Yes?"

"Oui, Abbé Le Loutre, I believe they will."

10 – DIX

Lieutenant Colonel Charles Lawrence surveyed and then began walking through the feverish construction activity that was occurring on the ridge on the south side of the river, across the broad expanse of marshlands from the French position. Already the palisades that would surround the military installation were nearing completion; thanks to the expertise of the engineers with which he had insisted that his mission be resourced.

The military buildings: the armoury, storerooms and barracks were already framed in. Outside of the palisade, construction of the commercial structures was also proceeding well. The brew house was coming along; soldiers didn't only march on their stomachs, but also their bladders. There was a trading post being finished off and the trunks of merchandise for sale were already awaiting the display of their goods.

He walked over to the trading post and chatted briefly with his Commissary, Joshua Winslow. Lawrence was most anxious for this building and the brew-house to be completed; he was accountable for the cost and benefits of the mission, and he had no concern if the mission's soldiers, themselves, contributed to the revenues. He would even encourage the Crapauds, if they wished, to spend their silver coins at his establishment. All warfare now was a commercial enterprise as much as a political one. He was pleased to hear from the commissary that he was already prepared to sell merchandise on request and that he would properly report any such transaction.

Captain Edward How was helping Joshua empty crates and arranging the ale mugs, pipes, and various other commodities and giftware on the shelves.

"Captain."

"Lieutenant Colonel."

"Had any contacts with your Acadians here?"

"I've met some, Lieutenant Colonel. Friendly. Don't seem to be all that patriotic to the Fleur de Lis."

"Not a bad idea to butter their scones, How. If they see us as friendly, when the Indians are burning their houses, they might be a valuable asset."

"Bountiful idea I think, Lieutenant Colonel."

Lawrence nodded and started walking to the door. "Indeed. Good Day."

* * * * *

Mati had one more homestead to check for hidden silver coins; they were at the residence of the old widower, Melançon. He had no heirs and no one to leave his life savings to, but had told his friend, Gabrielle Hébert, 'in case anything ever happened to him'. After he died, Gabi had told Mati about it and where it could be found. She also said that Mati could keep whatever she found.

So she decided to do it before the English finished their construction and began to look around the village ruins. The English were locating their fortress and ancillary buildings north of Beaubassin on the same ridge, so her trip would require her to pass by the English both ways to and from the old settlement. She would need to be ready for anyone, especially the half-breed who had startled her before.

She brought with her some coins as an excuse to be travelling across the river. She had heard that the English were opening a trading post and that could justify her visit. She also was interested to see what there was for sale; perhaps they had items that would be of interest to women! She had never been in such a shop. Mostly they only sold tobacco, alcohol, fishhooks and hunting items. She would like to see if what the English had to sell was different.

She borrowed the Hébert's old nag for the trip; it could travel the three-league distance in better than half the time she could and the less time she spent passing the English, the more likely that her trip would be completed successfully.

She saddled up the old mare and slowly trotted down the slope past the completed French army camp and crossed bridge and rode along the grasslands to the other ridge. She urged the old horse to go faster along the bottom of the ridge.

When she approached the British camp she couldn't help but be impressed with the level of completion of the palisades and buildings. In a few days, they were well ahead of the French fortress and it looked like the buildings outside the fort were even further along. She kneed the mare hard and quickly passed the English into the remains of the Beaubassin settlement.

She passed their old home and felt her eyes well up with tears. They had worked so hard and given up so much on the orders of a damned priest. And now it was rubble; only the foundation remained. She inhaled deeply and held the tears back and led the mare to the old Melançon shed.

It was not as badly burned as the rest of the homes; likely because the old man hadn't the strength to follow Le Loutre's orders. The roof was gone, but the walls were still standing. Mati pushed open the door and it creaked and was blocked; she had to push to the limit of her strength to open it. Finally she got through and she looked for the fireplace. She saw it and the hearthstone under which the old man's treasure was located. She doubted it could be very much.

She found an old metal stake and used it to lever up and move the stone and then to dig underneath it. There was a wooden box there and after considerable effort she was able to extract it from its clay prison. There was no lock and she opened it. It was filled with gold and silver coins; more money than she had ever seen in her entire life.

She gasped.

The old man had probably never spent a sou in his life. Everything he had ever earned was in front of her; enough money to keep an Acadian family for a lifetime.

There was no way she could carry the whole box and she looked around for something in which to carry all the coins. She found a dusty leather bag with a strap that would do and she filled it with the coins. She could barely lift it, but slung it over her shoulder. She stood and almost staggered under the weight. She had a thought. Les Maudits, even as barbaric as they were, would never bother a pregnant woman. She hoped.

She removed her blouse and undershirt and hung the bag around her neck so the coins hung in front of her stomach. She put her blouse and undershirt back on and over the fortune and looked down. A man, even one of the more clever ones, would almost certainly not see through her ploy. She wondered about the noise of the coins, looked around and found some old rags that she could use to pad any noise from the coins. She mixed it in, adjusted her tops and jumped up and down without a noticeable sound. That would do.

She walked toward the horse; the weight of the coins was so much, she felt like she was pregnant. She was about to mount when she noticed the frightening half-breed eying her from the edge of the English area. If she bolted, he would notice and likely see it as a sign of fear and perhaps even chase her.

She decided to be bold. She wanted to see the English trading post anyway. She slowly walked the old nag toward the English area, ignoring the presence of the half-breed. She looked for where the crowd was gathered and led the nag there. Without fear she confidently strode up to the place, tied her mare to a post and walked toward the door. She glanced back and noticed…she remembered he had said his name was Virgil.

She walked in. She looked around; there was a man who appeared to be a shopkeeper, his young assistant and a well-dressed English officer. The shopkeeper nodded at her genially, "Good morning, Madame, please tell me if there is anything you might like to purchase."

Mati nodded demurely back at him. The English officer also

nodded.

There was already merchandise on shelves. In her entire life she had never seen such things. All the trading places she had been in had catered to men; hunting and work items and pots and such.

Here there were shelves of fine pottery, ribbons, and fine cotton cloth, even fine stemware for drinking. She even saw what she thought might be perfume! She was fascinated when she noticed stacks of silk items in the corner. Who here could afford to buy silk? Were les maudits that wealthy they could buy such gifts? Who would they give them to? None of them could have wives here… Perhaps they would be purchased as gifts to take back to their wives in England.

She went closer to take a better look when she heard the door open. She glanced back and saw it was the half-breed. He was staring at her, and then started to walk toward her.

She snatched one of the silk items, put it under her arm, and moved quickly toward the door.

As she thought, the shopkeeper noticed and moved toward her, blocking her passage, which made the half-breed back off. The English officer also started to block her way. She redirected herself toward the shopkeeper and took out her purse from her pocket. The half-breed, seeing the attention paid by his betters, left.

She withdrew the silk handkerchief and put it on the counter.

The shopkeeper smiled and moved behind his counter and spoke in English. She made the universal facial expression that meant she didn't understand. She made a face to show fear and pointed at the door, and the English officer stepped in and made an indication that he understood her.

She withdrew some coins from her purse and put them on the counter. The shopkeeper examined them, took several and wrapped the silk handkerchief with fine paper, almost as fine as the silk itself. She felt guilty for a moment until she realized that, in a bag hung from her neck, was a fortune suitable for the Pope; if her purchase allowed her to return to her home.

She picked up the package and glanced at the soldier. He

nodded and introduced himself, but she understood not a word.

He offered his arm, and she, not sure what to do, put her hand on it.

He engaged her in conversation in French, and she just nodded and smiled. He allowed her to precede him through the door and out and down the steps. The half-breed was waiting a few yards away. The officer appeared to excuse himself, walked toward the half-breed and addressed him sharply. "Virgil" appeared to cower, and looked at her, then ran away in the opposite direction.

The officer returned and she looked toward the old mare.

He led her to the horse, helped her to mount. She was careful to sit side-saddle to show her care for her 'unborn child'. He saluted her, she smiled, and she began slowly trotting away from les maudits and their half-breed henchman. In less than an hour she was back in Beauséjour.

* * * * *

Danks walked over to Lord Miller. "Chief, would ya send out a scout or two and get a line on where those murderin' bastards went. Have them report back within the hour. Your men get the next collection of hair."

The Mohawk leader nodded and walked over to his men and spoke to one who was digging graves for their lost men. The Mohawk nodded, called to a fellow and they started trotting to follow the signs of Copit's Miqmaqs.

Danks' men were cleaning themselves up; some had found a stream going into the tributary that wasn't filled with mud and were washing themselves and their clothes. Others were cleaning their muskets and adjusting their weapon's attachments that had been damaged in the hand-to-hand combat. Many were bandaging up wounds, one was sewing up a gash in a friend's face with a needle and deer gut thread.

"Hez, let's look at the settlement."

The two rangers walked the half mile to the Nanpan

settlement in the little valley of the tributary along which their bloody battle had just taken place. They did not worry about their safety; Danks doubted that the Miqmaqs would have gone to a different place to resume hostilities. But Danks and King still kept their eyes peeled.

The settlement, when they arrived, was very quiet, there were a couple of cows and sheep grazing, but it appeared that many of the residents had left. The rangers walked down the hill into the collection of buildings. Like Beaubassin, the village had been razed and it was like a ghost town. Notable were the remains of a church close to the centre of the settlement.

They walked into the square and came across an old man and woman sitting peacefully in front of their house. He was smoking a pipe. They looked at the two obviously English men without fear. Danks and King walked up to them.

The old man spoke, "Mon nom est Leblanc, c'est ma femme, Domithilde. C'est notre maison où notre famille a vécu pendant plus de cent ans. Si vous nous dire de quitter nous ne ferons pas. Tout comme nous n'avons pas lorsque les sauvages est venu avec le priest. We souhaitez être laissé seul."

Danks did not understand a word said. But he captured the meaning. He had killed many other Crapauds just like these two. But there had been enough killing today; at least of innocents. He said, "You are at no risk from us this day. King, we'll go back."

Danks turned around and thought better. He walked up and gave the old man the jerky he had and his pouch of tobacco that came from Virginia.

The old man accepted the gift and nodded; Danks and King walked back to their men.

When they returned Danks looked at the dead bodies of his company; most were Mohawks, though there were a couple of his Massachusetts boys. He looked around and was troubled not with what he saw, but what he didn't.

He liked Josiah Higgins almost most of all; almost as a son. The boy was in his late teens, with a red face that had never seen a razor. And young Josiah wasn't to be seen.

* * * * *

Mati arrived back in the new settlement flushed, excited and a little bit apprehensive. She went to their shelter, removed her tops and placed the bag of coins on the ground and looked at it.

What should she do with the money? There was hardly a place to spend it.

What about Gabi Hébert? Should she tell her how much she had found? She likely had no idea how much money the old man had saved up.

Should she tell 'Quila? Normally, this would not be an issue, but with his recent attachment to that damned priest, would he want to give their new treasure to the church?

If they kept it, they could still do great works with the money; she knew that hard times were coming and the difference between life and death might just be having a certain amount of money. And the priest would probably only use the coins to get more power.

She came to a decision. She would bury it. But she had to be very careful to even do this. If the wrong people, soldiers or churchmen, saw her bury it, they would surely take it.

Yes, she had to be very careful. And yes she had to tell Acquila about it, but not where she buried it. And, yes, she would have to tell Gabi but explain that she was keeping it for emergencies for any of them, in case bad things happened. Mati knew herself well enough that if anyone in the settlement faced a real crisis that could be solved with money, then she would offer it.

She looked around their temporary shelter to see if there was a place to put it until she determined where it would be safe for a longer period. She found a niche under the log floor that Acquila had built and the bag fit nicely underneath it.

* * * * *

Acquila walked over to Camille Robicheaux and Simon Bourque who were starting to lay out on the ground the dimensions of their adjacent new home sites with rocks.

“Mes amis! Simon, how is your family?” Acquila knew from Mathilde that Simon’s wife was fearful of the future and was refusing to share intimate activities with her husband until things were more stable and the future was clearer.

“I am working very hard, ‘Quila, to keep them happy.”

“I have good news!”

Camille said, “We would like to hear good news, Quila. What is it?”

“We are to go back into building aboiteaux like our grandfathers.”

Simon stopped working, “That is only good news, ‘Quila, if we find food to eat when we begin digging.”

“Even better. We will be paid to work on it.”

“Vraiment?”

“Vraiment. l’Abbé Le Loutre has arranged funding for this. We will be paid for our time which we can use to buy food from les maudits until we are able to grow our own.”

Simon was always doubtful, “They will sell us food?”

“Les Anglais would sell their own mothers if the price was right.”

“When do we start?”

“As soon as we get our work crew together and put in a day’s work. There is one other thing.”

Simon said, “There is always one other thing…”

“You will need to train in the militia to help defend our settlement.”

“We’re not soldiers, and neither are you.”

“We need to become soldiers, Simon. Our futures depend on it. And the army will train us. And building the aboiteaux will make us strong.”

Camille said, “I will need to see the vast amount of bullion with which he will pay us, but if what you say is true, then I will be there to work.”

"You always work hard, ami."

Simon said, "I work not so hard, but I will still work for the money, 'Quila."

"You're a good man to work with, Simon, with all of the happy faces you never make."

"I will smile very widely if I can go make money and have comfort again with Philomene."

Acquila said, "I need to know nothing of such personal matters, ami. Mati… moi?… la même chose…"

* * * * *

While it was not yet mid-day, Jean Baptiste Copit was doing what he always did, sipping steadily from a bottle of brandy; he always purloined as many casks of the rotgut as he could get his hands on from settlements and the storehouses of churches. He shared it liberally with his camp members, women and men; it tended to keep them oblivious to the devastation around them.

The women in camp, several of whom were already soused, took particular interest in the captured English prisoner. The soldier, hardly more than a child, was sobbing and crying like one. The women wasted no time in tying the lad's hands to an elm tree branch that made him hang from his wrists so that his toes barely touched the ground.

Copit looked on as the slaughter started.

Copit had always believed that the women were the crueler of the two sexes. But he thought that this way was as was provided by Kisulkw. Not that Copit had much regard for anything spiritual, except when it served his purpose. In this case, allowing his women to exorcise their own suffering from the brutality of their existence in this way meant that he, their chief, would not be held to account.

He took a longer drink of his brandy and watched as the women started and fuelled a fire at the boy's feet. The women began dancing around him, whipping him with sticks and jabbing him with spears. One lit a torch from the fire and held it against the boy's crotch until it was aflame. The boy howled in horror and pain.

Copit grew bored of watching and thought about cutting him down, but let the women enjoy themselves and to continue to be distracted.

He wandered over to the cooking fire where there were fat, juicy trout hanging from a spit and dripping into the flames. He moved one from above the fire with his musket ramrod, removed it and ate it with his gloved hand while he watched the women.

They were growing tired from their efforts and were removing the boy from the tree. He was now inert with the appearance of a large rag doll. Copit watched as they removed his hair. And he noticed that the boy's arm was moving when they emasculated him.

* * * * *

Danks suspected the worst as far as Josiah Higgins. If the Miqmaqs had taken him, then he was probably already killed and likely very painfully. He would need to avenge the boy, if he was beyond being saved.

The friendly casualties had been buried while the Miqmaq dead were scalped and corpses left to be consumed by scavengers. Danks called the men to muster. "We are going to hunt down those black ducks and find young Josiah, dead or alive. Lord Miller, send your scouts to find our way and King, lead the column."

The Mohawk leader spoke to two of his men who ran ahead to find the path taken by the Miqmaqs; the rangers following in two columns.

After two hours of hard marching the scouts came hurrying back and conferred with Lord Miller; he came over to Danks and spoke. "Their camp is over that rise, in a small valley, but there are only women there."

Danks took King and they carefully went to the top of the rise and looked down. There was a terribly mutilated body hanging from a tree; likely Josiah. They went back to the column.

"Men, your friend is hanging from a tree over there," he pointed, "burned and mutilated. Have at them, boys. Make them feel pain and make bloody sure they're living when ya take their hair."

Danks and Hezekiah King, who had been Josiah Higgins' best friend, led the company on the slow approach to the top of the rise and the dash top speed down the fifty paces to the gathering of Miqmaq women. The women looked up but had little chance to respond. The rangers were upon them and the bloodshed and torture and lack of human mercy was extreme. Hair, then heads, were removed, but noses and ears were cut off first to maximize pain.

When it was all over, the noses and ears were collected on a length of cord that replaced the sad corpse of Josiah Higgins, whose remains were sent back to Fort Lawrence on a litter carried by a couple of rangers with three Mohawks for security.

* * * * *

Mathilde was almost too tired to make supper, but she was still excited by her close shave at the English trading post and she was bubbling with anticipation from her find; 'when and what will I tell Acquila?'

She had taken two large salted fish from their dwindling provisions and soaked them in water when she had first arrived home. Now she took them to the nearby stream to clean and rinse them thoroughly. She boiled some potatoes and the flesh of the fish, then crushed them with a wooden masher, a cup of flour, salt and some herbs. She formed them into cakes, covered them with a cloth and let them sit to properly congeal.

The coins. She knew that 'Quila would very likely want to share them with the community and give a healthy portion to the church. She was also sure that keeping the money for an emergency might save their lives someday, maybe even when all other hope was lost.

She would need to have Acquila see and understand the need to protect themselves first, otherwise they might not survive to help others.

She went to the edge of the hill and looked over at the new English fort, barely visible on her far right. There didn't seem to be any commotion between there and the bridge. She was glad; she had worried that the terrible half-breeds might have told the soldiers of her secret visits.

She called to the children "Emile! Maurice! Béatrice! Vite, aller ici!" and they ran toward her; hungry and tired from a full day pretending they were priests and Indians.

"Now go, you, and bring me a big pile of dry wood."

She went to the cooking pit and arranged some stones to hold her cast-iron cooking vessel and lit a fire within with birch bark kindling and fed it consecutively larger pieces of dried wood that the children had collected. Soon she had a roaring blaze and moved away to allow it to burn down and generate enough heat on which to fry her patties.

Acquila returned just as she had formed the patties and covered them in a light coating of lard. "Ma Chér, comment ça va?"

"Bien, bien, 'Quila."

She put the fish cakes onto the skillet, being careful to move their bottoms around briefly to prevent them from sticking.

She seemed apprehensive to him and he asked, "What is wrong? I have good news."

She responded cautiously, "Good news?"

"Yes, Mati. We will be paid to build the new aboiteau."

"That <u>is</u> good news. How much? Where is the money coming from?"

"I don't know yet, but it should be enough to buy food. The Abbé has arranged for it. "

'The Abbé…,' thought Mathilde. "Everything from the Abbé always comes at a greater cost than benefit. What does he expect of us, for this fortune he will pay?"

She flipped the fish cakes with a little extra emphasis.

“He expects us to build the aboiteau on the Riviere au Lac to allow us to get back to farming.”

“What does he want from you, Acquila Girouard?”

“He wants me to lead the men.”

“When will you have time to build our house and barns when you’re building his aboiteau? Would you do this if we did not need the money?”

“I cannot imagine how we could come up with such amounts, Mati?”

“We already have, Chér…”

“What?”

“Remember old Melançon?”

He nodded. “The man who died from poisoned roots.”

“Oui. I went to find his savings today.”

“In Beaubassin?”

“Oui. I went to the remains of his house, and ‘Quila, he had almost more gold and silver coins than I could carry. I’ll get them.”

She went over to the niche in their lean-to and withdrew the bag and gave it to him.

“The fish cakes!”

She hurried back to the fire and luckily the cakes were done perfectly. She called the children and distributed her mére's delicious specialties and they ate hungrily.

Acquila lifted the bag and felt its weight and shook it. Then he looked inside. “Mati, this bag is ten pounds! He opened it and put his hand inside and felt the many coins with his fingers. He pulled one out. It was a gold Spanish doubloon, worth a king’s ransom by itself. He pulled out another and another.

The food was forgotten.

“Mati, this is Spanish gold. How could the old man ever have obtained these?”

“Well, they say he was a mariner; that he used to serve on King Louis’ ships in the southern islands.”

“Do you think he was a pirate, perhaps?”

“Who knows? He kept to himself. Gabrielle Hébert said she

was his a relative and one time told me that he came here from Port au Prince, not from France. Perhaps he discovered a treasure?"

"Perhaps. It would make some sense. Should the money not go to Gabi and her family?"

"I think, peût-etre. But she told me to keep what I found there, because I had recovered the money for the other families."

"We will give her and her husband one-third. We still get more money that we ever dreamed of, she will get her due for being nice to an old man, and we will give one-third to the church."

"Quoi?"

"I will ask Abbé Le Loutre to relieve me of my duties with the aboiteau, appoint Camille to take the head-man job, so that I can build my house. I will offer our life savings in return for this."

"He will be curious, no?"

"Yes. But he knows me as an honest Roman Catholic and I will tell him that I will continue to form our militia. He will understand."

Mathilde nodded, showing some doubt and said, "Let me serve you supper, mon Chér."

11 – ONZE

After supper, and when it was getting dark, the Girouards heard noise from the Pont à Buot trading post. Acquila stood up and walked to the edge of the hill leading into the marshlands. He said to Mathilde, "Sounds like music, some of the people are having a party, either that or they're strangling all the geese from the river. Let's go and enjoy ourselves, Mati."

"What about the children?"

"Bring them too. After everything that has happened, it would be good for them to see their parents enjoying themselves."

"Oh, yes!"

"Mati, bring one of our old coins, from before. Let's use it to celebrate our community staying together and surviving."

Mati went over to her secret hiding place under the spruce boughs that made their beds, and dug around until she found their old bag of coins and took one out. She thought, 'I must hide our new fortune better…'

She woke up the children and let them wipe the sleep from their eyes before she led them down to join her husband and walk down to the party. On the way she called to Gabi who called to Philomene and they got their husbands, and so on until a party of a dozen or more were walking quickly toward the trading post; the children running and getting there before the adults.

Just next to the trading post a makeshift stage was set up and a group of men were dressed up in costumes laughing and shouting outrageous stories to each other. One stout fellow walked on stage, to an uproar of laughter; dressed in a red coat and white long johns with a tricorn hat over white rabbits' fur made to resemble a wig. He loudly took command of the troupe.

He walked around self-importantly; a few other men came out wearing red coats and tricorns and pretended to march in order, but were tripping over each other. Meanwhile the actor playing Lieutenant Governor Lawrence hit at them with a pretend riding crop and gave them orders to do silly things like trying to stand on their hands and get on each other's shoulders. Men from the audience hooted rude suggestions and comments.

There was a keg of cider with a porringer and Acquila led Mati over and he took a large drink of the potion while she took a sip. Acquila yelled out, "Monsieur Cyr, Monsieur Cyr, another keg!" and tossed the tavern owner the silver coin.

Simon and Camille were nearby and said, "Girouard, did you find the Holy Grail?"

"Non, amis, I just think we should celebrate. We are still here despite the British and the Indians, we should be happy!"

Camille, ever his dour self commented, "not to mention the priests."

Acquila ignored him.

A half dozen men went to the stage and began playing music again; two with whistles, one with a fiddle and two with sticks and started playing a fast paced song. The old men sitting near the stage kept pace by clicking the beat with their tongues; one plucked at a Jews harp.

Acquila grabbed Mathilde by the arm and along with a dozen other couples started dancing wildly around the musicians, with couples twirling around each other locked at the elbows.

The settlement children were imitating their elders, dancing without care and without much rhythm, but with equal enthusiasm.

The night went on and the bonfire grew higher. Mathilde looked away from the bridge, downstream toward the area where Acquila used to vault the river with the pole. In the moonlight, looking away from the fire, she saw a figure, just for a second; seem to fly over the water. She thought nothing of it.

The party went on for another hour, then wrapped up and the families, all tired, some with big heads that would be bigger in the morning, made their way to their beds.

Mathilde put her children to bed, while Acquila prepared their bedding. Just before she joined him in bed, she had a strange thought and decided to check their fortune hidden in her secret place.

It was gone.

* * * * *

Mati didn't sleep all night. She worried and squirmed around enough to waken and get several grunts from 'Quila. But mostly she wondered who had taken their cache. Worse, not only had their fortune disappeared, but 'Quila had thoughtlessly wasted one of their precious silver coins.

Suddenly, all the promise of their movement across the river disappeared. They had nothing and could not afford to buy anything. Acquila hadn't resigned from the works crew position, thankfully, 'Merci, Mon Dieu', but there was no guarantee that they would survive the winter, which would be bleak without having gold to buy food, safety and anything else they might need.

Finally, in the middle of the night, Acquila had wrapped her in his arms and she had felt safe enough to sleep.

When she awoke, Acquila was already up and moving about.

She went over to him. "Acquila, something terrible happened last night."

"What could be terrible, Chér. We are rich and even more important, safe."

"The money from old man Melançon, it is gone."

"Gone? Where?"

She started to weep, "I don't know, but it happened when we were at the fête at the bridge."

"Who could have stolen from us?"

"I think they came from across the river. I saw someone use your pole to cross the river last night."

"So it was a maudit?"

"It must have been; I don't thing anyone from our settlement would steal from us. Do you think the soldiers would?"

"I don't think so, although I would never trust them. Perhaps it was their savages, the ones not in uniforms."

"I think so. That gives me an idea." She brightened up when she thought she might have an idea who could have committed the crime. "The half-breed."

"Who?"

"There is a half-breed, there. I saw him when I was there before and he saw me yesterday. I think he was searching for valuables we left behind when we moved. He scared me, 'Quila, I think he knew I had found something and he followed me to their trading post. I was rescued by an English officer and I was able to come home safely with the horse. I think he might have been watching me and knew where we lived."

Acquila put his head in his hands for a moment and then rubbed them up past his forehead and to the nape of his neck. "We will get them back."

"How?"

"We will find him and take them back."

"And how will we find him?"

"I think we have an ally across the river."

Mathilde asked, "Who?"

"There is an English soldier, his mére is from Bretagne. He is very friendly and allowed me to bring the hearth and other things across the river. This may be the man who assisted you in the trading post."

"Where can we meet this man again?"

"He often visits the trading post at the bridge."

“Well, let’s not wait.”

“Ma Chér, I don’t think that even les maudits are awake this early in the morning.

* * * * *

Abbé Le Loutre carefully oversaw storage of the chest that he knew to be filled with bullion as well as stacks of French currency notes. One of the first constructions in the new fort was the secure armoury and the chest was being deposited there. He remembered his travel to Quebec to meet with the Intendant, François Bigot, to discuss what he knew was soon to be a problem. While the action of forcibly demanding the relocation of l’Acadiens to the defensible area across the Mésagouèche was necessary, he knew that it would not be without costs and had requested financing to build the new settlement.

They had left behind the aboiteaux and dykes that had made the other side of the river the most productive farmland in New France. As well, he expected, as he was demanding, that the new settlement at Beauséjour would soon attract refugees from all of the French settlements now in English hands. And there simply was not the capacity in Beauséjour to accommodate thousands of people. Also, the farmers, while they had been able to move their livestock across the river, had not the time or ability to relocate feed and there was little to forage on the high ground in the new place.

The church had been burned and his parishioners and Miqmaqs needed this symbol of the greatest of God to continue to follow the doctrine. Their losing of this monument was a sure way of losing the peoples' devotion. He had managed to save the massive bell from the Church of Notre Dame in Beaubassin, now he needed a place in which to put it.

So he had personally pledged repayment of a massive contribution of funds to support building the new church and new aboiteaux to convert the marshlands into productive farmland as previous Acadiens had done a century before.

He also needed to expand the number of settlements to Mémérancouque, Chipoudie, Gediak and Oueskok and along the Tintamarre River to accommodate more refugees from the old settlements. A community larger than a few hundred residents could not sustain itself with the demand they collectively placed on lumber, firewood and local food animals.

He had already designed the dykes and he had the original plans for the burned church in Beaubassin that could be used for the new one. Now he had the money.

But he knew that it wasn't enough.

The dykes would not pay dividends until at least five or more years after completion of the dykes and aboiteaux, and without food the people would starve and nothing would be built.

So he had purchased from l'Intendant Bigot a supply of food for the refugees, deducting the cost from the funds and also paid Bigot a considerable commission. But it was an investment in his people and their eternal souls, so worth it. He had no personal wealth to repay if this became necessary, but he would surely be dead before the note was called in.

He knew that he also needed to buttress the new settlement with military power so he was prepared to invest funds in the expansion of the fortress and there was no better source of potential labour than his Acadians. They were hard workers. They could also, if necessary, support the French army and the Miqmaq warriors, if it came down to that. So he would hire them to work and pay them so they could feed their families.

As they approached the fortress construction, Le Loutre noticed the young man, Girouard, walking with his wife in the same direction.

He called to the young man as they approached, "Monsieur Girouard, will you join me for the remainder of my walk?"

Mati started to say, "Non, 'Quila…" but she was too slow in responding and Acquila hurried toward the priest, looking back at her with an expression that told her it would be all right and not to worry.

She pursed her lips and was about to say something more, but stayed quiet and only showed her displeasure by putting her hands on her hips.

Acquila caught up to Le Loutre and had to walk fast to keep up with the shorter man's pace.

"Monsieur Girouard, the holy church is honoured by your sacrifices and your devoutness."

"I am a good Roman Catholic, your eminence, as we all are here."

"You may call me Abbé, Monsieur, his eminence is very far from here. We need you to put together work crews to finish building the fortress and our new church."

"Abbé, you know I will do what I can, but we men also have to look out for our families and build our own homes."

"Ayyyy. Oui. I know, Acquila. But that is where you and I, with the help of our Saviour, will come in. I have a solution. Come with me. We will talk more."

* * * * *

It was afternoon when Mathilde and Acquila took time off from toiling on their new home to go in search of the good Englishman. They found him near the tavern sitting on a roughly hewn bench speaking with Monsieur Cyr, the English keeper; the Frenchman's daughters giggling not very far away.

Acquila approached him, "Monsieur, I am Acquila Girouard, you were very kind to allow me to recover items from our homestead after it was burned. This is my wife, Mathilde."

"Of course, bien sûr, Monsieur Girouard, I may be English but I have a good memory. Good morning, Madam, we have met before."

Mati nodded.

Acquila said, "Monsieur la Capitaine, might we speak in private?"

"Yes, will you excuse us, Monsieur Cyr."

The tavern keeper politely excused himself and he called to his daughters to join him inside.

"How can I help you, Monsieur?"

"Monsieur la Capitaine, you were very kind to allow us to recover our goods before. Something very much more serious happened last night?"

"What might that be?"

"We believe someone from your side of the river came to our settlement and stole our life savings."

"What? Are you suggesting that an English soldier came to your place of residence and stole from you? With respect, impossible."

Mathilde said, "With respect, Monsieur la Capitaine, we do not accuse the English, we believe there is an Indian living in your settlement that did it."

"There are many of those. He is a Mohawk?"

"No. He is a half breed. Miqmaq perhaps!"

"But those are your allies… no? Ah… There are two Miqmaqs abiding in our camp. They are brothers. And they're not really Miqmaqs they are half breed French."

"That is it," she said. "One of them bothered me when I was recovering some of our goods and then again when I was…"

"Of course… you were the woman in the trading post, that purchased the silk handkerchief. It was only a couple of days ago."

"Oui! You saved me from a terrible event, I think."

"Why, that was Virgil Labreque and he is a renegade, certainly not associated with the English army, although I believe he is involved with our rangers in some way; as a guide or scout perhaps.

"Did you see him actually steal your goods?"

"No, but I believe I saw him escape across the river when we were enjoying a fête right at this very place."

"I was actually here myself for a short time, at least until the theatrical performance became a little rude."

Acquila spoke, "Monsieur How, can you help us?"

"I can certainly try.

"I can tell you that it is unlikely that Virgil will do anything that would not be a shameful act. He and his brother are terrible men; cruel and uncivilized. He certainly would not volunteer his guilt, nor would he even tell the truth about the matter."

Acquila said very softly, "We can take matters into our own hands, Capitaine How."

"Well, in that case, I'm afraid that I really can't do anything to actually help you, physically. Morally, oui."

"Can you tell us where we might find him?"

"They are very, very dangerous, these brothers. But if they disappear, they will not be missed. They are living in a basement of one of the buildings in your old settlement; the church, I believe."

Acquila said, "They are even desecrating holy ground. Will you forget about our meeting today, Monsieur Capitaine?"

"I have already forgotten, Sir. I believe I was not even here this morning."

12 – DOUZE

It was late afternoon when Acquila finished his duties to his family and went looking for his most trusted friends to try and convince them to assist him in his other duty to his family; to try and recover their lost fortune.

As usual, Simon and Camille were together, this time just smoking their pipes under a tree and talking; as always, Simon was complaining about something and Camille was just listening.

Acquila called, "Mes Amis!"

They waved him over.

"How are you?"

"Over worked, under loved and not paid," said Simon.

"Well, I may be able to help you get paid, Simon, but I expect you would just waste the money on food."

"I would waste it on brandy, mon ami. What brings you to this side of the hill?"

"I am here to see if I can find a man or two who can be trusted and is deadly."

Simon said, "Well Camille is deadly when he has eaten too much cabbage."

"Not that kind of deadly, but someone who can use a knife and perhaps a musket."

"You raising an army for Le Loutre?"

“No, I’m raising an army for me.”

“Are you going to war against Le Loutre?”

“No, Simon. I need one or two men to help me recover our fortune.”

“What fortune is that?”

Acquila told them and what had happened.

“I don’t know, Ami. Philomene would kill me if I ended up dead.”

“If not you, then who?”

“Camille?”

“Not me, ‘Quila. I’ve never even held a musket.”

“Who?”

Simon had an idea. “Remember that Grenadier? de Fiedmont?”

“Yes, yes I do. His first name is Gaeten, I think. No, Thomas.”

“That’s him. He is a good man, a little serious, but he’s very hard working and I saw him practicing targets and he is a very good shot.

“Where can I find him?”

Simon gave him directions to de Fiedmont’s tent.

“Simon, not a word to anyone.”

“I’m not much of a talker, ‘Quila, you know me.”

“Oh, I know you, Simon, but your middle name is parler!”

“I only ever say what needs to be said.”

“And always do, mon ami… I'll go to look for him.”

It was getting close to dusk before Acquila tracked down Grenadier de Fiedmont. He was sitting in front of his tent, behind a fire that was offering itself to a small animal, possibly a muskrat that had agreed to serve as de Fiedmont's supper.

"Grenadier de Fiedmont?"

"Oui?"

"My name is Acquila Girouard we met a few weeks ago when you first arrived."

The soldier laughed. "I remember you, Monsieur Girouard,

you were telling me I had to work much harder."

Acquila was embarrassed, "Well... I'm sorry, did you work much harder? I mean..."

"I think I have done my share, Monsieur. What brings you to our camp this cool evening?"

Acquila looked around. "Is it safe to talk here?"

The grenadier chuckled. "Are you planning to attack the fortress, Monsieur? If so, then it is not safe to talk here. Otherwise, I believe it is."

Acquila drew closer. The soldier offered him a small cigar that he accepted and allowed de Fiedmont to light.

"Grenadier de Fiedmont, I need a man who is very good with knife and musket."

"Why, are you a jealous husband?"

"Quoi? No, of course not. I mean, I would be a jealous husband, but there is no need for that."

"Then why are you looking for a dangerous man?"

"I have a special mission, for such a dangerous man, that pays well, if it is successful."

de Fiedmont removed the meat from its skewers and offered some to Acquila who refused. He put it on a tin plate and poured something from a wineskin into a pewter mug and offered it to 'Quila who accepted it.

He drank it; it was strong brandy and he returned the mug.

"I suspect it will pay a much greater amount if it is unsuccessful. Tell me about this dangerous mission."

Acquila told him about the theft, the half-breed who had likely committed it and where he and his brother were. "I will pay you one tenth of what we recover."

de Fiedmont shrugged and said, "I expect they are undisciplined and won't be alert to a quiet attack. I also expect they will have indulged themselves with alcohol, hopefully more than we have. They're untrained savages and will be like little girls against we two men. Let's do it."

Acquila was impressed that Grenadier de Fiedmont was so confident, but apprehensive because he, personally, had never done anything like this before.

"Girouard, don't be nervous. Those half-breeds will fold at the first hint of a serious assault."

He went inside his tent and came out with two musket pistols. He tossed one to Acquila along with two cartridges. "It's cleaned and ready. We'll load when we get close to prevent the cartridge from getting fouled. One more thing."

de Fiedmont went back into his tent and came out with two war hatchets. "These might be useful. I took them off some Abenakis last year."

Acquila hefted one. He felt powerful and dangerous just holding it.

"How will we get across the river?"

Acquila was a little overwhelmed, now that they were actually starting the raid. "I have a pole that I use to vault the river, but the half-breed used it."

"Then we'll bring another, how long does it need to be?"

"About twenty feet."

de Fiedmont left for about five minutes and came back with a pole about the needed length. "The Abbé likely won't miss this. I think he wanted it for his cross. Let's go."

de Fiedmont shoved his pistol in his pants, so Acquila did likewise. Acquila picked up the other end of the pole and they began trotting down the hill, toward the crossing point in the absolute dark.

They came to the crossing point and Acquila could see his pole on the other side. de Fiedmont said, "You go first. You've done this before. Throw your weapons across. Make sure you get them all the way across."

It was easy. Acquila tossed his hatchet and pistol high and long. He tested the pole; it was thicker than his, but he got across easily and recovered his weapons. He noticed that de Fiedmont had studied his actions intensely. He pushed the pole back; de Fiedmont tossed his weapons across the river and in a few seconds joined him.

They picked up and loaded and primed their musket pistols.

"Which way?"

"About one mile that way." Acquila indicated the direction.

"I'll follow you, keep a steady pace, and pretend you're a wolf. Be invisible. If the moon comes out hit the ground and don't move until she hides herself.

"Is the moon a woman?"

"Did you ever doubt it?

"When we arrive, if there are two men, I will take out the one on the left and you will take the other. If there are three, I will shoot the one on the left, you the one on the right. Let me move first, on mine, you then take the other. Let one live."

"What if there are more?"

"We let them fall asleep and then kill all but one."

Acquila had nothing more to say to that so he started trotting, like he had seen the Miqmaqs run. He could barely hear de Fiedmont behind him; the soldier was a ghost.

In fifteen minutes they had covered the distance and not been discovered by English sentries. Acquila turned around and slowed de Fiedmont to a stop. He pointed straight up the hill. They walked carefully to the hill and then crawled on their hands and knees to the top. There was no motion when they got there, but they could hear some noise coming from the old settlement.

de Fiedmont took the lead and they silently moved toward the remains of the old church. He held up his hand and Acquila stopped. de Fiedmont hit the ground and Acquila followed him. They were about twenty yards away; there was a campfire and two men with a huge keg of drink and each with a porringer.

de Fiedmont whispered, "Go on three." He lifted one finger, and then his second and then his third and they ran full speed into the clearing. The two men looked up but were too inebriated to react. de Fiedmont controlled his target and Acquila controlled his, knocking him over and putting him in a stranglehold. de Fiedmont pulled a knife from his belt and stabbed his target in his left eye.

Acquila could speak no English so quietly asked the survivor in French, "Ou est l'argent". His target was shaking with fear and didn't respond. de Fiedmont came over, with his bloody knife, "Ou est l'argent?"

The survivor pointed to the keg and there, lying on the ground, was the sack in which Mati had carried the coins. de Fiedmont said, “Kill him.” Acquila took his hatchet and caved in the side of the terrified man’s head. They picked up the bag and more carefully returned to the other side of the river, leaving the original pole so there would be no evidence of their visit.

* * * * *

Acquila and Grenadier de Fiedmont made their way to the French soldier’s tent and went inside. de Fiedmont lit up a lantern and Acquila placed the bag between them.

“Now what do you have there, Monsieur Girouard?”

Acquila opened the bag and carefully placed the contents on the ground so as not to make any noise. de Fiedmont was obviously astonished when he saw the gold coins.

“That, Monsieur Girouard, is a very… impressive sum.”

Acquila said, “A tenth is yours.”

de Fiedmont passed him the bladder of brandy and Acquila took a long swig.

“What would I do with so much money? I have no family, I have no place to spend it except on drink, but I expect I will die on behalf of King Louis before the wine does its work. Take the money to your wife and children; perhaps if you have another child you might honour him, or her, with my name.”

“I insist… That was our arrangement.”

“I got far more joy from sticking a knife in the eye of that half-breed than I ever could from money and what it would buy. Go home to your wife and be my friend, Monsieur Girouard.”

“My children will tell their grandchildren of you, Monsieur de Fiedmont.”

de Fiedmont took the wineskin back as Acquila gathered up the coins. The Grenadier saluted Acquila as he left the tent and Acquila nodded back.

Acquila was very careful returning to their shelter, the last thing he wanted was to be discovered skulking around the army camp with a lot of money. When he arrived back the children were fast asleep and Mathilde was sitting on the brow of the hill looking down into the darkness of the valley.

He snuck up behind her and went, "Pssst."

She was startled and jumped from her seated position. "Who… 'Quila, you scared me almost to death, you!"

He laughed, showed her the bag and they embraced, he lifted her up and spun her around.

"You're back and safe!"

"And wealthy!"

She was wide-eyed but was still herself, "Sssh, no one can know!"

She pulled him toward their shelter and whispered, "What happened?"

"Grenadier de Fiedmont, after who we will name our next child, helped me… Actually, I helped him. We got all the coins. And you never have to worry about the half-breed brothers again."

"Really?"

"C'est vrai, ma Chér."

* * * * *

Captain How awoke and dressed. His tent was at the point closet to the river, at a corner of the encampment.

He started a fire just outside his tent, left to do his toilet in the latrine and returned. He cleaned his boots and they were shining in the morning light. He filled a bent and battered teapot, placed it on a rock in his fire and waited for it to boil.

He took out his pipe, filled it, and lit it with a stick from the fire. He dropped a handful of tea leaves in the pot and sat to pull on his boots. Soon his tea was boiling and he took it off the fire to steep.

He poured it into his precious china cup that he kept stored in a box and wrapped in a feather cozy. The cup was a gift from his mother that he treasured more than any other personal item.

He blew on his tea and sipped at it while he chewed on a strip of dried jerky. He swallowed the last piece, emptied his tea in the grass and carefully washed out and replaced his teacup inside his tent.

He wondered what the Acadians might do about the Labreque brothers. He would hope that no one had seen his meeting with them, and he'd otherwise never mention it. If someone had seen them, he would carelessly dismiss it.

His Ensign, Chapman, arrived outside and called for him, "Captain How. It's Chapman arriving for duty, Sir."

How exited his tent and returned Chapman's salute.

"There appears to be a retinue from the other side who wishes a parley, Sir."

"Who are they?"

"I don't know. Looks like an injun or two with a proper frog or two."

"They are not frogs, Ensign Chapman. They are French soldiers and possibly more civilized than you or I. Let's go see them. Get Simpson and a white flag."

Chapman saluted and left the tent on the double returning with a grizzled sergeant in a tricorn hat with a white flag on a pole.

"Simpson, lead us to the delegation."

The three men marched in rank down the hill with How in the middle. As they got closer to the French group of three men, one in uniform, How noticed something unusual. The soldier's uniform was incomplete; rather than having white breeches as would be expected from a regular officer, the uniformed man was wearing what appeared to be leather trousers of some sort. 'Queer,' He thought.

Then he noticed that the white flag was attached to the bayonet of a musket. Even more queer.

Then the musket was pointed at How. It was fired, exploding a hole in the Englishman's chest into which a fist could fit. The three Englishmen had come unarmed and the survivors looked helplessly at their dying Captain and at the three French, now all revealed as Miqmaqs whooping and shouting as they ran away.

Simpson and Chapman picked up the corpse of Captain How and carried him as quickly as they could back to the encampment.

* * * * *

When Chief Copit returned to the redoubt he was met immediately by l'Abbé Le Loutre. "It is done, Father."

"Bless you, my son. We can not have an English be liked or respected by les Acadiens; they will have less love and respect available for their God and their King."

Chief Copit smiled broadly.

"Now, my son, we have to more strongly encourage those Frenchmen who have not yet left the English territory to do so; to join their fellows here.

"If they are seduced by the promises of the English, then they will allow our foes to afford more protestant invaders to come to our land that will poison your people's minds with heresy.

"Take your men and visit the other villages. Be kind if they agree to relocate. But do whatever is necessary to make them abandon their settlements. Destroy them as we did Beaubassin if necessary."

"Yes, Father. I will go now."

* * * * *

Mathilde awoke before Quila and walked outside in her night clothes. It was a cool but sunny autumn day and she was glad that their new house was coming along. With the money promised by the Abbé the men had been able to devote the last two weeks to building their homes rather than searching for food. All the foundations were completed with mortar set for thirty houses, the cold rooms dug, and the beams were erected. The side boards were stacked next to each house as were the floor planks. In two more weeks, God willing, they would be ready for move in, even if the structures were not entirely finished.

Her biggest fear was that one of those terrible cold winters with an early blizzard would arrive before they were ready. But she was hopeful that this would not happen.

Only two weeks ago, before they had gotten the coins, lost them and then got them back, she had been terrified that they would not be ready for the cold. But today she was able to finally start her winter preparations. She would ask Acquila's help in slaughtering and carving up two of the pigs. She would pickle the knuckles and feet and smoke the rest.

She took a moment and prayed that the weather would allow them to set up a smoke house for the other parts of the animals.

She thought she would also ask him about slaughtering one of their heifers for similar treatment. And she would ask him to capture a dozen or so of the big geese. She would render the fat from them and fill an entire earthen pot of them cut into pieces and covered in the almost clear fat the way her grandmother had taught her. The geese would be preserved until it was warm again and be delicious when they were removed and cooked.

They were short of vegetables for the winter although they had barrels of apples that grew wild on this side of the river that she would dry. But they had lost their crop of turnips and potatoes; the English fort was now sitting on their gardening fields.

It was too late to grow anything now. But they had money! Perhaps they could buy their own produce back from the English this winter.

All in all, she was very pleased with how things were turning out after all the violence and tragedies.

She heard a cough and some grumbles which meant that Acquila had risen. She walked back to their shelter.

"Good morning, Chér."

Acquila, like most men, was grumpy when just awake, but he managed a smile and said, "Good morning, Mati. Beautiful sunny day."

"It is. A beautiful day to build houses and slaughter pigs."

"Quoi?"

She explained to him what she hoped to do today.

"Well, can I get dressed? Although such dirty work should probably be done in the clothes we had at birth." He started pulling on his work clothes. He looked around for a length of rope, picked it up and tied it around his waist.

"That would shock the priest, 'Quila."

"I suspect the priest has been shocked before by worse things than a naked man. If we are going to do this, we might as well do it now."

Mathilde looked around their box of kitchen items and came up with a serious looking knife, not unlike the ones that the Miqmaqs used for taking off hair. She thought of this for a second, shivered, and quickly put it out of her mind.

He picked up the bucket of food scraps from their eating area and allowed her to lead them down to their pigs.

"Which one, Mati?"

"I don't like that one, there." She pointed to one of the year old boars. "He's pudgy and stubborn just like that priest of yours. I have even nicknamed him 'Loutre'."

"Now, Mati..."

They both laughed.

He removed the rope from his waist while she dumped the slop into a trough and the pigs came running. Acquila went over to Loutre and threw a noose around his neck. The pig fought against being pulled from the group, he was over a hundred pounds, but eventually Acquila forced him to move away helped by Mati waving a carrot in front of him. Soon enough they'd persuaded the swine to climb up the hill and under a tree to finally achieve the carrot.

When they stopped, Acquila tied the lead rope around a tree. The pig put up a fuss; he squealed loudly as if he knew he was at an end. Then Acquila went back to the shelter and found a longer rope. He returned to the pig and threw one end over a limb of a strong maple tree and made a noose. This he slipped over the hind legs of the sow and started hoisting it into the air, the pig squealing even louder and fighting fiercely to stay on the ground.

Once the pig was a few feet off the ground and struggling less fiercely, he took a hold of the lead rope, got the knife from Mathilde and slit the pig's throat. Mathilde put a bucket underneath to catch the blood. The squeals stopped and in a few minutes the boar hung limply, its blood filling the bucket.

The couple walked over to the stream and washed off and went to wake up the children and have breakfast. Mathilde boiled some oats which she mixed with butter and sugar made from maple sap.

When they were finished, Acquila said, "Emile, you come help us. Maurice you take Béatrice to play."

Acquila had piled dried hardwood, mostly maple, about fifty yards from the shelters. He'd also procured a large piece of canvas from the building site and Mathilde had sewn it into a rough cone shape that would fit over a teepee frame that Acquila had made. They put their cooking grill over four large stumps about three feet off the ground that covered a hole that Acquila had had Emile dig. They built a fire using the hardwood and tinder in the form of birch bark. Soon there was a roaring fire that initially flamed over the grill, but soon burnt down and barely reached the bottom of the grill.

They went back to the shelter and each took a large wooden bucket; Acquila gave his to Emile and went to get a large board about four feet by two.

The trio walked the fifty steps to the pig; Emile's eyes wide open when he saw the animal hanging stiffly, swaying slowing. Mathilde removed the bucket of blood; she would mix it later with herbs, scraps of meat and the oatmeal to make sausage.

Acquila put the board under the pig and released the rope. "Emile, help me." Together the two males manoeuvred the dead pig onto the board and the work started.

When they were finished and had thrown the feet and knuckles and hocks into a bucket and Mati put the heart, liver and entrails in a woven bag. Acquila and Emile carried the carcass the few strides to the cooking spot. Acquila went to work on the carcass, cutting off parts that would be used in sausage. The cool day kept the flies from appearing in great numbers which was a relief. But if they waited until it warmed up in the late morning, working with the carcass would be almost impossible. Mathilde seasoned the carcass with salt and powdered red peppers that had come from the French islands in the south and added scraps of what remained to the bag of organ meat.

When the flames had burned down to embers, Acquila put the seasoned pork shoulders, ribs, chops, ham and bacon onto the grill and Acquila and Emile lifted the framed canvas structure that Mathilde had soaked in the stream over the entire fire-pit, far enough away not to burn. She took the bucket of hocks and feet in the bucket back to the shelter to go into the pickling barrel and seasoned, cut up and fried the tenderloin for lunch that she served with a thick apple sauce.

It was Emile's duty to stay by the fire the rest of the day and make sure that he lifted the tent flap and added a handful of wet maple sticks as needed to maintain a low temperature with a lot of smoke.

13 – TREIZE

After lunch, Acquila was on his way to the new settlement **to** work on the house when he saw Abbé Le Loutre marching toward him in the company of a Miqmaq that was frequently in the priest's company.

Acquila waited until they came to a position directly in front of him.

"Monsieur Girouard. This is Jean Baptiste Copit, he is the leader of our Miqmaq brothers' militia." The two men nodded at each other.

Acquila took a look at Copit. He saw a muscular man, of average height with blood-shot eyes, wearing leggings, leather boots and a string of objects around his neck. On closer look Acquila saw they were desiccated ears.

"Monsieur Girouard, as the leader of our militia you will need to work closely with Chief Copit."

"Certainly, Father."

"As you are no are longer leading our work crews on the aboiteaux you are called to assume more responsibility in protecting our settlements. You will leave in the morning with Chief Copit on a special mission aimed at the heart of the damned English new headquarters."

"But, Father, with respect... I have my house to finish and

need to get our food supply ready in time for winter."

"And, Monsieur Girouard, how safe will your family be if you lose your soul? It is God's wish for you to protect His church and your country. I'm afraid you have no choice. God will protect your family, if they live under his roof."

Acquila felt chilled, not from the weather and not even from the demand from the Abbé. But from how he knew Mathilde would react to this.

"Whatever God wishes, I am his subject."

"Bien. Then you will meet Chief Copit at the Pont à Buot at daybreak tomorrow, Monsieur Girouard."

And with that, the Abbé turned face and led Copit to the construction site of his new church.

Acquila knew that he should have said no; he and Mathilde did not need to worry, with their cache of gold. But he was also a devout Roman Catholic. Mathilde was as well, but never at the expense of the reality of a day's temporal needs.

He decided he needed to think more about this and he would do this while he worked on the house. When he arrived, Simon and Camille were on the crew putting up the studs of the new houses. He joined them at the work, but they noticed that something very heavy seemed to be weighing on his shoulders.

When he arrived home as it was getting dark, Mathilde was serving supper to the children. He greeted the family, hugged Mathilde and filled a plate with the pork hash she had made. As always, there was no discussion to be made while eating.

When he finished, he still wasn't comfortable with telling Mathilde the bad news. "Emile, come with me, carry this bucket." He picked it up and passed it to his oldest son. "Mati, we will go and get the pork."

They arrived at the cookhouse and the embers were still hot enough to burn flesh if within a foot or two. They removed the canvas cone; the meat was obviously crispy and the aroma was enticing even though they had just eaten. The shrunken meat still filled the large wooden bucket and Emile had to use both hands and all his strength to carry it. After a few dozen steps Acquila reached over and helped his son for the rest of the trip.

When they arrived, the whole family ate cut off strips of the crispy pork skin. It was delicious.

Finally the children went to bed and Acquila and Mathilde were alone. Mati said, “let’s go for a walk, you.”

They left the shelter and walked to the brow of the hill. “Okay, you, Monsieur Girouard, my husband. What is it you are not telling your wife, you.”

He thought before he spoke. “I am in great trouble, ma Chér.”

“It is the priest, oui?”

She seemed to be able to always read his mind. He wondered if she already knew what he was going to say.

“Oui. It is the priest. He has given me orders.”

“We both knew he would. He uses people the way that a general sends young boys to die in battle.”

“I know... I can’t refuse, Chér, he will excommunicate us all and condemn us.”

“I suppose you can’t. We still live under his protection,. The families that chose to stay in their settlements or went to other places are starving, or being killed by les maudit’s Indians, I hear.

“But you can be careful and make sure you come back to your wife and children. What is it he wants?"

“I will be leaving with the Indian chief early in the morning to attack the English in their new headquarters in Chebouctu.”

“Mon Dieu!” This was beyond her worst nightmares. Not only would her husband be risking his life for the damned priest, but he was risking it far away. If anything happened he would have no place of sanctuary.

“Is there any way...”

“I wish there were, Chér. He is our priest, he controls our destinies here and now and hereafter.”

“What about Father Le Guerne.”

“He has no power over Pére Le Loutre.”

“Then you will be careful?”

“I will be careful, Chér; as careful as I can be.”

* * * * *

Abbé Jean-Louis Le Loutre's face, even when he was a small boy, always had an expression of determination. He was shorter than average and his large head, broad shoulders and full head of curly hair made him appear almost like a small bear who had adopted a human form.

He filled his priestly robes with some degree of majesty; it was evident to anyone in his presence that he was a man to be listened to, even if he was not the most senior church or military authority in a room. Today he was wearing his ordinary cassock with a large cross hanging from his rosary around his neck. Copit was following him.

Acquila was standing at the Pont à Buot at first light of day when Le Loutre appeared out of the dissipating gloom of dawn. The approach of the priest was almost supernatural. Finally, as if he had vanished for several seconds he was directly in front of Acquila.

"Monsieur Girouard, you rise early to serve God. That is good, very good. Are you prepared to make the ultimate sacrifice for your Lord?"

"I am at His command, Father."

"Bien. Now let's travel to Shubenacadie to meet our other acolytes and begin meeting His sacred demands."

They needed to avoid the eyes of the English; the lowliest sentry would know who Copit was and respond accordingly. Copit led the two men across the bridge and took a route over the rise north of the English camp. The Miqmaq set a brisk pace up the hill out of sight of the English and travelled all day. The men hardly spoke during the trip and as the sun was going down they arrived at the shores of an inlet. They made camp and awoke early the next day. Copit had a canoe hidden there and they crossed the inlet and paddled down a winding muddy stream for several hours. They arrived at the Miqmaq village, Jean Baptiste Copit's headquarters.

* * * * *

From the brow of the hill Mathilde had watched Acquila and the two others cross the bridge, walk through the grassland, and up the other bank until they were out of sight in the mist. She knew she had to support Acquila in this dangerous mission and didn't want him dwelling on their moments as being worrisome and upsetting.

But she was worried and upset. She had known from the beginning, since the priest had first introduced himself, that nothing good could come from it.

Now she was watching her life walk away with a murdering Miqmaq and an insane churchman.

What would it be like without him? She hated to think of this; l'Acadie was a difficult place and she had seen the fate of young mothers who had lost their husbands.

She did have the gold, but could never use it without gaining attention and without making people suspicious. She was tempted to follow her husband, to be there if he was injured. But she knew she couldn't possibly leave the children.

All she could do is move on and be prepared for the worst.

14 – QUATORZE

Acquila, Le Loutre and Copit had met up with a detail of Miqmaqs and a half dozen other Acadians after they had returned to dry land and were marching the final league toward the new settlement that les Anglais had constructed on the north shore of the bay at Chebouctu. The moon was full. The painted and feathered war party had canoed and portaged down from Shubenacadie with more than a half hundred Miqmaq warriors, along with Joseph Brossard.

Brossard was Le Loutre's military leader and everyone called him Beausoleil. His nickname was given to him for his smile and happy disposition when with his friends and family. He was an extremely handsome man and very charming, but he was also known for his short temper and his ferocity as a fighter and killer.

Major Geoffroy of the French army who normally was stationed in Fort Louisburg had come along as an observer. The Major had travelled a great distance only for this attack; it promised to have a great effect on the future of their control of New France. The French needed to stop the English before their efforts to populate the region were successful.

The British had begun bringing in civilian settlers as the French had over done a century before. From Le Loutre's perspective this was made worse because the civilians were

Protestants. Heretics.

The settlement was new and palisades had not yet been erected. It was probably suspected by the English that they wouldn't be needed, being so close to the large English garrison.

"Beausoleil et le Chef!"

Copit and the Acadian approached the priest. Acquila was nearby. Le Loutre said, "Divide your men into two groups. Beausoleil, you enter the town from the south, Jean Baptiste, you from here in the north. Beausoleil, use a fire arrow to signal the charge. Meet in the middle and kill everyone and burn everything. Go now. I will grant you and all your men absolution. Fifty livres for every scalp."

Acquila joined Beausoleil and about two dozen of the Indians and a few other Acadians and silently went to their place in a grove of trees about 30 yards south from the dozen of so buildings that made up the settlement. They were quite close to the inlet from the ocean.

One of the warriors took out his flint and tinder and started a fire and touched it with an arrow whose head was covered in oily pitch. When it was fully aflame all the men stood and freed up their weapons, ready for the attack. Several had lit pitch-covered torches to add to the mayhem and devastation. Acquila had his musket and the war hatchet that he had taken to get the gold back from the half-breed brothers.

Beausoleil nodded, the arrow was released and the killing began.

The warriors screamed their war cries and broke into the cleared area with at least three attacking each structure. Acquila watched. He saw the warriors breaking through doors with their axes, throwing their torches inside and following them into the houses. Cries, now the sounds of pain and sheer horror, began coming from the houses.

He saw women escaping through windows and being chased down and their heads smashed in with war clubs. He saw men try to fight back and be quickly clubbed to death. He saw small children, barely of an age to walk on their own, grabbed by their arms and scalped while still alive.

Acquila ran at the end of the pack of charging warriors; he was not anxious to enter the fray. Beausoleil pointed at a building and told Acquila to go there and kill. Acquila took a flaming stick from the ground and went to the house and looked inside; there was only an old man. He threw the torch inside and made his way with the house between him and Beausoleil.

In less than a half hour the small village was totally aflame and the only sounds were the victory cries of the warriors. Acquila watched as members of the raiding party passed alongside the dead English making sure that the scalp had been collected from each. A few of the dying lifted their bodies to try and escape but were quickly smashed in the head.

The Indians had tied a rope around the necks of a half dozen settlers, four women and two men. They would be kept as slaves or hostages or killed if they caused trouble on the trip back to Shubenacadie. One was in an English red coat. The soldier started to resist and he was quickly clubbed to his knees and had his head and hands chopped off. His murderer held the man's head by its long greasy pigtail and scraped it away from the skull.

The other Indians set fire to every building. A small blockhouse that had offered the Chief's men the strongest opposition was also set to fire with anyone inside burned to death. Acquila was relieved that he had managed to not harm anyone; he wondered how this brutality could possibly be ordered by the Almighty.

Beausoleil, the Chief and Le Loutre met in the middle of the small settlement. The Abbé spoke. "I suspect the English across the bay will have noticed the fires. Gather together the men."

The leaders did and Le Loutre confronted them and began a blessing. He finished with the words, "Je vous absous de tous vos péchés."

* * * * *

Danks and his rangers had spent months roaming across the peninsula from Canso to Grand Pre, Beaubassin, Remsheg,

Mines and even to the south shore. Every few weeks he and his subalterns needed to visit Chebouctu to conduct the commercial transactions associated with their excursions and enjoy some civilized recreation.

He and his cohorts, Hezekiah King and Charlie Hollis, arrived on the north shore of the Chebouctu harbour just after night had fallen. They came across the remains of what had been a small settlement that had been destroyed by an attack. The smell of burned flesh still hung over the place and the evidence of something traumatic happening was obvious. They looked around for any sign of life and found none until King looked into the burned out blockhouse. He called Danks over.

Inside was an old man; probably sixty. He was shirtless and his sunken ribcage suggested he hadn't recently eaten very much. His eyes were blank and he obviously hadn't washed or shaved for some time. Danks spoke, "Who are ye? And what happened here?"

The old man replied, "We was killed. All of us. The Injuns came and they even scalped the babes and womens. I tried to save some. But it were no good. They all got killed. They did."

"Have ye eaten?"

"Nae. There is naught to eat and no way to get across the harbour to get anything."

Danks said, "Hez! Give the man whatever jerky ye have. Here is mine." He handed King his reserve and left the building. King gave the man what they had and followed Danks when he left the blockhouse.

King and Hollis picked up the canoe and the three men walked down the slope toward the water, and pointed the boat toward their destination. They got in and made the trip across the harbour.

Benjamin Lloyd was there, as always in front of a small bonfire, and he greeted the men as old friends, "Ah, Capt'n Danks, welcome back to Chebouctu. I expect you came to sell your hair."

Danks grunted, "Not mine Lloyd, but I've got a bag full of others." He took out a cigar and offered one to the sentry, who accepted, nodded in thanks and used a pair of tongs to remove an ember from the fire. Both men lit up.

Danks said, "What is the news?"

"Well, Capt'n, the place is over run by bloody Germans." Then he said softly, "Which isn't a surprise, I suppose, considering German George." George II was the first German to rule England.

"Well, Lloyd, I suppose that German George pays for these cheroots."

"Indeed. In any case, the settlement is stuffed to the rafters with the clods; they drink too much and argue over prices and some don't pay their accounts properly. I think they've put the Guv'ner in a bit of a tizzy."

Danks chuckled for a second. "I hear they want to ship them out to take over the Crapaud settlements."

"Yes, but I don't think they will send any up your way, Capt'n, to Tintamarre. Word is that it's a dangerous place for anyone who isn't a hard tack scrapper. I hear that the Guv'ner is quite distressed with the entire situation, you see there really isn't enough food and rum to go around and there is terrible discontent. He's even resorted to a lottery to pay for things, but hardly anyone can afford to buy a ticket."

"Interesting, Lloyd. I reckon we'll be at Shippey's local for a jar of watered down ale after we conduct our business this afternoon. Join us if ye can."

"I will Capt'n. I'm usually there when I'm finished."

"Well, fare well, Lloyd."

"You as well, Capt'n."

Danks led his small crew to the church and Willigar; the two men had become friendly despite their differences. The paymaster was a chipmunk to Danks' wolverine.

Willigar was seated and bent over his desk examining ledgers, his nose barely above the surface despite his spectacles when they entered. He looked up, "Danks! Another pile of rotten hair, I expect."

"Hello, Willigar. I left it outside, care to count them?"

"I prefer to burn them, how many?"

"Three score."

"Quite a sizeable sum. All black haired this time, I assume."

"Aren't they always, mate." He passed Willigar a packet that contained the contents of the victims pockets and purses which was a sizeable sum by itself. "I suppose you will take care of this for me."

"Of course, of course. Would you mind just disposing of them for me?"

"Not at all." He pulled a ledger sheet from a desk drawer, made a notation and initialled and passed it to Danks to do so as well, which the ranger did.

Willigar said, "We've been expecting you and I have a missive from the Governor for you to stop in when you arrive. Evidently Colonel Gorham is indisposed and failed to make his monthly meeting."

"If I must. Lads, why don't you go to the Spread Eagle, I'll be along." The two younger men left.

* * * * *

Danks hated visiting Cornwallis, even in Gorham's company. This was no different than his other visits. Hinshelwood looked at him disdainfully and made him stand while he dealt with other matters. Finally, after almost an hour, the aide knocked on the Governor's door, entered and returned. "The Governor will see you in the yard, Captain Danks."

He motioned to the ranger and led him through a side door. Cornwallis was seated under a parasol on an elaborately made chair. There was no place for Danks to sit, so he remained standing.

"Captain. In the absence of Colonel Gorham, I will give you orders directly. We are establishing German settlements within 30 leagues of these headquarters. They will be in Chezzetcook, LeHave and Mirligaiche. They will require protection from the Indians, we expect, and you will provide that protection. You are to muster your company of rangers on our parade ground by day break two days from now. You may get your written orders from Hinshelwood. You're dismissed."

Danks assumed a military posture, saluted properly and returned to the Governor's ante-room. Hinshelwood looked up at him and held out a scroll which Danks accepted. The ranger turned and left and walked the few hundred paces from the Governor's apartments through the palisades gate and to the Spread Eagle tavern.

He entered and John Shippey, the tavern owner, greeted him by name. "Captain Danks, welcome back. Your lads are already comfortably seated."

"For now, Jimmy. We'll be on the move soon enough."

"We've got some ale, and some pease soup freshly made."

"Ya, bring us both for all and buy a round for all on me."

"Thank you, Captain Danks, we welcome your custom."

"I'd welcome a drink, Jimmy."

"Of course, won't you join your men."

Danks interrupted his sub-alterns and Lloyd's teasing of the bar maid, "Lads, leave the poor lass alone, I doubt she has eyes for poor peasants and bad musket shots such as you. We have our orders and they don't involve trying to get between the legs of a Chebouctu hussy."

15 – QUINZE

Thomas Pichon left his stateroom to examine his new posting as the sloop *"Bienfaisant"*, that had carried him from Quebec, entered the harbour of Louisbourg. Since the town had been returned to the French from the English by Treaty who had captured it only a few years before, it had been re-fortified to better repel English attacks. Pichon had been called by Intendant Bigot to his new posting to manage the expected expansion not only of Ile Royale, on which Louisbourg sat, but also the new fortress, Beauséjour, which was being built in Chignectou.

Pichon was a stout man who enjoyed fine living and while he had been well brought up in France, he enjoyed the rustic comforts of Canada; the stream of attractive strumpets that he could invite to his boudoir, the cases of fine wines and brandies from which he had his pick and the incredible selection of game: fowl, fish, wild boar and caribou. He suspected that while this new place would be less bountiful in his satisfying some of his lustful indulgences; it might well offer him more freedom of action in other ways.

The trip had been relatively peaceful; almost the entire length of the voyage terra firma had been visible from the ship and there had been no storms. Pichon was well rested.

The Bienfaisant dropped anchor and Pichon was the first to

board a tender and make his way to shore; he had ordered his considerable weight in personal affects to travel with him.

He was greeted by a small contingent of French soldiers. He pointed to a fat, slovenly soldier in dirty greys, “You, take my luggages to my quarters, where ever they may be.

“Direct me to the commandant!”

The soldier waved to some other fellows and they ran to the two massive steamer trunks and struggled to pick them up; Pichon, defying his stout stature, started walking quickly toward the gates. His fat guide had to hustle to catch up.

They came to the gates and the guards snapped to attention; obviously this was someone of great importance.

Inside the walls Louisbourg was impressively busy; construction on new casemates and barracks was swarming with workers and a large French flag was flapping in the offshore wind. Platoons of infantry were drilling intensely and the entire parade ground was surrounded by civilians pushing carts carrying huge baskets of fish and other potables.

There was, barely audible above the clamour, an orchestra of some type playing music of an unknown sort to Pichon. He walked toward it and saw a sextet of musicians playing rough-hewn fiddles, blowing whistles and hitting rhythm sticks while two men danced feverishly. Occasionally someone would toss a coin in the performers' direction. There were jugglers and acrobats performing their magic for coins and several women who were apparently available to the highest bidder.

Pichon looked to his guide and followed him to the building that obviously housed the governor’s apartments. It was the largest building, by far, was much better constructed than the others, and had an enormous well-cared-for lawn. His guide spoke with the guards for a moment and they were led forward. The guide used the ornate door-knocker to announce their arrival and it was quickly opened by a man-servant.

They entered and the servant said, “I am afraid his governorship is occupied, will you wait in the ante-chamber?” He pointed to an area just to the left of a staircase and opposite to the curved staircase.

Pichon was impatient and refused to sit down, instead walking around the room and admiring the fine art and statuary. While wandering he glanced at the upper hall, which was open to the lobby, and behind a finely crafted balustrade.

He noticed movement and on closer look saw a young girl of no more than sixteen, a peasant or servant in plain clothes, emerge from one of the rooms, look furtively around and stare at Pichon. She was flushed and dropped her eyes and hurried away, in the opposite direction of the staircase, probably to the servants' staircase.

Pichon made a mental note; not only of the Governor's proclivities, which might prove of benefit, but also opportunities for his own libido.

He was pondering the possibility of this when, with a clatter, came downstairs his colleague, Comte Jean-Louis de Raymond, who had assumed the job only a few months before. They had travelled to New France together, but Pichon had carried on to Quebec to meet with the Intendant. Pichon thought, 'didn't take Louis long to feel at home…'

"Thomas, finally you made it!"

"Louis, I see that you did, as well…," and smiled.

de Raymond blustered, "Well, ami, this <u>is</u> a long way from Angoulême."

"Louis, it is a long way from everywhere!" They both laughed.

"I come to be at your service, Louis."

"Well, Thomas, my servants call me Comte de Raymond."

"At the moment of maximum passion?"

de Raymond's face reddened.

"They are all peasants here, Thomas, even the soldiers. But some of these peasants are quite comely."

"Does she have sisters?"

"She is a good Roman Catholic girl, Thomas, she probably has several."

"Where will my quarters and offices be?"

"Come, I will show you."

* * * * *

The officers' barracks at the newly named Fort Lawrence, adjacent to the ruins of Beaubassin, was one of the first buildings fully completed in the English fort.

John Gorham had been assigned a small apartment on one end with a window. After sending Danks and his men off to Halifax and unaware of the violent events underway, he was managing his personal affairs. He had used much of his fortune to finance the operations of his rangers and he was preparing an accounting to receive recompense from the crown. In particular he had disbursed thousands of guineas in bounties for scalps on direct orders of his superiors. He worried about how easily he would be paid; often the Board of Trade that was financing the expedition authorized expenditures enthusiastically but paid begrudgingly.

Deep concentration had become difficult for him; he had begun to have splitting headaches and muscle pain. He thought he must have come into contact with a poisonous plant as in the last couple of days his hands and arms had become itchy and inflamed.

He had received a letter from his wife, Elizabeth, and her worries about their finances were carefully understated, but were also very clear.

His income from his Massachusetts' properties had declined with the hostilities and he had used much of what was a relative fortune on behalf of the crown. But were they good for it? He wasn't entirely sure.

He decided, despite the turmoil of the times and place, that he would need to settle his accounts himself, which required a trip to England. He also needed to express to his superiors in London that a much greater military commitment was needed to quell the savagery of the Indians and the mischief of the Acadians.

Although he had lost Bartelo to Indian cruelty and Danks was gone for several days, his younger brother, Joseph, showed promise. He had learned at his older brother's lap and he could assume control of John's rangers while he was in England.

He wrote a letter to his brother in Annapolis Royal to request that he come to Fort Lawrence to assume command of his company of rangers in his absence.

He finished his financial report, gave the letter to his subordinate for delivery on the daily sloop to Annapolis Royal, and prepared to meet with Lawrence to receive his authority to make the trip to London. He left that day on a supply ship that was returning to its home port in Liverpool. His fortune spent and never to be recompensed, he was never to return and died in the land of his great grandparents of smallpox.

* * * * *

Acquila stayed in Shubenacadie for several days and mostly he just ate and slept. No one had approached him, not even the dozen or so other Acadians, and he had stayed to himself. He noticed that Le Loutre spent his time talking with Miqmaqs, preaching the gospel and the need to eliminate the heretic Anglais from this land.

He felt unsure of his inactivity at Dartmouth... Was he a coward? Did he take the Lord's instructions against violence or was he sceptical of the value of the killing of women and children in maintaining Roman Catholic control of these lands?

He had met some Anglais at Pont à Buot, notably Captain How, and they had seemed like reasonable people. He had not met any Anglais not in the military, but would the general population of les maudits be less friendly or civil than their soldiers?

A week after the Dartmouth attack Beausoleil had called together the men. He explained how the group would conduct their next mission. Starting in the morning they were to stop the establishment of a new blockhouse at Chebouctu.

They made the trip back to the English capital as they had a week before, paddling most of the way. Beausoleil walked back to Acquila to speak with him during the last few miles of the trip.

"Monsieur Girouard. We do not have spectators in these attacks."

Acquila didn't know what to say.

"If you are to follow the orders of your shepherd, then you must become a warrior for God, not just an observer. Oui? We are crusaders, non?"

"I will try harder, Monsieur Brossard."

"Call me what everyone else does, Acquila, Beausoleil. But earn my friendship, try very much harder."

"I will, Beausoleil."

They arrived in the late afternoon, stopping in the brush surrounding the English camp, and settled in to examine their target. It was a new blockhouse guarding the land entrance to the Chebouctu settlement. There were a half dozen soldiers, shirts off, tending to the grounds removing the brush that might provide cover for attackers. They were too late.

Beausoleil nodded at Acquila, signalled to Copit and the Miqmaqs and Acadians rushed the English soldiers. They were unarmed and helpless and were overtaken in their panicked run back to their blockhouse. Acquila was caught up in the raid, his heart was beating and he lost all reason. He was a fast runner and was among the first to participate in the violence. He struck a soldier in the shoulder with his axe.

It was done. He had killed for God.

The massacre of the soldiers took only a few minutes, their scalping only a minute longer. Before the other blockhouse soldiers could respond Beausoleil's men, including Acquila, were making a retreat, leaving two men behind to discourage their being pursued.

* * * * *

Edward Cornwallis sat behind his desk, across from his aide Archibald Hinshelwood, and he was not in a very good mood. In fact he was extremely irritated. He had come to this terrible place, built a city from nothing, suffered through the murder and torture of close to a hundred civilians under his charge, and accommodated several thousand Germans in new settlements.

And yet the damnable Board of Trade had stuck him with a stack of unpaid bills enough to frighten the very King George, himself. The rum costs to distract the new residents from their hardships, alone, would cause the sovereign trepidation.

He hated having to deal with the low born wolves and weasels in the commercial world.

It was an extreme bother. He spent at least a third of every waking day in calculating funds spent and funds needed to proceed with the building of a great country. Then another third in dictating a demand for the replacement of the funds he had personally expended as well as debts for which he had provided his personal guarantee.

Furthermore, the damnable Crapauds and even more damnable Indians were proving themselves irresponsible and extremely disagreeable.

He had gone out of his way to accept them into the fold, agreed to allow them to practice their religion without interference, save their right to be married by the Roman Catholic officiates who were aggressively leading insurrection.

And yet, the previous day, he had received their deputies and they had stopped just short of expectorating on his visage. Their "petition" sought to provide themselves with the pleasure to leave Nova Scotia if they wished, or to stay if they desired, without pledging absolute obedience to the King. They had demanded the right to both consume their pudding and to retain it.

He had met with Council and received their consent to respond, and he was now doing so. He dictated to Hinshelwood a letter in response; that they could leave if they wished; he would even provide them passports for their safe conveyance. But that they remained English subjects even if they crossed the river at Chignectou; that that area remained British territory, notwithstanding the opinion of the French and their priests. He expressed his disappointment at their foolishness to believe the entreaties of the priests that had sent Indian savages to burn their farms. And he explained that if they decided to stay that they would act entirely and properly as subjects of King George.

"Seal it appropriately, Archibald, and have it delivered to them in Piziquid and Mines."

"I'm afraid that we may soon be parting company, Archibald. "Ere long, I will be called to travel to London to sort the financial situation out and I believe that I might well resign my commission while there."

"Very well, Milord."

* * * * *

Joseph Gorham was settling well in his first few days at Fort Lawrence. While there had been hostilities since his arrival, none in his area. His rangers were off with Danks trying to protect the new German villages being created by Cornwallis.

He had received the letter from London advising of the death of his brother. He was surprised, but death was something to which those in the warring class grew immune. He would of course help John's wife, Elizabeth deal with the loss; mostly financial. John had written in his letter that he had left for England and that the main purpose of his voyage had been to recover his expenditures on behalf of the crown. Joseph would see to it that these funds would be paid to his estate.

Failing an increase in the activity of the God damned priest and his more damnable Indians, he thought he would concentrate his rangers in his base of Fort Lawrence.

He went to see Lawrence at his apartments to confirm his plan.

Lawrence was drinking brandy when Joseph arrived, even though it was mid-day. He offered the new ranger leader a glass and he accepted.

"Please, have a seat, Joseph."

Gorham settled on a settee and Lawrence on a comfortable armchair. "So are you finding your accommodations suitable?"

"Yes, Colonel, very comfortable considering the wild place we are in. Much better than Annapolis Royal."

"Good, good. What do you see in our future, Joseph?"

"Well, the packets I get in from Danks suggests that he's getting rich with scalps. The Indians are common on the south shore."

Gorham sipped and enjoyed the warm aroma of the brandy.

Lawrence said, "I think our friend the priest has something else up his sleeve, other than pestering the Germans. Perhaps he will wait until their fortress across the river is completed to strengthen himself. Perhaps he's moving out of his Cobequid headquarters. I suppose there's a chance he's given up and gone back to France. I hear that he and his Indian Major are having some disagreements."

"Copit? My brother told me that he is a bit of a bounder; that he is usually drunk, always erratic and frequently over reaches his authority."

Lawrence said, "Well, what he has done is offer to treat with us, according to Cornwallis. That he wants to live and let live."

Gorham said, "I'll believe that when I see it. Danks told me what he and his women did to Josiah Higgins."

"Higgins was a good young fellow." Lawrence held up his snifter in a toast and Gorham followed.

Lawrence said, "We'll stay alert, Joseph, but I think we're about to see a little less excitement. Word is, from the Governor himself, that he's to return to England; evidently he's tired of the Board of Trade farthing and pennying him on his expenses. Hopson, I expect, will succeed him."

"Peregrine?"

"Yes. He's a good organizer with testicles the size of seeds. But he should be able to do the job."

Gorham laughed. "Well, I hope we don't need anyone with testicles the size of cannon balls."

"Well, if that need occurs, Joseph, I do wear extra large bloomers."

Both men laughed.

* * * * *

Mathilde had been without any word from Acquila for almost two months. Every day, when she wasn't looking after the children or working she would sit on the brow of the hill and watch for him. And every night she would go to bed and cry herself to sleep.

They had their first snow that morning, just a dusting but it was a sign of the beginning of hard times. She hoped it wasn't a sign of their fate.

Word had come that the Miqmaq and Acadians led by Major Copit for Le Loutre had committed many raids against the English; both against soldiers and innocent settlers. Casualties of the raiders from participating in these would never be reported to their family members; their families would be left with eternal longing for the return of their lost loved ones lost forever.

To their credit, Simon and Camille had filled in for Acquila in the construction of their new house and Mathilde was making the new house a warm home for her husband when he returned. It was bigger than their old place and there were two gable windows for their sleeping areas upstairs. Living in a new home should be a happy occasion, but how could it be, without Acquila?

It couldn't. He was her life even more than her children. She thought, as much as she loved her children, they were only half hers, while he was all hers; as she was all to him.

Emile had sprouted up during the fall, he was almost as tall as his father and every time she looked at him she saw her husband. Maurice was also a big help in doing the things in a homestead that only men should do.

Simon and Camille had been saints since 'Quila had left, filling in on doing the hard work. They had butchered and smoked or pickled another pig and one of their cows; she only had feed enough for two over the winter. She had not touched the gold; she had no place to spend it. She had shorn and spun the wool of their sheep and made Emile and Béatrice new winter clothes; Maurice would wear Emile's old ones that were now too small for the older boy. When the sun was just about to go down, everyone was inside. The men had even made new beds and they were in place with fresh straw mattresses. Simon started a fire for her and she offered to serve him dinner but he refused, explaining that he had to go home to his wife. But this only made her more lonely.

She cooked dinner for the children but didn't feel like eating. But she set a place at the table for Acquila. Just in case he might come home, but more a sign to herself that she still held out hope.

The new house was warm and she enjoyed the company of her children, but if only...

It was night and the children went to bed while she stayed up. She brewed some tea made from spruce buds and watched the flames slowly die. Then she went to bed.

* * * * *

Abbé Jean Louis Le Loutre walked the three leagues to Baie Verte alone, he did not wish anyone to notice that he had left l'Acadie. He needed more. His funds from Quebec would be used up over the winter, especially on Ile St. Jean whose settlers had taken nothing when they left and found there was nothing when they had gotten to their new home.

He would need to petition his Cardinal and the court of King Louis for more capital. He needed to provide his people more than food for this day and more than sustenance for their souls, they needed to build what their forbears had built before. They needed the aboiteaux and the farm land that provided food eternally; but this took decades to build and make fertile farm land.

Old l'Acadie, east of the new settlement and fort at Beauséjour, was lost. They needed to rebuild in the new land and finish the dykes in Pedditkoudiac, Chipoudie and Mémérancouque and Gediak. The funds with which he had originally been provided were gone feeding the exiles and building houses and the church.

He expected he would be in France for at least three months; he hoped nothing bad would happen until he returned. He had instructed Major Copit to continue his adventures but would not suggest, if asked, that anyone should trust the Miqmaq leader.

* * * * *

Mathilde had left the fire burning in the fireplace before she went to bed. She had wanted to keep the warmth overnight so that her children would not shiver and the hot coals had done their job.

It had snowed and she was relieved that they had gotten settled in the new house in time. She allowed the children to sleep in and she spent the early morning sorting things out and putting them in the right places. One thing that hadn't been built, though, were shelves and closets; she would need to have Acquila build them when he got home.

When he got home.

The day went quickly and by the time it was getting dark she had made the place a little more liveable. She swept up the wood dust and shavings remaining from the construction and put them in a box next to the fire to be used as tinder. She scrubbed the floor with sand and carefully removed any splinters and laid down a sheen of linseed oil and it shone.

When she was done she stood back and admired the collective work done. While the house was larger than their old place the main floor ceiling was less high. But this allowed the upstairs cubby-holes for sleeping to have a little more height, almost enough to allow her to stand up. As she was organizing their things she noticed the keepsakes and other sentimental items that had been left behind.

She opened the door slightly and looked outside; it was frigid and the wind was blowing off the bay. She needed more firewood in case they were snowed in completely. She draped her heavy woolen wrap over her head and shoulders and put on a pair of woolen mittens and went outside.

The wind took her breath away and she wrapped her cape more tightly. It was surprisingly light as the moon reflected off the snow. She walked over the dozen or so steps to the woodpile, odds and ends of the lumber that had been used to build the house.

For some reason, there was a snow bank two or more feet high a few yards from the pile. She thought it unusual as it hadn't snowed much yet and no one had shovelled. She picked up an armload of wood and on her way back to the house gave the snow bank a kick.

It moved, she shrieked and dropped the wood in her arms.

She bent down and brushed the snow away. It was Acquila's fall sweater. Then she realized in shock. It was Acquila! And he showed no signs of life.

She brushed the snow off of him and touched his forehead; it was cold, too cold. She tried to move him, it was hopeless. She tried to drag him but his clothes were stuck to the ground.

She rushed back to the house and yelled for Emile. The boy was of an age that it was almost easier to waken a corpse. She climbed upstairs and pulled him by his foot. "Emile, come, quickly, your father needs your help."

Emile grumbled and moved stiffly and slowly.

"Come NOW! Mainténant!" She shouted in his ear.

That gave the boy a start and also woke up Maurice.

"We have no time. Come downstairs. Put your sabots on. Hurry!?

She went on without them to Acquila's lifeless body and laid upon him, trying to warm him at least a little to see if he was alive, and if he was, to stir him to consciousness. But it seemed to be a lost cause.

After a few minutes the two boys arrived. While her body heat had not awakened Acquila, at least it had separated him from the frozen ground.

Between the three of them they were able to half carry and half drag their husband and father into the house and they put him in front of the fire. Mathilde stoked it and added some logs.

She removed her woolen cape and put it on her husband and held him close for several minutes. Then she got down on her knees and began to pray.

The children joined her.

16 – SEIZE

Peregrine Thomas Hopson felt comfortable in the Governor's apartments in Chebouctu. While his predecessor had shortcomings when it came to keeping records acceptable to the Boards of Trade which were financing the expansion of settlements in this Nova Scotia, he had constructed a most impressive citadel and village.

Outrageous amounts had been spent on rum, he noticed, but that would be necessary to avoid the natural demonstrations resulting from the deprivations of newcomers in a wild place such as this.

He was dressing for a meeting with the Miqmaq leader, Jean Baptiste Copit, who had agreed to discuss a treaty and possibly bring to an end the savages' murderous attacks on the settlements and military outposts.

His instructions from his superiors were clear. End the Indian problem and deal with the French peasants once and for all. They could leave if they wished, but they could not stay without swearing absolute fealty to King George and England. First things first; settle the Indians. Then settle the French.

When Hinshelwood finished dressing Hopson, the new governor lit his pipe and waited. "You're excused, Archibald." The diminutive Scot excused himself and went to the Governor's office to fulfill other duties there.

Soon enough, just after he had tapped his pipe out, a knock came to Hopson's door and he commanded, "Open".

His aide de camp, Caruthers, entered. "We are prepared to leave, Milord."

"Excellent." He donned his tricorn and followed Carruthers. Outside of his apartment waited a full company of perfectly kitted and attired members of the 40th Foot. Hopson took his position as Governor, Admiral and Captain-General of Nova Scotia and Colonel of this very regiment. He allowed Carruthers to command and direct the company to the harbour for the short whale boat voyage to George's Island, at the entrance to the harbour that separated Chebouctu and Dartmouth.

It took almost two hours for the company of soldiers and the Governor to cross the harbour and establish themselves ashore using the simple pier that had been constructed to build an advance defense post on the island.

Hopson noticed that there were several large Miqmaq canoes leaning sideways and pulled onto shore about fifty yards from the pier. He was disappointed that the Indians had arrived first. Carruthers led the company formally in two ranks while Hopson marched at their front.

In less than a quarter hour they came to the high point on the island where fortifications were being constructed. The Indians were sitting around a fire smoking and didn't stand until the English column arrived and were set at ease by Carruthers.

"Now see here, I am Governor Hopson, who is this Chief Copit?"

One of the Indians stood and walked toward Hopson. Copit was immediately put off by the appearance of the Indian Chief. He had expected to see a noble character, but what was before him was a filthy, stinking savage whose alcohol laced breath could be smelled two paces away.

"Carruthers, the document, please."

The Governor's aide came forward with a wooden portable secretary and placed it on a level spot on the ground along with a feather pen and inkwell.

Hopson bowed to Copit. The aide translated the Governor's

comments into French. "Chief Copit, greetings and salutations from his Royal Majesty, which I offer on his behalf. Carruthers, read the treaty first in English for my signature and then in French for Chief Copit."

Carruthers proceeded to read the parchment document which explained the duties of the Miqmaq to protect the peace and to assist and not harm British soldiers and settlers. It was based upon a treaty drawn up a few years before in Kennebec in the Province of Massachusetts and provided safety for the Miqmaq, if they behaved, as well as annual tributes of food and hard goods.

When Carruthers finished reading, he placed the document on the surface of the wooden secretary. Hopson signed in the appropriate place and had Carruthers witness his signature and add a seal.

The aide then read a translated version of the treaty in French and indicated to Copit where he should make his mark. Carruthers initialled the X and noted beside it: Chief Jean Baptiste Copit, his mark.

Copit held up a hatchet which for a moment startled the British officers and a couple of the infantrymen even raised their muskets, but Copit shook his head and pointed to Hopson's sabre.

Copit then pointed to a hole that the Indians had dug. He placed his hatchet in the hole. Hopson was reluctant to leave behind his blade that had served his family for several generations. "Carruthers, your sabre."

His aide provided the less treasured weapon and Hopson placed it in the hole adjacent to Copit's. Carruthers and one of Copit's men together filled in the hole. Copit held up a pipe.

"Well, Carruthers, that does it. Chief Copit, I appreciate very much your willingness to bury the hatchet, literally. Carruthers, my chair."

Hopson sat while Copit came forward with his pipe which he had filled with some dried leaves and lit. The Miqmaq mumbled a few words and held the pipe toward the ocean, then in three other directions. He placed the bit of the pipe in his mouth, inhaled and passed it to Hopson.

The Governor took the decorated pipe, sniffed the smoke and coughed. Then he inhaled and blew the smoke out and tried his best and successfully not to cough, but only barely.

"Very well. Carruthers, take us back." Hopson bowed while Carruthers ordered the men to attention and they turned about face and removed to their whale boats and Chebouctu.

* * * * *

When she wasn't praying, Mathilde spent the day washing Acquila and trying to keep him warm, but was getting no response. She was worried but knew that she had to keep trying to save her husband as well as keep her sanity.

Eventually Mathilde fell asleep lying next to Acquila and didn’t awaken until the sun shone in her eyes the next morning. She immediately checked on her husband, his condition didn’t seemed to have changed. She even wished he would snore to prove that he was still alive.

She started praying again and the strangest thing happened.

Acquila’s eyes opened.

She gasped in shock too stunned to immediately react.

Then she began covering his face in kisses.

And he moaned.

“Emile, Maurice, Béatrice! Your pére. He is home!”

The children awoke and the two younger ones rushed down the ladder, while Emile, as an adolescent boy, took a little longer.

Acquila came to consciousness slowly.

He stared straight up and appeared to not notice anything.

Then he lifted his head up and stared at Mathilde and appeared to recognize her and appeared to be wanting to say something and opened his mouth, but said nothing and his head slumped back on the floor and he fell back into a deep snoring sleep.

Mathilde wrapped her husband in woolen blankets and allowed him to sleep. A few times she tried to waken him to have him drink some water, but this was mostly unsuccessful. Finally, knowing that he simply needed water she had gotten Emile to hold him in a seated position, and she managed to have him drink a full cup while he was partly conscious. At least his ability to drink showed her that he was living and would get well eventually.

Both his ears were black and blue and she wondered if his time in the freezing weather had made him unable to hear. She wrapped warm cloths around his head to try and keep them warm.

The children had stayed inside, it was a blustery day and although slightly above freezing, very cold and damp.

It was little Béatrice, Mathilde thought afterwards, who then caused everything to happen.

She had started to sing a little song while next to her pére that Mathilde's mother had taught her when they had visited Nanpan one time. It was lilting and the little girl voice made it sound almost religious. Without noticing, or making any effort, Mathilde had started humming the song too while she was darning holes in the boys' winter pants.

She heard a sound, and stopped sewing. It wasn't Béatrice or the boys. It wasn't her... She got up and hurried to Acquila's side. He was humming her song with his eyes closed.

Should she disturb him? How could she not!

She began kissing his face and Béatrice joined her.

And Acquila's eyes opened, not wide, but they fluttered. "Mat..."

"Yes, 'Quila. It's me and Béatrice, your little girl sung you to awakeness!"

"Chér, water, please water."

Mati hurried over to the cistern that was almost empty, its minimal contents had come only from melting snow in the last day. She called upstairs, "Emile, you come now and you get water for your pére. Mainténant!"

The older boy hurried downstairs, "Papa, he is better?"

"He will be better, Emile, when you come back with this bucket filled with water."

Emile said, “Hello, papa! I go to get you water to drink.”

Mathilde called upstairs to her younger son, “Maurice, bring down all the pillows and blankets, vite!”

The boy almost fell downstairs in his hurry, but appeared all the same in a few seconds.

“Chér, help me up.”

“’Quila, you’re okay where you are, you. Here, I have pillows and blankets to warm you.”

He got a slight twinkle in his eyes and said quietly, “I think I need some of Bertrand’s mixture and my pipe.”

“No, you, you need sleep.”

“Why sleep? I’ve been asleep. I am home with my wife and family. I don’t need sleep I need to be with the reasons that I am still alive.”

Mathilde helped him rise and to his chair, then she wrapped him in a goose down duvet.

He told her how horrible his time with les sauvages had been; beyond his ability to comprehend or even describe. He had murdered. He had done so under the direct orders of his superior, if he was a soldier; under the orders of his priest and in the name of the Heavenly Father if he was not.

But he had murdered, all the same.

He reported how Beausoleil had led them through a number of raids after the ones in Dartmouth and in Chebouctu. They were not as violent as the others, but Acquila had attacked and defended himself and killed English soldiers without being wounded himself; at least physically. Thankfully he had not been forced to attack any fellow Acadians.

Beausoleil had even made him a lieutenant; while Acquila was embarrassed by his own fear and reticence to kill, it turned out he actually had been more brave and ready to get into the action than almost all of his comrades.

Then, being fed and having a healthy portion of moonshine, he had slept some more.

After a week had passed, the only remaining effect of the icicle that he had been was his left ear, that had been exposed to the snow when he had collapsed. It had been numb for a couple of days and then turned black and wizened and the lobe and lower half had fallen off.

He was shocked by it and Mathilde had looked distraught, but not for long; she was happy that his ear was the only cost to him of his awful adventures. She joked with him about never listening anyway, and her humour had comforted him.

He awoke in the middle of the night, not sure where he was. He thought of his terrible times in the last two months and decided, for the time, he needed to put things behind him. He had a family, and God's providence had allowed him to survive to look after Mathilde and the children. And he had work to do.

So he rose and carefully folded the feather quilt. He could tell that it was still dark outside, there was no light through the tiny gaps in the door and windows. He knew that Simon and Camille would be getting dressed and having breakfast and preparing to go to the new aboiteaux on the Riviere au Lac, just west of their new settlement. Acquila had missed working on the dykes and sluiceways; he hoped that his friends would welcome him back.

He looked around the kitchen and found the great loaf of bread that Mathilde had cooked the night before. He pulled off a healthy portion, placed the remainder on the table and smeared lard and preserved plums on the large hunk of bread. He had barely eaten for several days and he wolfed it down. The kettle next to the fireplace was always hot and he poured some hot water over some herbal tea to help his digestion.

Before he finished eating, and not surprising to him, he heard creaks from upstairs and looked up to see Mathilde climbing down the ladder. She could hear a mouse scoot under a table from fifty feet away.

"Acquila, you should come to bed and rest."

"I've recovered, Mati. Thoughts of your love kept me warm when I was away and when I was frozen in ice. I need to go back to work, the other boys have been doing my job and I must again get back to doing my share."

"Well then, let me pack you your dejeuner." She bustled around the kitchen area while Acquila finished his rough breakfast."

"The house is very nice. Did Camille and Simon do the work?"

"Oui. Along with some other men, but mostly it was them."

"We are in their debt. Do you still have our coins?"

"Of course. There has been no need to spend them."

"Perhaps you can give them some... No, give some to Camille and some to Simon's wife. My friends would not be able to stay quiet. Simon, anyway."

"Bon idée. I will. I have some smoked pork, I see you found my new loaf of bread. Take it with you. And here is a bottle of spirits to warm you." She put the pork in a bowl and wrapped it all up in a cheese cloth and tied it with a knot. "Would you like me to raise the children to see you off?"

"No, let them sleep. I will see them tonight."

He stood and she came into his arms and they held each other for several minutes. "I was empty without you, 'Quila."

"I only survived because I knew you were here, Mati."

"Now go, you. And come back early, you need to catch up on your rest."

She didn't know that sleep brought back his memories of horror and violence.

"I will come back when I can."

He kissed her deeply, pulled on his heavy coat, tucked his mid-day meal under his arm, opened the door and left.

The sun was halfway over the horizon to his left as he turned to walk north down the hill toward the new work area. Before he got very far he was called to. "Girouard, you lazy cow, wait for us, you can't avoid your work this time by going to fight women from England."

Acquila knew it was Camille and Simon and he knew that he would have to put up with their teasing and jeers at least until they ate their mid-day meal.

"I just got tired of doing all the fighting for you two old women." Acquila was glad to be home. Warring against the English with the Miqmaqs was a horrible thing; they were too violent and sometimes they stared at him as if he himself was at risk of losing his own hair. But his friends, although they teased him mercilessly, made him almost be able to forget his experiences in the last months.

"Come on, Acquila, less talk, more work." Camille took a running start and slid down the slippery grass of the hill, followed by Simon and finally, laughing, so did Acquila.

The men worked feverishly with their spades on the very edge of the bay at low tide, which kept the ground from freezing, and digging six feet down on a dike that had existed for over a century. Once finished they broke for food; Camille had a bladder of cider which complemented the pork that they had all brought with them.

They resumed working until dark. On the way back to the village Acquila realized that he had forgotten the bowl in which Mathilde had given him his dejeuner. He shrugged and thought he could retrieve it the next day.

* * * * *

Benoni Danks and Hezekiah King watched the activity of a new village being built at Mirligaiche, about a full days march south of Chebouctu. It was a rocky place but had a decent enough harbour, although where the place on which Danks would put his camp barely had enough soil in which to put a tent peg. He wondered what crops these German farmers would be able to plant in this rocky ground.

Their men were camped on the outskirts of the new town being built. A sturdy blond man was approaching, his clothing was clean, his hair carefully cut and his face appeared to be well scrubbed.

He held out his hand and spoke with a strong accent, "Hoffman."

Danks shook. "Danks. This is King." The visitor nodded cheerfully and shook King's hand energetically.

"Guten Morgen, meine freunde. I am head man here."

“Morning to you. How many are ya?”

“Ve haff over four hunderd.”

“Do any of them have cheroots?”

The German settler looked confused.

“Is the Colonel Lawrence among them?”

“Ya. Ya, Colonel Lawrence…, ya, Herr Danks.”

“Take us to him, Hoffman.”

The two rangers allowed the German settler to lead them through the town to a small collection of white bell tents that were acting as Lawrence’s headquarters for his visit. The Lieutenant Colonel was sitting on a folding stool, smoking a small cigar and reading some paperwork. He looked up. “Mister Hoffman, who have you brought me? Danks! About time you arrived.”

“Sorry, Lieutenant Colonel. We travelled overland and it was more difficult than usual without knowing the water way.”

“How many men ya bring.”

“As many as we could muster, two and a half score. A third Mohawks.”

“Well. Very well. Any contact with the local savages?”

“Not since Nanpan, they've not been that easy to find for some reason, Colonel. We did destroy a group of their doxies in Cobequid.”

“No Indians, no scalp money, Danks.”

"I know that, Sor."

“You’re to protect this settlement until it’s completed and fortified, Danks. Should be six to eight weeks minimum. Scout around and look for trouble. I don’t think either the Miqmaqs, the Acadians or King Louis wish us to settle this land. So I expect trouble.”

“Will do, Sir. Same bounty if we find any renegades?”

“That’s still undecided with the new Governor. He believes he has made peace with them, but I believe this not. And he’s as tight as a beaver’s bung hole. Save them up if you get any, they’ll be made good at some point.”

“Very well, Colonel.

"Sor. One more thing. Any chance I could rob a cheroot from you, Colonel."

"They're in short supply, Danks. You're dismissed."

The two rangers turned and walked back to their camp.

* * * * *

Several months after Acquila's return, Le Loutre came to the Girouard homestead early, before Acquila left to work. As was his way, he opened the door and walked in without knocking. The house and lives of these people were in God's domain and he was His soldier.

Mathilde was serving breakfast, fried pork belly in oat porridge with maple syrup. They were finishing their morning prayers waiting to drink the still warm milk for which she had gotten up early to take from Celia their cow.

When the door opened, her first thought went back to a few months before when the sauvage had come into their house and her man and little boy had saved them all. She picked up the pot in which she had cooked the bacon to defend her children. Acquila, although he was still recovering from his wounds, in a second, picked up the fireplace poker next to him to attack the intruder.

When they saw who it was 'Quila replaced the poker and calmed down while Mati strode toward the priest, pot in hand. "Why are you here? We are having breakfast, Mon Dieu!"

"Never take His name in vain, Madame! I am here to speak privately with our head of militia. I am sorry if I interrupted your dejeuner, but my mission will not wait. Monsieur Girouard, you will come with me."

"He will not! He will finish his breakfast. Because you are our priest you may join us, but you will not speak about your mission. We do not speak at meals in our family."

"I will wait outside, Madame, for your husband. I do not need to eat in the mornings, it is a time for inspiration."

Le Loutre left.

"Acquila, you will not go with that man, you!"

"Mati, we have been over this. We have a responsibility to our community and our church. I was called to this. It is not my choice. If les maudits are not stopped we have no future, except in the hereafter."

"And Acquila Girouard, if you die we may have no future."

"Mathilde Girouard, your bravery gave our family a future with or without me."

"But, Acquila Girouard, my bravery will not keep me warm at night!"

Acquila finished his porridge and stood, "Ma Chér, I will always keep you warm at night, I hope, even if I am not with you."

Mathilde felt her eyes well up with tears. "You come back to me, Acquila, you."

"I will, Mati, I will."

They both stood and she came toward him and they embraced. "I love you, Acquila Girouard, and I will always love you."

"Et moi, ma Chér, et moi."

They kissed passionately, stared in each others eyes for a full minute. Acquila started to leave.

"You take your winter coat, you. It is still cold at night."

She hurried over to get it and helped him put it on.

"You come home soon. There is something I have to tell you."

"What?"

"I will tell you when you return."

"What?"

"Come home, Acquila, as soon as you can."

He left.

Mathilde ate her serving of porridge and then Acquila's, as well and then some more.

When Acquila left his home, he didn't dare look back. He looked around the settlement and saw that Le Loutre was on the edge of the ridge, looking across at the English fortress a half league away. The priest turned around a few moments after he heard the door close. He waited for ‘Quila to join him.

“Father, what am I to do?”

“My son, our comrade and ally, Major Copit, needs to be encouraged to resume our struggle. He was seduced by his temporal authority and lost his spirituality and obligation to our Father. We will re-engage his interest.”

Acquila nodded. "Monsieur, can you recruit some of your militia members, perhaps two."

Acquila went to find Simon and Camille who had finished their season of work on the dykes and aboiteaux and were doing chores around their adjoining houses. When he arrived they were removing large rocks from the ground with a lever.

"You work hard early in the morning, mes amis."

Simon said, "Well, you were not here to help, so we decided to start without your constant complaining about hard labour."

"I have come to take you away from your all your travails."

"And lead us to the land of milk and honey, I suspect."

"In a way. Pére Le Loutre has ordered us to accompany him."

Simon harrumphed. "Pah. To a nicer place, I expect."

"To a nicer hereafter, for certain."

Unusually for him, Camille spoke. "Moi? I like the here and now even if it comes with sore muscles."

"Mes amis, it is an opportunity for us to return the violence to those who have been terrorizing our families for our entire lives. Come. The priest orders and we are good Roman Catholic men and we follow."

Camille asked, "For how long?"

"A week, it might be less or more."

Simon said. "It is a good week for Philomene and Therese to be left alone. My wife and daughter are meaner this week than all the priests in Acadie. I'll go."

Camille said, “I already do the work of two men, I won’t be able to do the work of four, so I will join you.”

A few minutes later the two friends joined Acquila and they

went down the hill to the abbé who was still looking across the marshes intently. They marched toward Baie Verte and joined a small group of Miqmaqs who had set up a camp upstream and headed east. Along the way they were joined by Beausoleil Brossard.

Copit's encampment was in a village called Remsheg and it stunk of burned flesh and Acquila could see a post in the ground surrounded by burned logs and bushes. He turned his eyes away and silently whispered a prayer for whomever had suffered there.

For a change there was not witty commentary from Simon and Camille, as always, was stoic in seeing the horrible people and surroundings.

There were a small number of warriors in the camp, the rest were most likely foraging or raiding. A half dozen women were working around the small settlement, piling firewood, smoking fish and tanning skins. Jean Baptiste Copit was sitting next to his son on a stump smoking a pipe in front of a tipi covered in skins. Leaning against the lodge was a musket and a long handled war axe. He stood when Le Loutre approached him. His hair was tangled and filthy and even from six feet away Acquila could smell his body doors.

"Père."

"My son, what is this I hear about you?"

"What do you mean?"

"You are being friendly with les maudits, I have been told, and that you have promised them that you would no longer do them harm. Is this true?"

Copit didn't answer and looked like he was frightened.

"Jean Baptiste, you are a sinner if this is true. The cost of sin is damnation and eternal suffering."

"What can I do, Father?"

"You are a Roman Catholic, Jean-Baptiste, you are very well aware of how you can avoid this penalty. You must confess your sin and make restitution."

Copit stood and prostrated himself in front of the Abbé and began speaking rapidly and explaining how he had agreed to peace with the English for provisions for the winter and for peace to allow his people to gain strength.

"Did the Holy Father tell you to do this, Jean Baptiste?"

"No, mon Père."

"Did I give you authority?"

"No, mon Père."

"Do you have this false document?"

"I will get my copy." Copit rummaged through his meagre belongings and withdrew a badly crumpled large piece of parchment."

"Now burn it."

Copit did as he was told; he threw it into his campfire.

"Jean Baptiste, you will pray for forgiveness for one full night, starting when the sun goes down and not stopping until the sun rises. Then you will go to the village of the English a days march from Chebouctu and you will wreak revenge on the heretics you find there, and after you are completed with this, I will absolve you of your sins. Do you understand?"

"Yes, Father."

"These men, Monsieur Brossard, Girouard and the others will accompany you and return to tell me that you have completed your act of contrition."

"Yes, Father."

"Beausoleil, Capitaine Girouard, do you understand your duty? Beausoleil, you will accompany him." Acquila nodded.

"Then settle here until the Major has completed his penance, then go and destroy as many Anglais as you can. Bring me their scalps." And with that, Le Loutre turned away and left.

Beausoleil spoke, something he seldom did. "Get your things, Chief. I know where we can find the maudits."

Copit looked a little panicked and quickly pulled together a group of a dozen of his men who went frantically around the village collecting their travel items; weapons, tobacco and alcohol.

Beausoleil motioned for the Acadians to sit. Beausoleil went to a campfire, lit his pipe and returned, squatting on his haunches.

"There were some maudits, to whom some other Miqmaqs

offered comfort when their ship wrecked further down the coast. About two days travel. Our people's reward was to be murdered and scalped. They are heretics and as a reward they will be sent to hell, a destination at which they will feel comfortable."

* * * * *

The crew travelled by canoes for two full days, almost to the great ocean, on the shore of Ile Royale, and arrived in the early morning. They saw smoke and carefully made their way toward it. The settlement of a dozen or so houses were quiet and there were tents for likely a dozen men with signs of it being a military camp. A small schooner, its sails furled, was at anchor just off shore.

Beausoleil looked at Acquila. "Take half the men and begin the assault. Kill them all. We will support if needed."

Acquila nodded to his two friends. They both had war hatchets. Then he motioned to a group of Indians. They started quietly crawling toward the tents. When they were about twenty paces away there were signs of movement in the camp. Acquila raised his hands and the group all rose and started running at full speed, the Miqmaqs uttering their blood curdling war cries. The tent flaps opened and men began leaving their tents in various stages of undress; most only in their breaches.

They were set upon; one came running directly at Acquila with his musket, bayonet attached and deadly. When the Englishman moved to stab him Acquila smashed the barrel of the musket to the side with his hatchet and then crushed his opponent's head with it. He fought with a frenzy, caught up in the blood lust, almost fully decapitating one English. All around him were the sounds of wars: the screams of agony and pain and hatred and fear; the sounds of hard weapons hitting soft flesh; the field covered in blood, their own and their opponents.

Acquila sensed and felt nothing but the violence aimed at him and the violence he meted out. Until it was done. He stopped. There were no more to kill. He looked around and already Copit's other men had joined the others and were looking through the tents, digging through their victims' clothing and taking scalps.

He looked over at the small settlement and saw the inhabitants escaping in terror, much as his family and friends had only little over a year before.

He checked on his friends and they were standing much as he was, quietly and looking around and trying to not focus on the barbarity all around.

17 - DIX-SEPT

In his months at Louisbourg, Thomas Pichon had found his apartments comfortable but not nearly as ostentatious as de Raymond's; but then again the Count was the acting governor.

He was also enjoying the company of some peasant girls who were very devoted to the hierarchy. He relished the wonderful selection of food available, although it was poorly cooked by the chefs here. Luckily, Louisbourg was the first stop off for ships travelling from St. Malo to Quebec, so he and de Raymond had the first chance to be supplied with fine wines and excellent cognac.

An aide of some level should have staffed the entry area of his work place, but the chair and desk had not been occupied for several weeks. There was a stack of unopened correspondence.

He sat at the chair and opened the many weeks' worth of correspondence that was folded and sealed with wax. He stacked them face up in one pile and discarded the basic reports and accounting records. There were many reports and letters from the Abbé in Acadie, Le Loutre; Pichon thought he must either be very busy to write so many reports, or be not very busy to be able to write so many reports.

One report detailed the expenditures of a substantial amount to build new aboiteaux north of the boundary river; in Au Lac,

Chipoudie, Pedditkoudiac and Mémérancouque as well as to build a church at Beauséjour. Interesting, he thought. He wondered if all the cash that had been disbursed had actually ever been received, and, if received, actually how much would actually ever be spent on its intended purpose; this collection of projects would take a decade at least to complete.

Finally he opened one from his patron the Intendant in Quebec, François Bigot. It opened as usual with a series of salutations.

He was taken aback. After the pleasant opening comments he was given new orders; he was to go as commissary to the fort being constructed at Beauséjour after only two years.

His first thought was to his appetites; he didn't suppose any of wine, food and women could be as available as at Ile Royale. But then again, he would have more freedom of motion, conveniently being situated some distance from any oversight. 'I can make out like a Paris pickpocket', he thought.

He put on his jacket and hat and went looking for some assistance in packing his luggages; his orders required him to be redeployed in his new headquarters within a fortnight and it would take him at least that long to get his things together in trunks and travel.

* * * * *

It was spring and Acquila had been away for months without any word. Surely, with the work needed on dykes and aboiteaux he, Simon and Camille would return soon. She knew her baby would arrive soon, but she hoped not before her husband.

It happened when she was hanging clothes to dry one cool April morning. Béatrice was playing near her. Her water broke and she gasped, "Béatrice, ma petite, get Emile, vite."

The little girl ran to the fields where Emile was herding their sheep to a better forage area. When he arrived he was terrified, "Maman, what can I do?"

"Quickly, get Philomene, hurry!"

Mati made her way inside and painfully made it upstairs to her bed. The baby wanted to arrive, but Mati wanted it to arrive where it had been conceived and where the bassinette and swaddle clothing for the baby were.

Philomene Bourque arrived with Emile and Maurice and was all business. She put a pot to boil on the fireplace rack and ran up stairs.

"You two, you stay down here and look after your sister."

Mathilde was in agony. Philomene removed Mati's underclothing and pushed her skirts up over her waist. Then she hurried downstairs. She rummaged in the kitchen and found the sharpest knife and applied the whetstone to make it even sharper. She dropped it in the hot water in the pot on the cooking rack for a minute, poured some cold water from the cistern into another pot and went back upstairs. Mati was sweating profusely and Philomene could see the baby's head starting to appear.

In less than half an hour the little boy made his loud announcement of his birth to all and Philomene performed her midwifery and wrapped the tiny dark haired boy in a warm cotton blanket and placed him in his mother's arms, who was exhausted and gasping for air after the exertion.

Meanwhile there was a commotion downstairs and in a minute Acquila came charging up the stairs and hit his head, stunning him for a moment. But he shook his head and kissed Philomene and went to Mathilde's side and kissed her forehead and laid beside her with the little baby in between. Louis-Thomas was busy having his first food on earth.

Mathilde was almost out of breath but said, "'Quila? What shall we name him?"

"Louis-Thomas, after the Grenadier, my dove."

She said, "I love you Louis-Thomas. And you Acquila Girouard."

"Why didn't you tell me?"

Mathilde was weak but was smiling that her entire family was together for the first time in months and spoke softly. "I tried to, but your maudit priest took you away from us before I could. Where have you been?"

"It's not important, Chér. I am glad to be home and with you and with my family."

"Was it terrible?"

"Yes. It was very terrible. But we all came home safely."

"Your ear looks funny, but it will stay with me forever as a sign of how desperately you wanted to come home to us."

"I have no place to go for now."

"Bien, then we can finally celebrate our Christmas. We were waiting for you."

"I prayed every day that God would allow us to share Christmas, but it took very long for me to have my prayers answered. Go to sleep, Chér."

"Non, Attender. Have the children come and meet their new brother!"

"Emile! Bring Maurice and Béatrice to meet your new brother."

The boys made their way clumsily upstairs while Béatrice was helped up by Philomene."

Acquila said, "This is your new brother, Louis-Thomas." He presented the baby to the other children.

The children started to gather around Louis-Thomas cooing and making gentle sounds.

Then Béatrice turned her attention a foot to the left and said, "Oh, Bonjour, Papa!" And then Louis-Thomas burped his dejeuner on his father's shoulders and all the children laughed.

* * * * *

Thomas Pichon's travel from Louisbourg to Beauséjour was without incident except for the grumbling from the soldiers having to carry his substantial and very heavy luggage from Baie Verte to the fort. The weather was cool and there had been a light dusting of snow with which to contend. Overall, though, cool days with thawing ground was easier to transverse than hot days on swamp.

He arrived to a bustling construction site. The fortress had its outer palisades installed and fossed, the barracks were completed and the casemates with timber roofs were being assembled from local stone to underlay the earthen walls of the citadel. A well had been built to supply the fortress with fresh water.

The garrison was now being commanded by Jean-Baptiste Mutigny de Vassan, although Pichon knew that his days were numbered; that Louis du Pont du Chambon de Vergor was to be appointed by Pichon's own sponsor, Intendant Bigot, to replace him before long.

DuPont would bring with him a hundred and a half veterans from the Colonial Marine to supplement the Royal Army soldiers, Miqmaqs and Acadiens for the battle that was sure to occur.

Pichon was generally pleased with DuPont's pending appointment to the fort under construction because there would not be any oversight of his own expenditures, but disappointed that so many funds had already been expended without his involvement.

He noted the settlement outside of the fortress was proceeding well; the church, in particular, was developing and a large church bell was waiting on a pedestal to be hung. There appeared to be two dozen or so houses with roofs and smoke coming from their chimneys. He doubted that this place would offer him much in the way of his more animalistic desires, but the money that he could acquire... ooh la la.

While his luggage was being located in his quarters he had yet to approve, Pichon decided that he should visit the commanding officer and put him in his place.

He had never spent time with de Vassan, although the officer had undoubtedly been through Louisbourg while Pichon had been there. The new Commissary wished to see first hand what wiggle room he might have in his new job.

Pichon blustered his way to the Commandant's apartment, ignoring glances and comments from lower level officials. It was a short walk of less than a few dozen strides to his destination across the parade ground to the newest and largest barracks, the only building in the fortress with two stories.

The fort compound was very small and was already saturated with people even before the full complement of the garrison had arrived. Everyone appeared occupied with their tasks.

He boldly lifted the latch and entered. A lone ensign manned the roughly hewn desk in the small anti-chamber of the commandant's office.

Pichon passed his orders to the young French soldier, "I am to serve here under the terms of my orders from the Intendant of New France and under the authority of the Governor of New France, Marquis Duquesne de Menneville."

"Bonjour, Monsieur Pichon. These seem to be in order. The Commandant is currently overseeing some of the constructions that are going on."

"We cannot be too prepared, Ensign, the English are less than a league away."

"Oui, Monsieur le Commissaire."

Just then the door opened and a small man appeared; almost totally consumed by a huge tricorn hat festooned with embroidery that topped off an oversized blue and grey full set of formal clothing and great coat.

He looked at Pichon.

"You would be Commissaire Pichon, I expect. Welcome to our military headquarters, as I enjoy calling it."

"Bien sûr, and I expect you are the Commandant that I have heard of, but never met." Pichon bowed.

"I am Jean-Baptiste Mutigny de Vassan and pleased to make your acquaintance." He returned the bow. "Come into my office, I shall need to give you our books of account, as they are; I am afraid we have not kept our records as well as we might."

Pichon almost smiled; any deficiencies during his term could be blamed on his predecessor. "I trust you will make note of this... discrepancy."

"Provide me with a balancing and I will acknowledge their acceptance."

"Very well."

"Come in, come in, Monsieur la Commissaire."

De Vassan sat at his desk and indicated to Pichon that he should sit in the chair across from the desk. He reached into a drawer and removed a stack of papers. "This is the accounting papers."

"Merci, Monsieur. I will review them for acceptability. What does… what does one do here for a distraction?"

"Monsieur Pichon, this place itself is a distraction. There is nothing here… but here."

"Hmm. Is there no, I don't know, place for relaxation, a dining place or such."

"Well, there is Caisse's trading post, of course, at the Pont à Buot. Although Monsieur Caisse has been gone many years. Actually, officers from the English garrison frequent the place. It is a distraction to exchange frivolity with one's eternal enemy, I suppose."

Pichon wondered how he might profit from this. "I suspect it offers an opportunity to evaluate the readiness of one's enemy."

"Or for them to evaluate ours. I have forbidden men of our garrison to frequent the place. I allow our officers to visit and recreate there. We bring up a keg of ale or rum from there to celebrate our festivals when our supplies have not been refreshed."

"What need I concern myself with, Monsieur le Commandant?"

"It's not what, Monsieur, it is who."

"Who then."

"It is a priest by name of Le Loutre who has a very close relationship with the local aboriginals."

"I have heard of this priest. And why should I be concerned?"

Pichon was well aware of the considerable sum that now resided somewhere in this outpost under the priest's protection.

"He acts outside of any authority. He is like Moses in the way he leads his flock. He has a compatriot, a sauvage, Copit, who acts totally beyond any standards of decency with regard to the local French peasants and for that matter what few English settlers there are. But I have been directed to offer them both every courtesy, and I am and shall do so.

"Perhaps worse, we've seen some members of our garrison disappear, I am afraid they may have found a place with the English across the river. If I get an opportunity I'll trade for them, but so far none of the English have seen cause to look for succour here.

"But my main purpose is to get this fortress constructed and to prepare for the conflagration that we will no doubt see before long."

"Well, Monsieur Commandant, I appreciate your frankness, I have no doubt we will become fast friends. Please allow me to assist you in your mission in any way I might. I will review and approve your accounting records as necessary."

Pichon stood and bowed deeply and de Vassan did the same. Pichon left. He needed to get to that trading post as soon as possible.

* * * * *

Charles Lawrence waited outside the Governor's quarters in Chebouctu. The settlement had grown considerably in the time since he had last visited; there were easily twice again as many buildings and the port area at the harbour had a number of new warehouses. There was also the start of a larger fortress at the summit of a hill that dominated the landscape behind the current village.

The door to the Governor's chambers opened and Archibald Hinshelwood entered the ante-chamber. "Colonel Lawrence, so sorry for the delay, Governor Hopson and I had to review some documents and I'm afraid with his eyesight as it is, that it took much longer than we had anticipated."

Lawrence stood. "Then might I see him now? I do have other duties while here in Chebouctu."

"Yes, please come in."

Lawrence followed Archibald into Hopson's chambers. Hopson was looking at documents with a magnifying glass, he looked up when Lawrence entered. “This infernal thing! Charles, I’m glad you could come to collect your orders. I thought it best that we don’t delay.”

He stood to shake Lawrence’s hand.

“Don’t delay what, Peregrine?”

“My constitution has suffered here in the colony, Charles. I’m afraid I’ll have to go back to Kent to renew my health.”

“I’m sorry to hear this, Peregrine. Is there anything I can do?”

“There certainly is, here are your orders.” He passed a sealed document to Lawrence who broke the seal and scanned the document.

“So I’m to be Acting Governor in your absence? Fair enough. What should I consider and act upon?”

“I think it’s up to you to settle the French and Indian affair. They’ve broken their treaty obligations and have been terrorizing our German settlements. I would hope that it won’t be on-going when I return.”

“When should I assume office.”

“I will be leaving on the tide tomorrow on the Torrington, Charles.”

“Then I suppose I should send a crew to Annapolis Royal and Chignectou to retrieve my belongings.”

“Yes, Charles, that would be sensible, I expect I’ll be gone a year or more. I’ve had Archibald send out missives to all the regional commanders to advise them of your assumption of this office.”

"Very well, Peregrine."

* * * * *

Pichon had arisen late; it was near noon when he was dressed and he left his apartments to begin his day. It was a cool morning; the snow mostly melted over the course of a sunny day except on the lee side of rises in the ground, but the stubble on the low-lying fields of the marshland was still frozen and stiff on this morning. The oak and elm trees were denuded of leaves, the sky was a clear blue and the offshore wind was chilling, but, it was far from the coldest day that would be survived in this winter season.

He could see the smoke rising from his destination and he quickened his pace. Few of the peasants he passed knew who he was, nor did he know them, so he was uninterrupted in his trip.

The area around the redoubt and trading post was well populated with soldiers, trappers with their skins and a collection of purveyors of foods and homespun on stools, some with tables. There was a small group of soldiers, both English and French, outside of the tavern waiting to get in and Pichon thought he would need to impose his authority to get inside.

He admired some of the French maidens in the crowd, selling trinkets and other items but sadly, he thought, not themselves. These saintly Beauséjour maids had been very offended when he had offered his pleasures and he had not exercised his libido since he had arrived. He was frustrated by this and responded by deciding to boost his ego instead.

He bolstered his bulk and strode confidently toward the door of the log building brushing past a ragged line of soldiers and civilians, explaining, "Let me pass. I am the Official Commissary of Beauséjour."

A couple of the trappers eyed him aggressively but let him pass and Pichon entered. The interior of the log tavern had room for about two dozen patrons and it was full; mostly with rough looking men in roughly made clothing, many wearing beaver coats. A few French officers were sitting around a table, tri-corns off or tilted to the side, passing around a small keg of rum and awkwardly pouring portions into pewter mugs. There were two Englishmen sitting quietly in one corner and another sitting alone, with the only vacant seat in the smoky room next to him against one wall.

Pichon recognized the solitary man,; his presence was the reason for Pichon's visit. He approached and said loudly in English, "Sir, might I join you? My name is Thomas Pichon." Pichon bowed.

The English officer stood and met the bow and also raised

his voice, “I am Captain George Scott, and I am pleased to make your acquaintance.” He offered his hand and Pichon shook it and sat down. The Captain signalled to Françoise Cyr who brought two pewter mugs of hot buttered rum and placed them on the table. After Scott gave her a coin, Pichon watched her smile and offer her thanks and then studied her rear end as she seductively walking away.

Scott whispered, “Thomas, it is pleasant to see you again.” He picked up a mug and gave it to Pichon and then his own. They clinked their mugs.

Scott had met Pichon the year before in Louisbourg when the English soldier had accompanied a flotilla of boats that went there to secure rum and other goods from the French West Indies for the settlement in Chebouctu. He and Pichon had made out very well from this transaction and had stayed in touch whenever they could with apparently innocent written messages.

“I hope you have been well, George. What brings you here?”

“As well as one can be in this place. Well, it seems that someone high up decided I should take over the garrison here. Charles Lawrence has been sent off on some other great mission to tame the heathens. What about you, Thomas?”

“Well, welcome here to both of us. Bigot saw fit to send me to a place that would better suit my skills but unfortunately may not suit some of my temptations.”

“We are but pawns, Thomas.”

“Poor pawns indeed.” Pichon sighed and surreptitiously reached into his coat and removed a handkerchief that contained a letter. He passed it to Scott under the table after assuring himself no one was paying attention to them. “It is from my dear friend, Mister Tyrell.”

Scott smiled, “I hope my friend Mister Tyrell will start having better fortune with the maidens of Beauséjour, Thomas.”

“I hope so, as well, my friend. He is feeling quite unfulfilled and lonely.”

The men continued chatting and drinking until the skies started to turn dark and then bowed to each other and Pichon finished his rum and left.

* * * * *

The entire village was in love with little Louis-Thomas. The women of the village all visited regularly to see the only baby born in Beauséjour for the entire year and brought food every day and volunteered to do household chores and look after the little boy if Mathilde wished a break.

After many months of regret and prayer since his return, Acquila was becoming reacquainted with peaceful living. He had accepted his awful acts and the Abbé had given him and the others absolution for the killings they had committed. He was settled and happy and loved watching Louis-Thomas becoming a little boy that was starting to try and walk and laughed at any little event that occurred.

Acquila was back working with Simon and Camille and there was considerable progress being made on dyking and building the sluice gates on the Riviere au Lac. When he had been in the Miqmaq camp Acquila had kept his hair short, since fleas and lice were so common in the filthy hovels in which they had been billeted. But he had started growing his hair long, like the other men, not only to follow the fashion but to disguise his badly injured ear, although Mati had said it was a sign of his love for her.

The boys were growing into men before Mathilde's eyes and were starting to help out their father on the dykes. Béatrice was becoming very useful in cleaning up after the males who came home exhausted and covered in mud. She was also showing interest in the church and promising to be very devout, if not keen enough to enter a convent. Acquila was questioning his own faith, however. He did not understand how the violence he had seen, and even been an active participant in creating, could come from the Father. He was suspicious that the abbé was acting for his own purposes and that of the King, rather than from divine inspiration.

By sheer might and weight of population the English had taken control of Acadia. The efforts to disrupt the new English settlements had failed and Le Loutre's efforts were now devoted to expanding new and stronger settlements west of the Mésagouèche River. He no longer called on his Acadian militia to cause havoc and this made both Acquila and Mathilde very happy. Acquila had always found himself a reluctant participant in the terror.

Things were back to what Acquila and Mathilde hoped would be normal. For now, at least, they could live, love, work and raise their family among friends.

At times, though, he felt almost bored. The dyke and aboiteaux work was hard and Mathilde was devoted to the baby and spent little effort welcoming Acquila in bed. She had expressed her concern many times about having another baby because of the English still existing across the river and the risk of another dislocation. He knew she prayed every night that they would never need to move ever again and that he would never be called on to leave his family.

Simon had changed since their time chasing the English having killing many. He was much more serious and less talkative and all and all less enjoyable to be around. Camille was himself, taciturn as always, but seemed to be enjoying cider more than normal and worked less hard.

For the last day or two Mathilde had been cooking and fussing around the house. It was time for Béatrice's confirmation which was a reason for celebration in their community. The service was to take place this afternoon after mass, which was to be just after Louis-Thomas' christening, so it promised to be an exciting day for all the children and a lot of work for the adults.

Mathilde had made her Grandmére's seafood ragout and it was staying warm on the hearth. She had baked a huge boule de pain and a pie with apples and plums. The boys were dressed in their Sunday clothes and Béatrice in her white confirmation dress.

The family all left when the house was all set up for the feast.

Father Le Guerne had scheduled the christening for the half hour before mass and all the family friends were in attendance. Acquila had held his precious son while Simon and Philomene, as Godparents, affirmed their faith and trust in God.

Then the father indicated to Acquila to hold Louis-Thomas over the font, and poured holy water on the boy's forehead, "Je te baptise au nom du Père, du Fils et du Saint Esprit."

Two choir boys presented the four adults with candles. "Briller comme une lumière dans le monde pour lutter contre le péché et le diable."

The couples, with Acquila in the lead carrying his son, walked in a line outside where all the parishioners came to offer congratulations and small gifts that Béatrice accepted on Louis' behalf.

After mass all of the friends came to the Girouard house and enjoyed the family hospitality. For the first time in years, things seemed safe.

18 - DIX-HUIT

Abbé Henri Daudin was accompanied by a small retinue of English soldiers on his cross peninsular voyage from his new parish in what the English called Annapolis Royal, to the English stronghold of Chebouctu. It was an unpleasant trip; while the four men had a large canoe, they had little opportunity to use it and it was more excess baggage and a hindrance than a travel convenience. The soldiers were also unpleasant.

While in the canoe, taking advantage of one of the few opportunities for water transport, to his destination, he thought back to his meeting with Jean Louis Le Loutre a few months before...

Le Loutre had made a trip to see Daudin at his previous parish at Piziquid after his visit to a Miqmaq camp in Cobequid. As the Abbé always did, he had marched non-stop on his own, not-sleeping and seemingly daring any natural or human elements to slow him down.

When Le Loutre arrived at Piziquid in the mid-afternoon he had been all business. He entered l'Eglise de l'Assomption as if he owned the place and marched purposefully to the front where Abbé Daudin had been sweeping up the altar.

"Daudin, why are you wasting your time doing janitorial work when you should be guiding your flock to our new settlements."

"Bonjour, Louis. It is nice of you to visit. I enjoy doing the more simple acts of love for Our Father."

"When we have settled our people in a place where they can flourish and worship you can do your cleaning, Henri. I need you to do something important."

"How may I serve, Father?"

"We need all of our Acadians to move north to Chipoudie, Mémérancouque and Pedditkoudiac. Many are cowards without faith and some even wish to return to their farms here. A few are even travelling to the Governor in Quebec to try and override my authority and receive permission to return to their own farms."

"How can we do this?"

"We will get the English to assist us. You will visit the English Governor and you will have him believe that we are having the Acadians leave this place and resettle north to the new colony. Which is true. You will tell them that they are very unhappy being here and may even get up in arms and stop providing les maudits with sustenance. He will then cause them more hardship and make them more accommodating to our desires."

"I will try and do this, Louis." Daudin moved to pick up his broom but Le Loutre intercepted him.

"You work too slowly and do a poor job." Le Loutre then had picked up the broom and began sweeping the floor.

Daudin had gone to Chebouctu, and he had been quite warmly received by Governor Hopson. Indeed he had been almost fawned upon. Hopson had made promises to protect Daudin, his priests and the Acadians that had remained behind. He had even pledged to allow the French churches to be fully supplied with priests! Daudin hadn't know what to say, except nod and agree.

Then, a few days ago, the commander of Fort Anne an Annapolis Royal had visited Daudin. They had argued, with the Englishman demanding lower prices for agricultural goods, while Daudin had warned that the French settlers could just as easily let the English starve or treat them as unwelcome invaders.

And yesterday a messenger had arrived from the English Governor along with three soldiers. They had in hand orders for his appearance at Chebouctu and before the new Governor, Charles Lawrence. Daudin doubted that this visit to the English Governor would be as congenial as his previous one.

When they arrived the soldiers treated Daudin aggressively and marched him through the palisades gates and directly to the Governor's apartment. When they entered the secretary sniffed and entered the Governor's chambers and returned in a moment. "Enter, the Governor has been waiting."

Lawrence was standing when Daudin entered, a soldier on each side of him.

"I am tempted to throw you in the stockade." Daudin had no idea what Lawrence was saying. One of the soldiers translated.

"Porquoi? I am but a humble priest."

"You humble priests are causing your Acadians far more hardship than we English, acting lawfully under the terms of a treaty. We have every right to dispose of your Acadians as we wish. I warn you now, Monsieur, and formally, that those fomenting rebellion will be treated severely, and your collar offers you no protection from being a party to any rebellious actions, nor any penalty that we might decide to impose under the authority of His Highness. Am I making myself clear?"

The soldier translated: "Perfectly, Governor Lawrence."

"I warn you. I am not Peregrine Hopson. There will be hell to pay. Your Acadians are providing sustenance and comfort to the Indians that burn our villages and scalp our settlers. And we will have no more of it.

"Get out of my presence. Should I see you again, it is most likely that you will be in chains. Leave and tell your hellish, Godforsaken leader Le Loutre to not cause any more trouble for me."

The soldiers each put a hand under Daudin's shoulders, turned him around roughly and marched him through the gates and pushed him forward. "Leave, Papist."

After Daudin left in the company of the soldiers, Lawrence exited to his ante-chamber in which Hinshelwood was seated.

"Archibald. Damnation... Damnation! Those Frenchmen are as treacherous and obstinate as snakes in the grass." He poured a glass of sherry from a decanter on a side table and drank it down.

"Take a letter to the Board of Trade with a copy to Governor Shirley at Province House. I think we will be far better off if those French are away from here."

* * * * *

Pichon left his quarters and took with him the paperwork associated with the latest shipment of stores that had been received from Quebec and strode toward the buried casemates underneath the parapets to do his inventory.

He was of modest height so barely had to lower his head to enter the small stone encased caverns and count the barrels that had been received in the magazine. There was a score of kegs of gunpowder and as many crates of four pound balls and a crate of fuses. There were also ten cases of new muskets all accompanied by bayonets. He checked them off his list and thought it was curious for a shipment of armaments of this size to be shipped to Beauséjour in this current time of peace.

Undoubtedly there would be a conflict; it was impossible for two ancient enemies to have fortresses less than a league apart and not deploy them. But would it be that soon that the munitions would have already arrived?

There were no signs that the English had any intent to change the current stalemate. He wondered if the French had designs to take their lands back? But he knew this was an impossibility. The English were too strong and the Miqmaqs had seemingly even entered a treaty with them. He wondered about this and left to report to the Commandant.

Louis du Pont du Chambon de Vergor had just assumed the job of Commandant as Pichon had learned prior from their mutual patron, l'Intendant Bigot. In a way he was disappointed; there was only so much room for procurements to be... managed, and if this Vergor were a friend of Bigot's then certainly he would also be looking to benefit financially from his new posting which would mean less for Pichon's own purse.

He walked to DuPont's quarters and entered. The Commandant was chatting with his aide de camp. "Monsieur le Commissaire? Comment allez vous? Je suis Chevalier Louis du Pont Duchambon de Vergor." DuPont spoke with a pronounced stutter.

"Very well, very well, Monsieur le Commandant. Je m'appelle Thomas Pichon. May we talk for a moment.?"

"Of course, Monsieur Pichon, please come into my quarters."

After they entered his quarters Pichon looked closer at his new commander. DuPont's visage was very pale and between his deep-set beady eyes his large nose had a map of red blood vessels revealing one of his pleasures; the strained buttons of his doublet revealed another.

DuPont signalled to Pichon to sit and he went to a sideboard and poured two healthy portions of cognac. He gave one to Pichon and sat behind his desk.

They toasted each other with their libations.

Pichon said, "How is our friend, Monsieur l'Intendant?"

"He speaks well of you, Monsieur Pichon."

"S'il vous plâit, Monsieur, call me Thomas."

"I, then, am Louis to you. Monsieur Bigot continues on with his struggles to finance all of the demands of running our outposts in this lost place. But he is pleasant in his attitude. He requested that I offer you his greetings. Now, what should I know, Thomas, about our conditions here?"

"I see we have received a large shipment of munitions, Monsieur Commandante. This seems unusual. The English and les sauvages seem to be acting like doves this past year or so."

"Those red doves are very ambitious, Thomas. We do not expect that the situation can be sustained. They are moving aggressively toward Canada and we expect they will also move more aggressively in that direction through us here in Beauséjour. We will be receiving another company of Royal soldiers in the near future to make our garrison more muscular."

"Where will we put them all?"

"Some will go to the fortress at Gaspereaux at Baie Verte, we will increase our garrison at the redoubt at Pont à Buot and we are going to establish an encampment near Pedditkoudiac. This will allow us to have a nearby reserve as well as a place to fall back if we need to."

"Very intelligent, Monsieur le Commandant."

"Thank you, Thomas. It also provides us the flexibility of, perhaps, pre-empting their aggression with out own. Do you have the inventory document? I will send it on to the necessary channels."

Pichon stood, removed the document from an inner pocket and unfolded it. du Pont took a pen and signed it without looking. He passed the pen to Pichon who did the same. Pichon returned it to the Commandant. du Pont said, "Good day to you, Thomas."

"And you, Louis."

After Pichon left the new camp commander, he took a turn to the right and hurried toward the gates; this news could not wait. He passed through the sentries nodding at them as be walked by and strode as quickly as he could along the draw bridge and toward the Pont à Buot.

As he made his way bypassing the Acadian village he saw that he was on a collision course with an equally stout figure; the Abbé that he always thought of as Moses. He had come to privately refer to Abbé Le Loutre as the great Hebrew leader because he seemed to have an equal level of control over his Acadians.

He maintained his pace and in a remarkably short time the two men came almost nose to nose.

"What do you hear from the Commandant, Pichon? What secrets is he keeping from me?"

"Abbé, with respect, the affairs of the state are not the business of the church."

"Pichon, we are French not English, and there is no distinction; the affairs of the state are the affairs of the church. We are not les maudits, bless God. After all, your King was chosen by God and owes all his power and all your finances to

Him."

"Ah, Abbé Le Loutre, I must say that I have become fond of your ability to avoid social niceties and be direct."

Le Loutre looked back sceptically unsure if he was being complimented or insulted.

Pichon smiled in his toad-like manner, "No, seriously, Monsieur, I am very impressed that you always get to the point and don't waste breath with jibber jabber."

"Well, then? What is that lazy Commandant doing? What does he have planned to help our settlers here get their crops and get our aboiteaux built? Hien?"

"Monsieur Abbé, the Commandant has told me that the state of your Acadians is among his highest priorities. If he has information that he wishes to share with you, I have no doubt, whatsoever, that he will. You should ask him yourself."

"I will do that." The priest quickly turned and walked toward the fortress.

Pichon watched the priest huff away and believed he was late for his liaison so he picked up his pace. He definitely did not wish to be late. After about a half hour he arrived at his destination, regretting that he had not appropriated a horse from the stables to assist him in his journey. He would be tired and uncomfortably hot by the time he returned to his quarters. He suspected he would also be a little bit affected by a quantity of rum or brandy he was about to consume and the return trip back and up the hill would be very difficult indeed.

He arrived at the eating place. The usual merchants were outside and he ignored their entreaties to purchase beaver skins and other apparel items and entered. His friend Captain Scott was in his customary corner table. While the place was buzzing with conversations between all combinations of English and French soldiers and civilians, it was not as raucous as usual so the two men offered their greetings quietly. The maiden server brought over a mug of hot buttered rum and Pichon immediately took a healthy swig.

"So, Mr. Tyrell, what greetings do you bring for me from Beauséjour today?"

"Well, we have been provisioned for the winter, so while our civilians might starve, we will not." He leaned forward and whispered, "We have received an enormous supply of muskets and field pieces and ammunition."

"Really? How strange. Never thought we'd ever get down to needing much of these any more. The peace has been quite pleasant. We're settling Germans, of all sorts, on the old Acadian farmlands. Quite unpleasant people, them. Rude and short tempered."

Pichon said, "We have a new commandant. Very tiring sort, unpleasant and from his appearance not very capable. It seems there may be some orders coming from Quebec."

"Hm? What might they be."

"I think Moses the priest might wish to relocate his entire flock to new fields. And if he did that, it would quite certainly end any of the financial benefits you get from your lands here. You would need to bring in many more Germans than might wish to leave Germany."

"We continue to have Indian attacks on some of our settlements, some quite brutal."

"That would be of Moses' cause, I expect. But I think it goes beyond that. We're growing our garrisons from here to Baie Verte, I think the fools who govern us might be planning to take Acadia back."

Scott showed his surprise and took a draught of his rum. "Do you have something for me?"

Pichon passed him a folded note under the table and Scott surreptitiously secured it in his boot. Then he reached into a pocket of his redcoat and pulled out a deck of cards and they began to play a game of piquet.

* * * * *

Back at Fort Lawrence George Scott examined the note from Pichon; it reported his friend's revelations on French military expansion in Fort Beauséjour written in his hand on the margin of actual correspondence of the commandant, du Pont, intended for the Governor of New France in Quebec.

It described how many of the Acadiens had been fomenting rebellion against French command and planned to return to their old farmlands. They would seek protection from the English rather than the French garrison in Beauséjour north of the River Mésagouèche. How some had even already left the new settlements.

It also revealed that the French army should be prepared not only to defend their own lands north of the river, but to be prepared to march back into Acadia if and when an English assault on Fort Beauséjour failed.

This was shocking.

The English had never considered the possibility of such events. Cornwallis had clearly informed the Acadian deputies that they would not be allowed to return to their farms without accepting the obligation to defend the land against aggression from their own countrymen. And the French army, without a convenient supply line to a main base of operations, had never been considered a threat to actually try and recover their former land.

He called to his adjutant. "Morse, come in here."

Morse appeared.

"Take this message with all speed to the Governor in Chebouctu. Take two men with you and avoid any hostiles."

"Aye, Captain."

* * * * *

John Winslow was huffing and puffing as he made his way through the narrow streets of Boston and up the hill to Province House, and then up the steep circular staircase past the floor of traders in the lower floors. After almost two years back in civilization he was anxious to again get away from his pleasingly plump but shrewish wife and leave it all behind.

He had managed to avoid the exotic diseases of the

Caribbean when he had been there and had ignored the savage women in Nova Scotia when he had been posted in that primitive place. But the risks he had faced in Dominica and Annapolis Royal were much less frightening and more pleasant than being again ensconced here in the Massachusetts Colony. Between the boredom of trying to achieve legislative victories and finding ways of hiding from the eternal demands of his wife, it was unbearable.

He shuddered.

Even his time in the northern part of the province, near the border of the wild country where the Massachusetts Colony met the northern ones, even all the clouds of mosquitoes and teeming black flies, were preferred to being here among the slovenly whores, the bickering burghers and beggars of Boston.

He finally made it to the Governor's floor, totally out of breath, and took a moment to compose himself. Governor Shirley's attaché, seated at a desk and sorting papers, nodded to Winslow and toward a richly brocaded settee. Winslow nodded back and took advantage of the invitation for a respite. The aide brought over a pitcher of water and a glass on a tray and placed it on the side table.

Winslow took a healthy draught and was pleasantly surprised that it was well flavoured of gin.

"Welcome back, Major General, I hope that your trek up our mountain has not depleted you totally of energy."

"No, thank you," he raised his glass in salute, "this has made up for my travails, Ensign. Will the Governor be soon available?"

"Very shortly, Milord. Finish your glass of water. Have another if you wish. His agenda is reserved for you."

"You are very kind, Ensign."

Winslow finished his glass, set it on the tray and stood.

"I'll arouse the Governor, one moment, Major General." The aide opened the door, entered and closed it behind him.

Winslow straightened out his clothes and brushed back his hair with both hands and waited for only a moment before the ensign returned. "Major General, the Governor is ready to see you."

Governor Shirley was standing and came forward when Winslow entered his private office.

"John, tired of all the peace are ye? Come in, come in.

"Please, have a seat.

"Will ye have a cognac?"

"Of course, William. I looked over the bay before I came inside and the sun is starting to peek over the yardarm, I noticed."

The Governor poured a healthy portion and refilled his own crystal snifter and passed one to Winslow. He sat in a chair adjoining Winslow's indicating the expected informality of their meeting.

"How can I serve you today, John."

Winslow sipped. "Well, William, your know Mary is getting less comely as she ages and the boys are requesting less of my time as they conduct their schooling. And, Governor, I'm bored."

"Ready to get back into the fray, are ye, John?"

"I wish to get out of this fray, William."

"Consider it done. What do you have in mind."

"Where the action is expected to be the most interesting, I expect."

"Well we have something. Back in your old haunts."

"Dominica?"

"No. Nova Scotia!"

"Of course."

"I needn't tell you why, but we've decided to clear the place of the French. Not only have they established themselves, in a manner, in the northerly part of our colony there, but they seem to be spreading out. Led, of course, by their bastard of a priest. They're close to finishing construction of one of their cathedrals, and are breeding like mice in a barn. We wish to end their encroachment and we need good men to do it. Interested?"

"I'd swear off gin, William."

"Well, we certainly won't ask you to do that. We'll ask Monckton to join you in mustering a force. Put together a plan and bring it to me and I'll see that it's done. You should be banging the drums in a two weeks."

The Governor offered a toast and they clinked glasses and finished their brandies.

* * * * *

The Abbé was examining progress at his church.

The first thing he had done was to have some of the men dig a well so he would have water he could bless for masses. He had wished he could have built a church of stone, but that had been impossible, so he had used wood from the local oak, elm and maple trees which was almost as solid a building material as granite once it was seasoned. He had tried as best as he could to reproduce the cathedral he had seen in Quebec, but given the limitations of both workers and time he had made it half scale. But he had designed a steeple high enough to be seen for miles and large enough to house the bell he had rescued from the church in Beaubassin before it had burned.

He had noticed the extra shipments of armaments arriving at the fort as well as the arrival of dozens of marines from Quebec. It was obvious to him that the Governor in Quebec, Duquesne, either had knowledge of events that would escalate the conflict here in Beauséjour or had plans for the French marines to do so themselves.

In either case, this would create insurmountable problems in his plans to grow the settlements north of the Mésagouèche. He thought it might also encourage his Acadians to flee back to their old lands in what the English now called Nova Scotia. This was not acceptable. Such a military action could only cause destruction and harm, it would be a stupid decision, would clearly violate the unconfirmed peace and encourage the English to attack his new settlements.

He turned his direction toward the fort and marched quickly through the main gates and up to the commandant's apartments. He entered without knocking. DuPont was wigless and coatless and chatting with his secretary, Deschamps. He turned around when the door opened. Le Loutre was pleased to see him without his trappings of authority; he would feel less powerful.

"DuPont, tell me what you are doing to protect our settlement here. What difficulties will you cause me?"

DuPont despised Le Loutre, not only for his presence and his arrogance, but for his very name; it was impossible for him to say with his impediment and he always started out at a disadvantage and with a feeling of inferiority. And the harder he tried, the worse it came out. He stuttered his greeting: "Bonjour, Abbé L… L…Le Loutre. I cause you no difficulties."

"But neither do you offer me assistance. I have insufficient food to feed my parish and you seem to be wasting money on preparing for war." Le Loutre didn't know that DuPont had been in receipt of substantial amounts of food that he had sold to the English.

"Well, Abbé, what might you request f…from your k…king?"

"We need to build new settlements on this side of the river to accommodate the king's people here and we need to provide them protection. That is what God demands."

"How many new settlements, Abbé?"

"I will expand the small settlement in Chipoudie and establish others in Gediac and Memramcook. We'll also need to dyke and build aboiteaux."

"This is impossible, Abbé. I simply do not have the manpower to even think of this, given that we have this fortress to build and this settlement to protect."

"Then, Monsieur Le Commandant. You will pay a different price, beyond the cost of providing safety to God's people. Good day. We will talk again."

19 - DIX-NEUF

The drums were beating along the streets of Boston while John Winslow sat in the offices of Charles Apthorp waiting to arrange for the logistics of transporting and provisioning his expedition to Beauséjour. The offices of Apthorp and his partner Thomas Hancock were less than a minute's walk from Province House.

Apthorp bustled into his office. He was a bit untidy and his clothing a bit worn, though the opulence of the finishings of the offices suggested significant wealth.

"Hello, John. Thank you for coming. I have the papers; just retrieved from my solicitors."

The two men shook hands.

"Now, the Governor has authorized a substantial amount for this expedition, the letters of procurement are complete and authorized by the Governor, the warranty from the Board of Trade executed and I have in hand a promissory note to my benefit. What shall you require? I'm sorry. Brandy?"

"Yes."

Apthorp poured two snifters, gave one to Winslow and sat.

"So we have three frigates, John, The Success, The Mermaid and The Syren to carry you and your officers, and another thirty odd transports to carry your men and material. The crew of these transports know their way well, as they have been buying on our behalf much of the Crapaud's agriculture over the years.

"Much of what you need is in local stores, though I'm afraid to say we have a severe shortage of musketry, but the order has been placed in London."

"What about outfitting the recruits?"

"Here is a letter of credit for you to outfit your recruits with their basic needs."

"Then that is it?"

"Seems so."

"Well thank you, Charles."

"I must admit, these conflagrations are painful for many, but very rewarding to others."

Winslow left the offices on Merchant Row and followed a large assortment of brigands, ne'er do wells, ruffians and pious looking churchmen to the Common grounds where the battalion would be formed. The beating of the drums had filled the streets with the desperate, the mercenary and the curious and they were all walking swiftly to make sure and not miss any of the excitement.

By the time Winslow arrived the Commons was packed with people, perhaps as many as two thousand. He pushed his way through the throngs with the assistance of a small group of soldiers to a huge stump fully five feet across and five feet off the ground. He climbed up a set of steps, and joined John Jenkins, the town crier. Winslow retrieved his spectacles and removed a document from an inner pocket. He confirmed its contents and handed it to Jenkins.

Jenkins began ringing his bell to summon the attention of the crowd and they began to surround the speaker's stump: "Oyez, Oyez. Now Hear Ye!

"In the name of His Royal Majesty King George, may God continue to bless him with health and good spirits. I speak for Major General John Winslow who is here present. To wit:

"On orders of the King, I am to recruit a regiment or more of able fighting men to participate in a mission to stop the encroachment of French squatters on the King's land in our possession of Nova Scotia.

"I am allowed to offer remuneration to each enlisted man the sum of ten pounds in old legal tender for an enlistment of one year, with two pounds at the time of enlistment, then the remainder when mustered. Each enlisted man will be allowed a camp kettle, a bowl and platter, a spoon, a blanket, a knapsack and a bandolier. Each will be provided with the King's arms, as appropriate and other accoutrements. And boots.

"All recruits will be commanded to behave very orderly on the Sabbath Day, and either stay on board their transports, or else go to church, and are not permitted to stroll up and down the streets.

"Those who wish to enlist here and now should line up here, the rest disperse.

"Affirmed on this day, 13 March in the year of the Lord, one thousand seven hundred and fifty-five at eleven of the clock, forenoon."

Winslow took the speaking notes from Jenkins, returned his spectacles to his inside pocket and dismounted the stump, the soldiers making room for him. A burly sergeant arrived with several officers and some additional regulars to set up tables and begin the task of signing up the Nova Scotia expeditionary force.

Near the front of the crowd was a carpenter from Newbury who had heard of the desire to recruit men. He was descended from sailing men, but was tenth eldest in a family of eleven and with little left for him by way of inheritance he had become a bit of an adventurer and made small amounts from doing itinerant woodworking. He was a single man and still had the wanderlust of his ancestors and had signed up for previous expeditions with Winslow against the Abenakis at the edge of the Massachusetts province. He was close to first in line.

"Adams, Nathan, Maybury."

The sergeant looked at him, "Think I've seen you before."

"Kennebec, Sergeant."

"Indeed. Bit calmer here than there. In this rabble ye'll be a Captain, I suspect." He passed over the recruitment book and Adams signed where indicated. "See the paymaster at the end."

"Yes, Sergeant."

* * * * *

Several weeks later the proprietor of the *Bunch of Grapes Tavern* welcomed the four men all but one in uniform, to his establishment with his usual bonhomie. "Come, come, have a seat, fellows, and enjoy our victuals and libations." He signalled to his serving wench to bring over mugs of foaming ale.

Winslow had taken a room at the tavern to avoid the irritation of the half day trip to Marshfield, as well as avoid the demands of the homestead. The public house was adjacent to the Long Wharf and a convenient carriage ride to his regiment's encampment at the common grounds.

Shirley said, "Thank you, Mr. Waite."

"We are honoured to have your company, Governor Shirley."

"I think we'll all have the venison stew."

"With alma pudding?"

"Yes. We'd be much obliged."

The ales arrived and the men, including Winslow, Colonel Monckton, and Charles Apthorp, all toasted the King, England and St. George.

Monckton led off the discussion. "So what exactly is the problem, John."

"Short of not having any muskets. The men have been sitting and training for almost a month and have likely already spent their two pounds on frivolity. It was good that we had the extra weeks in training, however; they are all ruffians and most couldn't bayonet a pumpkin.

"Charles, what about the muskets."

Apthorp, as always, smiled like a serpent. "Oh, they'll be here soon. The Snow is expected daily, the weather has held it up."

Monckton replied in his usual superior manner, "I expect

they have been audited properly and we won't have any musketry missing and have our boys go into battle with sticks."

"Certainly not. Mr. Hancock was there to oversee the loading and the count. They're to be here."

Monckton said, "I hope so, Mr. Apthorp. We are billeting over two thousand men, they are getting restless and the cost of keeping them provisioned is outrageous! I tell you now, Charles, the tides are proper on coming Thursday and we will leave then or deduct the cost of our keeping our host here in Boston from our payment to you."

Apthorp with an expectation for such a delay had already priced such an increase in. "Of course, Robert, as always we will make good on our contractual obligations."

The dinner came and was delicious and was served with an excellent claret and followed by port. The men smoked pipes and left to remove to Deer Island; Pastor Philips was preaching and it was good, prior to an expedition like this one, to ask for strength and dispensations for future acts.

* * * * *

Winslow rose before the break of day; there was a slight chill in the air as he dressed, walked downstairs and signed off on his account with Waite, the tavern owner. His baggage had been aboard "The Industry" since the last favourable tide almost a month before and he had made arrangements for his kit that he had kept with him to be sent home to Marshfield. He had written a note to his wife to excuse his not returning prior to the expedition departure.

The regiment had been billeted aboard ship for two weeks awaiting the muskets and several men had died from illness or mishap and the tension and delays had resulted in a number of cases of insubordination and disagreements that had been settled physically. There were a dozen or so men that had to be released from the brig for the voyage.

The wind was freshening as he began the walk down the

Long Wharf as the sun was just leaving the horizon to being what would most likely be a pleasant day to sail.

"Winslow!"

He turned his attention toward the call, it was John Thomas, the surgeon. They both maintained their residences in Marshfield, about ten leagues south of Boston.

"Hello, Thomas."

"Might I walk with you?"

"Of course."

"We're on the same sloop, Jacob Goodwin's "Industry", I understand."

Winslow was in no mood for idle conversation so just grunted in agreement.

The two men made the remainder of the walk in silence. They came to the gangway to the tenders; Winslow noticed that much of the flotilla appeared ready to weigh anchor.

In a few minutes they were rowed to their transport, "Permission to come aboard, Master?"

"Granted. Honoured to have you travel with us, Major General."

"Hope it won't be for long, Jacob."

"Should be a reasonably efficient trip. Southwest wind, quite favourable. Your luggages are secured in your stateroom."

"Thank you, Master. You may weigh anchor."

Goodwin said, "Very well," and left to execute his duties.

Winslow noticed the flotilla of more than two dozen transports had already weighed anchor and were raising their sails and that his ship's master was so instructing his crew.

* * * * *

After nine days of erratic travel, the expeditionary force was nearing its destination with dusk approaching. Winslow retired to his small stateroom to catalogue the day's progress, carefully read the dispatches from the fleet commander John Rous and write his missives for distribution to the other staff officers in each of the ships. Rous had ordered the fleet to weigh anchor at dusk. Winslow studied the charts and tide reports and a final trip of ten leagues and making landfall in the late afternoon made eminent sense. The tide would be high which would allow the whale boats to unload their cargo conveniently in the rivers on either side of Fort Lawrence and avoid the disaster that had occurred on the mud flats three years prior.

Winslow folded and sealed his instructions to each of the other command ships, gave them to an aide for delivery and prepared to sleep.

* * * * *

DuPont was angered that someone roused him from his bed in the middle of the night especially since he was lying next to the wife of one of his servants. She was older, squat and had a slight moustache, but for some reason he was drawn to her comforts.

"How dare you!"

Then he recognized it was Brossard, who was a man to be taken seriously so he toned down his anger. There was another man with him, strong looking and handsome but missing half of one ear. "Monsieur Brossard."

"Commandant, I thought you might wish to be informed that les maudits have just entered the bay. I don't expect they would come under the cover of darkness if it is just to provide a show of strength."

"Of course. Get me Pichon and allow me to get dressed. And de Fiedmont."

Beausoleil and the man left. Two others entered, just as DuPont had dressed. It was the commissary and the grenadier soon followed by the two Acadians. Pichon was still in his sleeping clothes while de Fiedmont was properly uniformed.

"You have heard the news?" DuPont had applied his wig but it was a little off centre and showed too much forehead.

"Oui." Pichon spoke. "We knew this day would come, that is

why we have formed the militia and strengthened our defenses."

"What shall we do, Lieutenant? You are our engineer."

"Ahh, Commandant, I am actually just a plain grenadier, but I understand some skills of engineering."

"Well, what shall we do."

"I think we are only prepared to surrender and not cost lives needlessly."

"How can you say that?"

"Well, Monsieur le Commandant, I have witnessed that very little of what has been received here to strengthen the fortress has actually been spent strengthening the fortress. And now, we have at most, assuming that les Anglais dally with the maidens or enjoy the warm beaches, is one day."

"What can be done?"

"Not much, Monsieur le Commandant. We might empty our bomb-proofs of everything so we can use them as shelters. We might get some diggers putting more soil on the roofs of the bomb-proofs. We might strengthen our complement at the Pont à Buot and establish some breastworks strategically to try and delay their moving their field pieces within effective range. And if we pray very loudly we might have enough time to be reinforced by a company or more from Louisbourg."

"Then that is what we will do. Thomas, will you send the missive to Ile Royale, make it sound urgent. And Lieutenant, will you immediately start the reinforcements.

"And, Monsieur Brossard, will you muster all the Acadian men to come inside the fort and prepare to defend against les maudits."

"I will, Monsieur le Commandant."

The four men nodded and left; none with any confidence that their efforts could be successful.

* * * * *

Acquila left DuPont's apartment with Brossard. The older man was walking quickly and talking rapidly. "We must see l'Abbé immediately, we will need him to bring our people inside. Many will resist."

They left the fort through the front gate and walked quickly down the hill toward the church and the adjacent rectory. Given the time, they expected that Le Loutre would be asleep and they were correct. Brossard knocked and they entered.

Le Loutre and Pére Le Guerne shared the main room in the modest rectory. Brossard spoke quietly, "Mon Père. Levez-vous, s'il vous plait." The Abbé stirred.

"Quoi? Ou est vous? Qui est-ce?"

"It is Beausoleil, l'Abbé Le Loutre. There is urgent news."

"Quoi?"

"Les Anglais are landing their men at the other Fort built on the old settlement. Perhaps one thousand or more."

"Mon Dieu! We must get ready. Is that you? Girouard?"

"Oui."

"Rally your men. Have them bring whatever arms they have to the Fort. The families… The families should also be brought to safety. Bring them to the church."

"Go now, Monsieur Girouard."

The men left and Beausoleil said, "Acquila, wait."

"Acquila, we will lose this fort. We need to prepare for this. I am requesting the militia and any other men to come north to the small settlements. When the fortress is lost I will come and visit the English and offer to assist them in order to give us time."

"I will join you when my family is safe."

"Bien. Go to your family."

Acquila ran down the hill to his own house. Mati was still awake after being disturbed by Brossard's collection of her husband. "Mati, ma Chér, we must gather the children and go to the church."

"Why?"

"The English are preparing to attack from across the river."

Her jaw dropped, remembering the stories of her grandmother and the lobster coats. "Oh…. No… Mon Dieu." She looked toward heaven and whispered, "Save us."

She immediately went upstairs and awoke the children. The two eldest boys were now large enough to help the men, while Béatrice could cook almost as well as Mati. Little Louis-Thomas, was still gaining confidence in his walking and would stay with her. "Vites, vites, mes enfants. Get dressed. Hurry!"

The children could sense the panic in her voice and responded quickly.

She went back downstairs. "Quila. What about the treasure?"

"It will be more important than ever. Now. What can I carry it in? Get it."

Mati went down into the cold room and came up with the leather bag and gave it to Acquila. He rustled through it. "Here are eight coins. Put them in your shoes. I will hide the rest."

"Go now, ma Chér. I must tell the other families." They embraced. The children had come downstairs.

"Quila, take the oldest boys with you. They can help. I will take Béatrice and Louis-Thomas."

"Yes."

Acquila and Mati embraced again. He said, "I will see you soon, ma Chér."

"I will be waiting."

He called to the boys, "Garcons! Viens avec moi. Allons y." They joined him. He ran next door to Simon's house and banged on the door. Emile, you and Maurice, go waken the other families. Tell them the Abbé has instructed them to go to the church. The men are to go to the fort and take their weapons if they have any. Understand?"

"Oui, Papa."

Acquila had the treasure to worry about. He could not put it where anyone could ever find it. But would need to be able to get it if the worst happened. He thought for a moment. The well; the Abbé's holy well. It was too far from the village or fort to be used for any other purpose. Almost no one knew it even existed.

He ran to the Bourque house. Simon came to the door.

"Acquila Girouard? Why are you awakening me in the

middle of the night."

"You're lazy. The English have come and are preparing to attack our settlement. The Abbé has ordered men to the fort and families to the church."

"You think the English would burn down the church?"

"Chér Dieu. I would hope not. They could not be that evil."

"I pray not."

Simon called inside, "Philomene, dress the children. Go to the church. The English are attacking us."

"Simon, help my boys wake the other families. Tell the men to go to the fort and bring their weapons. I will see you there."

"Yes, my friend. May God above save us."

Acquila turned away and started running quickly to the far side of the Butte. It was dark and he didn't know this area of the settlement very well. He had only been there to help dig the well itself. He wandered around looking for landmarks and he found the path that the workers had used when digging. In a minute he was there.

He picked up a stone and dropped it in the well and he heard a splash in less than a second. The water table here was very high and they had only needed to dig less than ten feet to hit water. The well was reinforced with stone three feet above the ground, had a roof with a windlass and a strong rope with a bucket. He dropped the leather bag into the well, said a brief prayer, and returned to the settlement to continue to rouse the families.

20 – VINGT

Winslow awoke to the sounds of a large naval fleet preparing for action: the loud commands of the masters' mates shouting out orders to prepare the rigging for the "Industry" and slightly more distant commands from the other warships in the flotilla, the rapid movement of many men, and the lifting and dropping of heavy objects. He dressed quickly, feeling slightly guilty for being tardy, knowing that Monckton would notice and criticize him. Winslow despised the younger man who Shirley had placed in command of the entire expedition.

He left his stateroom and exited to the main deck and surveyed the preparations. His own men were taking their mess and his sub-alterns, Bradford, Gay and John Thomas were also so engaged. On his way to join them he came across a familiar face, "Adams?"

"Yes, Lieutenant Colonel. Nathan. From Maybury."

"You were with me at Kennebec."

"Yer, Sor."

"I recall you're a scrapper, Adams. Good to have you with us."

"Thank ye, Major General."

"Well, to your duties, Adams."

"Yes, Sor. I have a missive for you, Sor." He handed Winslow a folded and sealed note who opened it. The command came from John Rous on the "Success" to weigh anchor and Winslow went to eat while the sales captured the wind and they made their way to Chignectou.

After Winslow was finished eating a boiled salt pork, potato and cabbage stew the sun began to set and the flotilla arrived in the bay offshore of Fort Lawrence. The ships dropped anchor and began unloading men and material to the whale boats.

Winslow was on the first whale boat to hit the shore and immediately took temporary command, directing the companies as they landed to form into rows and ranks. Eventually Winslow's rival, Robert Monckton, arrived.

"Brisk voyage, Robert."

"Yes, Winslow. Where will you stay? In the officers' quarters?"

Winslow was about to lie when Sylvanus Cobb arrived. Winslow had previously arranged to stay on his farm. The last thing he wished was to be in Monckton's company any more than the impending conflict would require.

"Gentlemen, you will stay at my farm, of course."

Monckton said, "Very kind, Syl, very kind. We'll put our men abed and be over. You still have claret, I hope."

"About three hundred gallons!"

Monckton said, "Well then, we will give our orders quickly and loud and clear." Winslow tried hard not to grimace.

It took several hours to off load the men and get them counted. It was dark when the men were released to look for places in the fort to spend the night. They stayed in barns, stables and under any roof they could find, and many drank rum to warm them through the cool night. Some read their Bible by candlelight. Some didn't sleep.

* * * * *

Mati was sitting on a pew in the new church with Louis-Thomas on her lap talking with Huguette and Philomene about their situation. All the effort of three years to build it and the bell had not even been installed in the steeple. Béatrice was beside her listening intently.

"We can't stay here, Huguette. The lobster coats cannot be trusted. They have burned families in churches before!"

"But Abbé Le Loutre has promised us sanctuary, Mathilde."

"His promises are shallow and only are used to control and manipulate us. We must look to our own men and ourselves for our safety."

"So what will you do?"

"I will get my husband and my children and I will hide in the forests like my grandparents did when the English came before and killed the grandfather of my mother."

"What should we do?"

"Philomene, you will need to make your own decision. But I'm leaving. Will you look after Louis-Thomas et Béatrice while I find Acquila?"

"Of course. If you see my Simon, will you tell him that I worry for him?"

"Yes."

Mathilde kissed Louis-Thomas and Béatrice and gave Huguette and Philomene quick embraces and left. The church was only a few hundred yards from the fort and she could hear the work going on inside. There was just a hint of a sunrise from her left. She hurried past many men feverishly digging several trenches many yards in front of the fort entrance. She could tell it was hard work as the ground just under the sod was still partly frozen in the spring climate.

She had to wait in line behind other settlers but after a few minutes walked through the palisades and over the first bridge to the gate, "I am the wife of head of the militia, Commandant Acquila Girouard. I have an urgent message for him."

The guard blocked her way. "Give me the message, we are not allowing civilian women inside until the fortifications are completed."

"I cannot. He speaks a different dialect than you and he

would not understand. I must tell him directly."

"Go ahead, then."

Mathilde passed the guard and walked down the ramp past the guard houses and into the parade ground. It was filled with people carrying logs, digging into the embankments and stacking sod from the sides on top. She looked around for her husband, but couldn't see him; the only person she recognized was the Abbé who was busy bossing people around. She walked around the outside edge of all the activity and finally found him cutting sod with a dyke spade. Emile and Maurice were pulling the piles of sod in a sledge to its destination.

He saw her, smiled, and finished his sod and tossed it on a pile with the others. He plunged his spade into the soil.

"Chér, what are you doing here?"

"I came to take you away, 'Quila."

"To where?"

"Someplace where there are no English soldiers."

"I think that might be England. Their soldiers all seem to be on their way here. Why? This is our home."

"Acquila, my grandmother told me of the last time the English army arrived. They burned my grandmother's village and killed and scalped my old grandfather. I fear they will do this again."

"We will not let them do that, this time."

"But they are so many."

"Probably not more than us."

"But they have cannons."

"So do we. And we have no option except to defeat them. When we repel them, they will just return to New England. I think you will be safe in the church with the women and children."

"They burned the church in Nanpan."

"That was a long time ago, Chér."

"What if we lose?"

"Then things will be as they are now. No worse. Les maudits want us to stay and farm. They just want our army to leave."

"If any of you fire a musket at them, Acquila, they will treat you and everyone else as traitors, not just enemies."

"That's not a worry. Beausoleil has arranged for us to be given a letter that we are under threat of death if we do not assist in the defense of the fort."

"Acquila, Beausoleil and that priest have taken my husband away from me."

"No they haven't, Chér. I am doing what your older grand pére would have done. Fight back."

"What if you die?"

"I won't die. I'm too smart for them."

"But I may not be, Acquila. We will not be safe in the church, and I will not take any chances with our children. Where can we go that is safe?"

"I have heard that there are some families at La Coupe further north a league or two. Otherwise, Beausoleil is working to build more settlements north of here. I think many other families are going there for safety. Would you go there?"

"If we go there we will not have you to protect us. And les maudits will probably go to all the villages."

"Then you will need to stay with me in the fort. I will protect you."

"That's what we will do, then."

* * * * *

Nathan Adams suddenly awoke to the rude pounding of drums. He was bivouacked along with a score of other men in a barn outside of the palisades of Fort Lawrence. It had been a cold night but the hijinks of young men, rum and bad singing had made it bearable.

The sun was just rising as he hurriedly pulled on his breeches, tunic and coat and donned his tricorn.

He and the other older men all kicked at a few of the young bucks who were deep sleepers.

"Hie, there shall be no rest for the lazy on this day, soldiers. Get your bat and clobber and get to parade! Now! Outta yer kip! Get on yer smalls!" shouted a sergeant to no one in particular.

Adams was the first to leave the barn, which was a good thing because the first thing he saw outside was John Winslow. "Adams. You're up early. Good. Ye're a Captain and this morning you'll lead the vanguard. Be sharp and ready."

"Yes, Major General."

The sergeants were following around the drummers and shaking men out of their sleep and drunken stupors. As the sun was fully in the sky and temperature began rising, so did the expeditionary force. Men were frantically cleaning up their mess, pulling on breeches, counting their cartridges, pulling on boots.

"Officers to the front! Single columns, ranks of three. Now! Hie to it! Faster! Move! "

It took almost an hour to get all two thousand men in a column and ready to march.

Finally they were in three columns, each in a rank of three, Monckton's regulars were in the front, Winslow's First Battalion of Provincial militia behind and George Scott's Second in the rear. Trailing behind were carts with large structures made from long tree trunks that had been awaiting the expedition for weeks.

Monckton said, "Mr. Adams."

"Yes, Lieutenant General."

"Lead the vanguard to the front."

"Yes, Lieutenant General."

"Mr. Adams, follow the top of the ridge to the bridge area."

"Yes, Lieutenant General."

Adams, "Expeditionary Force right.... turn. In ranks of three, March!"

It took almost three hours for the eight hundred men to follow the high ground and get to a point immediately across the river and about five hundred yards away from the Mésagouèche River, the Pont à Buot and French redoubt and blockhouse.

"Expeditionary Force.... Halt!"

Monckton stiffly marched to Adams.

"Captain, Take your vanguard down in three ranks to maximum musket range and draw fire from the enemy. We will follow with our regulars to kill, install the bridge and cross the river. Go now."

Adams gave the command and led his men carefully through the bare trees, some of which still had snow at their base, down the slippery grassy hill. They reorganized their column at about two hundred yards from the French position and right wheeled until they were parallel to their opponent. The ground was soaking wet and many men found their feet getting stuck in the muck.

Adams stood at their centre and ordered the men to stop. He continued on to the end of the column. He looked across the river to his opponents. The French launched undirected fusillades with the musket balls not coming near the New England lines. The New Englanders could hear the loud hoots and hollers of the savages across the river and, with the bridge destroyed, could see some of the Indians splashing across waving their bows and flintlocks shouting and making rude faces.

Adams ordered, "All ranks, open pan."

"Prime and load."

"First two ranks, kneel."

"Third rank, make ready."

The Indians were running toward the New Englanders with blood curdling screams.

"Third rank… fire."

Fifty muskets opened fire at once and tore apart the dozen or so Indians that had approached to within a hundred yards. The few remaining stood and looked confused. They started walking back to the French line and were taken down by the French fusillade.

"First two ranks stand and advance. Third rank to follow."

Within a minute Adams' vanguard was within effective musket range of the French and their balls whistled overhead. Their adversaries were on slightly elevated ground, but they would soon adjust.

"First rank, kneel."

"Second rank, shoulder arms."

"Third rank, prime and load."

"Second rank, Fire."

A deadly fusillade of fifty well maintained Brown Bess muskets fired at once, all identically on plane. A wall of lead five feet high tore apart those French standing and preparing to shoot.

"Second rank, kneel."

"First rank, stand."

"Fire."

"First rank, kneel."

"Third rank, Fire."

The French were badly injured by the steady and unassailable hail of lead sent their way by the British and the Indians and Acadians dropped back leaving only a few dozen French regulars to defend the crossing. But they loaded their swivels with grapeshot and the New Englanders took their first casualties. From behind, Adams could sense movement and he saw a column of over two hundred British regulars led by Monckton starting to cross the field. At the tale end of Monckton's column was a train of carts carrying the portable bridge.

As had Adams before but with more men, Monckton arranged his men in rows of one hundred in each of three lines. They delivered twice the devastation to the French position than had the vanguard. Monckton yelled, "Captain Sturtevant, your cannon, please."

The captain quickly brought up his six pounders on small carriages and they further tore up the French installation until there was little left. There was silence for a few moments and then some explosions and the French breastworks, blockhouse and even the tavern were no more. The French soldiers that had remained were running full speed up the hill on the other side, up the Butte à Roger. They quickly buried their swivel guns to try and keep them out of British hands.

By one of the clock Monckton had his portable wooden bridge crossing the Mésagouèche River and the English were following the route of the French retreat, dealing violently with their adversary's attempts at skirmishing to slow them down.

Winslow followed up with his battalion and relieved Monckton's regulars to begin establishing a base camp for their siege. Monckton and his men crossed back across the river and joined Scott's reserves for the return march to Fort Lawrence. They used the carriages that had brought the cannon to the battlefield to take back the casualties.

Engineers and carts carrying construction tools passed Monckton and Scott's men en route to the new siege camp.

* * * * *

Louis-Thomas Jacau de Fiedmont had had his hands full getting soldiers up in the middle of the night to work on the fortress. He knew exactly what had happened to all the money that had not been spent. But there was nothing he could do about it.

He found his way to the officers' quarters and roused a couple of captains from their beds. He told them, "Les Anglais sont venus ici. Mainténant!" And soon enough they got dressed and made their way to the barracks and he got more men to start the reinforcement of the casemates and bomb-proofs.

As he finally got the men pointed in the right direction and told them what to do, Jean Louis Le Loutre appeared, looking bedraggled and dressed in peasant clothes rather than his cassock. Jacau thought this was unusual as Le Loutre always insisted on being recognized and commanding appropriate respect. Nevertheless the grenadier appreciated having the priest and the dozen hard working men that accompanied him. de Fiedmont was a veteran, not quite an “old moustache”, but experienced. He knew that the fort had no hope of withstanding the siege that the English would bring against it. So any divine support that could be requested would be appreciated.

Then the cannons roared from further down the river; probably by the bridge. de Fiedmont pushed the men harder knowing he only had hours before they would be under bombardment. He saw Acquila working hard as always and hurried over to him.

"Monsieur Girouard, thank you for all the hard work."

"Grenadier de Fiedmont, I do this for you and to protect the church and people, not for the fool who manages the military affairs."

"Thank you for helping me, then. We will need to bring the wives and children into the fort. As much as they might be safe in the church, they will be in direct line of the English artillery and at some point we will need to put fire to the settlement and the church so the English cannot use them against us."

"I understand. I will have them come in."

* * * * *

Louis-Thomas Jacau de Fiedmont took it upon himself to put fire to the settlement. He had helped settle the Acadians four years before, and he would continue to protect them now; but the settlement had to be razed. The English would otherwise use the buildings in their assault on the fort.

He called to a few men he knew to be dependable, "Philippe, Jean-Rene, Henri-Maurice, venir ici. Light torches, we need to put fire to the settlement. Hurry!"

Louis waved the men forward toward a small stack of torches that he had prepared for the overnight reinforcement of the fortress, but had never been used. They each took two and lit one from a bonfire. "Allons-y!"

They rushed over the drawbridge and down the hill toward the village, passing the female settlers, now refugees, on their way to safety in the fort. They came first to the church. The Abbé stood at the front door.

"What are you doing?"

"Pardon, Monsieur Abbé. I am afraid we must raise the church and village before they are used by the English."

"I will not stop you, but I will need help removing the bell. It is not hung yet."

"Rene, Maurice, take men and remove the bell to safety."

The two men followed the abbé into the church. Fortunately the bell was still on a skid and they were able to pull it into a place near the holy well. There was a large area of freshly turned soil that appeared to have been dug and refilled recently which would make the digging easier. Le Loutre brought shovels and followed them and stayed to make sure it was buried properly.

Louis and Philippe set fire to the church and moved on to other homes, kicking in doors in their urgency and lighting whatever was flammable inside. When the two others joined them they soon had the dozen or so other houses fully aflame and returned to the fort.

* * * * *

The two days since the initial assault across the river Winslow's company had been preparing a siege camp on the Butte à Mirande; eight hundred paces from the French fortress and a few hundred from the now smouldering settlement. They had needed to defend themselves against raids from Acadians and Miqmaqs since locating here but had avoided casualties.

John Winslow was surprised to see Sylvanus Cobb's sloop, the Coverley, making its way along the Mésagouèche River toward their position. The tide was high and the wind favourable and the ship was slowly and carefully manoeuvring along the winding river. He wondered how it had managed to navigate past the French fort and suspected it proved how badly prepared were his opponents.

He was relieved because at least his men would stop complaining about being low on cartridges and food. He really needed to see them relieved; they'd been on a state of high alertness for days with little sleep and had to respond to steady sniping from Acadians and Indians. Winslow had sent Ensign Hay to request relief from Monckton and he was hoping that Cobb carried with him orders to prepare to be relieved.

As the ship approached, musket fire erupted from dykes and

the remains of the French village that had been burned the night before. The houses and church were still smoking which served to make the shooters indistinct as targets.

"Adams!"

Nathan Adams responded to Winslow and rushed over.

"Adams, take a company and go and clear out those French muskets."

"Aye, sor."

Adams collected ten of his best men and they skirted the edge of the trees toward the French. In just a few minutes the French attackers were sent scrambling back to their fort.

Once it was clear, Cobb's crew and the men from Winslow's battalion took down carriages and sledges and returned with provisions, cannon and balls and a massive mortar. The mortar balls were so heavy that two men had to sledge each of them up the hill to the new position.

The last sledge brought up two large kegs of rum and a message sealed with wax for Winslow from Colonel Monckton, himself. He opened it gingerly.

He cracked the seal and unfolded the note. It was not from Monckton himself, but from an adjutant. The pompous ass had refused his request for relief; had even stated that if he could not hold his position, that he should retreat to a secure one. Even worse, Monckton had appointed an underling to deliver his orders.

Winslow tore up the note in anger. Monckton expected him to retreat and then, likely in the morning, endeavour to take back the ground he had already secured. The missive also ordered Winslow and all his field officers to meet at the bridge at ten of the clock the next morning with work crews to improve the road.

* * * * *

Commandant du Pont and his cousin, Lieutenant de Vannes, Thomas Pichon, the Abbé and a few other officers met for breakfast at first light as they had every morning for over a week;

in the bombproof casemate farthest from the British lines.

The grounds of Fort Beauséjour were soaked from several days of rain; they were a morass of blood, gore and water filled cannon ball holes. Several of the bastions had been destroyed by English cannon. Only one of the barracks buildings remained standing and the addition of the Acadians to the population had created stress so great that soldiers were volunteering to take on dangerous missions against well defended English positions.

As it was, every square foot of covered space in the fortress was over at least one nervous, hungry and desperate head.

As they were having their tea poured a messenger arrived. Du Pont took it, broke the seal and examined its contents. It was from Commandant de Drucour in Louisbourg, *"Monsieur Commandant du Pont, I regret to inform you..."*

"Damn him to hell."

Le Loutre responded, "What?"

"de Drucour refuses to reinforce us. He says that the English are guarding the passage from Ile Royale and he can not be assured that any support he might send would arrive here. All is lost... We must offer terms."

Le Loutre said, "We will offer them nothing! Rien! We will win this fort for God and King or should be buried in its walls."

Pichon commented, "We are indefensible. We must try to save what we can."

"Monsieur Abbé, you do not have a wife and family who would suffer by losing you. And your Acadians seem to have become much sparser in the last few days. We are too few in men and ammunition to defend this fort.

"Monsieur de Vassan, if you will, please prepare your parchment and ink."

21 – VINGT ET UN

Even in the rain de Fiedmont was pushing the soldiers and hard working Acadians to repair defences, scrounge for food and even launch guerrilla attacks on the British lines when they could. He had noticed the population seemed to have dropped in the last few days and had mentioned this to du Pont who had sent out a small company to explore this. They had brought back over a dozen Acadians who had tried to escape over the northern ridge and the Riviere Au Lac but had gotten stuck in the marsh.

The previous day had seen an escalation of the might of the English bombardment, they obviously had installed a heavy mortar and were lofting huge missiles in from only a few hundred yards.

de Fiedmont knew it was only a matter of time. He hoped he'd at least be able to rescue the Acadians. Thankfully du Pont had already given Brossard a letter that the settlers had been forced to defend the fort or face death.

Then de Fiedmont heard and felt it coming; the bellow of cannon and the upset to the air. de Fiedmont, as an artilleryman, had always been told that you never heard the cannon ball coming with your name on it. But he heard this one. He looked for cover and leapt into a ditch and covered his head. When the cannon ball landed, barely twenty feet away, he felt the earth shake. The debris of earth and stone and timbers went a hundred feet in the air and came down in a shower. A piece of timber three feet long and a foot across bounced off the back of his head and he was stunned for several moments.

When he recovered he noticed the rain had stopped and the air was perfectly still. He shook his head and ran into the rubble. The huge cannon ball had landed flush on the bombproof casemate and collapsed its roof.

Others also came running, he noticed Le Loutre and du Pont, themselves, and a dozen others, running from their own shelter. They began pulling at timbers, moving rocks and pulling on arms and legs to extricate bodies.

They pulled out bodies until they determined if they were lifeless or not and then moved on to another. When they were finished there were two alive and four dead; all unidentifiable. Finally they identified the casualties; only one of them was a French soldier and de Fiedmont crossed himself in thanks. An English prisoner was one casualty, who was no loss, and the other dead men were of no account. Two other soldiers survived.

Le Loutre took command; shouting over du Pont. "We must not give up. We must rebuild our redoubts. I will be buried in this ground before I will surrender to les maudits!"

du Pont responded, "Lieutenant de Vannes, bring me your letter of terms suitable for us to surrender the fort and raise a flag of truce."

Le Loutre began to protest, but du Pont interrupted him. "Monsieur l'Abbé. This is a temporal decision, not a spiritual one. We have lost this ground."

* * * * *

Robert Monckton quickly reviewed the offer of terms from the Beauséjour commander, given to him by a French messenger under a white flag. He wadded it into a ball, and threw it on the wet ground of his command tent at the siege camp. "This popinjay believes HE can dictate terms to ME! I'm tempted to raise the bloody red flag and cry havoc and KILL THEM ALL!"

"You go back, ensign, and inform your commander that I will dictate terms of surrender; not he. Inform your commander that we will enter the fort at seven of the clock and present him our terms. If he chooses not to accept we English as victors of this campaign, then inform your commander that we will reload our batteries and we will turn he and his men and his fort into powder. So begone and give your commander this."

He quickly wrote and then handed the messenger a folded document.

The messenger saluted properly, turned and left.

Monckton turned to Scott: "Captain Scott, we regulars will march into the fort this evening at seven of the clock, fully armed in battle array. You and Winslow should build your encampments outside of the gates."

* * * * *

Abbé Jean-Louis LeLoutre had watched the disaster unfold from the safety of one of the remaining bomb-proof casemates. His entire past and future were rooted in saving this land for his king and god, but everything was coming apart before his eyes. He had survived almost two decades of turmoil in his Acadia and had expended every last bit of his energy. He was as ragged as his torn and dirty cassock and he could see no way to avoid the ultimate humiliation of being put in chains by the God be damned English.

He had few belongings and little gold; probably not even enough to afford a fare aboard a commercial vessel, if any ships were planning to return to France. As of only a few hours ago, he no longer had the leverage to demand to be taken to safety as one of the most powerful men in New France. He was definitely not safe here at Fort Beauséjour. He had to leave. The English would not respect his position and would surely hold him as an agent provocateur.

Fortunately he had been able to bury the gold that had been

sent from Paris to build the new settlements well hidden under the church bell to try and keep it from being found. He doubted he'd ever be back to reclaim either.

He could try and get transport from Baie Verte, but he expected the English would soon re-deploy their forces from Beauséjour to there. And if there was no transport from there, he would be caught and hung for sure.

His option was to go to Charles Bois-Hébert for protection at Fort Menagoueche, a much longer overland trip, but one that would be much sooner out of eye sight of les maudits. Then he could move on to Quebec and, he hoped, be welcomed by the Bishop. But he decided to accept the risk and began his trip to Baie Verte, if God looked down on him, there would be a boat that could allow him to go somewhere else.

He carefully avoided drawing attention from any of the Acadians and scouted around until he found a ragged shawl, a bonnet and a length of stick that could serve to disguise him. He picked up a canvas bag of his important papers and worked his way carefully out of the fortress, bending over and walking as if he were an ancient. He passed the English camp that was already being reinforced with more men. The line of red coated men and materiel crossing the bridge stretched as far as the eye could see, back up and over and along the ridge on the other side of the river.

He walked up to the top of the ridge that separated the two marshes and began his trek. It took him most of the day and when he arrived he genuflected when he saw that Fort Gaspereaux was still in the hands of the French and Rouer de Villerary was likely still in charge. He removed his disguise and dropped the walking stick and recomposed himself.

He walked to the gate and was surprised to see how few French soldiers there were behind the small palisades; perhaps a few more than a dozen. He spoke to the guard: "I am Abbé Jean-Louis Le Loutre and desire to see the commandant."

"Oui, monsieur. Go ahead. I am sure you will have no problem finding him."

Le Loutre passed the small collection of soldiers at the entrance and a dozen steps to the warehouse that was the only building within the small palisades. The guard at the door presented arms and then went to attention and saluted. Then he opened the door and Le Loutre entered.

Benjamin Rouer de Villeray was no friend of the Abbé; if anything he held him with some animus because of his interference and controlling nature.

"Abbé Le Loutre, to what do I owe this honour."

"You will provide me transport to Quebec or at least Louisbourg."

"Abbé, the French navy, last I heard, does not exist as carriages for churchmen. Especially since you and the rest are all assured a pleasant hereafter."

Le Loutre held up his bag. "Monsieur de Villeray, I have here papers that are critical to the protection of New France. I demand transport or will see that you are held personally responsible for any harm that comes to France as a result of them being captured."

de Villeray sighed. "There is a ship now at Port la Joye on Ile St. Jean that is leaving for Ile Royale on the tide tomorrow. I can have one of the local fisherman take you there. I would as soon be rid of you when the British come."

The commandant called for his guard and instructed him to arrange for Le Loutre's travel across the strait.

* * * * *

Louis du Pont du Chambon de Vergor looked at the terms of surrender as they had been written by Monckton. He got absorbed in them and didn't notice that the messenger was still standing in front of him.

The terms were actually quite fair. They would surrender with honour and be passported under the protection of and in the ships of England to Louisbourg. He could really ask for nothing more. Monckton had even agreed to pardon the Acadians who had defended the fort.

"Merci. You may return to the headquarters of Colonel

Monckton and tell him that his terms are acceptable to us and that we offer him our hospitality at supper this evening."

The messenger saluted and left.

* * * * *

While de Vannes was delivering his commander's list of terms to the English lines under a white flag, chaos was reigning within the palisades of Fort Beauséjour.

Louis-Thomas Jacau de Fiedmont was dismayed to see French officers, as well as Acadians, filling baskets and bags with anything of value they could get their hands on. Almost all the soldiers were drunk, many to the point of sickness and even unconsciousness.

He saw Girouard, empty handed, walking toward the gates.

"Acquila Girouard!"

"Grenadier de Fiedmont."

"I have something for you, Acquila." He handed the Acadian a paper with a formal signature of the commandant.

"That allows you and all the others all to avoid any charges of treason by les maudits. It says that you were ordered to defend the fort or be executed for failing to."

Acquila scanned it.

Acquila put his hand on de Fiedmont's shoulder and looked him square in the eyes. "This is precious, Louis. Merci beaucoup. But I think you should give this to Brossard or Le Loutre. I am not a politician. Have you seen my wife and children?"

"No. Keep it with you. Le Loutre is nowhere to be found and Brossard already has one. They are trying to find safety from all the troubles, I think I saw your family in the casemate over there." He pointed.

"Thank you, Louis. May God bless you in the next few days."

Acquila picked up his musket and a bag of flints and cartridges and walked with some speed across the parade ground, now a morass of mud and cannonball craters and rubble. He avoided the drunken soldiers and other Acadians as best as he could and entreaties for him to help with one task or another. He needed to get his family away from here now; before the English exercised their control from the pending surrender.

He found the boys outside watching the panic all around. Mati was huddled in a corner of the casemate trying to calm down her screaming two year old boy with Béatrice seated next to her. When she saw Acquila she carefully placed Louis-Thomas on the ground, gave him a leather teething ring and ran into Acquila's arms. "Where were you?"

"I was organizing our way out, Chér. We have a schooner to take us to Chipoudie. We have to go now, to ensure there is room for us."

Acquila noticed a shiny object in the corner of the casemate, under some rubble and fallen beams caused by the English bombardment. He moved the rubble aside and found a sabre, with the top foot of its blade broken off, but still a very useful weapon. Its shorter length made it more valuable to him; he could conceal it better.

He looked outside to see if their path to leave was clear. It wasn't; they would need to make their way out of the fort as far from the gate as possible.

He found some sackcloth on the ground, wrapped the broken sabre in it and concealed it inside his trousers then he led his family out. He pointed to the top of the redoubt farthest from the English and took Louis-Thomas from Mati. "Allons y. Vite!"

The two boys led the way and helped their sister and mother up the fosse hill and down into the dry moat and then up the other side. Luckily, their escape was opposite to the direction of the anticipated English attack and the wooden palisades were low and poorly constructed. The boys and Acquila were able to help Mati and Béatrice scale the pointed timbers.

Once on the other side they felt safe and collected themselves. "Attendre ici. Mathilde, do you still have the coins?"

"I have six left, I needed to spend two for food."

"I am going to try and recover the rest. Wait here and try not to be seen. Emile, if I'm not back when the schooner arrives take our family down and get them on the boat. Mati, it will cost one of your remaining coins."

"Boys, be careful, there are sinkholes and other dangers between here and the boat. Protect your mother and your brother and sister. I'll return as soon as I can. Emile, you keep my musket and cartridges."

He looked at Mathilde, embraced her, and left.

* * * * *

Acquila carefully hurried back towards the burned settlement and Le Loutre's holy well, now near the English encampment,. He went far enough north and down the hill to be out of the line of sight of the English and deserting French soldiers and ran as fast as he could. He removed the sabre from his trousers to allow him to run.

He was confident that he'd be able to lower himself in the well and recover the bag of coins. But he also cursed and thought how stupid it was for him to put them there for safekeeping in the first place. It was so safe he might not even be able to recover them. All the danger and risk to get them but now that might have been worth nothing.

After about twenty minutes he slowed; he thought he heard a group of men. He moved behind a copse of fir trees. There were three English soldiers smoking their pipes and laughing, passing around a small earthenware jug. He waited and listened. They were talking about places that Acquila knew of but had never visited: Mémérancouque, Chipoudie, Pedditkoudiac. Why?

Just when he thought he would have to return empty-handed to catch the schooner the group broke up and two of the men walked back toward their trenches.

He thought and waited. He had to get back within about a half hour to be sure and make the boat. Without the money his family would struggle, with or without him. He decided he had to make the attempt. He quietly followed the English soldier who walked toward the well. When he arrived the soldier put the jug on the ground and began unbuttoning his breeches to urinate.

Acquila moved. He withdrew the broken sabre and ran at the soldier who heard him coming and just had time to turn before Acquila struck him just over one ear, almost removing the soldier's head.

Acquila dropped the sabre, sat on the well and swung his legs over the edge and grabbed the rope holding the bucket and jumped into the water. It came up to his chest and he tried to feel around with his feet. In a panic, just when he wondered if someone hadn't already taken it, he felt something with his right foot that seemed like it might be the bag. He took a deep breath, lowered himself into the water, felt around, found it and stood. He pulled himself up the rope to the top, looked and saw all was clear and climbed out. He lifted the English soldier over the edge of the well into the water and started running.

He ran down the butte to the edge of the marsh to be as far away from the English as possible and ran as if his family's lives depended on it. Because they did.

* * * * *

Acquila's family was just boarding the schooner from a rowboat when he made it to the brow of the last hill before the slope declined to the marsh and Riviere au Lac. He was exhausted but ran even harder while watching the ship begin to leave. They were starting to tie the tender to the schooner to allow it to follow in the larger ship's wake. He saw that Mathilde was vociferously talking to the sailor and that the sailor seemed to be ignoring her and even pushing her away.

Acquila arrived at the muddy shore just as the schooner was starting to weigh anchor and open the sails. He yelled to get Mati's attention and slid down the mud into the water and started splashing toward the ship. He was about twenty feet away when the anchor cleared the water; he was in water up to his waist and starting to sink in the mud. He stopped and threw the bag of coins toward the ship. It looked like it would make it, then the ship moved and it looked like it was falling short.

Mati stretched toward the coins and they hit the side of the schooner and caught on some rigging. She looked at Acquila only to see him step into deeper water and disappear.

The sails caught the wind and started moving the schooner out into the bay. The sudden movement caused Mati to fall and she was slightly stunned when she hit her head and she didn't see Acquila recover from his fall, just as he didn't see her stand, bend over the side and recover the bag of coins.

She quickly secreted the bag in her bodice while placing the bag's drawstring over her head. She looked around and saw Béatrice holding little Louis-Thomas and the two boys up near the bow.

She looked back at her lost home. Again.

It was here that she and her husband and their neighbours had built their homes and raised their family. But on the orders of the damned priest, Le Loutre, their homes had been burned and her family had needed to flee for their lives in terror.

Maybe this place, this Tintamarre, was not a place for family and for love, but a place for war and hatred. Maybe it was accursed ground and maybe they were blessed to be leaving it.

She knelt on the wet deck and prayed.

* * * * *

Thomas Pichon busily went about packing his necessities in his dresser and his barrel staved trunks. He had arranged with George Scott to exchange his bullion and silver coinage for pound sterling which he had carefully secured and hid under false bottoms.

By his actions, Thomas Pichon had ensured himself of a pension, not from his loyalty to France (although he had rewarded himself extravagantly from managing its procurements) but from his disloyalty. Whether or not his divulging of the state of French defenses in Beauséjour had any effect on the outcome was of no consequence; he was paid for services not results.

To avoid recognition he removed his wig and donned simple peasants clothes without any adornment.

He had arranged with Scott in the days before to travel to England via Boston on one of the sloops with the returning militia. While the English were preparing to march toward Fort Beauséjour to assume control, Pichon anxiously went to the ramparts to observe their progress. He looked at no one and avoided contact with any soldiers that he passed on the way. He tried to look like an innocent civilian in the middle of a terrible place and he was ignored.

* * * * *

Mathilde was seated amidships leaning back against the bilge of the schooner, the bag of coins safely hidden and protected inside her tunic. The older boys were still at the bow, fascinated with the experience of being on a boat for the first time in their lives. Béatrice was huddled next to her mother hugging her doll and Louis-Thomas, in Mati's arms, was screaming at the top of his lungs in discomfort.

The schooner was crowded with two dozen other family members all in similar situations of confusion and terror, all the others with an adult male helping to manage the children. Mati was worried almost to the point of desperation by having Acquila fall behind. With all the panic on the schooner she hadn't been able to see if he got out of the river or not.

'Is he alive? He had never been much of a swimmer. How would she ever even know?'

She thought again about what happened to women and their families who had their husbands die young. Their lives became desperate; they were unable to do all the work required to grow and harvest and manage livestock and maintain the well and fireplace and all the other things.

The lucky widows had found another man to do the heavy work, often decades older and cruel or a drunk or violent. The unlucky ones died or had their children die.

She had never been more than a few miles from her home and now she was being taken to a place she had only ever heard of; where she knew no one. She prayed that the people there would be willing to accept her and their children, at least until Acquila tracked them down. If he was still alive.

She had to be strong. She had four children and enough gold to support them, if she could protect them, and it.

* * * * *

Acquila's mouth filled with muddy water when he slipped into the Au Lac River after tossing the bag of coins toward Mathilde. He had no idea if she had been able to catch them; he had slid on his back in the greasy mud the second he had let it go. He wretched and scrambled for ten minutes to try to get out of the red silt: there was almost nothing solid to hold onto. Finally, when he was approaching exhaustion, he grabbed a handful of roots of marsh grass and pulled himself to safety.

He laid on the shore for many minutes, his clothing soaked and covered in sticky mud. He dragged himself high enough to avoid the tide coming in and removed his clothing and washed it as best as he could along a less muddy point of the river. He had lost his moccasins.

Where could he go? Are Mathilde and the children safe? Did she catch the bag of coins that could possibly enable her to buy her way to safety? He could only pray that she did.

He heard drums coming from the direction of the fort, and stood and crawled up the bank of the palisades until he came to a point where he could see what was happening. A column of redcoats, led by a pair of drummers, was making its way toward the fort.

He knew that Beausoleil was moving away from the area to join some other refugees who had left when the Beauséjour village was burned: north across three more rivers to Mémérancouque. He decided he would make his way there and then travel to Chipoudie to find his family.

22 - VINGT-DEUX

That evening, at precisely seven of the clock, Monckton led his two hundred regulars of the English 40th Regiment of Foot properly in array up the marshy ground from their encampment and over the moat and through the gates of what had been Fort Beauséjour. He had purposefully not invited Winslow nor any of the Massachusetts militia to participate.

When they arrived the French, unarmed and looking the worse for wear, were lined up in three ranks. Monckton smiled when he saw what a small and pathetic group he had defeated. He was surprised at the damage that his artillery had caused; the barracks were almost completely destroyed: only one still had all four sides and part of a roof.

A small, fat and unpleasant looking man in a much too grand hat and too large a uniform coat stepped forward toward the equally fat but the much better dressed English Lieutenant General. He was accompanied by an older soldier, probably a translator, Monckton thought.

"Monsieur, Je suis Capitaine Louis du Pont du Chambon de Vergor et Commandant de la Fortress Beauséjour."

"I am Colonel Robert Monckton, Commander of the 40th Regiment of Foot."

"Monsieur Monckton, nous nous engageons à vos termes de la capitulation et vous demande respectueusement de bien vouloir faire affaire avec nous.

"We surrender and ask for kind treatment, but we are yours to dispose of, as you will."

"You will be treated well. Travel has been arranged to remove you to your Fortress Louisbourg leaving tomorrow with the tide on transport from the Bay Verte north of here. You may leave under your flag, with drums and in full uniform."

"Monsieur Lieutenant General, may I invite you and your officers to join us and enjoy our modest hospitality in appreciation of your gentleness."

"That would be very welcome, Capitaine."

"Captain Murray."

A ruddy faced sub-altern properly came up to Monckton.

"Sir."

"Have our men man the bastions of this Fort Cumberland."

* * * * *

Acquila had escaped a league north of the British positions to the village of Tintamarre without being discovered. He knew a family there, the Landrys, whose home was on the edge of a large freshwater lake. Before he approached their house in the dark he cleaned himself as best he could. Any caked mud on his clothing was mostly dry and he was able to remove his pants and shirt and shake them until they were reasonably clean.

His feet were a mess, filled with nicks, bruises and cuts. Now that he had stopped his trek, the pain was approaching his tolerance level. He undressed and walked into the lake and washed himself as well as he was able. He tore off the tails of his shirt and bound his feet as best as he could.

After he was dried off he went up to the Landry house and knocked on the door.

Bernard, who had worked in the fields in Nanpan when Acquila had first arrived, carefully opened the door a crack. At first he didn't recognize Acquila.

"Girouard? Acquila?"

"Oui, c'est moi."

"Come in, come in."

Acquila pointed to his feet.

"Mon Dieu? What brought you here without shoes?"

"I had to leave quickly, Bernard."

"Come in, come in, and let me get you some sabots."

Acquila entered; there was a roaring fire and he was anxious to warm up. When he was fully inside, Bernard hugged him, then his wife, Janette did as well.

"Asseyez-vous. Sit. Sit."

"Are you hungry? Have you eaten? Would you like some fricot? Some chokecherry wine?"

What happened to your ear?

"It came from listening to l'Abbé, I think."

Bernard and Janette both laughed.

"You are very kind and an excellent hostess, Janette. I would much like some wine and soup."

She rushed across their small main room and ladled a healthy portion of whatever was in the cooking pot into a clay bowl. Bernard appeared with a small jug and two pottery mugs and filled them with his home brew.

"Would you have a smoke, 'Quila?"

"I'm sorry I lost my pipe."

"You can use mine, you look like you need it."

Janette brought the fricot. Acquila was starving and he made short work of it, finishing the entire bowl of strongly seasoned thick broth, vegetables and chicken before he said another word. He took a big swig from the wine and let out a deep breath. Bernard passed him his pipe filled with tobacco and a twig to light it. Acquila lit and inhaled the strong smoke.

"Why are you here?"

"Les Anglais. They have taken over the fort. Mathilde and the children have gone to Chipoudie, I escaped to come here."

"You're not the only one, ami. Every family but ours has someone sleeping in their barn. How are Mati and your children?"

"They are well, I pray. They left just before dusk on a schooner. I will go and find them once things are quieter."

"Where are you going now?"

"There is an Acadian leader named Brossard, dit Beausoleil. Do you know of him?"

"I have heard of him. I believe he is in Mémérancouque."

"So I have heard. How far is it?"

"Not far, perhaps 5 leagues. It is on the crooked river, of course, northwest of here. You can follow the moon."

"I will move on, Bernard."

"Are you sure? You can stay here and rest, if you would like."

"No, I think I will go. I still have things I must do before I find my family. Your hospitality will never be forgotten."

Acquila stood and passed Bernard the pipe. His friend said, "No, you keep it. And here's a packet of tobacco."

"Thank you, ami. Janette, thank you for supper."

"Oh! Shoes. Try these on."

They were a little large so Bernard gave him a pair of thick woolen socks. Before he put them on, Janette rushed to her mantle and came back with a salve made from lard and boiled spruce needles and applied it to his wounded feet.

"Thank you, Janette. This is very helpful to me."

"Come back again, Acquila. We will pray that you find Mathilde and the children."

Acquila left and started walking toward the moon.

He walked through the night often stumbling in wet ground and having to walk around wetlands. Finally, as he was approaching exhaustion, he saw a light and walked toward it. He came to a small house, already with its candles lit: the family preparing to start the day.

He knocked on the door and it was opened by an old man, grizzled and unshaven, wearing only his pants, that were held up by rope suspenders, and his wooden sabots. He was smoking a pipe.

"Bonjour, Monsieur, come in. I am Gaetan Bourgeois."

"I am Acquila Girouard of Beaubassin, Monsieur. Thank you." Acquila entered the house, it was barren but had a roaring fire.

"Would you like dejeuner?"

"Coffee or Tea?"

"Tea. Please sit." The old man took a pewter mug off his fireplace mantle, a pot from a rack next to the fireplace and poured some steaming liquid into the mug. He passed it to Acquila. It was too hot so Acquila blew on it before drinking.

"Are you visiting someone here in Mémérancouque, Monsieur Girouard?"

"I am hoping to find my friend, Joseph Brossard, dit Beausoleil."

"I know of this man. He is settled with the Poiriers not far from here with some other young men."

"Where is that?"

"Walk to the river and then go to the right and walk, you will find them."

"Thank you, Monsieur Bourgeois."

Acquila finished his cup and left and the rising sun and the tea re-energized him and he was able to walk the extra few hundred yards along the river and followed it until he came to a small cluster of buildings. There were men in the yard wandering around, sitting and smoking and talking. Beausoleil was standing and chatting with a shorter but sturdier and older man with long curly grey hair.

Acquila walked toward them and Beausoleil noticed and touched his friend on the arm and indicated they should go toward the visitor. They met and Beausoleil embraced Acquila and stood back leaving his hands on Acquila's shoulders and looked at him.

"Ami, where have you been?"

"Brossard, I have a family I had to look after."

Brossard laughed.

"But I have several!"

"Don't tell the priest." Both men laughed.

Acquila looked at the other man.

"I am Acquila Girouard."

"Charles Bois-Hébert."

Acquila nodded and shook the man's hand.

"Monsieur Bois-Hébert. Why are you here?"

"Monsieur Girouard. I am here to kill English.

"I have heard of you, Monsieur Girouard. Brossard says that you have killed your share of les maudits as well."

"Some. What do you plan?"

"We are gathering muskets and axes and men. We will keep as much of this land north of the Mésagouèche as we are able for us and not allow the English to come here."

"They have many men, Monsieur Bois-Hébert."

"But the English have only more to gain than to lose, but our men... we ... have everything to lose. We will fight harder."

Brossard said, "Girouard, here, he will fight hard."

Bois-Hébert said, "Tres bien! We need hard fighters. Come along, Acquila Girouard. Help us prepare."

* * * * *

The regiment of French Marines, short a dozen men who had been lost in the siege or deserted, formed three lines and followed their drums past the English encampment toward the north shore at Fort Gaspereaux where an English transport ship waited.

Louis-Thomas Jacau de Fiedmont felt a deep sense of loss more in sympathy for the Acadians than for the defeat. He had joined the army to see the world; walking in the footsteps of his father. And he had visited France, but had been stationed here in Tintamarre for four years. He had been born in Ile Royale, now he was to return there; to probably join the garrison at Louisbourg. He would have liked to have stayed; he had developed good friendships among many Acadians and would like to be able to protect them.

But he had the feeling that his days facing the damned

English across ramparts were not over. He was not mistaken.

* * * * *

Robert Monckton was reading a letter just arrived from Charles Lawrence.

"The Deputies of the Acadians of the Districts of Annapolis, Mines and Piziquid, have been called before the Council and have refused to take the oath of allegiance, whereupon, the council advised and it is accordingly determined that they shall be removed out of the Country, as soon as possible, and, as to those about Beauséjour, who were in arms and therefore entitled to no favour, it is determined to begin with them first...

"You must proceed by the most rigorous measures possible, not only in compelling them to embark, but in depriving those who shall escape of all means of shelter or support by burning their houses and destroying everything that may afford them the means of subsistence in the country.

"If these people behave amiss, they should be punished at your discretion; and if any attempt to molest the troops, you should take an eye for an eye, a tooth for a tooth; and, in short, life for life, from the nearest neighbour where the mischief should be performed."

Monckton folded the letter and sent a messenger to his chief subordinates.

* * * * *

Winslow, on his way to see Monckton, ran into Captain Alexander Murray.

"Hello, Alec. What do you think we are about to see and hear."

Murray, replied: "Well, I can't imagine that the Crapauds will be allowed to stay around here and continually bite at our heels."

Winslow said, "I don't think we'll be putting down the muskets any time soon. Not if good General Robert has his way."

When Montgomery opened Monckton's door to allow the visitors to enter. Monckton didn't stand or even offer salutations. George Scott was already there.

"Well, we're done with those who wear uniforms. Now once we get rid of the savages and remove the peasants we may be able to make something of this place."

"Winslow. Murray. Scott. We are losing our men, and I want it to stop. We don't even dare send our men out even to forage for firewood. Now who is responsible for this?"

Scott, since he had been resident here for a longer period offered a response.

"Hmmp. I believe it's Copit's Miqmaqs, Lieutenant General."

"He's the one Peregrine treated with, no?"

"I believe so, Sir, but I have heard from our French spy that the priest, Le Loutre, had forced them to again turn to violence and terrorism."

"Who is this spy?"

"He went by the name Tyrell. But he's removed under our passport of safety. Back in England or France I suppose."

Monckton said, "And the Acadians? There were several hundred, I believe, that we allowed to remove because they had been pressed into service. What became of them?"

Scott said, "I believe they removed across the river to other French settlements."

"Well, let's bloody well bring them back. I've ordered Gorham and Danks to come and effect that.

"Cyril."

His secretary shifted his chair around to face his Colonel.

"Yes?"

"Draft up a formal letter addressed to all Acadians lately removed from Beauséjour and invite them to return to work on the reconstruction of the fortress and on roads. Tell them that they will be generously paid in silver coin. Translate it and be clever and figure out how to get it in their hands."

"Yes, Lieutenant General."

"Winslow, I have here orders from Governor Lawrence. He directs that the Acadians be sent away from here. We'll send them to our colonies in the south and hope they are absorbed and converted from the Roman church. You, Lieutenant Colonel, will be responsible for this. But first, we must collect them.

"We will order all Acadians to report to their nearest British command. Here at Fort Cumberland I will command with the assistance of Colonel Scott; Winslow, you will direct the operation in Grand Pre and Mines and are instructed to send as many as two thousand rebel subjects to the North Carolinas, Virginia and Maryland. Murray, you from Fort Edward to Pennsylvania and New York. Scott and I will look after this collection to go to South Carolina and Georgia."

"Now allow me to ensure that there is no misunderstanding. We will treat these French Acadians as traitors and rebels and we will neither spare them nor show them any mercy.

"Am I clear."

Winslow resisted showing his distaste for the pompous prig. "Yes. General."

* * * * *

After sailing through the night, as dawn was breaking, the schooner was nearing shore. A high mountain, for these parts, could be barely seen through the fog in the emerging daylight. One of the schooner's officers had a spyglass and was sharing it with passengers. To the right of their destination, at low tide, there seemed to be huge flowerpots just off shore: islands fifty feet high with trees on top. The shouts of the ship's crew were awakening any sleeping passengers as was their scrambling around the deck to adjust sails. Mathilde had been awake all night with Louis-Thomas who had taken well past midnight until settling in to sleep by the gentle rocking of the ship.

But, like any mother, she was indefatigable when she was responsible for tending to her children. She would rest when it was safe to do so.

Louis-Thomas was whiny when he woke up, but he returned to his version of his father's serenity once he had breakfast. Mathilde wanted her family near when they finished their voyage and got Béatrice to track down the boys and bring them to join her.

When they arrived the two boys, now both a foot taller than their mother, put their arms around their mother and sister and pulled all the family members together to look at their new home. From the schooner it didn't look like much. They could see a church steeple and a cluster of houses around it. There were another half dozen buildings spread out around the small village. Béatrice quietly said, "Maman, will we be okay?"

"Oui, ma petite chou. We will be fine."

"I want papa."

"He will be here soon, Béatrice. We want to make sure we are happy when he comes. We will be safe and happy in our new house."

There was a pier built for the settlement so the travellers didn't have to take tenders to shore which relieved Mathilde; she had enough on her mind to not worry about managing the children getting on and off boats. She got the boys to carry what few belongings they had and allowed all of the other passengers and her children to proceed her down the gangplank.

When they made it to dock, Mathilde waited with the other mothers with young children to avoid the rush. Other than her children, the only thing that really mattered was hanging from her neck. It promised to be a hot and sunny day. She hoped it was a happy one.

The boys, as she expected, ran down the gangplank to shore, whooping and hollering. Béatrice carefully collected her dolls and put them in a bag and followed her mother. Louis-Thomas was acting like a two-year-old and showed his upset by screaming as she tried to concentrate on faces on shore. When almost everyone had left she reached in her moccasin and extracted a gold coin and held it tight in a fist, lifted up Louis-Thomas who would soon be too heavy, walked down the short gangplank and gave the coin to the ship's captain. He accepted it, looked at her suspiciously, and pushed it into a pocket.

Mathilde looked around to see if she knew anyone who had not arrived on the schooner. She called to the boys, "Emile, Maurice, settle down. Help me find who is in charge here." The family walked toward the church, assuming they would find someone there with a knowledge of the situation.

She was surprised to find Abbé Le Guerne, the priest from Beaubassin, welcoming people in front of the church.

"Bonjour, Bonjour!"

When it was finally her turn, the priest smiled and tickled Louis-Thomas under the chin.

"Bonjour, Madame Girouard, what a lovely family you have here. And your boys are so big and strong now."

"Thank you, Pére Le Guerne. I am very happy to be safe here away from all the problems. Do we have a place we can stay?"

"Since the English came, everyone here in Chipoudie has been preparing for the refugees. The men have started building more houses that should be ready before it snows, meanwhile, people will stay with relatives, or others who have space, or in the church."

"We have no family here."

"Then, at first, you will stay here in the church. If Acquila comes here, then perhaps we can have a new home for you very soon."

"We had to leave without him."

"I am sure he will find you, Madame Girouard. He is a good man and father. Come, come. Settle yourself and your family in the church. We have plenty of oatmeal, bread and salt fish."

"This is a blessing, Father."

* * * * *

It was an overcast but not unpleasant day when John Winslow landed in Grand Pré in the company of Nathan Adams, two other adjutants and two dozen men in three schooners.

"Hobbs, go ahead and make sure that my quarters in the priest's house are suitable for my presence. Have my belongings secured there. Good Father Chauvreulx is visiting Chebouctu so I would expect he has no further need of it."

"Yes, Sor."

"Adams, we shall establish out military headquarters in the mass house. Our provisions should be secured there along with the allotment for Acadians.

"Oh, and get the men to work building pickets around our encampment and those two buildings and another much larger one for the Acadians. Order all the men to not leave the vicinity nor to make themselves a menace to the locals."

He sniffed.

When Adams returned he and Winslow wandered toward the dike lands where the Acadians were fully occupied in harvesting. He thought to himself of his orders, 'this is no work for a soldier.'

"Adams, pull their head man, Therriot, away from his endeavours and confirm the location of the cattle we have appropriated.

* * * * *

Louis-Thomas awoke Mathilde in the morning at first light as he always did. She rolled toward him on their shared straw and calmed him down. When he was fell back asleep she gently placed him back on the mattress next to her.

The boys were snoring loudly and Mati watched Béatrice, snuggled up in her goose feather duvet, managing to softly snore sweetly herself, ignoring the cacophony just a foot or two away.

Mathilde took a moment to wonder about her husband. She was doing that a lot. She wondered if he knew they were here and were safe. Her baby was fast asleep, she didn't want to wake him, it was still early, so she cuddled him and went back to sleep.

She dreamt of the time that Louis-Thomas had been conceived. It had been a hot summer day, just like this day would be. Acquila had gotten the boys and Béatrice to go out on the marsh and pick the crows' feet greens that they all enjoyed. The children would likely be gone an hour or two.

Acquila and she had sat by the little stream that was next to their original temporary shelter when they had been forced to abandon their home in Beaubassin. Mathilde had brought along a loaf of bread and some rough pate that she had made from the liver and scraps from the pig they had butchered. Acquila had a jug of chokecherry wine he had made. It had been a warm summer day and her husband had removed his shirt. She had stirred with passion, not only from her love for him and her attraction, but the wounds on his shoulders and arms that he had suffered in his campaign against the English invaders. He would do anything and sacrifice everything to protect his family and community. He was fearless and brave.

She could almost feel his arms wrapped around her from behind, both lying on their sides on the soft mossy ground, with the warm wind embracing them. The trickle of the stream providing music; the lowing of cows in the valley; the trees whispering privately to each other. He had moved his hands up to her bosom and caressed her and then lower, moving aside her nightclothes. But she was not wearing nightclothes. She was wearing her shirt and petticoat.

She felt his kiss on her neck and shivered.

She awoke.

He was here. She could feel his manhood firmly but gently press against her and she lifted her cotton shift to help him. She muffled her sounds as he muffled his; to not wake the children or other people in the church. When they finished she lay in his arms for it seemed hours, until Louis loudly announced his intention to dominate his mother's attention. And, soon after, everyone was awake.

Béatrice was the first to run into her pére's arms; the boys were reticent and stood awkwardly until all the women were done and then came forward into Acquila's embrace.

"You boys have grown just since I left. You look stronger than me." In truth, Maurice was already taller than Acquila, although nowhere near as strong. Emile resembled his mother and was developing a barrel chest and large forearms.

"Let me look at you." He shook his head in amazement. Only a couple of days had changed his family. He directed his attention to Béatrice who was tiny like her mother but had the nose that Acquila had inherited from his mother. She was beautiful to him, though, perhaps, she would not be the coquette of the village.

"Could the damned priests or lazy men here not find you a house?"

"This was very comfortable."

"Not comfortable enough for my wife and family. We have to work. Emile. Get two axes, we need to build a house."

Acquila said, "Maurice, get dressed and ready. Come. Allons-y!"

They found Pére Le Guerne outside, walking between the various homestead sites, getting people to help each other out and to find various tools and hardware that were necessary to do a task.

Acquila approached him.

"Monsieur Girouard. I told your wife that you would find her and your family and God answered her prayers."

"I am happy that He did, Pére Le Guerne."

"I have already found the place for your new house. Come."

Acquila followed the priest to the lot he had set aside. It was a good site, close to a stand of maple and elm trees that could be felled and easily trimmed and put into place in the new house. Maurice and Emile showed up with the axes and he and Acquila started choosing and limbing trees that were straight and about a hand span in width.

Acquila began to think of his boys differently as the work proceeded; they could do the work of men. He could now be proud of them and he was. Emile would be massive and powerful when he was grown and Maurice was willow thin, but would be tall and add different strengths to work.

By the time the sun was starting to go down, they had limbed, felled and stripped the bark off of thirty trees. Mathilde and Béatrice helped out as much as they could, while they shared looking after the baby. Their new house would be small, but it would suit their needs until they determined where they would settle. Perhaps it would be here in Chipoudie. Perhaps not. Acquila would take some of their gold and buy the hardware that Mathilde would need to make a place their home. He spoke quietly, "Mathilde, do you have our gold?"

"I carry it with me, Chér."

"Can I have one gold coin?"

She hid behind him and removed one from the bag and gave it to him.

He went to find Father Le Guerne to trade this gold sovereign in for smaller currency that he could use to buy basic household goods from anyone with the ability to sell something. What he didn't need he would donate to the church.

23 - VINGT-TROIS

Philomene Bourque was hanging her wash when she saw in the distance redcoats coming up the hill. When the English had first marched toward the fort, and the village had been razed, she and Simon had travelled a league north to stay with their cousins in Pré de Bourque. The homestead was crowded, and she was hopeful that they could build their own place soon and Simon had already started to take down trees to dry and season in time for next spring.

Now les maudits were coming again. But now Simon and her and their family had nowhere to go.

She held her hand to shield her eyes from the sun and noted that the score or two of British soldiers were breaking up into twos to visit the various homesteads in the area.

Two came up to her and the older soldier bowed respectfully.

"Madame, I am Captain Nathan Adams." She only understood that his words were an introduction and that he was an officer.

"I am unable to speak French, but request that you read this document and act accordingly." He handed Philomene a piece of parchment. She looked at it briefly. Adams bowed again and signalling with his hand to his cohort, they walked toward the next homestead.

Philomene looked at the parchment; like almost everyone in her community she could not read. They did not have a family Bible, nor any other book, for that matter; and reading was not something that affected their daily lives. She didn't think anyone she knew could read, either. Simon barely remembered his catechism. But obviously this was an important piece of paper. She folded it and put it in her apron and went about her duties.

On the following Sunday, Philomene and Simon and their three children awoke early and met Rene and Marielle Gallant to walk the league to the Tintamarre church. Simon had examined the letter closely and had thought that he was able to translate a few words: "travail" and "paiement", which would suggest that there might actually be something of value, something good for them.

They arrived and the parishioners were in deep discussions in small groups. All had received the notice and almost all seemed excited.

"We can return home! We will be given jobs!"

Only old Abelard Robicheaux was cynical, explaining that les maudits can never be trusted and anything to do with them could only turn out bad. But Robicheaux le Vieux had been a widower for decades and had lost all his children to disease or to les Anglais and never, ever, had anything hopeful to say.

Father Jean Menach walked among the parishioners and drew their attention.

"Today we celebrate Saint Roger of Nanpan, and the fact that we still exist to worship on this earth because of the grace of our Father that worked through him. It is not a time to ponder our temporal existence but to celebrate our spiritual existence."

"Come in, come in, and prepare to worship."

After the service Philomene led Simon over to their friend, Abelard's nephew, Camille Robicheaux to ask him what he thought. He seldom talked but when he did he had the strongest opinion, and he was the one most likely to not be hoodwinked, which was probably the reason he had stayed a bachelor.

"Well, I trust les Anglais not at all, but I barely trust myself most days. I am living in the barn of a family that does not make either ale or wine, and they do not even have a daughter to entertain my eyes. So when someone offers to give me silver coins to do work that I am used to doing for no coins at all, I pay attention."

"So you think we should go to work for our enemies?"

"I will. It is up to you to do as you wish."

* * * * *

Benoni Danks had been scrapping with different collections of Miqmaq warriors for over five years, most lately while protecting new settlements on the south shore of Nova Scotia. While he had been handsomely rewarded financially, there had been a considerable cost to his company. All of his Mohawks were either dead or disappeared and many of his New Englanders had received their just rewards.

So when he arrived back at Chignectou he was down to seven men, including himself, which hardly provided him any capability to be too rambunctious. He knew he'd have to join with another company; hopefully led by a high born toff who would not be anxious to get his own hands too bloody by collecting scalps.

So when he arrived at the newly named Fort Cumberland, he was pleased when he saw Joe Gorham walking in his direction. Gorham was his brother's successor but was much more civilized.

"Danks."

"Capt'n."

"Travels been well?"

"Profitable."

"Seems you're short some bodies."

"We gave better than we got, Capt'n."

"I doubt that not. You're to bring what ye have with me."

"Where we to go?"

"The other side of the bay. The Crapauds have escaped there, and we're to bring them back and discourage their settling at places of their own choosing."

"Where will they be put?"

"I think the Charlie Lawrence has plans for them. We'll muster in the morning. I think there will be mess in the parade yard at dusk. Pitch your tents somewhere on the hill."

* * * * *

The Acadian men gathered in the parade ground at what had been Fort Beauséjour. The demolished buildings had been rebuilt and the destroyed bombproof shelters restored and the bastions re-fortified. Simon noticed that even the palisades had all been improved; it seemed sure that these English were here to stay.

Uncomfortably, Simon noticed that there were ranks of armed English soldiers along the outer walls of the fort. In essence, the few hundred Acadians who had reported to work were surrounded. He hoped their presence was only to assist in organizing the work crews.

With great pomp and pageantry a senior officer exited one of the buildings and marched in full parade to the front of the unorganized collection of Acadian men. He came with a translator and removed a parchment from a tube and unrolled it officiously.

"Here ye! Former residents of the former settlement of Beauséjour. The King of England declares you as rebel. Your lands and all other goods are forfeit. You will be retained as prisoner here until your disposition is ordered."

After a moment of silence among the Acadian men, they slowly comprehended the treachery against them that they would now endure, then started a hew and cry in protest of the order. Then, came an order to the English soldiers: "Order Arms! Fix Bayonets!" The sound of flintlock muskets being raised and bayonets being attached silenced the protest.

"Here ye! You will be fed and protected until the means and place of your peaceful disposition is determined."

* * * * *

It had taken only three weeks but the Girouard men had built an excellent house. The two boys were very good workers and, with the help of the neighbours, had been able to fell even more trees and the house, while smaller than before, was twice as large as Acquila had expected it would be.

The house already had solid birch floors and elm walls and a birch-bark roof. They hadn't yet been able to come up with the stones necessary to build a fireplace, but had made a rough fire-pit for cooking outside.

The family was sitting around the fire in the morning eating fried pork belly and bread toasted in the fat when there was a bit of a commotion. Acquila looked around and saw Beausoleil coming through the village. He always attracted a crowd with his enthusiasm, charm and good looks.

Acquila knew that Brossard was here to see him. Acquila had told Beausoleil that he was to be here for two weeks and it had been three.

He stood.

"Acquila?"

"I have to go, Chér. We have to keep the English from taking everything we have built for over a hundred and fifty years."

"But why does it have to be you?"

"Because I can, Chér. And somebody has to."

"We need you."

"You have me. I will return as often as I can to visit you and the children and your boudoir."

Brossard appeared.

"Girouard! Where have you been? We have missed you."

"I have a family, Beausoleil."

"As I said, I have several."

"But your children are all older than I am!"

"Not quite, but they will not reach your age if we do not defeat les maudits."

Acquila said, "Where will we go?"

"Back to Pedditkoudiac. The English have been raiding villages. Even taking scalps again. We want to build as large a group to repel them as we can. With Bois-Hébert we have almost two hundred, but have too few to lead our men."

"With muskets?"

"No. We have few, but everyone has a killing weapon and we will attack them quickly and with great violence. You can come back to your family in a week or two."

Acquila said, "D'accord. Give me your musket and axe. I will say goodbye to Mati and join you in a few minutes."

Brossard gave both to Acquila along with a leather bag of flints, gunpowder and balls. Acquila went back to his home.

Mathilde knew he was leaving again.

"Don't say anything, 'Quila. Just let me look in your eyes so that I know you will return."

"Emile. Maurice." The boys came and he gave the musket and bag to Maurice who was a better shot and the war axe to Emile who was strong.

"You will protect your mother and sister and little brother, oui?"

"Oui, papa."

Acquila looked at Mathilde and fully wrapped her in his arms and kissed her deeply. Then he looked her deeply and steadily in the eyes for a full minute. Then he left.

* * * * *

With the arrival of three transports, which was half of what he had been promised, Winslow had his orders.

The village of Grand Pré was in turmoil. The redcoats had marched into the village the previous week in force and had immediately began nailing notices to doors of the public buildings.

The notices ordered all residents of the village to collect this evening at the church for an announcement. It was stated that any who failed to attend would be arrested and put in jail. Everyone was gathered in the village square speculating and gossiping about what might be demanded by their hated occupiers. Some thought that the English might allow them to sign an oath of allegiance that would not take away their rights to practice their Roman Catholic religion; some even that they would not be forced to take arms against fellow Frenchmen. But most were pessimistic and many of these fled to the forest.

The church was full when John Winslow arrived along with a protective force of twenty men and a translator. He strode to the area just in front of the altar and removed reading glasses and began reading from a sheet of fine paper.

"Messieurs:

"I have received orders from his Excellency the Governor and he has given to me the responsibility to give resolution of the situation to the French inhabitants of Nova Scotia.

"For a half century your rulers have granted you indulgences, and you have not acted in your own best interests.

"It is very disagreeable to my natural temperament to have to invoke these resolutions, but it is my duty to do so.

"Therefore, all your lands and tenements and cattle and livestock of all forms and all your other personal effects are hereby forfeited to the Crown.

"The order of his Majesty is that all French inhabitants of this province be removed. But in his goodness, he is allowing you to retain any money or household goods in your possession.

"I will see that you are protected prior to your departure and will endeavour to see that entire families shall go in the same vessel and that your relocation will be made as easy as His Majesty's service can allow. I hope that wherever you may land, that you will be faithful subjects and be peaceful and happy.

"I must also inform you that it is His Majesty's pleasure that you will remain in security within the confines of Fort Edward under the direction of the troops that I have the honour of commanding. You have been declared rebels and prisoners of the King."

Winslow watched as the translation was made and the Acadians began to appreciate the penalty to which they were about to be made to pay. He folded the paper and replaced his reading glasses in his pocket.

Once he did this, the church broke into an uproar with many of the Acadian men shouting loudly and a few rushing Winslow himself. Then the sound of bayonets being fixed quieted the crowd and they were forcibly marched into custody.

* * * * *

Danks had slept well on the soft ground of Chignectou after having to suffer the rocky ground of Lunenburg for over a year. Even better, when he had arrived the previous evening, Joe Gorham had given him a handful of cheroots. These had been rare in Lunenburg and he had badly missed them. Before going to bed the previous night he had lit his match case fuse and smoked one.

He rolled out of his canvas paillasse that he had stuffed with marsh grass the night before, and immediately lit another stinking cigar. The other men in the big bell tent paid him no notice. The smoke likely improved the smell given off during the night by eight unwashed men who had been fed beans and ale the night before.

He thought back to the men lost. He had liked Lord Miller; for an injun he was good company and was brave and didn't drink. Josiah Higgins had been like a son and his death was as cruel a one as the devil himself could invent. Many had just disappeared, most likely abducted and desecrated while wandering only a short distance from the camp looking for an apple tree or a place to defecate in private. He suspected most of the Indians had just wandered away, attracted to other pursuits or distractions or higher rewards. He had none of the Indians left; even the half-breeds, the Labreques, were gone. Just Hez King, Nehemiah Black and Charlie Hollis, who had all become real scrappers, and three Germans who had taken better to fighting than farming. The Germans had been proven in their travel to

Chignectou when the rangers had been attacked by a small group of Copit's men. Danks expected his cabbage-eaters would wish to continue their pursuit of wealth by removing hair from adversaries rather than sowing seed on rocky ground.

He pulled on his moccasins, lifted himself up by his musket and trekked the few hundred lengths to the Fort. He announced himself to the sentries at the drawbridge gates.

"To see Gorham."

"In the officers' barracks, last seen."

Danks continued on and found Joseph standing in the parade ground where his company of rangers were at ease, smoking and playing cards and talking.

"Ben. Where did all yer men get to?"

"Aye. The injuns all left when the scalps started getting less. Most of the rest wandered away and a few of the scraps were hard on us."

"Well, ye can look for the rebels with my fellows. Ye have mess yet?"

"Not yet, Capt'n."

"See what ye can forage around here. I had some pork belly and hard tack.

"Frye's come up from Boston with some men, he'll take command of our excursions against the Crapauds. Ye'll be joining him to track down and bring back them that don't come back on their own. Raze their shelters, if they don't. They are in rebellion against the king and are outlaw. Dispose of them as ye will. They're mostly north of here, in settlements along the rivers. Ye might want to start further up and work your way back. Pedditkoudiac I think they call it. Get Syl Cobb to ferry ye up there. You can herd them back this way."

"Aye… Bounties, Colonel?"

"Mikymakys only this time. No redheads, Danks."

"Yes, Colonel. Permission to take command."

"Given."

Danks walked over to the motley crew of men in their filthy blue bonnets and tattered kilts, breeches and coats.

"Rangers! Fall in!"

The men knew Danks; he was famous for how much in bounties he had allowed his men to earn, although few were still around now to spend it.

"You know who I am, I expect. Get your kit and muster back within the hour."

24 - VINGT-QUATRE

Nathan Adams arrived at Winslow's quarters in the former parsonage at the break of day to receive his orders. Winslow was fully dressed and quite formally. His boots were polished, he had shaved and carefully braided his pig tail.

"Top of the morning, Captain."

"To you as well, Major General."

"Well, it seems that our good friend Robert Monckton has failed to provide us the transports we are expected to fill with outlaw Acadians. We only received three, so it will be quite crowded."

"I wouldn't ken, Major General."

"Well, I've come to expect such from that git. Did you muster a small company? "

"Yes sir."

"Let's find Landry the Elder and advise him that it is time."

The two men left Winslow's quarters followed by two hundred fully armed men and walked toward the fields where they found Landry with a group of other Acadians preparing to go into the fields.

"Bring him to me, Adams."

Adams returned with the community elder.

Landry was the only person in the village who could understand even a word of English.

"Bon matin, Génerale."

"Elder Landry, we will begin locating your inhabitants on the tide in one hour."

He appeared shocked. "But, Monsieur Génerale, we still have the crop to bring in."

"The crops are no longer your concern, Mister Landry. Your duty now is to bring together all the residents of this settlement within an hour and present them at the mass house or we will surely bring them at the point of a bayonet.

"Adams, send men out to empty the houses of their population; all women and children and elderly. Force them if necessary but have them appear within the hour. They are entitled to take with them their currency and clothing, nothing else. When they are removed, raze there homesteads and barns."

"Elder Landry, your wives and children and grand parents will be on those transports in an hour, whether you and your men are or not. We will provide you sustenance for your voyage. Am I clear? There is nothing to parley about."

"Yes, Génerale."

"See that it is done, or suffer the consequences."

Winslow went looking for the ships' masters; he expected to find them in the mass room having mess and he did. Thomas Church, the master of the "Leopard" was smoking his pipe and drinking tea.

"Church."

"Winslow."

"You will be embarking within an hour for Mary Land and will wait upon the Lieutenant Governor there, Horatio Sharp. You are to ensure that your cargo has not an offensive weapon of any kind on his body and guard against any possibility of any attempt to take control of your ship. Throw difficult people overboard if necessary."

"Understood."

"Furthermore, only permit a small number of your stowage on deck at any given time, perhaps only to do their toilet.

Provisions are being loaded now for the voyage. Nightingale is leaving Mines directly, you might benefit from his convoy."

"Very well, Major General."

"I am not pleased with this task, Thomas. The Acadians are religious people and good workers, but found themselves in the wrong place at the wrong time. Bon voyage."

Winslow, not having eaten, took a cup of tea and bread and butter and walked outside; he could smell the smoke and the sounds of collapsing buildings, the shrieks of livestock. When he left the church he entered an inferno and heard the shrieks of fear and pain from the women taken from their houses. He watched as the men rushed up from the fields, to cause trouble or at least to try and comfort their families. But Adams had done his job, there were several dozen of his men with fixed bayonets waiting for them.

Winslow was not at all tempted to watch the hundred men, women and children, all in desperation, and agony walk the mile to the wharf. He went back inside the mass house and refilled his tea and had another piece of bread and butter.

* * * * *

Charles Bois-Hébert was sitting in front of his shelter when Acquila and Beausoleil arrived back in Mémérancouque. He was freshly shaven and was braiding his bushy hair next to a campfire. On the ground next to him was a war axe and a metal breast-plate. It was obvious for what events he was preparing.

There was a swarm of men in the resistance encampment; at least five dozen more than when Acquila had left. He and Beausoleil walked quietly over to Bois Hébert who was smiling. He sipped from a pewter wine cup and rose.

"Mes amis. 'Quila, how is your wife and family?"

"Charles, my boys are so big now, I almost thought of bringing them with me, but Mathilde would have killed me, I think, if I had suggested it."

"We need strong young men, Acquila, their time will come."

"It would be nice if their time never needed to come, Charles. But, I think it will."

Bois-Hébert took a pipe from a pocket and filled it with tobacco, then lit it with a faggot from the fire.

"The English are coming, my friends. They have a company of about three score that loaded on a ship at Chignectou yesterday. I expect they will be coming this way. I expect they know we are here and will want to visit us. They'll likely split their forces on either side of the river.

"We'll relocate the camp today, there's a place further up and across the river that will serve as a protected place for our civilians. We'll mass our forces and meet them where we wish; on the other side of the river where many of our men have already begun preparing our battlefield. There's a stream there that we can use to trap them, I think. Go to your men and bring the barges to the shore.

* * * * *

Danks didn't much like Joseph Frye; found him a toff that thought he knew it all, although he was new here in Nova Scotia. Frye was also from the gentle town of Andover while Danks had grown up with a hard scrabble life in the mountains in western Massachusetts.

He would accept his commands, if necessary, but not look to stop a musket ball for him. He was pleased that Frye was on a different ship than Cobb's sloop on its way to Pedditkoudiac; the long trip would have been unbearable otherwise.

The tidal force was strong and they had been making a rough and slow voyage since leaving the Nova Scotia shores and battling the tides and the wind across the bay. Danks always suffered discomfort at sea and this voyage was no different; his stomach had emptied within an hour of leaving Chignectou and he hadn't bothered trying to refill it for the day of travel since. He gripped the gunwale and made it back near the stern where Sylvanus Cobb was working the tiller.

"How much longer, Syl?"

"What ya feelin' sad, Ben?"

"Sick. Never was suited to the sea, Syl."

"Better tie yourself down, then, Ben. We're crossing the tide for about another two hours to anchor, it'll be rough, sure."

"Got any whiskey or any of your fancy claret?"

Cobb reached into his coat pocket and pulled out a skin.

"Rum?"

"Argh. That'll have to do." Danks took a long pull of the vicious Jamaican liquor, coughed, and handed the skin back.

"That's a start. Got a cheroot?"

"God's balls, Danks. Didn't ye bring any supplies wi' ye?"

"I drink everything I get me hands on, Syl, and smoke everything that'll catch a flame. It comes with the business."

Cobb chuckled and adjusted the tiller to better manoeuvre in the strong winds.

"How ye feel about going after these Crapauds?"

"I'm paid well to do it, Syl. Don't feel one way or t'other."

"I feel kinda sorry for them. They're just peasants like my kin were."

"And mine. But peasants killin' other peasants for the king, that's always been the way."

"And 'spect shall ever be, Ben. You best go hunker down, we're about to hit a rough spot."

"Aye."

"Ye got yer pipe?" Danks nodded.

"Here's a pouch and my match case. I won't need it til we land."

"Thank ye, Syl."

* * * * *

Major Joseph Frye sent his sloop, The Warren, up the river called the Pedditkoudiac at high tide and watched with his arms folded as his men transferred to land by shuttling on the single whale boat that they had brought tethered to their sloop. He had his own fifty men, brought with him from Massachusetts. Joe Gorham and his company of rangers made up the balance. Frye had only a rough map and estimated that their destination, the village marked on his rough map called Mémérancouque, was less than a half league further up river.

He ordered his men into ranks and they began the march along the river bank until a small settlement came into view. It appeared empty. Frye was disappointed. He had come for action, to escape civilization and prove to others and himself of his strength and character under fire.

"Gorham!"

Joseph came to his commander and saluted.

"Take the men and burn what there is to burn."

Gorham properly marched to the front of this company, "Company, f'ard, march!"

Gorham was disgusted at his duty and wished he was almost anywhere else, except that he knew similar events were occurring across the colony. They arrived, and Gorham looked at his Sergeant, "Hodgins, light a fire and burn this village to the ground."

Gorham's Rangers began the effort of burning the deserted village, lighting torches from the fire and throwing them inside of buildings and on the thatched roofs. The church took the efforts of a quarter of the men to set aflame. The firing went on for two hours until the last barn was burned. Gorham noticed some movement on the other side of the river, "Major! Look!"

Frye looked across. There were two men, probably Acadians, fleeing from a copse of trees along the river, barely a hundred strides away.

"There they are! Gorham, have the men bring up the whale boat! We'll get our hands bloody this very day."

Gorham said, "Lieutenant Endicott, when ye get the whaleboat shuttle fifty men across the river. Find out who those renegades are!"

Endicott sent a small crew down to bring up the whaleboat.

The sun showed its first signs of setting as the whaleboat arrived and shuttled his company the thirty paces across the river. The banks were muddy and several of the soldiers slipped and got covered in the dark brown mess when they tried to scale the river sides.

Gorham, no coward, was glad that he had not been ordered to make the crossing. Frye walked to the edge of the river, and, the ranger commander had been pleased to see, had slipped into the muddy river bank and covered his breeches with sticky grime. The delay in rowing the unwieldy boats back and forth gave Gorham a chance to look and think. He noticed that no more than fifty paces to the left from their landing area on the opposite bank, there was a rivulet leading into the larger river. It was only a dozen paces across, but would be an obstacle for someone forced to move along the river. He smelled a rat.

* * * * *

Mathilde was organizing her living area. She and the Béatrice had made straw mattresses for themselves and she had made an extra soft one for Acquila for when he returned. Emile and Maurice had crafted chairs and Béatrice had used her skills to weave comfortable seats for them. They had a rough-hewn kitchen table and with the help of a few of the men had constructed a fireplace with a chimney that wasn't as good as the two they had left behind, but would do the job.

The door opened. It was Emile.

"Maman, the Doirons have invited us to share a pig if we do the smoking and butchering. Can we do this?"

"Of course. We need to prepare for winter. See if you can go fishing with someone as well."

"Oui, Maman."

Mathilde already had filled her small cold room under a trap door with turnips, carrots and potatoes. In a day or two they would be sure that they would not starve this winter.

Mati walked outside into the brisk fall morning to watch her boys. 'Men', she corrected herself. Maurice was carrying a hundred pound pig on his shoulders and Emile was pulling a huge sledge of dried maple toward the community smokehouse. Mati thought for a second and went inside and found the broken sabre that Acquila had taken with him from Beauséjour and left behind when he had visited. While it had likely served a violent purpose, she had cleaned it thoroughly and it would be perfect for chopping up the pig once it was fully smoked. Louis-Thomas was sleeping in his cradle.

As he had been taught, Maurice hung the carcass by its feet on a maple tree near the house, got a bucket and placed it beneath to catch the pig's blood. Mathilde came and gave him the sword and Maurice did the gruesome deed. Mathilde said, "Good work, my son. Will you relax and enjoy a cool drink?"

"I can't, Maman. I have to practice."

"Practice what?"

"With my musket. Before long I will join Papa to fight les maudits and I will need to be a good shot."

"I understand, Maurice. Please be careful to shoot your musket someplace safe, you."

Maurice smiled, "I am a good shot, Maman, I just wish to become better."

She stood on her toes to kiss his cheek.

"You are still my little boy, Maurice."

"I'm not little any more."

She laughed, "No. You are not mon petit any more."

* * * * *

Danks roused himself from the quiet place he had found to settle in with his pipe and try and minimize the effect of the waves and shifting tides on Cobb's sloop, "The York and Halifax". His pipe had gone out and he had stuffed it from Cobb's pouch and lit it with the smouldering fuse in Cobb's match case. There was a commotion aboard "The York" that he knew signified a ship preparing to heave to.

The ship was in the midst of a swirling, muddy, mess of water and silt heading toward a narrow rivulet with slick banks of sodden mud that appeared able to devour anyone so unfortunate as to fall into it.

Cobb was working hard on the tiller when Danks came up to him.

"Lend me a hand here, Ben. I'm trying to manoeuvre her into that tidal stream ahead port. Cobb was straining to hold the tiller against the tide and Danks grabbed a solid hold and together they were able to force the sloop directly into the mouth of the stream.

"Will save us anchorin' and havin' to use tenders for the men. Will also keep the Crapauds from seein' us."

The crew had dropped all but one sail to slow the ship down and support the tiller's direction. Finally, after the determined efforts of a half dozen strong men on the sheets, the ship righted itself and moved slowly upstream, surrounded on two sides by the muddy banks, until it came to a sudden halt, stuck in the mud of a lowering tide. Cobb's crew set out a row of planks to solid ground and the several dozen regulars and rangers and their muskets and kits of the expedition were soon on terra firma. Danks was among the last to depart and the first to light up another pipe.

* * * * *

Mathilde stirred. Her nightmares had been painful; she had been back in the time of her grand-mére when the red coats had butchered Mathilde's great grandfather. She could almost feel the heat from the firing of her grand mére's house. She sensed something was not right.

"Maman!"

"Emile!" She rose from her bed in a start.

"Quoi! Emile?"

"Maman, there are raiders!"

Mathilde rushed to the door and opened it a crack. She could see fires burning at the far end of the settlement and there seemed to be people running. She was terrified. She could not allow her nightmare to come true.

"Béatrice!! Levez vous. Prepare Louis. Vite! We need to prepare to run. Emile get your axe; Maurice, your musket."

Mathilde started to rush to her fireplace, but then remembered the coins were in the cold room. She lifted the trapdoor and started to climb down and slipped, falling six feet onto the dirt floor. She gathered herself and quickly tipped over a barrel of potatoes and pulled out the leather bag of coins. There were twelve left. She hung the strap around her neck.

She hurried upstairs. The boys were waiting and helped her come up and slammed the door shut. Emile, holding his axe, asked her, "Maman, what should we do?"

"Here are two coins each if you need them." Mathilde reached inside the money bag and handed them the coins and tried to think about how they could go to a safe place; she couldn't move quickly enough on her own to escape with Louis-Thomas. Would the English be more likely to harm women and children than two strong young men?

"Emile, we will be alright. You and Maurice, go. Go find your father. Tell him we will join you later."

"But, Maman… We promised our pére that we would protect you."

"You just go, you. We will be safe. Les maudits, I don't think they will harm women and children. Go!"

Maurice started to go to his mother, but his older brother pulled him away.

"Load your musket, Ami, and come. Ma mére? Are you sure?"

Mati hesitated for a brief moment and looked at Béatrice who was holding Louis-Thomas who was sobbing.

"Yes. It is important that we survive to find your father and tell him of this. Now go."

She put out her arms and the boys both hugged her, tears rolling down their cheeks. Emile felt his eyes well up but forced himself to leave. He pushed Maurice out the door, followed him and closed it tightly.

* * * * *

A minute later, at the sound of musket fire, Mathilde carefully opened the door. Outside she saw dozens of her friends and neighbours running in a panic. At the other end of settlement, a hundred paces away, barns were burning and she could make out the tricorn hats and red coats of English soldiers in the glow of the fires. There were others as well; wearing flat pancake hats, who looked dirty. A small group of these were coming her way, recklessly throwing torches onto building roofs and shooting at crowds.

For a moment she considered running, but there was no hope of escape for her with Louis in her arms. She made a quick decision.

"Béatrice, come." Mathilde picked up a coat and a pair of moccasins by the door and she led her daughter the few paces to the back of their house. Mati opened a shuttered window that led off into woodland only a half dozen paces behind.

"Go, ma petite. Take off your petticoats and put these on and run as fast as you can and hide in the forest."

Béatrice looked terrified and was crying but nodded and took off her heavy clothing and was left with just her slip and stockings and coat. Mati gave her the moccasins, helped her daughter through the window frame and closed the shutter behind her.

Mati was stuck in a quandary. She could surrender with Louis and put her destiny in the hands of the hated English, hide in the cold room hoping that they did not search her house and didn't set fire to it, or hide in the woods herself.

The English settled it for her: she could hear them yelling orders; they were coming closer. If she waited a minute longer she would have no choice to make. She had to go now. She pushed a wooden crate over to the window, climbed on it, and managed to sit on the window sill while holding her son. She bent her legs, used all her strength to hold Louis-Thomas and dropped the few feet to the ground and stumbled into the foliage of the forest just as a torch landed on the roof of their house.

Louis-Thomas was bawling in fear and Mati hoped that the English were too busy and there was too much other noise for him to be heard.

She hadn't run two steps before she felt horrible pain in her left ankle and almost stumbled. She gritted her teeth and forced herself to keep going. She managed to make it into the brush just as the roof of her house caught fire and lit up the ground around it. She huddled in a nettle bush and resisted the urge to cry from this new pain. Louis, wouldn't help and continued to bawl, and Mathilde muffled him and prayed that the English would not hear.

Looking through the brush she could see English everywhere. A small group with the flat blue hats were passing by her house on all sides. She took off her white bonnet and sunk down lower hoping that they would not notice her and she tried to stay perfectly still and tried to keep Louis silent. When she sensed they had moved on she carefully backed up and got as far away as she could.

* * * * *

Emile held his younger brother back for a moment before rushing away and they might be noticed. There were red backs some distance away who seemed to pre-occupied with burning, but others seemed to be looking inside and around buildings. The elder brother led them away from their home skirting the settlement along the tree line. Soon they were clear of the terrible acts in their village and began to relax in their voyage when Emile remembered his pledge to his father.

"Maurice, we must go back."

"Maman told us to go to father."

"But Papa told us to protect our mother and sisters. Our mother is very brave, Ami, but we'll go back."

They were almost back to their village and standing on the edge of forest with the sun now shining when a shot rang out. Emile was startled. Then he saw his brother fall to the ground, hit square in the chest by a musket ball, the light already going from his eyes. Emile picked up the fallen musket and the cartridge bag and looked for a target and could find none. But he saw the group of men with flat blue hats only a hundred paces away and coming toward him. Another shot barely missed him. He quickly said a prayer for Maurice and made a cross on his forehead as he had seen priests do, then ran into the woods, knowing that trying to help his brother could only cause his own death. He ran as if the devil was biting at his heels, as surely it was.

25 - VINGT-CINQ

Although she had no idea where her boys were and she had not found Béatrice at least she and her little boy were safe for the moment. In the morning light she could see through the trees that the entire village was gone, smoke rising from all the destroyed homesteads, brown bundles on the ground that had only hours before had been cattle.

She picked up Louis-Thomas and carried him as far as she could to the north, away from Chipoudie and toward the base of the mountains. Then she saw a commotion a hundred paces away. One of the blue-hatted English was lifting a body up by the hair and doing something with a knife. She thought back to her own nightmare, only hours before, that had happened almost a hundred years ago.

Now it had become real. The past had become the present.

She knew what the English were doing and her heart fell when she felt sure she knew to whom they were doing it. She waited until the English were gone then walked over and found the desecrated body of her second oldest son. And she placed Louis on the ground and fell to the earth and cried and cried until she could cry no more.

* * * * *

Jean Louis Le Loutre had managed to find transit back to France after a month stuck in Louisbourg and another begging for penance from the bishop in Quebec. Not only had he been rebuffed, he had been charged with going beyond his authority!

He had been pleased to see the last vestige of New France on the port side about three weeks ago. Soon he would be in Paris; he hoped he arrived there before the bishop's missive did.

He had lost weight during the turbulent times of the last few months and not eaten much on the voyage. But even worse, he had lost his treasure. While he had depleted it considerably, he still had left thousands of livres in gold buried beneath the church bell near the Beauséjour settlement when the English had invaded. The bishop had been very peeved about this and had threatened to have him excommunicated, even though he had not spent a sou on anything but the interests of the Holy Church. If he had let his flock starve, would this have served God? And He had received His church and his King his aboiteaux.

He did spent almost all of his time on his voyage in his small cabin praying for his flock, spread as they were across Acadia. He didn't pray to try and affect his own destiny; the Holy Father would judge him appropriately.

He packed his sparse belongings into a simple woven bag as he felt the ship start to heave to, probably preparing to enter the harbour of St. Malo. When it came to a full stop he rose and exited and climbed the few steps to the main deck.

When he arrived on deck he was surprised to find it in turmoil; there were a half dozen swarthy men, obviously English, starting to swarm around the decks, directed by a uniformed office who was in the company of a better dressed officer, likely a ship's captain.

Le Loutre thought that nothing good could come from this and started to withdraw to his cabin.

"You! See hear. Stop. Come here."

It was the more senior officer.

"I am Captain William Mantell of His Majesty's ship Centurion. We are blockading French ships who sail through our waters and looking for contraband and criminals. Who are you?"

Le Loutre indicated his supplication by showing his palms and approached the Englishman.

"Je suis Jean-Louis Le Loutre."

"You are a priest."

That was obvious; Le Loutre was wearing a cassock.

"Oui".

Just then, the sailors searching the French ship returned. One looked at Le Loutre, "You bastard," and drew a knife and rushed toward the abbé, but was held back by two of his shipmates.

"This priest wished to have me scalped by the red Indians, he did, and had several of my mates done in that way. I will have my revenge."

Captain Mantell said, "Hold on now, sailor. Le Loutre. I know of you. You're the one who caused so much trouble in Dartmouth when we were at Chebuctou. I think we might want to bring you back to England."

"I'll have me revenge I will."

Mantell said, "Sailor, you will finish our voyage in the brig. Next to Mister Le Loutre. Captain, you will bring your ship to follow us to port."

* * * * *

Mati cried through the rest of the day and an entire night. All was lost. Her little boy, Maurice, who had been so filled with joy and tried so hard to be just like his father had been massacred.

Her oldest boy had disappeared, she feared the worst.

The red coated devils would likely follow him like dogs until he collapsed with fatigue. She prayed that Emile would make his way to find his father.

And she prayed that Béatrice was safe.

She was without strength and prayed to St. Roger of Nanpan to provide this to her.

She found Maurice's rosary in his pocket and grasped it as hard as she could to her chest and prayed for the soul of her lost son and worried how he would be buried.

This prayer and her worry gave her strength to try and save the mortal body of her son from more violence from scavengers. She placed Louis-Thomas carefully on the ground and looked around for stones. They were plentiful and she covered her Maurice's body as best she could and tearfully blessed him.

Where could she go?

Whatever her destination, she needed to find Béatrice; she was still a girl and could not make her own way. Mathilde mustered her energy, prayed to Saint Roger one more time, and set off back toward the village.

She tried her best to keep the sun over her left shoulder when its rays reached her.

It was difficult travelling with Louis-Thomas; he was too heavy to carry and walked too slowly and wouldn't remain silent. She couldn't move very quickly or make any sudden movements, nor could she allow him to go hungry and get whiny. So it took her at least twice as long to return to the settlement as it would normally. But silence was more important than speed, although she came across no sign of the red-coats.

Finally she saw smoke through the trees and knew she was close. She carefully worked her way to the edge of the trees and looked out on total devastation. Every building, the church and all the homes and barns, were still aflame or heaps of smouldering wood. And worse, there was a group of the red coats at their old house eating the pig that they had hung. For a moment she hoped that the pork was undercooked and they all caught disease.

Then she heard a noise behind her and her heart dropped. She stood preparing to flee and turned and it was Béatrice and she gasped, "Oh. Thank you, God. You're alive."

"Yes, Maman. I hid well and came looking for you. Where are my brothers?"

Tears started to flow from Mathilde's eyes, she had thought she could cry no more.

"They killed Maurice and desecrated him."

Béatrice started to cry and they embraced with Louis in

between who started crying.

"And Papa? Emile?"

"I think Emile is with your father and I think that they are at the camp of Beausoleil.

* * * * *

Emile knew generally where his father was, but no idea how to get there. He knew from discussions with his father that it took about five hours to walk to and in what direction. He cried as hard as he ran when he left Maurice, running as fast as he could directly away from the English. After an hour he thought he was safe and slowed down, awash in tears, but he kept walking.

He walked until the sun started to set and he came to a river at high tide. It appeared to thicken to his right, he had never even tried to swim, so he turned to his left and followed the river upstream. When the sun began it's decline he considered stopping, but the moon was bright and sky was clear and he kept walking until the river became a stream and he jumped across.

Once across the stream he came to steep hills. He knew that his father's camp wasn't in the mountains so he walked along the edge of them until light came and he was walking along the shore. With the sun in his eyes he walked by what looked like huge mushrooms in the bay. On closer examination he realized they were islands. He knew he was on the right track as his father had talked about these. He carried on until he came to a large river and walked along its shore until he saw a ship filled with red uniformed soldiers sailing upstream.

He must be going in the right direction, he thought, the English were probably going to attack his father's camp. He needed to hurry and began to jog. While he fell behind the ship he soon caught up as the river began to narrow, then he saw the English stop their boat and go across to the other side and begin setting fire to a village. It might be his father's encampment. The chance to warn his father gave him more energy and he ran faster. He saw a group of men hiding behind some mud dikes on his side of the river. It must be his father. He was careful to not be seen by the English and came up to the Acadians. He noticed his father's friend Beausoleil in the group and quietly came up to him and whispered, "Monsieur Brossard...".

Beausoleil was shocked and turned and pushed Emile down, "Who are you? Le garcon de Girouard?"

"Oui."

"Be quiet. Your father is nearby."

* * * * *

Gorham watched as Endicott's company crossed the river and was forming into ranks on the other side of the side. He ran south along the river's edge and tried to stay low, until he got on the other side of the dike and belly crawled to the very edge of the river and carefully studied the dike. Nothing. Then he saw a movement. Could have been a marsh bird. But he couldn't take the chance.

He started running back toward the crossing point yelling, "Major Frye! It's a trap! Bring them back! Bring them back!"

Frye heard Gorham's yell and looked to him and then across the river. The men were forming normally. Had Joseph gone mad?

As soon as the last English soldier was ashore and in ranks a fusillade of musket balls from the dike on the other side of the small stream tore into them, taking off arms and exploding heads. Endicott's company ran in the opposite direction looking for cover and right into a second fusillade that knocked down a dozen more. They were in a cross fire.

The English troop lost all discipline, many going back toward the river to find cover, others even looking for cover from their slain comrades. Frye yelled at Gorham, "Captain, get our men here under cover."

Gorham barked his order.

"Company. Take cover in the village!"

The redcoats remaining on the north side of the river hurried to cover among the smouldering ruins and were joined by Gorham and Frye. Joseph looked at the massacre unfolding on the other side of the river. The English troops were only surviving because the Acadians were poor shots and poor muzzle loaders. Most of the English had retreated to the slippery banks of the Pedditkoudiac River for protection, some sliding into the water.

"Major, we need to send troops to cover the retreat. Ten across from the two Acadian positions."

"Make it done, Joseph."

Gorham hurried to the largest cluster of soldiers under cover and gave the order. The fusiliers moved instantly into position and began firing. Soon the Acadians had to change their positions to avoid musket fire from across the river. This gave the surviving English a chance to slide down the river bank, and flop and swim and crawl awkwardly cross the muddy water to the safe side and get under cover. But the field on the other side was littered with more than half their number dead with survivors screaming and moaning in pain.

The firing across the river continued until both sides were totally out of cartridges. Then Gorham and Frye watched as the Acadians rose from their positions and waved their muskets in the air hooting and hollering. One stood and held up his musket and shouted in French, "Vive l'Acadie!"

Gorham gathered the remaining men safely behind what remained of the church and did a count; at least three dozen men were missing. It had been a slaughter. He had learned to respect Brossard and despise and almost fear his brutality from previous engagements. The Acadian was a fearsome opponent.

Nathan Adams was one of the survivors.

"Adams assay our ammunition supply."

Adams returned after walking among the men.

"We have fewer than one hundred cartridges in total, Captain."

Gorham went to Frye who was shaken and silenced.

"We don't have the ammunition or men to pursue the attackers, Major. We should depart the field and avoid another engagement."

Frye nodded. "Make it so."

* * * * *

After decimating the English at the river the Acadians regrouped at their camp at Le Cran in the mountains, only a few hundred paces from the scene of the battle. Emile was wrapped up in the adrenaline and excitement and frenetic run back from the spectacular victory. He ran along with the rest of the resistors while looking for his father. Despite not sleeping for a full night and day he was filled with energy and regretted not arriving in time to participate in the battle.

At the camp the hundred Acadians who participated in the raid attacked a pig that had been roasted and hung from a tree and cracked open barrels of chokecherry wine and lit their pipes. The drums and spoons and sticks and whistles and fiddles were taken out and soon the triumphant victors were clogging and dancing with each other in reels, swinging each other around like dervishes; stopping for a moment to refill their pottery cups.

Emile got caught up in the celebration when he received a hard slap on the back and he turned to see his father, his hair now long and tied in back.

Acquila grabbed his son, pulled him close and kissed him on the forehead and embraced him hard.

"Emile! Beausoleil! My son has joined us!" Acquila began introducing Emile to other resistance fighters and it was a blur for the boy and he remembered none of the names.

The older man grabbed his son, picked up two mugs from a table and filled them with wine and gave Emile one.

"Come, tell me about your mother and brothers and sisters." He pulled Emile away from the crowd and behind some rough buildings.

Acquila could tell something was wrong. Emile was seldom excited and usually quite calm. While he had been excited only a few minutes before, now he seemed morose. He only sipped at his wine and after all the excitement was behind them the heavy weight of the terror he had seen and the fatigue he felt deflated him.

"What is wrong?"

Emile hung his head and shook it sadly.

"Tell me, Son."

"The English. Les maudits. They came." He broke into tears.

Acquila took a deep breath and closed his eyes…

"What? Tell me, Emile."

"They burned the village. And… killed Maurice…".

Acquila was silent and wished he had known this before the battle just ended. There would not be a single English left with his hair.

Acquila had seen so much violence and butchery that knowledge of any more was an expectation not a surprise. But he would make them pay.

He remained silent for several minutes; getting his emotions organized.

"Your mother? Sister? Louis?"

"I don't know. We separated. She told me to find you."

"They're alive?"

"When I left them."

"We need to go there. Let me get some fellows to go with us. Come."

Acquila stood and Emile, downcast, followed.

Beausoleil was seated under a large elm tree speaking with Bois-Hébert both with their pipes, sharing a jug of rum.

They stood when the Girouards arrived.

"Beausoleil, you know my older son, Emile."

"I met him before the attack. He kept very quiet and still as I asked him to."

"Charles, this is my son, Emile. This is Commander Bois-Hébert."

"It is a pleasure to meet you, Monsieur Girouard. We need strong young men to assist us in our struggles."

"Emile brings some bad news from Chipoudie."

"Tell."

Emile gathered his strength, "The English came yesterday morning. They burned the village and killed my brother. I don't know how many others, Monsieur Bois-Hébert."

Acquila said, "Charles, how shall we respond?"

"We have received word that the English have gathered the residents of Beauséjour, Pré du Bourques and La Coup and other nearby settlements in their fortress."

"For what purpose?"

"Have les maudits ever done anything that is not evil, 'Quila?"

"Never."

"The first thing is to protect our families, and you to protect yours. And we will continue to bite at the heels of les maudits. But we also need to find a haven, a safe place that we can defend ourselves when they continue their terrorism. I know of some places north of here."

"I will go to find my wife, daughter and son. Can you help?"

"Monsieur Girouard, recruit as many men as you need to save your family and go now before the English do any more harm."

* * * * *

Danks and his company were drinking rum in their camp next to Cobb's anchorage in the river near the destroyed Acadian settlement. They had feasted on the roast pig and were awaiting the high tide in the morning to transport their two dozen prisoners to Fort Cumberland. Most were women and children; many of the Acadian men had been killed, some probably had escaped.

There was a ruckus near the mouth of the river, now at medium tide. Cobb stood and looked.

"It's 'The Warren'." Frye's sloop had laid anchor just off shore.

Men from the sloop were pulling up the tethered whaleboat and three men boarded it and rowed to shore. Frye and Gorham came ashore leaving behind one of the rangers with the boat.Cobb and Frye were friends so Sylvanus approached Gorham who met him half way.

"How be ye, Joseph. Ye look a little troubled."

"More than a little, Syl. We almost got massacred up near the French settlements on the river."

"God's blood! What happened?"

"We were razing the settlements along the river and got ourselves ambushed. They are snakes, these Acadians. They hid in wait, behind some dikes. Teased us to cross the river and got us in a cross fire, they did."

"How many lost?"

"Half the bleeding company. More than a score, but less than thirty. That many are missing, but we left quickly once the bloody French retired."

"God's blood indeed. Any officers?"

"Billings was wounded from Winslow's battalion and March from Scott's was lost. Other than that ordinary soldiers and provincials.

"Joe, Have ye got any provisions? We're out of cartridges, the bloody monkeys were hollering and hooting at us from across the river once they realized we were helpless. Truthfully, we were lucky that they didn't pursue us. None of us would be here, anow."

"God may end up having been with ye, Joe."

"Could have been worse."

"Any Mikymakys."

"Could've been. Hard to tell them apart these days. Renegade Frenchmen and savages all look the same."

"Who led them?"

"Not sure, but we were tracking to try and find Brossard and Bois-Hébert. Probably them."

"I'll get ye some supplies. Danks! Come over."

Danks joined the two men, and Cobb offered his regrets.

Danks said, "We've the remains of a pig the Acadians left behind. We're not done our mission but could spare some cartridges, if needed."

Frye said, "I pray we won't need them."

"Rum?"

"We have plenty. Our mission ended early."

"Then can you take our prisoners back? Will save us having to ferry them and keep looking for more."

"Done."

"Danks, send the prisoners to Frye's sloop. He'll take them back to Fort Cumberland for us."

"Yes, sor."

* * * * *

Mathilde and Béatrice took turns carrying and helping Louis-Thomas as they carefully avoided making any sound or noise that the English might hear in the still night. Louis-Thomas had been good all day, clinging to his mother which helped her carry him and being perfectly quiet when he walked on his own. But after a day of motion he wanted to sleep and couldn't and let his mother know. A few times he cried out loudly as they were escaping and she trying to muffle him, but the more she tried the worse he squirmed and more noise he made.

She wasn't sure where they should go. She hadn't eaten in over a day and she was dealing with her grief by trying to set it behind her. If she kept moving she could try to focus on now and forget the pain and tragedy from the day before.

Béatrice prayed enough for both of them, but when they had settled down for the night, when she prayed for St. Roger to provide them food, Mati knew they couldn't continue to wander through the wilderness. She needed to find food. But she had never, ever had to find food; only cook it. She looked around the forest floor for greens that she recognized as edible but could find none. At home, she had lived near a forest, but had never foraged there because the greens that she enjoyed were found in marshlands.

They didn't dare go near the marshes or tidal streams to catch fish; the English would surely see them. It was autumn, so birds nests would be empty. She hadn't been in Chipoudie long enough to have secret places for mushrooms or crabapples. They would need to find a crabapple tree! She thought they must grow wild here as they did in Beaubassin. She knew apple trees were lower and bushier than the elms, maples and oaks in the forest and their leaves were a lighter green; if she focussed on looking for the leaves, she could find the apples!

This got her thinking. There would be berries of various types and there would be other forest greens that her grandmother would include in meals. Dandelions and mustard and mushrooms; she had seen these in the forest, but her mother had warned her to ensure they were not poisonous. She explained this to Béatrice and her daughter went one way while Mati went the other. Thankfully, when they had stopped, Louis-Thomas had fallen asleep, which made her task easier. She concentrated on bushy light green leaves in the air and looked for yellow flowers on the ground and white mushrooms. After concentrating she was amazed at what she was able to collect and store in her apron. Then she saw an apple tree on the edge of a clearing and walked up to it. She noticed she had worked her way back to the edge of the old settlement. She heard a noise. It was probably Béatrice. But it came from the wrong direction; it came from the clearing and she looked through the foliage and there were six English soldiers only a few dozen paces away.

* * * * *

Acquila walked around the camp and Beausoleil, Bernard Haché, Henri Doucet and Jacques Robicheaux grabbed their muskets and joined him and Emile. More than six men would be difficult to maintain their silence and stay hidden.

They were cautious in the travel along the river, suspicious that the English might be organizing a counter attack. Robicheaux reminded Acquila of Camille Robicheaux, who he thought must be trapped in the English fortress.

"Jacques, are you family with Camille?"

"Cousin."

"You remind me of him."

"He is very dour and opinionated."

"Oui. He is."

Jacques barely said a word, but in their battle the day before he had been very fierce and had even taunted the English after they had retreated. Haché and Doucet he knew from Beaubassin. It took them a half day to get within eye sight of the old settlement. They climbed up the hill north of the settlement to get a better view. First they noticed the burned buildings, smoke still rising from some. Then their eyes were drawn to movement of people further south. Bernard had a spyglass and looked more closely.

"It is English. Maybe some others."

"May I?" Bernard handed the glass to Acquila.

He saw about two dozen English in tricorns and another dozen in flat blue hats. But there were also others, civilians. His eyes narrowed but he couldn't identify Mathilde or Béatrice; he saw no one carrying a child. But there were more than a dozen people in Acadian clothing; men and women.

"They're not there."

Bernard Haché said, "But others are."

Acquila said, "Should we try to save the ones that are there?"

"If we had more men. We can do no good now."

"Then we must look for Mati and Beatrice elsewhere."

"Oui."

Just then there was motion from crowd and Acquila raised the spyglass. The English were moving toward the river where the rising tide had lifted a ship off its muddy course. They were preparing to leave.

"They're boarding a ship."

Just then Acquila noticed some movement and pointed the spyglass. A small troop of the blue hats were pushing two woman from the wooded area across the clearing, toward the ship. One might be carrying something, perhaps a child.

* * * * *

Mathilde backed up slowly and quietly both to avoid making any noise herself and to keep Louis-Thomas from awakening. After she had retreated about ten yards she moved more quickly to escape. She was safe, she thought. Then Béatrice came crashing through the woods and called to her mother. Mathilde tried to quiet her, then whispered loudly, "Run!"

She held Louis-Thomas tightly, raised her skirts as best as she could and began running. Béatrice looked shocked and stood still for a second and then joined her mother and ran as quickly as she could away.

26 - VINGT-SIX

Benoni Danks and three of his rangers were making a last search around the vicinity of the village for any stragglers. Danks was anxious to return after his week on patrol. His scalping had not gone as profitably as it might have; the population of the village they had visited was small and most of the Acadians had surrendered peacefully. He expected he would see more of the same on this side of the river. Because it was difficult to get to, most of the escapees were likely not here.

He was about to go back when he heard some sounds in the wooded area. He signalled to his men and they broke into the forest.

"There are some over there!" He pointed and his men went after the two women. Mathilde and Béatrice tried their best, but Mathilde with a child and in their long skirts they had no chance. Mati stopped and prayed that the English, as evil as they are, would not harm women and children.

"Come on, women. Come with us. We're takin' ye home."

Danks' men took Mati and Béatrice by the arms and led them out of the forest without any resistance.

* * * * *

Acquila was frantic and picked up his musket and started to leave to go after his wife and children but Haché held him back.

"Ami, you can do nothing. The English, they will only kill you and they will take your family anyway. At least now, you have hope they will survive and that you will find and free them."

"I am watching them leave. I cannot sit here."

"You must. We know where they are going. They will be taken to Beauséjour, which you helped build. You know secrets from that you might use to rescue them. If you are killed, then THEY will lose all hope, and what is worse."

They returned to Le Cran and Acquila went to find Brossard and told him he would go and rescue his wife.

"Beausoleil, will you help me?"

"I will help you, but I think I am too well known to be possibly seen around you if you are near the English to save them."

"But, Girouard, for you? We will leave tomorrow after we have planned our mission."

* * * * *

As they were being loaded onto the whale boat to be taken to the ship Mati looked back. She strangely felt that Acquila was watching her. She was sure that he would be doing anything he could to save them. She knew he would not be foolhardy; he was brave but even in gambling games he would never place a bet he did not have more than an equal chance to win. Some of the men on the boat were weeping and all of the women. Béatrice was sobbing and Louis-Thomas was bawling.

Mathilde was stoic. The women in her family history had all faced times like this and all had survived. She would as well. Their last voyage on a ship had promised hope and a new life. This one had only a glimmer of hope provided by a strong and brave husband that loved her and her children.

* * * * *

After Acquila and his group got back to Le Cran and got a jug of chokecherry wine and a bag of tobacco the men sat around a fire. Beausoleil and Bois-Hébert joined them and spoke first after everyone, even Emile, had a mug of wine and lit up their pipes. Bois-Hébert was even more experienced at war and intrigue than Brossard.

"Girouard, we will rescue your wife and children. Do we know of any other family members of any of our men who might also wish to rescue theirs? Find out.

"Do we know what they plan to do with them? They cannot keep them prisoner forever; they must have other plans. We need to capture a prisoner who would tell us this, and we will need to know before we plan very much. Brossard, you will send some men to capture us an English and find out."

"I will do this myself."

"Bien, start now." Beausoleil left to find two good men to help take an English soldier.

"We can rescue them from the inside, or the outside. We know the ground there probably better than les maudits do.

"We can use assault strategies or covert ones. We cannot do this by force; they outnumber us at least ten to one. From inside we escape with them, from outside we help them escape."

"Girouard, what do you think?"

"I can get inside."

"How could you get out again?"

Acquila shrugged.

"Tunnel. We're diggers. We've been digging all our lives."

Bois-Hébert stood.

"Then that is what we will do."

* * * * *

Joseph Brossard took two men and timed their travel to arrive at dusk in Au Lac, just north of Fort Beauséjour and hidden from it by a ridge and forest. Beausoleil, himself, had killed by his own hand several English who were foraging or exploring in places where they should not have been. And it had always been at dusk, when lonely soldiers wandered away from the barking of their officers and desired peace.

He suspected they would be much less cautious with the Acadians removed or in custody.

The small village at Au Lac had been razed but they found a barn that was not completely destroyed and was dry and they rested there. Joseph Landry was with him who spoke a little English that he had learned during the peaceful time by blacksmithing at Cyr's trading post.

At dusk the men went up to a place in the forest that allowed them to oversee the English fort and watch for opportunity. They did not have to wait long. They watched an English soldier walk slowly away from the fort and separate himself from others who were avoiding their superiors.

The English walked toward the burned out settlement, possibly to look for loot among the ruins.

The Acadians, keeping themselves below the line of sight ran down to the remains of Le Loutre's church and waited. As they suspected the soldier was soon rooting around in one of the ruined houses. Beausoleil had a Miqmaq war club. He looked around the corner of one side of the church and waited. When the Englishman stopped to light his pipe he ran to him and hit him on the head. Two other men followed and dragged him behind the remains of the church. Then they carried him to the barn at La Coupe, gagged him and tied him spread-eagled on the ground.

Landry went to wet his shirt in the river. When the English was secure Landry placed his sodden shirt over the soldier's face until he began choking and coughing. He awoke and was terrified. Beausoleil held up his scalping knife in front of his face and sliced his cheek. The soldier kicked and tried to free himself and Beausoleil pulled down his breeches. They learned what they wanted to know and finished him, throwing the corpse into the Riviere Au Lac, and started their return trip.

* * * * *

Mati was devastated and she and Béatrice huddled together during the entire overnight trip back to Beauséjour. Her daughter was sobbing. Mathilde felt an urge to, but would not allow herself to do so. Her mother and grandmother had been through times as horrible and survived and had been able to raise their families with joy. She would be resolute; while this moment was terrible she would not allow it to weaken her.

She tried to remember Maurice as if he were alive and waiting for her back in Beauséjour. To avoid thinking of his brutal murder she concentrated on keeping Louis-Thomas entertained. His innocence strengthened her resolve; for him this was just another new day and another adventure. She had to think and feel like her child.

At least the English didn't bother them. She couldn't find anyone she knew on the ship, she hoped Father Le Guerne and the people she knew from Chipoudie had all escaped. She still had the coins. Was it possible that she could use them to bribe an English or somehow ease their imprisonment?

She had spent very little time in the fortress, what did she remember about it that might help them survive, or, pray to God, possibly help them escape? Where was Acquila? Was he still alive? She had to think he was. His times fighting the English with the Abbé had made him tough and very able to both protect himself and others. She also absolutely knew that he would go to his death to save her and the children.

She wondered about Emile. She had seen him escape the English and believed that he would have made his way to Acquila. Any other event was unimaginable. He was his father's son.

After a while the three slept, even Louis-Thomas responded to the soft rocking of the ship. Then she was awakened by the shouts of the crew members and their frantic movement around the crowded deck. She looked over the prow and could see the mound of the fort. The elms and oaks were starting to lose their leaves and it promised to be a warm late summer day.

She saw two tender boats coming out to move the human contents to shore. She waited her turn and they and the other twenty Acadians eventually arrived on shore and were marched up to the front gates and over the drawbridge and into the fort. Awaiting her was Philomene Bourque who hugged her and Béatrice.

"Mathilde, I am so glad you are safe. We have heard terrible rumours."

"The truth is very terrible, Philomene. The English killed Maurice and desecrated his body. Acquila, I believe, escaped them and I pray that Emile is with him."

"Oh, I am very, very sorry."

"The crying is over, Philomene. We now have to worry about the living. What is it like here?"

"The English have not been doing us any more harm and they are feeding us sufficiently, if not as well as we would feed ourselves."

"What are they going to do with us? They cannot keep us here forever."

"Come away from here, where we will not be noticed."

They walked away from the entrance and toward a more private place.

"There are stories that they will send us back to France."

"Pah. Back to France? I have never been to France and neither have any of my parents and grandparents. How can they send us back. Are Simon and your children unharmed?"

"Yes. For a change Simon is very quiet here and has not gotten us in any trouble. The children are accepting this as a new home."

Mathilde looked around for the first time, almost the entire parade ground was filled with bell tents.

"Are all of our people here in the fortress?"

"Those that survived? I think they are also holding others prisoner in the other fortress across the river, but I'm not sure. Come. I have some tea and we have some bread and cheese."

* * * * *

Beausoleil and his men dog-trotted all night to return to Mémérancouque and slept for a few hours before crossing the river at high tide in a canoe and returning to Le Cran at mid morning. They went to find Acquila.

Bois-Hébert was sitting on a stump smoking his pipe alongside Acquila. He looked up at them and said, "Bonjour."

"We know."

"Well... please tell us."

"They are planning to send our people on boats to New England."

"Quoi? There are thousands of us."

"They have all their fortresses in Acadie acting as temporary prisons until they bring in ships."

"Did they tell your dead English friend when they planned to do this?"

"It is expected to begin within the next two or three weeks."

"Well, Acquila, how would we do this? You know the fortress best."

"We are diggers. If we got 2 dike spades over the wall, we could dig under the walls in a night."

"Then that's what we will do. You and Beausoleil will find yourself a way to be captured and do it. We will start a distraction to draw as many of their soldiers away as possible and you will escape with as many of our people as possible while les maudits are occupied with defending themselves. D'accord?"

"D'accord."

* * * * *

Acquila and Beausoleil found some paper and ink and quill pens in the remains of the church across the river and Acquila started sketching out a diagram of the fortress. Acquila knew it intimately and suspected that the English had not fortified its weaknesses on the bay side of the fort in the short time since the Acadians had left or been captured.

He chose a spot in the star shaped earthworks that he knew to be hidden from the parade ground and main gates by the new barracks and was poorly constructed as it had been away from the English positions when it was being prepared for the siege. It was the place where he and his family had escaped before.

He did a detailed map with landmarks to identify exactly where the spot of the digging could be identified on the other side of the rampart so that they could have diggers on both sides. The tunnel would only need to be about twenty feet long. With diggers working in shifts on both sides, it might be completed in just a few hours.

Acquila worked for almost a full day on his sketches, drawing a map that showed how he and his family had escaped before and detailing it down to small trees. He thought he might hide a rope of some sort in his clothing that he could throw over the rampart to show the exact place to dig on the other side.

The more he thought about it, the more sure he was that it could work. The fort was designed to keep armies out, not keep people in, and once outside the main wall, all the angles of the fort made that side of the dry moat invisible. It would be unlikely that there would be guards on the nearest bastion nearest the bay and their escape path.

Once the tunnel was built, if there was a distraction, it would take less than five minutes for a small number of people to be safely on the other side of the palisades. And if there was a boat waiting, they could be out of musket range and to safety in only a few minutes more.

He spent another hour going over his plan, before he showed it to Bois-Hébert and Brossard, making sure that he had covered all the contingencies.

Finally he did one quick look through all his drawings. He corrected a few mistakes. It was ready.

Acquila hadn't eaten all day and he took his plans to Bois Hébert and Brossard who were having a fish stew and gave some to him. Acquila invited Joseph Doiron and Jacques Robicheaux to come to the meeting because he knew that they were excellent diggers.

They went over the entire plan until it became dark and then lit torches to make sure they had covered everything.

They decided that Acquila and Beausoleil would arrange to be captured and that Bois-Hébert would arrange two diversions. They would recruit Miqmaqs to attack the fortress at Baie Verte and require the English Commander to reinforce it with as many troops as possible. Then at night they would attack the northeast side of the fortress with as much musket fire and noise as they could. Brossard knew where the previous French defenders had buried swivel guns near the Pont à Buot and they would use these to make as much noise as possible.

Acquila would recruit Camille in the camp and offer to take him out with his family. Doiron would throw two dike spades over the sloped earthen glacis mounds and the men would get to work.

They would have a boat hidden out of sight of the fort on the Riviere au Lac ready to pick up the escapees. The Acadians were experts on tides and knew exactly the night when the tides would allow the ship to be quietly hidden upstream to be brought downstream the next.

They stayed up almost all night talking through the plans and looking for flaws and identifying risks and ways it could go bad. One thing they agreed on was that no one, not even their family members they were rescuing, could know until the diversion was underway and the digging was almost finished. In four nights the tides would be at their highest and the moon at its darkest. It was also very likely that it would rain or possibly even snow. They would do it then.

* * * * *

Beausoleil and Bois-Hébert spent the next two days organizing the diversions.

Beausoleil travelled north to the coast to look for Jean

Baptiste Copit, who he found in Richibuctou, and arranged for him to attack the English Fort at Baie Verte in three days with as many warriors as he could, and found another fifty Acadians who would join them.

He returned and directed any Acadians he met on the way back to come with him for an attack on the English.

Bois-Hébert prepared his hundred and fifty men to assault the English fort directly and they set to work wrapping cartridges for muskets, making torches and powder. He used the maps drawn by Acquila to explain to his captains how the diversion would be staged.

Acquila talked to Doiron and Jacques Robicheaux about how they would dig the tunnels; the two others would work from outside of the fort. Acquila explained how he would toss a rope over the ramparts to identify the line and how the tunnel should be built two spade lengths from the bottom and one spade length high. The rampart was sloped wider at the bottom so digging higher meant a shorter tunnel.

They also discussed who among those inside the camp they would invite to join the digging team. Acquila recommended Camille, who was Jacques' cousin, and the others agreed that Camille was among the best diggers in the settlement, if he was inside the fort. They discussed including Simon, but although he was like a brother to Acquila, he tended to talk too much and couldn't be trusted not to tell someone he shouldn't, although Acquila thought he would invite him and his family to escape at the last moment.

It was time. Beausoleil and Acquila prepared enough food for their travel and filled wine skins. Acquila spent some time with Emile and explained what they were going to do.

"Papa, can I go with Bois-Hébert and participate in the diversion?"

Acquila thought for a moment.

"Emile, we are going to rescue your mother and sister and baby brother. We each have to play our role. And I am proud of you wanting to do your part. It is very brave. I will leave it up to you, if you wish to do this. But if the worst happens and we are all captured or worse, we need someone to tell our story and to carry forward the memories of our family. So do not get killed."

"I will go with Bois-Hébert."

"Be brave, my son. I pray I will see you here in a few days."

Acquila talked to a few of the other men while on his way to meet with Beausoleil and thanked them for volunteering to help him save his family. They were all enthusiastic, after their success of a few days before, and eager to do more harm to les maudits.

Then it was time to leave and he and Beausoleil started out.

27 - VINGT-SEPT

It took Acquila and Beausoleil and the two diggers only half a day to make the trip even after needing to walk several miles out of their way to avoid the Riviere Tintamarre. They arrived at Au Lac in the warmth of an afternoon threatened by rain and walked up to the ridge to survey the fort. From the higher elevation they could see the tops of the large bell tents that housed the captives. But they were both surprised that the tents were outside of the main fortress in the fosse, the ditch below the ramparts.

Acquila crawled over to Joseph Doiron and Jacques who were seated on the ground next to Brossard.

"Amis, we should dig down on either side of the wooden pickets, only about our own height, then we can dig toward each other. But it will be much less difficult than we thought."

"I think we can do this."

The two men nodded with broad smiles.

"I had thought they would be holding our families more securely. But this proves that they are not planning to hold them for a very long period; that they are going to take them away."

Beausoleil said, "Bien, and the tents will make it even more difficult for our digging to be seen. This might make our escape easier in some ways, but more difficult in others. If we are discovered by our own people, they might attempt to escape all at once, meaning the English will be alerted and perhaps no one will escape."

Acquila said, "I know it will be difficult, but until we have the tunnel dug, no one in the camp must know of our plan.

"Joseph and Jacques, Bois-Hébert and our main force will arrive tomorrow night after dark and will meet you at Au Lac. Make yourselves invisible until then." The men nodded confidently.

"Beausoleil, are you ready to become a prisoner of les maudit Anglais?"

"As good a time as ever." He crossed himself. "Allons y."

The two men stood and calmly walked down the hill toward the main gates of the fort, getting odd looks from the English soldiers they passed on the way. When they came to the drawbridge Acquila went up to the sentry and slowly tried to explain that they had come to join their families and work on the fort. The sentry left and went to find an officer who spoke French. He soon returned with an officer and while he didn't fully comprehend the Acadians' request, he allowed them to pass. It would save some of his men having to apprehend them later.

The two men entered and saw a refugee camp surrounding the military one. Soldiers filled the area inside while the Acadians were outside the main ramparts but inside the wooden palisade on the other side of the dry moat.

"Your family will be found there." He pointed to the tents and indicated they should walk down the earthen rampart.

When they were away from the soldier Beausoleil said, "I would think they would have a much larger garrison. They came with, we believe, as many as two thousand, but there are less than a quarter of that number; if that many."

Acquila said, "I suspect they have sent some back to the hell they came from and put others in the field trying to find and capture the two of us!"

Both men laughed.

They looked around for familiar faces. It was obvious that everyone knew Beausoleil, but he knew very few.

Finally they came across Simon Bourque whose jaw dropped when he saw Acquila. He hurried over.

"Girouard, What in God's name are you doing here. We thought you were safe."

"I missed you, Simon."

"Well, I missed you too, Girouard. Come, Mathilde and your children are here. They will be excited. She told me you were probably with Beausoleil in the forest."

"This is Joseph Brossard. Beausoleil, this is my friend Simon Bourque."

"Pleasure to make your acquaintance. I have heard of you. But why are you here, Acquila?"

"I decided my war is over, and I want to be with my family to protect them. Les maudits murdered Maurice, I did not wish to lose any more family members and my destiny is with Mathilde, and she is here. So I came to her."

"Come, let me bring you to Mathilde."

"No, Simon, please not. You are my brother, but I would like to find her so we're both surprised."

"Can I follow behind?"

"Yes, but please allow me to find her."

"I will be as quiet as a palourde."

Acquila and Beausoleil wandered around the camp and captured the eyes and attention of everyone. Many came to introduce themselves to Brossard and he was polite but stayed very calm and discouraged conversation.

Acquila noted that the Acadians looked healthy, but seemed very sad as if living was a struggle and there could be no happy ending. Acquila looked for something in the crowd that he would recognize as his wife, but all the women were wearing the same clothes and bonnet so it was impossible to do so by looking at their dress. Then he tried to identify tiny women with a young boy, but there were none.

Finally he heard a child cry behind some tents and walked toward the sound. As he got closer he became more careful until he peeked around one and there she was; standing next to Béatrice talking to some women. He treaded quietly until he got a couple of steps away and then moved quickly and embraced her from behind and she shrieked.

"Non, ma Chér. C'est moi!"

She turned around and smiled and started crying while staying in his embrace.

"Quila, you scared me, you. What are you doing here?"

"I missed my wife and babies."

Béatrice came toward them and joined the embrace, crying as well and soon all his family were crying while Acquila was smiling broadly.

Mati said, "Chér, come to our tent."

"Let me see my little boy."

Acquila lifted Louis-Thomas and looked at his smiling face and kissed him on his forehead. "Louis-Thomas, you will make your papa very proud some day."

"Show me where you are imprisoned."

Acquila carried Louis-Thomas to their family tent and ran into Philomene who gave him a kiss on the cheek. He also met and was welcomed by many other friends from Beauséjour and Beaubassin.

Mathilde led them into their tent; it was large for the family and he was happy that there was room for him.

They sat on their straw mattresses and Mathilde got Louis-Thomas ready for his dinner.

"I'm happy you came, Chér. But I am very suspicious. I expected that you would try to save us, I had no idea how. So how will you save us from here? I kept expecting you to show up and take us before we arrived here at our prison."

"You know me too well, ma Chér. Of course, I came to save you and our children. We will be leaving tomorrow night, but you can tell no one."

"How?"

"We are diggers, Chér. We will dig our way out."

"But that will be impossible. There are guards; English soldiers everywhere. You will be caught!"

"We are not going to do it in the light of day when all les

maudits are standing around watching, Mati. We will do it in the middle of the night when they are asleep. And we will have some distractions for them to keep them occupied worrying about their scalps more than their prisoners."

Mathilde said, "We still have coins, too."

"Hmmm. They may be very useful. For now, Chér, the important thing is that you and the children be wide awake tomorrow in the middle of the night. Do you think we can be alone together tonight?"

"I will make sure we are alone tonight."

* * * * *

While Acquila, Simon and Camille were sitting outside Simon's tent smoking and drinking rum in the early evening, Robert Monckton was reading an urgent dispatch from their Fort Monckton at Baie Verte that they had taken from the French only a few weeks before.

It seemed that there had been three soldiers the night before whose scalped heads had been thrown over the ramparts after they had been out foraging for firewood. Then a company of Miqmaqs had attacked and begun to lay siege to the fort. This was serious as it had been assumed that the Indian problem had been eliminated. He sent for Nathan Adams who arrived in quick order.

"Lieutenant General."

"Adams, the Mikymakys are back and are killing our men at my fort in Baie Verte. Take a full company of one hundred there immediately and stay until the problem is solved for good."

"Yes, Lieutenant General." He saluted, spun on his heels and left.

* * * * *

Gérald Landry was one of the few survivors of the Chipoudie

attack and the only one that had a sailboat and he was expert at using it. It was light and about sixteen feet long with a keel and could carry a dozen people and was manoeuvrable and fast. He usually fished with it but had occasionally used it successfully to skirt around English camps. It had saved him and his family and several neighbours when the English had attacked; he had seen their sloop coming and had quickly taken his family and friends down the coast and hidden them.

On the tide, at the request of Brossard, he took his sailboat from their hiding place near Chipoudie to Beauséjour. In the pitch-dark middle of the night, when Acquila was lying next to Mathilde, the boat made its way up the swollen Riviere Au Lac out of sight of the fort to the very end of the river where he took down the sail and camouflaged it.

Then he met up with Jacques Robicheaux and Joseph Doiron and waited.

The next morning Bois Hebert travelled overnight to Beauséjour bringing Emile and sixty men to La Coupe and joined up with the men that had already arrived. A lot of the men he had in the camp at Le Cran had returned to their families, but Bois Hebert wasn't concerned; they weren't travelling to win a battle, just to cause a distraction.

When they arrived and met Robicheaux, Doiron and Landry and made their way to the former site of the Pont à Buot. It was a league from the Fort and out of sight and sound from it. They looked for signs of something being buried and dug up the two swivel guns that had been buried a few months before. An unexpected find was a crate of one pound cannonballs.

* * * * *

Before he joined Mathilde in their tent Acquila lit his pipe and walked outside by the torchlight. He could see a lot of movement on the drawbridge, a large number of English soldiers, perhaps as many as one hundred, were leaving, marching north along the road to Baie Verte.

Acquila noted this and went to bed. He and Mathilde had planned to sleep in but Louis-Thomas interrupted them with his loud morning welcome to the world. She picked him up and rocked him in her arms while Acquila started a fire and they warmed themselves around it.

The adults, with Louis-Thomas in Acquila's arms, and Béatrice joined others in getting porridge and bread from the English and were on their way back to their tent when they ran into Camille. Their stout friend smiled when he saw Acquila and rushed up to him and they embraced each other.

"Girouard, what are you doing here?"

"I came to visit you, Ami. I missed our conversations."

"Hmm."

"Camille, come to see me this afternoon, oui?"

"Bien sûr." Camille Robicheaux was his usual self and quietly marched off.

Acquila lifted up Louis-Thomas and they all went for a walk along the dry moat so he could find the best possible place to dig. He hadn't seen Brossard since they had arrived and suspected he was staying out of sight.

There seemed to be many fewer English soldiers in the compound.

With Acquila leading the family, they walked around the fringes of the Acadian tents occasionally talking to people they met, but mostly to appear innocent so he could look for sentry positions on the parapet ramparts. There were none on the two facing the bay! There were not even cannon on those. He suspected that the English believed the French threat was over and they had greatly reduced their defensive measures or moved them to different fortresses. He smiled.

"Bien!"

They went to the last tent in the cluster, it was about thirty paces from it to the unoccupied parapet and battery near the location of their planned tunnel. He looked around to make sure no English were paying attention, then examined the palisades. They did not appear to have been reinforced since he and his family had climbed over them, but they were still eight feet high.

He stopped and looked at one closely. He had worked on reinforcing the fort and knew that the palisades had horizontal support structures underground that reached at least four feet inside that would affect his work.

But it was still easier than digging through the wide, sodded glacis mound. The base of the palisades were at the bottom of a six foot slope; the diggers would be hidden as long as they stayed on their knees.

Better still, they needed to only dig about a dozen feet; four down on each side and four underneath the supports. He was pleased and felt more confident.

When he went back to their tent Camille was outside of their tent waiting for them.

"Camille, how did you find yourself here? Where are all the other Acadiens? There must be more than are kept here."

"The English, they went to our new places. I had moved to Pré de Bourque after they came. Then they promised to pay us in silver coin for working on rebuilding the fort, and I am always in need of silver coin, so I came here and here I have stayed. The others are kept at the English fort, across the marsh.

"What do you think the English will do to us?"

"I hear rumours that they will send us back to France, but I know of no one from here that has ever even been in France."

"Come inside. Mathilde, can you bring us some tea?"

They both lit their pipes from the fire outside the tent then Acquila allowed Camille to precede him into the tent and they both sat down. While they were chatting Mathilde came in with two mugs.

"So, Camille. Would you like to leave here?"

"Of course, we all would."

"We are leaving tonight, but need your help."

"Of course, what can I do?"

"We are digging under the palisade and you are our best digger."

"But that will be very difficult, the English…".

"The English will be too busy to notice us."

"I am bored, Acquila, so I will help you. What should I do?

"You will know when this is about to happen, there will be a great deal of noise. So go to your tent and sleep, and when you are rudely awakened, come here."

"I will. Should I eat supper first?"

"If it helps you sleep."

* * * * *

Bois-Hébert, careful to stay out of site of the fort, looked for the place from which to start the diversion.

Near Le Loutre's holy well were trenches that the English had dug and they were perfect; they were close enough to allow the small swivel gun cannon to drop balls near the fortress without harming the Acadians within. It also was on the down slope away from the fort so that the English could not easily see the muzzle flash.

They would set up their musket positions along the ridge near the fort and would bring enough cartridges and musket balls to maintain a wall of lead for at least three hours.

* * * * *

Acquila, despite requesting everyone else to sleep during the day, couldn't do so himself. After supper, when the sun was starting to set, he and Mathilde had brought the children into the tent and they had played games with Béatrice's dolls.

It was pitch black when Acquila left the tent to have a walk around. Most of the people were in their tents, some were making music.

He walked to the last tent in the direction of their dig site; there are no sentries anywhere near it.

Bien.

28 – VINGT-HUIT

Major Thomas Dixson was officer of the guard for the last shift of the day and took his tea to the guardhouse before he was to retire. He yawned and chatted with the sentry who was also set to retire for the night. By the light of a single candle he read a few Psalms. While he was far from home he tried to stay connected to Massachusetts by reading verses that he remembered from previous services in his mass house at Newbury. The moon could not be seen through the rain clouds, and sure enough, drops of rain began falling on the roof.

As he rose to order the changing of the guard a volley of muskets came from outside the fort. Then a cannon ball exploded a hundred yards or so in front of the front gates.

"Trooper, sound the alarm and then alert the Lieutenant General to have him rise."

The fort had a bell just outside the guardhouse and the trooper rang it aggressively and men began pouring out of the barracks in various stages of being dressed, hats were falling off, muskets were being dropped and men were tripping over men picking up their muskets and hats.

The musket and cannon fire continued.

Dixson went to the small powder magazine to see that the armoury sergeant was ready with cartridges for the fifty troops left in the fort after Nathan Adams had taken a company to Baie

Verte.

Meanwhile, the English soldiers bivouacked in tents in front of the fortress were grabbing their muskets and running in their night clothes over the drawbridge and into the fort.

Dixson ordered the men to ranks and files and stand ready and looked for the other two sentries on duty. They were still at their stations and Dixson went to the northern battery.

"Ensign, what see you?"

"Seems musket fire from the ridge over there," he pointed.

"I would guess somewhere around fifty, maybe more or less. Also small cannon fire from the other side of the ridge, a little more westerly. So far they seem to be very poor shots, Major."

Dixson walked toward the men assembled in ranks.

"Battalion. Check bandoleers and count cartridges. Shoulder arms if supplied, if not, fall out and report to the armoury sergeant."

A half dozen red coats hurried to get ammunition, and then fell back in.

Dixson walked through the ranks.

"I smell rum.

"Battalion, those who have lately consumed alcohol report to the brig."

Almost a dozen men sheepishly fell out and so reported.

"Battalion..... Right... Dress." The men shuffled to their proper position to fill in the gaps.

"First Platoon. To take positions on the three northerly batteries. Second and third platoons take prone positions outside of fortress. Fall... out."

The parade ground almost emptied as the troops took their positions.

Robert Monckton arrived, donning his hat as he came to a stop.

"What do we have, Major?"

"We believe we have fifty muskets shooting regular volleys at the fort with musket and small cannon."

"Casualties?"

"Not to the moment, Sir."

"Who the devil are they? And what is happening that the crows come out of nowhere and attack at Baie Verte and now an assault as us here?

"There is something behind this, Dixson. What do you recommend?"

"I think we send two platoons out and try to come in from behind them."

"Order it so."

* * * * *

Acquila had been awake before the first volleys had been fired but he was still startled when the tent flap opened and Beausoleil entered.

"You awake, Girouard."

"Oui."

Camille Robicheaux then appeared.

Mathilde was fully alert and gave Acquila a kiss on the cheek. Then Louis-Thomas started crying.

"Chér, I will return in about one hour, have the children ready. And keep Louis-Thomas crying, the English will not notice it when we leave here."

Acquila looked out the tent flap, there was the steady staccato sounds of muskets going off almost in unison and every minute the sound of a small cannon. He took a length of cotton rope that Mathilde had made from petticoats.

He kissed Mati and the men quietly and calmly left. Beausoleil had his scalping knife in his hand.

They were confident that all was proceeding as normal when they hurried smack into three English soldiers rushing toward the front gates, muskets in hand. Each of the Acadians took the nearest maudit, but except for Beausoleil's scalping knife, they were unarmed.

Camille was knocked in the head with a musket barrel, but

was built like a bull and shook it off and got inside the musket and head butted his opponent. Beausoleil cut the throat of his adversary but not before he yelled out a warming. Acquila struggled with his, but with the other two English finished, the other Acadians made short work of the third soldier.

The English were wearing white breeches and another risk was that more Acadians would have heard the struggles and appear. If word got out that they were escaping then most likely no one could escape. Silence was their friend. They quickly pulled their enemies over the edge of the fosse and out of sight of the camp and took cover. Luckily no other Acadians had noticed their struggles; many were closer to the action, near the north part of the fortress, looking to see what would unfold.

When they got to the chosen spot Acquila tossed the rope which had a rock wrapped on an end over the palisades. Instantly they heard a "psst" and two dike spades were dropped over the wall.

Acquila showed him where to start and Camille set to work, digging down feverishly but silently.

Beausoleil whispered to Acquila, "I will go to look for English who might come this way." He left.

Once Camille had the tunnel well started, Acquila began working with him and expanding the hole. They came to the underground supports and then started digging horizontally. The work was extremely easy, the ground was without rocks and not hard packed; much easier that installing an aboiteau.

They came to the end of the supports and knew they were more than halfway through.

There was the steady noise of war coming from the other side of the fortress, but it was muffled by the rain.

Then from behind there came a command in English.

"Who goes there?" The English must have decided to send sentries to this side of the fortress. Two more English were coming down the site of the ramparts. "Who is that, what are you doing?"

Then Acquila saw Beausoleil come up from behind wielding an English musket by the barrel and Acquila could almost see

English red coats falling down the parapet; Brossard had made short work of them.

Then, with Camille inside the hole and passing dirt backwards between his legs, the hole opened.

Camille whispered.

"We're through...".

Acquila whispered back, "I go to get the others, you go through."

Then he went back to collect his family, he noticed Brossard crouched, ready to take care of any English who happened to get close.

Acquila hurried, every second mattered as he knew that Bois-Hebert would be nearing the end of his ammunition and would need to withdraw.

He came to his tent and Mathilde and Beatrice were ready and the baby appeared to be sleeping as if dead.

"Come, we go now. I will get Simon and Philomene and their children."

He hurried in the rain to Simon's tent; with all the noise from the battle, his friend was standing in front watching.

"Bourque."

"Acquila, it's late. Someone is attacking the fort."

"Quiet. Waken Philomene and Marie. We are leaving now."

"Where?"

"To freedom, you imbecile."

"What?"

"Doesn't matter. Come, hurry."

Simon went inside the tent and returned quickly with his wife and teenage daughter followed him.

"Where are your boys?"

"They are watching the attack, I think."

"Philomene, go to Mathilde and wait for us."

Simon's wife took her daughter's hand and led her toward the Girouard tent.

"Simon, let's get your boys."

Remarkably there was a large crowd of Acadians near where the English were firing up the hill with muskets and every minute the air was shattered by a 3 pound cannon. Simon looked around and saw his sons. He grabbed them by the shoulders and said something to them and the three Bourque men hurried back.

Once they joined Acquila he said, "Walk slowly and calmly, like you are coming for dinner."

"Well, I am hungry, Girouard."

"Come, quietly, no noise, Simon. Or we will all die."

Simon heard the last word and nodded and they made their way past the other tents without anyone else waking up. They passed Brossard who nodded and followed.

Then they were at the tunnel and Mathilde pushed Beatrice through ahead of her and then followed and handed her the baby. Acquila heard her gasp when she got through, but she stifled herself.

"Philomene, hurray!... Simon, Marie, vite. Garcons! Vite. Vite."

Acquila looked at Brossard, "You next."

"No, Girouard, you.

"Once you are through I am going to get as many others as I can to escape with us."

Acquila pushed Camille toward the hole, turned and embraced Beausoleil and dove into the pit and through the tunnel and in less that ten seconds he was through.

He wiped his face and looked. There was Emile hugging his mother and sister along with Doiron and Camille's cousin.

Emile said, "Papa, vites, allons y. We have the boat."

Acquila took Louis-Thomas and the family ran quickly through the rain to the identified spot from which Mathilde and the children had escaped only a few weeks prior. The sail was up, Gérald Landry was ready and the women and children followed by the men boarded. Landry untied the tether and the sails filled with onshore wind and they left.

The family all embraced and watched the explosions and muzzle fire appear like fireworks celebrating their salvation as they went farther and farther away from the only home that they as a family had ever known.

* * * * *

Joseph Brossard worked feverishly, bringing one family after another to and through the tunnel. Soon there was a large cluster outside of the palisade and they had to leave. He led them along the course of the Riviere Au Lac and as they continued they were joined by most of Bois Hébert's party; a few left behind to continue the appearance of an attack and discourage pursuit.

The refugees continued on their trek to freedom on through the night; most had had some sleep and adrenalin drove and sustained them as they walked through Tintamarre toward Mémérancouque. Brossard counted his rescued Acadians; there were almost seventy that would not face the awful justice of the English.

* * * * *

When daylight arrived Major Thomas Dixson recalled his advance parties. An ensign named Thomas had led the reconnaissance platoon and came to report.

"Casualties, Thomas?"

"No, Major, not a one of ours. None of theirs for that matter. At least found no corpses. Did recover a swivel cannon."

"Odd."

Then, later in the morning, he saw Adam's company marching along the high ground, returning from Fort Monckton; they seemed to be in a very healthy state of repair. Dixson walked toward Adams and met him very near the rubble of the old Acadian church.

"Major."

"Adams. Casualties at Fort Monckton?"

"None, Major. Carried on a steady series of musket

engagements, but there was no hand-to-hand combat. I think our overpowering numbers kept them at bay, and would suggest we eliminated a dozen or more."

"Well done, Adams."

Dixson walked back toward the fort gates and saw a very angry Monckton marching rapidly toward him.

"Dixson! They're gone!"

"Gone, Lieutenant General? Who's gone?"

"The bloody Frenchman, half of them are gone!"

"Impossible. Where?"

"I have no bleeding idea. Come see for yourself. There will be hell to pay, and you, Major, shall pay it if it comes to that."

Monckton led Dixson to the drawbridge.

"See for yourself."

Dixson looked down on a small group of Acadians remaining in an area that had only a few hours before been occupied by over a hundred.

"If anyone ever hears about this, Dixson, you will be the one to fall on a sword, not me. No one shall ever hear of this! You are ordered to complete no report that tells of this fiasco."

All Dixson could say was, "Yes, Lieutenant General, if that be your pleasure, Sir," knowing full well that Monckton would make sure the story about the escape of dozens of Acadians when they were in his custody would never be told.

* * * * *

Jean-Louis Le Loutre took the tender boat to his place of imprisonment. He had faced trial in a language that he not only did not understand, but one that he loathed. He protested that he was a priest following the commands of the Holy Father, but his defense was ignored.

After two months in a cold military cell in Kent, he was manhandled by English sailors up a flight of stone stairs and marched under armed guard to a waiting schooner.

He had been ignored by the French government and army, forgotten by his church, and betrayed by the Acadians for whom he had sacrificed and spent more time in prayer and politics than he had to save his own soul.

The Isle of Jersey was ten miles away from where he was detained and seven years away from France for l'Abbé de les Sauvages de l'Acadie.

* * * * *

Captain Benoni Danks had his reckoning two decades later. He supported the new British North American provinces of Nova Scotia joining the American colony's rebellion against Great Britain. In a short but fierce siege of the renamed Fort Cumberland he and the other rebels were defeated. Danks was charged with treachery and thrown into the hold of a ship, breaking his leg which festered badly and resulted in his death. It was said that he was buried with little better circumstances than a dog and that he had lived under general dislike and died without anyone to regret his death.

* * * * *

Six months after their escape Acquila Girouard and Mathilde Leblanc watched Béatrice and Louis-Thomas play along the dikes near Le Cran; at the site of the great victory over the maudit "dos les homards".

He remembered the time that he and his compatriots had slaughtered two dozen hated Englishmen on the very grounds. The grounds were not, in his mind at least for now, soaked in blood, but soaked in freedom.

The winter had been brutal which had provided some saving grace in that there had been no sign of the hated English. Spring had arrived.

"Emile, get your brother and sister. We are going on a long trip."

"To where, Papa."

"You will see."

Acquila had borrowed a wagon and a horse and he threw a dyke spade in the wagon along with a carved elm wood monument and a basket of food and a bottle of chokecherry wine. Then he went to get Father Le Guerne who was joining them.

They travelled on solid ground as best as they could for about a half day. Mathilde and Béatrice were soaking up the sun while Acquila and Emile took turns leading the horse around wet areas.

They finally arrived.

Acquila hugged and kissed his wife after they arrived and lit up his pipe and enjoyed the sun beaming strongly down on his family.

He had come to this spot the day before with Emile and they had completed the work that had been needed to be done.

"Mathilde, Béatrice come."

He helped his women off the wagon, while Emile lifted and carried the heavy monument and they walked toward a carefully made mound of large granite rocks.

Mathilde and Béatrice unloaded the food and drink they would enjoy while the men installed the monument they had worked on over the winter.

When they were finished Acquila nodded to Pére Le Guerne who opened his Bible.

"La grâce et la paix de Dieu notre Père et du Seigneur Jésus Christ soient avec vous."

Fin

AUTHOR'S NOTES

Tintamarre! is historical fiction. This genre generally involves interweaving fictional stories about fictional people with real events and actual people.

As many original sources as could be secured were studied in its associated research: dispatches, journals and other documents about events that related to Acadia during the period of the book.

And the legendary historians who devoted lives to studying and reporting on the period, including: Trueman, Milner, Parkman, Beamish, Webster, Fowler/Lockerby and a few others were all read. I was careful to not read other stories of the period, both to offer a new light on the events and to avoid borrowing of plot lines and characterizations.

The top historians on the subject matter were interviewed: Ronnie Gilles Leblanc of Parks Canada, Ruth Whitehead: the esteemed Miqmaq historian, Francois LeBlanc at l'University de Moncton and Juliette Bulmer at Fort Beauséjour. Local historians were cross examined including Don Colpitts, Ron Trueman and Colin Mackinnon who still, every spring, go out on the marshes and look for relics.

But, Tintamarre! is fiction and there are many variations from the historical record as well as deliberate flights from reality. I ask the reader's forgiveness for this. Any mistakes herein are my own.

Actual events are re-ordered in any way the author wanted them to be to tell the story. Some time frames were extended while others were condensed; many events were ignored while others were invented.

Personalities were devised for real people that are in the book based as much as possible on contemporary accounts. But a few suffered from fictional biographies more than others. Benoni Danks, in contemporary reports, was not a very scrupulous man. He eventually was charged with treason. But there is no indication that he was even around during the time covered by Tintamarre; most likely he appeared around 1758. But Danks - as a figure in the novel - is a consolidation of many different characters. He was chosen to be the composite character because his biography was one that captured the author's imagination early on in the research.

The rather terrible depiction offered of the Miqmaq leader, Jean Baptiste Copit, is based upon observations mainly by British opponents of the day, but are supported by other aboriginal leaders of the time as reported by the top historians.

Jean-Louis Le Loutre is a highly controversial figure and was probably studied more than any other character in the book. Many of his personality flaws were invented, but the book probably describes his conflicted positions on the Church, the King, the Miqmaqs and Acadians fairly well.

The aboriginal people in the eastern Provinces are referred to as "Miqmaqs" although there are many variations similar to this. Miqmaq is reported to be a derivation by the English of the welcoming phrase used by aboriginal people of the time. According to the top historian, the word the local aboriginals most likely used for themselves was probably "L'nu'k" or "Onoog".

It's generally accepted that "Mohawks" did not join with the Rangers / Massachusetts Fencibles / Militia. The aboriginals who traveled with them were called this, but were likely Mohegans and Massachusetts area tribes.

My last big escape from reality is my use of Tintamarre as the title. Tintamarre was the name of the Acadian community that is now called Upper Sackville and perhaps four miles from the scene of most of the action. It is also the name of the marshes northwest of the Fort and the name of my High School. It was not the name of the place where all this occurred.

Also, careful readers will notice that the author reversed the accents over the letter "e"; what would be "accent agues" became "accent graves", etc. This was on the advice of Acadian linguists who advised me that this was a characteristic of the Acadian dialect.

The last major conflict with reality... There isn't really a buried treasure at Tintamarre. Or is there?

ABOUT THE AUTHOR

Brian Lloyd French is a writer in Toronto. He is author of "Mojito! A Novel of the Next Cuban Revolution". He studied English Literature and Canadian History at the University of New Brunswick.

He grew up within a few miles of the scene of "Tintamarre!" and used to play on the fields and Fort Beauséjour. His family, before he was born, lived very near the site of Abbé Le Loutre's "holy well".

www.brianlloydfrench.com

ABOUT MOJITO!

A Novel of the Next Cuban Revolution

Alec McCaul is a sinister security operative living in Havana, hired by the CIA to do a threat profile on the faltering Cuban regime. He connects with his mission partner, Lucien Ruel, a deadly commando with ulterior motives. Then he runs into his lost flame Kate Adams, now a reporter with CNN. Together, with an heroic Cuban chopper pilot, a street kid and the head of Havana's mafia, McCaul and Kate dodge Cuba's security apparatus and find a terrorist camp in the mountains. When a Miami Herald reporter is killed by the Cuban secret police, the White House is in a panic. Over the course of a week Alec and Kate take on the Castro regime, Islamic terrorists, the CIA and barely manage to survive the treacherous outcome.

www.mojitonovel.com

CPSIA information can be obtained at www.ICGtesting.com
Printed in the USA
LVOW10s0552130815

449752LV00007B/280/P